LOWER EDUCATION:
A TALE OF PASSION, PERSEVERANCE, AND MISSING MEATLOAF

Dr. Meander Swotty

Copyright © 2021 by Dr. Meander Swotty
Cover design by Cherie Fox

Between the Lines Publishing
9 North River Road, Ste 248
Auburn ME 04210
btwnthelines.com

First Published: December 2021

ISBN: (Paperback) 978-1-950502-44-8
ISBN: (Ebook) 978-1-950502-45-5

Library of Congress Control Number (LCCN): 2021951234

LOWER EDUCATION:
A TALE OF PASSION, PERSEVERANCE, AND MISSING MEATLOAF

Between the Lines PUBLISHING

This book is dedicated to everybody who has ever killed themselves during a staff meeting.

Chapter 1

Rob Chudinski smiled at the brass plaque on the door to Room 605—*Dr. Rod Chudinski, Assistant Professor*. Sure, they got his first name wrong, but that couldn't smother the pride erupting within him. After four years of undergraduate work, two getting his master's, and five in his doctoral program, he was finally an academic. Not only was he an academic, but after signing his contract with Eastern Wisconsin University earlier that summer, he was now an academic with a paying job—unlike many in his graduating class.

Balancing a cardboard box full of books, family photos, and various memorabilia from the University of Illinois on one knee, Rob tried the knob, but it was locked. Looking for anybody who could help him, he followed the hallway until he came to a partly open door. The brightly polished plaque on it read: *Dr. Craig Grubber, Professor*. Under that, another plaque said: *Department of Special Education*. Below that, a third plaque had the word: *Chair*. And below that, a fourth plaque said in tiny, engraved letters: *Twelve-time winner of the OFM Teaching and Research Awards*. Inside, a rotund man sat reading a newspaper. His black oak desk was so massive it practically filled the tiny office.

Knocking, Rob stepped inside. "Excuse—"

"What the hell is wrong with you?" Dr. Grubber pointed to the floor. "Watch your feet!"

Looking down, Rob found that he was standing on masking tape partitioning the office from the hallway. On it were the words: NO STUDENTS BEYOND LINE!

"But I'm not a student. I'm—"

"I don't care! Get out!"

Juggling his box, Rob retreated to the hallway.

"You probably don't recognize me with shorts and a t-shirt on, Dr. Grubber. But I'm Rob Chudinski. You hired me for the assistant professor position. Severe disabilities?"

Dr. Grubber looked over the top of the newspaper, his walrus mustache twitching in irritation. Rob couldn't help but think of Mr. Dursley from the *Harry Potter* films.

"What are you blathering on about?"

"You hired me." Rob adjusted his hold on the box. "In May."

It suddenly occurred to him that this was probably some sort of hazing ritual that all the new faculty went through. His smile became less forced.

"I know we don't start the fall semester for a couple of months, but I wanted to move in and get an early start on—"

"Out! Out! How many times do I have to tell you? Are you stupid as well as illiterate?"

Rob inadvertently crossed the line again. He scurried to the safety of the hallway.

The department chair stared at him; his face scrunched in disgust. "You're... You're that holy roller, Mr. Change-the-World."

Not knowing how he was a *holy roller*, Rob considered extending his hand again. "It's Rob... Rob Chudinski. You hired me to teach—"

"No, we didn't!" Dr. Grubber slammed his newspaper. "We hired the girl from some Podunk college in Florida, or California, or some such place. Tanned skin, blond hair."

Tucking the box under his arm, Rob groped through it. Hazing was one thing, but this was bordering on abuse. He kept hoping Dr. Grubber would crack a grin and let him off the hook, but the department chair's scowl only grew more sour. "I have the letter right here."

A man in a robin-egg blue polyester suit strutted up and shouldered Rob aside. He poked his head into Dr. Grubber's office, careful to make sure his feet didn't cross the tape.

"Hey, Big Guy! Having a good summer?" He watched Rob attempt to shake papers loose from a manilla envelope. "Who's this?"

"He's that idiot we interviewed in spring." Dr. Grubber stood and twisted his bulk through the narrow gap between his enormous desk and the office wall. "He thinks we hired him."

The man in the blue suit snapped his fingers. "I remember you! You were that Albert Schwarzenegger who kept going on about changing the world by producing caring educators." He mocked in a whiny voice, *"We can change the world one teacher at a time!"*

"It's Schweitzer, you moron. Albert Schweitzer. Arnold Schwarzenegger is a bleeding actor. Honestly, Bert, I don't know why we keep you around." Dr. Grubber snatched Rob's letter. "Give me that!" A wave of confusion spread across his flabby face as he read it. "This isn't right."

Down the hallway, a scrawny, ferret-like man stood in front of another office, slipping furtive glances at them as he sorted through his keys.

"This isn't right!" Dr. Grubber said again as he reread the letter. He checked the return address on the envelope, flipped through its enclosed material, then read the letter a third time. "Mary must've screwed up. Well, I'll fix this. I'm not going to allow some radical, two-bit hippy to teach in my—!"

There was a great whooshing sound. Turning, they found a white cloud billowing into the hallway. The ferret-like man stumbled out of it, covered in what appeared to be flour.

"Craig..." He choked. "They booby-trapped my door!"

Dr. Grubber and Bert raced over to him. Wondering what the hell was going on, Rob trailed close behind.

"Damn those constructivist bastards!" Dr. Grubber shook his fist at the blizzard raining around them. "We have to get them for this and get them good!"

"I know!" Bert hitched his blue pants with authority. "If we take their copier paper—with the budget cuts and everything—they won't get any more. They'll be dead in the water! And here's the kicker." He leaned in confidentially. "We won't run out this year!"

Dr. Grubber considered this. "Yes, but that hardly strikes the fear we need. I want them to rue the day they stepped foot onto the sixth floor! I want them to cower before us! We need something good. Something better than good. Our prank has to be brilliant! Now, think!"

They bent their heads in thought.

Rob took a tissue from his box and offered it to Les. "You all right?"

Les took the tissue and cleaned his glasses. His eyes were the only parts of him that weren't white. "Yeah, I'm—" He looked at Rob as if seeing him for the first time. "Who are you?"

Dr. Grubber snarled, "He's nobody. Mary made a goddamned mistake. As soon as I talk to her, he's gone."

"What?" The box almost slipped from Rob's grasp. "What do you mean *gone*? I just got here!"

Dr. Grubber thrust a meaty finger at Bert. "See if you can get ahold of the key to their storage room. Then steal every god-damned office supply you can. Everything! I don't want them to have a single piece of paper, pen, or paperclip to their names!"

"No problemo." Bert saluted. "You can count on me, Big Guy."

"You!" Dr. Grubber jabbed his finger at Rob. "Come!"

Rob scrambled after him, coffee mugs and picture frames rattling in his box. "It says I have a one-year contract. The letter they sent me… I have a contract!"

"Shut it!" For a heavy man, Dr. Grubber lumbered down the stairs with surprising speed. "It's a mistake. She's always making mistakes. I don't know how she became School Director. She must've slept her way to the top. Or blackmailed somebody. That's probably it. That's the only way to get ahead around here. Nobody cares about hard work anymore! Nobody!"

They reached the fifth-floor landing.

"But," Rob said, "I… I moved here! I… I bought a house!"

"Then you'll have plenty of time to spend in it, because you're not sticking around my department."

They reached the fourth-floor landing.

"But," Rob gasped. "Give me a try. I'm a terrific teacher! And I've, I've won two research awards!"

Dr. Grubber bristled. "I'm not having some no-good, Pollyannaish—" He struggled to find a fresh insult, "—*idiot* in my program!"

They reached the third-floor landing. A faint odor of marijuana lingered in the air.

"But I can contribute. I have ideas. And I have loads of experience. I taught in a residential school for—"

"I heard all about your newfangled ideas during the interview. We don't need nutjobs like you ruining all of my hard work."

Arriving at the second-floor landing, they were both sweaty, their pace little more than a stumbling crawl.

"When I got the letter," Rob said, "I turned down other interviews. I… I thought I had a position here!"

"I'm not talking about this anymore. The answer is no."

Reaching the first floor, they burst into a brightly lit corridor.

Breathing hard, Dr. Grubber leaned against a wall lined with hundreds of faded portraits of past deans sneering at them. "I'll get to the bottom of this. Mark my words! You'll see. Hire you? The last thing our students need is to hear your fanatical philosophies."

They entered a cavernous room partitioned into a labyrinth of cubicles. Sitting in front of their computers, scores of people played solitaire and scrolled through Facebook pages.

"I'm here to see Mary," Dr. Grubber told one of the administrative assistants. Without waiting for a response, he barged into an office decorated with every variety of cat knickknack imaginable. "Mary, I want a word with you!"

A tiny woman in her sixties sat behind a tidy desk, typing away. She looked up at them through coke-bottle glasses that magnified her dreamy brown eyes. "Oh, hey there, Craig!" she said in a thick Wisconsin accent. "How you doing? Having a good summer? Ready to get back to the old grind, ay?"

"Never mind that!" Dr. Grubber pushed the now-crumpled letter at her. He doubled over, trying to catch his breath. "He—" He flung a hand in Rob's direction. "He thinks you hired him!"

Mary wiggled her fingers at Rob, still clutching his cardboard box. "Oh! Hey there, Dr. Chudinski. Welcome aboard! How're you liking Wisconsin? I know it's hot and muggy now but wait until winter. It's beautiful. Do you ski?"

Relieved that he hadn't somehow misinterpreted the university's contract, Rob started to answer, but Dr. Grubber cut him off. "Who cares if he skis?" He seized the letter and shook it. "This… this is a mistake! We didn't hire him. We voted for Brittney… or Brianna… or whatever her name was!"

"I'm sure you know who you did and didn't vote for," Mary said diplomatically. Her face lit up as if she'd had the best idea in the world. "I know! Let's have a meeting!" She reached for a day planner that had a picture of a tabby kitten on its cover.

"No! No meetings!" Dr. Grubber waved his arms like a vampire warding off somebody with a silver cross. "Just tell him it was a mistake. Rescind the offer!"

"Oh, I couldn't do that. I don't think it'd be legal. He has a contract, don't you know?"

"People break contracts all the time," Dr. Grubber growled.

"That wouldn't be very nice of us, now would it?" She flipped through her day planner. Every page was blank. "Let's get together and chat this out. You know, see what's what."

The department chair stomped his foot again. "I already know what's what. There's nothing to—"

"The next opening I have is September 25th at six in the morning." She reached for a pen. "I can block out four hours so we can hash this out."

"September—?" Dr. Grubber spluttered. "Mary, that's two months away!"

"You don't want to meet?"

"No!"

"Very well." She put the pen back and shut her day planner. Turning to Rob, she said cheerfully, "Welcome to Eastern Wisconsin University!"

Rob groaned, "Thanks."

"Don't unpack that box," Craig told him. "You won't be staying long!"

After waiting for an elevator that never came, Rob scaled the stairs to the sixth floor. He found the door to his cramped office open. On a green metal desk that dated from the early 1960s sat a wicker gift basket. Judging by the holes in the cellophane wrapping and the gaps between the packages of cheddar cheese and cheese curds, somebody had taken several items. Hugging the box to his chest like a life-preserver, he slumped into a rickety chair that squealed and tottered.

"I won't be staying long?" he said aloud.

What the hell was he going to do? He'd bought a house. And a car. And he had student loans to pay back! Plus, nobody was hiring this late in the summer. If Dr. Grubber got rid of him, how would he pay his bills? He'd lose everything!

"How did this happen?"

"It happened," a harsh voice said, "because I made it happen."

An elderly woman smoking a cigarette shuffled into his office.

"Hey, Mrs. Larsen." Rob stood. During his interview, she'd attended all of his presentations and teaching demonstrations. She'd also helped him find a realtor after he'd been offered the position. "Good to see you again."

"Sit," she croaked. "I'm the departmental secretary. Not the fucking queen."

"Yes, ma'am." Rob set his box on the floor and sat. "I'm sorry, but you can't smoke in here. It's a smoke-free campus."

She gave a great, rasping cough as she settled into the chair across from him. "They can fire me. And it's Thelma. Nobody calls me Mrs. Larsen."

"Thelma. Right." He suddenly digested what she'd said as she entered. "Wait. What do you mean, you made this happen?"

"They wanted to hire some bimbo with big tits." She tapped her cigarette. Its smoldering ash fell to the cracked linoleum floor. "I wanted you."

Rummaging in his box, Rob found an old Purdue cup. He handed it to her. She tapped more ash into it.

"So, you—what? Convinced the other applicant not to take the job?"

"I told the school director the department voted for you."

"Why?" Rob found himself getting to his feet again, his voice rising with him. "Do you know what you've done? You had no right to screw with my life like this!"

"Relax." She broke into a violent coughing fit that racked her fragile body. "Don't get your panties in a bunch."

"This is my career we're talking about! I bought a house!"

"I know." Thelma took a drag on the cigarette and blew a stream of bluish-grey smoke into the air. "I sold it to you. Gave you a good price too, though I was willing to go lower. You should've haggled more."

"You sold me your house?"

"It was one of my rentals. I knew having a house would keep you here."

"Keep me here?" Rob repeated crossly. "Dr. Grubber wants me to leave! He told me I wouldn't be staying!"

"Don't you worry about Craig. I'll deal with him."

"How?"

Her expression turned sinister. "I know where the bodies are buried."

"Thelma! I can't be somewhere where I'm not wanted."

"Believe me, Dr. Chudinski." She tapped more ash into the cup. "You're wanted. I want you. And every family with a severely disabled child in this town wants you."

"That's very kind of you to say, but—"

"My husband created this department," she said. "He got a grant from the Kennedys and developed the entire curriculum. Every single class is from him."

"The Kennedys?"

She took another long drag, then exhaled. "He taught their little girl. The one they kept in St. Coletta."

"Rose?" Rob knew the story well. President Kennedy's eldest sibling had chronic seizures and intense mood swings. Doctors performed a prefrontal lobotomy to control her behavior, but it didn't work. She was left even more disabled than before and was committed to an institution in Jefferson, Wisconsin.

"That's her." Thelma crushed her cigarette butt into Rob's cup and then lit a second. "This was in the early '50s. '53. Maybe '54." She sent another stream of smoke above her. The office was filling with its hazy reek. "The President used to call Anders every Sunday to see how his sister was doing. My husband called him Jack. The President called him Dr. Larsen."

"You're kidding," Rob said, amazed. He cracked open the window. Humid July air poured in.

"When Anders told him how bad things were for special needs kids, the President gave him money to start this program. We were the first in the country to teach teachers how to work with the disabled."

Rob blenched at the lack of people-first language but decided not to push the issue. He had a good idea what Thelma would say if somebody attempted to make her more politically correct.

She looked directly at him. Whether she was tearing up or the smoke was bothering her eyes, he couldn't tell.

"My husband was a good man. He was kind and decent and thoughtful. He would do anything for anybody. And he had a dream. He wanted to change the world by creating educators who'd go forth and teach the disabled by using the most up-to-date techniques possible. He used to say he could illuminate a dark world by lighting a million candles."

Rob gaped. During his interview, he repeatedly said the same thing. It was his mantra. "I still don't understand why you—"

"This place is a shit hole, Dr. Chudinski. If Anders were alive today, he'd kill himself. All of his hard work... All of his campaigning... All of his research..." She let smoke trickle from her nostrils. "It's become nothing more than a cesspool where ignorant faculty collect paychecks for producing even more ignorant students, students who go out and teach kids like Stella."

"Stella?"

"Our daughter."

For several moments, they sat in the warm smoke-filled office—Thelma staring out the window, Rob watching her. Eventually, she went on.

"When you interviewed… When you gave your presentation… you sounded like Anders. You have his vision. You have his desire to create a program that produces educators who will not only use the most advanced strategies available, but also demand that the disabled be treated with the dignity and respect they deserve."

She peered at Rob again, her tired eyes defiant and resolute. "We need you here, Dr. Chudinski. The curriculum is out-of-date. Everybody gets accepted into our program, whether they should be in college or not. Everybody gets A's in every class. Then they go out and spread the disease that has been incubating here over the past twenty years. It needs to stop. And you need to stop it."

"I'm sorry," Rob said, deeply moved, "but I'm not sure what I can do."

"First of all, don't be sorry. Ever. It's a sign of weakness and the vultures here will eat you alive. Secondly—" Thelma hoisted herself out of the chair, cigarette clenched in her wrinkled lips. "—don't give up. That's what you can do, Dr. Chudinski. Don't ever give up. Too many lives are at stake."

Chapter 2

Over the next few days, Rob gradually got his office in order. The walls were still an institutional white and the ancient furniture was barely serviceable; however, with the plants his mother had sent him lining the windowsill and a new rug covering the cracked floor, it was beginning to feel like home.

As Rob hung his diploma from the University of Illinois, a haggard, middle-aged man wearing a threadbare tweed jacket over a black Grateful Dead t-shirt stuck his head into the room.

"You Rod?" he asked.

"Actually, it's Rob. The sign's wrong."

The man offered his hand. Rob shook it.

"I'm Pete. I teach the language development and reading classes." He fell lazily into the guest chair and propped his dirty cowboy boots onto Rob's ugly green desk. "Welcome to EW-U, where dreams go to die."

"You're in special education?" Rob sat as well, his chair squealing as it pitched to one side. "How come I didn't meet you when I interviewed?"

"I'm a full professor."

Rob had no idea how that answered his question, but he nodded anyway. "Right. Of course."

"Personally—" Pete picked through the remains of Rob's gift basket. "I'm surprised Craig hired you. I thought he'd offer the job to some woman with big breasts and no self-respect."

"Yeah, well… I believe she took a position elsewhere."

"Unlucky for you."

An awkward silence settled around them.

"Hey!" Rob lowered his voice. "Tell me about Dr. Grubber. What's he like?"

"You can call him Craig. You have a Ph.D. now."

"Sorry. Force of habit."

"Craig?" Pete unwrapped a pastrami log he'd taken from the basket. "He's a dick. At least, he is to anybody who will take it."

"You might not want to eat that. God only knows how long it's been sitting here. Everything is warm and half-melted."

Pete inspected the lunch meat, then shrugged as he took a bite. "We all have to die sometime—if we haven't already." He chewed. "The thing you gotta know about Craig is that he's an overbearing blowhard who loves to have his fat fingers in everything. Likes to believe he's in control, like a god. Everybody hates him."

"Is he?"

Pete swallowed. "Is he what?"

"In control?"

Pete took another chomping bite. "As much as any chair, I suppose. He usually gets his way. It's like that in small programs. Fewer people to give a rat's ass."

He usually gets his way...

Rob groaned. That couldn't be good.

"If everybody hates him, how did he become department chair?"

"Ever hear of the Dilbert Principle?" Pete asked.

"The comic strip? No. Why? What is it?"

"It's where incompetent people get promoted to positions where they can't screw anything up by doing actual work."

As if on cue, Craig sauntered into the office. He tossed a bunch of papers into Rob's lap. "Your teaching assignments, Pollyanna. Have a good term!"

Rob scanned the top sheet.

"Wait a second," he said before Craig could leave. "This says I'm teaching five classes. I thought I was supposed to have a load reduction my first year."

"You do, hippy. That's *with* your load reduction."

"But..." Rob flipped through each class roster. "I have over four hundred students!"

"I'm sure there'll be more come September." Craig added gleefully, "Freshman haven't registered yet!" He left, chuckling.

"Five classes!" Rob riffled through the course descriptions. "How am I going to have time to write the research from my dissertation?"

Pete gnawed on the pastrami log. "Why do research? You've got the job. No need working yourself too hard."

"I have the job for now, you mean."

"That's the spirit!"

Rob studied his schedule. "Oh, great! Not only do I teach every day, but I teach both the early and late sessions. I'll be here from eight in the morning to ten at night!"

"Tough break." Pete inspected the pastrami log as though he had misgivings about eating it. "What's the fat ass having you teach?"

Rob read his teaching assignments. "Introduction to Abnormal Children... Characteristics of the Severely Crippled... Assessing Disabled Students... Curriculum for the Educable Child... Controlling the Behavior of the Disturbed... Who the hell created these titles?"

"What's wrong with the titles?"

"Abnormal children?" Rob read again. "Crippled? Disturbed? Their offensive." Underneath the catalog descriptions, he found the course syllabi. The most recent was dated May 4th, 1971. "These haven't been revised in over fifty years?"

"You know how it goes." Pete returned the half-eaten lunchmeat to the basket and leaned back, his hands behind his head. "Terminology keeps changing. One day it is 'imbecile.' The next, it's 'feeble-minded.' Then 'mentally retarded.' Tomorrow it'll be something else. No sense in correcting them. It's too much work. Besides, they all mean the same thing anyway."

Rob thought he saw a golden opportunity to make himself useful. "Maybe that's something I can do for the program."

"What?"

"Update the courses. You know, change the titles to something more appropriate. Maybe go through the syllabi and make sure there isn't too much overlap in content. Align the courses with current state standards. That kind of thing."

"Knock yourself out. The paperwork is a bitch, though."

Rob considered this. If the paperwork was as bad as Pete indicated, Craig would probably appreciate Rob's efforts even more. And the more he saw Rob's value, the more he'd want him to stay.

"How many students are in your Abnormal Child class?" Pete asked.

Pulling himself out of his thoughts, Rob consulted his roster again. "Two hundred and seventy-two!"

"Sounds like Craig combined all the sections."

"Geez." Rob scanned the lists of students enrolled in his courses. "Look at them all. How am I going to have any group activities?"

"Group activities? Look, newb. This is what you do." Pete leaned forward. "You pick a textbook or two. Every week read the little monsters a chapter. Then give a final exam at the end of the semester. Make it easy. Happy students mean a happy career."

"I was hoping to have thought-provoking essays."

"Essays—?"

Pete's laugh was cut short by a blood-curdling scream.

They bolted into the hallway and found Bert and Les retreating from Craig's open door, hands covering their horrified faces.

"Those bastards! Those God-damned bastards!" Craig stood over his beautiful black oak desk. Somebody had cut it in half with a chainsaw. "That's it! That's it, I tell you. Those TLs have had it. I'm going to kill them! I swear to God Almighty I'm going to kill them!"

"TLs?" Rob whispered to Pete, who seemed to think the state of Craig's desk was amusing.

"The Teaching and Learning faculty." Then, seeing Rob's puzzlement, Pete added, "They prepare general educators."

"It's funny you should mention them. I was wondering why they weren't part of our program."

Craig wheeled around. Bert and Les froze, even more horrified than before.

"What... did... you... say?" Craig asked, his walrus mustache quivering.

"It's just that..." Rob said sheepishly, "in most schools, regular and special education are in the same department. It helps create the inclusive environment we want to model for our—"

"Now, you listen to me, hippy." Craig's face turned a pulsating shade of purple. "If you ever say something like that again, I'll have you out of here before your contract is up! Do you understand?"

"Sorry."

"Sorry doesn't cut cheese, hippy! Got that?"

"Sorry doesn't cut cheese," Rob repeated as if making a mental note. "Got it."

Craig glared at him.

"What are we going to do, Big Guy?" Bert asked. "We can't let those constructivist punks get away with this!"

"No, we can't," Craig agreed. "We can't let them get away with this… this…"

"Infamous assault?" Les suggested.

"Yes! Assault! That's what it is. A vicious, personal, unprovoked assault. First, the flour. Now my precious, handmade desk!"

"I know what we can do to them," Bert said. "We could put some sort of virus on their computers and make it look like they've been downloading porn. Get them all fired!"

"Virus, eh?" Craig mulled this over. "Do either of you know anything about computers?"

Bert and Les shook their heads.

"Maybe one of our students does," Les said, hopefully.

"One of *our* students?" Craig replied. "Come on, Les. Think!"

"Yeah! Think, Les!" Bert huffed. "Idiot."

They stared at the jumble of lumber that used to be Craig's desk. Somebody had drawn a smiley face in the sawdust covering the floor.

"Did you manage to get ahold of the key to their storage room?" Craig asked Bert.

"Not yet. But I'm working on it."

"Forget about it." Craig gritted his teeth. "We need to do something better than stealing their office supplies. Do you understand? We need to do something brilliant! Nothing sophomoric. Have your ideas in my mailbox by the end of the day!"

The snicker slipped out before Rob realized it. Everybody looked at him.

"Sorry," he said. "You see, during my undergrad, we had this practical joker, Vince Gossage. He convinced my roommate that the girl he'd met at a frat party was only fourteen and the daughter of an F.B.I. agent. Vince hired actors from the theatre program to dress up in dark suits and sunglasses. They even had bulges under their jackets and wires hanging from their ears. For two weeks, they chased my roommate all over campus. He went into hiding and was too afraid to go to class." Rob laughed again. "He ended up failing out."

Craig drew so close; Rob could smell the sardines he'd eaten for lunch. "I may have to put up with you this year, Polly. But keep your stupid stories to yourself." He stomped into his office, his face still purple with anger.

"FBI agents! What kind of goddamned moron did Mary curse me with?" He slammed the door.

"FBI agents?" Bert rolled his eyes. "Moron."

"Yeah," Les chimed in. "Moron!"

They drifted down the hall; their heads bent close as they whispered conspiratorially.

Pete clapped Rob on the shoulder. "I thought it was a funny story." Then his expression contorted. He belched. "Bad meat." Holding his stomach, he sprinted into the bathroom.

Rob went to his office and chucked the remains of the gift basket into the garbage. Sinking into his wobbling chair, he wondered how the hell he was going to survive the year.

Chapter 3

"And they gave me five entirely different preps!" Rob said to his computer.

He was sitting at a glass, L-shaped desk he'd put in the extra bedroom of his recently-purchased 1920's craftsman-style bungalow. He made this room his home office because the windows faced Lake Winnebago, and the vast stretch of rolling water was both beautiful and calming; however, at that moment, the view wasn't lessening his anxiety any.

His doctoral advisor, Frank Russo, adjusted his camera so that he appeared in the middle of Rob's screen. "Didn't you ask for multiple sections of the same course?"

"No," Rob admitted. "I didn't think that was going to be an issue."

"Rookie's mistake."

Rob exhaled heavily. "I'm going to hate it here."

"Why?"

"For starters, my department chair is an ass!"

"They're all asses. Anybody who wants a position like that is either an ego-manic or a sadomasochist. Trust me. If you ever get a chance to be in administration, run the other way screaming."

"I don't think I'll have to worry about that," Rob said miserably. "I probably won't even get tenured."

"Don't be melodramatic."

"I'm not being melodramatic! My chair is going to make my life so miserable, I'll have to leave. He's practically told me that."

Rob stared at the stars twinkling above the dark lake. Downstairs, his grandfather clock chimed ten. God, he loved his house. With its pristine wood and built-in cabinets, it felt like someplace where he could retire. He hated the idea of living anywhere else.

"Tell me about this chair of yours," Frank asked. "What's he like?"

"He looks like a big fat walrus," Rob replied.

Frank chuckled.

"Seriously!" Rob said. "His mustache completely covers his mouth. He'd make a great ventriloquist."

"That doesn't help. You need to understand him in order to get along with him. What else do you know?"

Rob thought. "He had this enormous desk. It was really something. It took up his entire office. But somebody cut it in half."

"What?" Frank leaned forward as if trying to determine whether he'd heard correctly.

"Evidently, there's some sort of feud going on between the different programs," Rob explained. "The faculty play these mean practical jokes on each other. When I first got here, a fifty-pound sack of flour exploded. Flour went everywhere. They're still cleaning it up. Then, today, somebody took a chainsaw and cut Craig's desk in half. It's a shame. It was beautiful, like something the Amish would make."

"Hand-carved?"

"Probably."

"What else?"

Thinking, Rob twirled a pen in between his fingers. "He doesn't let anybody into his office. He doesn't even have any chairs for people to sit in."

"Smart! You let a student sit in your office, and they'll stay there all day, complaining. Remember that. And if you have a female student come in—"

"I know. Always keep the door open."

"Exactly." Frank adjusted his computer's camera again. "What else can you tell me about the Walrus?"

"His office walls are covered in awards. But they aren't plaques or anything substantial. They're sheets of colored paper with calligraphy. They're the kind of thing you'd get for competing in a third-grade spelling contest."

"Then don't put up your research awards," Frank told him.

"Why?"

"Because clearly, he regards himself as some sort of alpha male. The big desk. Not letting people in his office. A wall full of cheesy awards. Men like that don't appreciate competition. You put up your awards and he'll feel threatened. Another cock in the henhouse and all that."

"Great!" Rob exclaimed. "I already put them up. They're right next to my diplomas from Purdue and U of I."

"Then take them down. No big deal."

Rob looked out into the night. Despite the gorgeous view, he couldn't shake the feeling he'd made a horrible mistake coming to Wisconsin.

"It can't be that bad," Frank said.

"It is! Craig keeps calling me Hippy and Pollyanna because I believe we can make a difference in the world. And he gave me the worst teaching schedule possible. I teach from nine in the morning to ten o'clock at night nearly every day! I don't know how I'll keep awake, let alone when I'll have time to do my research."

"Make time. I mean it, Rob." Frank's earnest face filled Rob's computer screen. "Don't let your data go stale. That's critical! You don't want to have spent five years collecting data and then have everything go to waste. Besides, if you really want to make a difference, you have to publish. It's that simple."

"I'll try."

"Don't try. Do." Then Frank added, "Or I'll kick your ass!"

"Thanks, Master Yoda."

Somebody off camera said something to Frank. He indicated he'd be done in a minute. He returned to Rob. "Have you made any progress on your research at all?"

"I'm almost done with the first study," Rob said, exaggerating more than a little. "I have to write the conclusion. Then I'll submit it."

"Good. I want you to have all three papers submitted by December."

"I'll do my best." He watched the moonlit waves roll into the shore.

"Come on!" Frank exclaimed. "Don't look like that. It can't be that bad."

Rob sighed. "It isn't pleasant."

"You have to have somebody there on your side. Somebody who can go to bat for you. A mentor?"

"No. Not really."

"All right," Frank said, getting down to business. "This is what you do. You have to think strategically. Ever watch *Survivor*?"

"The television show?"

"Yeah. They should have a season based on higher education. That's how cut-throat our business is. Men like your chair have enemies. Find out who they are, then kiss up to them. Form alliances. Make yourself useful, and other people will want you on their team. Understand?"

"Yeah," Rob said with a little more hope. "There's a guy named Pete. He's a full professor in our program. He hates Craig too."

"Good! Get to know him. Take him out for drinks. Show him you have value and get him on your side. Who else?"

Rob considered the people he'd met over the past few days. "There's the department assistant, Thelma. She seems to think I'm worth something. She's the one who put my name in for the job."

"The secretary?" Frank cried. "Hey, hotshot, then you're untouchable. Nobody screws with the secretary!"

"Really?"

"Absolutely! Christ! They know everything about everybody. Keep on her good side, and you'll be fine. Bring her flowers once in a while or maybe candy for the candy dish on her desk. And compliment her hair or something. Don't be phony! Be genuinely thankful for all the crap she does for you and everybody else. She'll appreciate it."

Rob imagined giving Thelma a dozen red roses and her throwing them in the garbage. "I think she'd prefer a carton of Marlboros and a bottle of bourbon."

"Whatever. Seriously, secretaries run the entire university. If you ever need something, they're the people to ask. They're also paid shit. So be nice to them, and you'll be good to go."

"All right," Rob said, his mood brightening. "I'll keep all that in mind. As a matter of fact, she specifically told me not to worry about Craig."

"There you go! Things will be fine. But remember what I said about your research. It's publish or perish, man. If you want to make it to the big leagues, you have to show everybody you have a robust research agenda. That means publishing your butt off."

"I will." Rob took a deep breath. "Thanks, Frank. I appreciate the pep talk. I needed it."

"Skype any time you want. And don't worry. Keep your head down, mouth shut, and eyes open. And above all, young Skywalker—publish!"

Chapter 4

Fighting to keep the heavy stairwell door open, Rob rammed the box containing his new office chair into the sixth-floor hallway. Breathing hard and soaked with sweat, he surveyed the empty corridor. None of the other doors were open. Everybody was probably enjoying the last few weeks before the fall semester began. Not that it mattered. He didn't think any of his coworkers would help him anyway.

Pressing his shoulder against the box, he drove it before him like a blocking dummy, the cardboard sliding reluctantly against the tiled floor. When he finally reached his office, he collapsed upon it, panting.

"What kind of building doesn't have a working elevator?" He dragged the sleeve of his University of Illinois t-shirt across his brow. "How do people in wheelchairs get around this place?"

For a moment, he considered filing a complaint under the Americans with Disabilities Act but decided against it. He wanted his colleagues to see him as a valuable team player—not a whiner.

He opened his door. Then, with an effort, rolled the clattering box inside.

It took him over an hour to put the blasted chair together, but it was well worth the effort. When he sat, his butt sank into the soft leather. The lumbar support hit him exactly where he needed it. When he swiveled from side to side, there wasn't so much as a squeak.

He glanced about his office.

He'd replaced his research awards and diplomas with artsy black and white photos of the rural Wisconsin countryside. His shelves contained various homey trinkets and books on special education. He'd even purchased a large bamboo plant for the corner.

He noted his desk.

Oh God. What a monstrosity.

Weighing at least two hundred pounds, it was made of dark green metal and had a white top that was so scratched and dented it might have been used for a butcher's block. Further, the drawers had no handles. Rob had to pry them open with a screwdriver—and even then, they only moved a few inches. He had to kneel and reach his arm in to pull anything out.

He stared at his desk, wondering if he could paint it.

Paint…

He regarded the dirty white walls. Perhaps he could have them painted as well. A friendly canary yellow would certainly brighten the place. He'd have to check with Thelma to see if that were possible.

Standing, Rob rubbed his aching spine. Then he piled the remains of the shredded box and the Styrofoam packaging onto his old chair. With an ear-splitting squeal slicing through the quiet, he dragged it and its cargo to a garbage bin by the stairs.

He went into the restroom, peed and washed his hands, then tried to straighten his hair in the mirror. When he returned to his office, his beautiful new chair was gone. The old ratty one was perched triumphantly on top of his green desk, a spring protruding from its worn cloth seat.

"What that—?"

From down the hallway, the stairwell's fire door thudded shut. Rob darted into the corridor, but nobody was there.

Chapter 5

Rob sat in his squeaking chair, papers scattered about the desk in front of him. In two weeks, the fall semester would start, and he was frantically trying to get his courses ready.

Somebody knocked.

A stunning young woman with bubble gum pink hair stood in the doorway. She was wearing what appeared to be a black headband for a skirt and a white sports bra that strained to contain her ample breasts.

"Hi!" Rob fought to keep his gaze fixed firmly on her pretty face. "May I help you?"

"I'm Tiffani. Tiffani Miller." Strolling about, she inspected his office. "With two 'i's.' Not these eyes—" She pointed to her head. "I mean, I do have two of them. I meant the letter i. In my name, that is. It's T-i-f-f-a-n-i. I'm the student worker, by the way. If you need any copies or anything, let me know!"

She sat on the edge of his desk as if it were a Lamborghini and she was a model in a smutty truck stop calendar.

"Great!" Rob managed to say. He'd been in Wisconsin for the better part of two months and was feeling lonely; however, he knew full well that getting involved with a student, no matter how attractive, would be the worst thing he could do for his burgeoning career. "Thanks!"

"No problem." She crossed her shapely legs. "You're Rod, right?"

"Actually," Rob said, looking everywhere but at her. "It's Rob. The sign on the door is wrong. And I prefer Dr. Chudinski if you don't mind."

"Really? Everybody else likes me to call them by their first name."

"They do?" At all the universities he'd attended, faculty never had students call them by their first names. It somehow defeated the purpose of having a Ph.D.

"So…" She twirled a strand of pink hair. "Is there anything I can do for you?"

The degree to which she was leaning over his desk made Rob feel uncomfortable—and more than a little excited. He was about to say *no* when he thought of something.

"If you could order a new nameplate for my door, I'd appreciate it."

"Why? What's wrong with that one?"

"As I said, the first name is misspelled."

"No, it isn't. That's how you spell Rod." Then she said proudly, "I checked!"

"Yes, but—" Rob rubbed his forehead in frustration. "—my name isn't Rod. It's *Rob*." He stressed the 'b.'

"Really? I was told it was Rod. That's what I've been calling you."

"Well, it's still Rob. And I'd appreciate it if you'd call me Dr. Chudinski from now on."

"Okay. Whatever you want." She arched a seductive eyebrow. "Dr. Chudinski."

"Thank you." Then he added because he thought he should, "Ms. Miller."

She giggled.

Trying to demonstrate that he was busy, Rob rearranged the syllabi in front of him.

"I'm in special education too," Tiffani said, not taking the hint.

"I bet."

"I was supposed to be in one of your classes this semester. But I get course credit for working here."

Rob stopped what he was doing. "You get course credit for working in the office?"

"Yup! Twelve hours."

"Twelve hours?" Most students only took fifteen hours per semester. "How do you learn the material covered in those classes?"

She shrugged. "It probably doesn't matter. I know everything I need to know. I've been babysitting a retarded baby. He's really cute. He has that disease that makes him look Asian. Anyway, I'm going to be a great teacher! All the professors say so."

Rob dropped the papers he'd been holding.

"Okay, first of all—" He tried to maintain a professional tone. "—the baby has Down's syndrome. Don't call it a disease. It's a genetic condition involving the 21ˢᵗ chromosome. Second, don't use the term retarded or any of its variants. Use intellectual disability."

"Variants?"

"Right. Don't say mental retardation, mentally retarded, or retarded. Say intellectual disability. Third, use people-first language. You don't say 'intellectually disabled kids.' You say, 'kids with intellectual disabilities.' Put the person in front." Then Rob conceded, "Unless you're talking about the deaf community. They usually prefer to be called deaf."

Tiffani's brows furrowed. "Okay…"

"Finally, you need to know what we cover in those courses. Teaching kids with disabilities isn't like babysitting. We don't simply occupy their time. We're teachers. That's what we do—we teach!"

"Oh!" she said as if seeing his mistake. "I'm going to be working with kids who are really crippled. You know, the ones who can't learn? The droolers?"

His fingers tightening, Rob crumpled one of the syllabi he'd been working on. "Droolers?"

"That's what Pete calls them." She giggled again. "He's really funny—when he's normal, that is."

Rob struggled to exhale. If the only faculty member he got along with was that ignorant, working in the department was going to be far harder than he imagined.

"I'm sure he's funny. However, please don't refer to children with disabilities like that. They're people, okay? Treat them like it."

"Sure thing!"

Tiffani scanned the office, then picked up a vase filled with daisies and black-eyed Susans. "These from your girlfriend?"

"What? No. No, they're for Thelma." He smoothed the syllabus he'd inadvertently rumpled. "She helped me out after I got hired. She even sold me one of her rental properties. I thought I'd thank her, but I haven't seen her in a couple of weeks."

"That's because she's dead."

"Dead? What—? When?"

"I think it was Monday. Maybe Tuesday." Tiffani put the vase back and began inspecting a picture of an old-fashion covered bridge on the wall. "She had lung cancer." Her nose crinkled. "She stank of cigarettes. It's how I smell after I perform."

"Dead?" Rob had only spent a few minutes with Thelma, but the news that she was gone felt like somebody had given him the Heimlich maneuver.

"Oh, that reminds me." Tiffani handed him a business card. "This is where I work when I'm not here." The card had the words "Big Willie's" emblazoned in gold above a silhouette of a long-haired woman swinging on a pole. "It's up in Appleton. Since you're a colleague, you get the discount."

Between Thelma's death, the fact his student worker was a stripper, and that people from the university got a discount for… something, Rob didn't know what to focus on.

"When's Thelma's service?" he managed to ask.

Tiffani took a textbook from a shelf and flipped indifferently through its pages. "I don't know. Probably today. When my grandmother bit it, we buried her as soon as possible. Want me to find out?"

"Yes, please."

"Sure. I'm happy to help." She returned the book to the bookshelf. "After all, I might be your new assistant. I have my audition with Craig tonight." She sat on the corner of his desk again and laid her hand on his. Her fingernails had little unicorns painted on them. "When would you like to audition me?"

"What?" Rob jerked his hand away. "Never. I'm… I'm good. Thanks! But, if you could get me the information about Thelma's wake, I'd be grateful."

Craig waddled by the open door. He harumphed as he passed.

"Okay!" She sprang from Rob's desk. "I better get going!"

"Ms. Miller," Rob called after her. "Remember, I also need a new nameplate."

"Sure thing," she said over her shoulder. "Anything for you, Rod."

Chapter 6

According to Tiffani, Thelma's service was that afternoon. Although he didn't look forward to socializing with his coworkers, not to mention missing all the work he needed to finish before the semester began, Rob still felt obligated to go. For a brief period, Thelma was his only friend in the entire state.

Wearing his best suit, he entered the darkened funeral parlor. Nobody seemed to be around. Continuing along a wood-paneled passage lined with fake potted plants, he found a room containing a coffin flanked by two modest bouquets of white peace lilies. Thelma lay inside, her bony, liver-spotted hands folded across her stomach, a light shining upon her mannequin-like face.

Bowing his head, Rob walked up to the coffin.

This was stupid. He barely knew her. Why did her death bother him so much? After all, she tricked everybody into hiring him.

Then again, most of his classmates hadn't found positions yet. He was one of the lucky ones. He should be thankful. Not to mention the fact that she sold him a beautiful little house right on the lake. She probably could've gotten more than what he paid for it. A lot more. And she seemed to believe he could make a difference in the world. Nobody else did.

Rob gazed down at Thelma. She appeared different than what he'd remembered. Perhaps it was because her skin resembled wax. Perhaps it was because she didn't have a cigarette dangling precariously from her mouth.

He exhaled heavily, then said, "Thanks for everything, Thelma. I appreciate it. I'll take good care of your house. And… I'll try to help people with disabilities around here. I promise."

Not knowing what else to do, he patted the coffin and turned around. All the chairs behind him were empty.

An employee carrying a leather-bound book passed by.

"Excuse me," Rob said, not knowing why he was whispering. "When does the service start?"

The employee checked his watch. "About an hour ago."

"I'm sorry I'm late. I found out she'd died this morning. Did everybody else go home already?"

The employee gave a wan smile. "You're the first to arrive."

Rob wondered why this made him so angry—and sad.

The employee offered him the book he was holding. "Would you like to sign the guest register?"

"Sure."

In a large script, Rob signed the first line. He felt like John Hancock.

"Feel free to visit," the young man said. "I'm sure she'd be grateful for your time."

Rob thought that *visit* was a rather unusual choice of words, as was *she'd be grateful,* but he guessed it was simply how people in the funeral business viewed such things. It made the endless parade of death somehow more palatable.

He took a seat at the rear of the parlor.

He'd been sitting there for a few minutes, pondering how long he should stay, when somebody said, "Pardon me."

Rob jumped as a thin man in a black suit leaned in toward him.

"I'm terribly sorry for startling you," the man said. "Did you work with Mrs. Larsen?"

"Yes," Rob replied. "Yes, I did. I worked with… well, I suppose we never actually worked together. I'm new, you see. I joined the faculty at the university a couple months ago. Anyway, I thought I'd come and pay my respects."

"I understand," he said as if Rob had confirmed his suspicions. "There was a hospice worker here earlier. She thought you might attend. She left this for you." He offered him a business envelope with the Lakeview Hospice Care Center's logo in the upper left-hand corner.

Reluctantly, Rob took it.

"Are you sure it's for me? I mean, I… that is, we—Thelma and I—we never really knew each other. I might have spoken to her four or five times if that. Less face-to-face. As I said, I'm new to the university."

"You signed the guest book as Robert Chudinski."

"Yes, I did, however—"

"I was instructed to give this to a Dr. Chudinski."

Turning it over in his fingers, Rob inspected the envelope. It felt empty. "Thelma left me something?"

"That is my understanding. Now, I'll leave you with your thoughts. Please stay as long as you like. If you require anything, don't hesitate to let us know."

"Thank you."

Rob stared at the envelope. What the hell could she have left him?

Tearing open one side, he slid out a faded black-and-white photo of a young couple standing in front of a 1950's Studebaker, the sun in their eyes. The man looked like an intellectual, his spine ramrod straight, short curly hair crowning a rather broad forehead. The woman was an attractive, twenty-something-year-old Thelma wearing a pencil dress and a pillbox hat. Between them, squinting at the camera, was a little girl who might've been five or six. Her left arm was contorted like somebody with spastic cerebral palsy, her mouth open as if in mid-laugh, drool dribbling from her chin. Behind them, a sign spanning two wrought-iron gates said: *St. Coletta Institute for Exceptional Children.*

Rob turned the photo over. Stuck to the other side was a yellow post-it note. On it, somebody had scrawled—*Don't ever give up*. Ever was underlined twice.

Chapter 7

Rob entered Agnew Hall's main conference room. It was the morning before the start of the fall semester, and he had nine meetings scheduled. According to the e-mail he'd received, the Dean's session was supposed to start at seven. However, it was now six minutes to, and nobody was around.

Coffee in one hand, laptop in the other, Rob turned on the lights and took a seat toward the far corner. He waited.

Seven o'clock came and went. Then 7:05. And 7:10.

He reread his e-mail, then checked his phone, making sure he had the correct day. He did. It was Monday, the day before school started. He was sure of it. With students going here and there, noisy frat parties blaring from every other house, and endless lines of mini-vans blocking the streets as parents moved their children into their dorms, the sleepy campus had suddenly sprung to life over the weekend.

At 7:12, Rob got up, walked into the hallway, and checked the room number. The plaque above the door said: 124. He checked his e-mail. It still said the meeting was in Room 124.

He sat in a different chair, hoping it would somehow change his reality.

At 7:18, Rob stood and started gathering his belongings. He stopped. He was clearly in the right room on the right day at the right time. He couldn't have missed the meeting—could he have?

He stepped into the hallway again, wondering if there was a sign indicating the meeting had been moved. There was nothing posted. Perhaps the notice had fallen. He searched the ground. He couldn't find anything.

Crap! How could he have missed the meeting? His first meeting with the Dean, nonetheless.

Then he heard people approaching.

"Excuse me," he said to two middle-aged men appearing from around a corner. They both held cups from Starbucks. "Is this where the faculty meeting was supposed to be?"

"Yeah," one replied less than enthusiastically.

Following them into the conference room, Rob laughed with relief. "I thought I'd missed it. My e-mail says it was supposed to start at seven."

"The Dean wants everybody to be on time, so he schedules the meeting to start a half-hour before it actually begins."

"Well, knowing that," Rob said, "don't people simply show up even later?"

"To tell you the truth, only department chairs and non-tenured faculty usually attend." The oldest professor glanced disappointedly at an empty table by the door. "I'm here because there are usually donuts."

"With the budget cuts?" His companion scoffed. "We won't be seeing another donut until the Democrats take control of the statehouse."

"Wouldn't that be typical? Solving our financial issues by not buying a ten-dollar box of donuts? They should try cutting the number of assistant and associate deans they keep appointing."

"Then where would all the incompetent people go?"

A few more bleary-eyed faculty filed in. Some stood around talking, exchanging stories about their summer, or complaining about the lack of pastries. Others collapsed into the folding chairs, yawning. They all clutched cups of coffee.

At 7:22, Craig, Bert, and Les swaggered in. Craig noted Rob sitting toward the back, lifted his nose in disdain, then sat in the first row, directly in front of the podium.

Rob watched the various groups of faculty members. He marveled at how each faction had its own characteristics. A circle of men standing by the empty donut table all wore Birkenstocks. Another group sitting to Rob's right had dark suits. Each woman in a cluster strolling about wore her hair in a bun. Nobody interacted outside their herd.

At 7:28, somebody by the doorway hissed, "He's coming!"

People dashed to their seats.

Moments later, a tall, muscular African American man with a crew cut entered the room. Glowering, he rolled up his sleeves, revealing tattoos of snakes intertwined around bloody daggers on his sizable forearms.

"All right," he growled as he stepped behind the lectern. "Let's get this damn thing over with. I've got better things to do."

He rifled through scraps of paper, then raked the seats with his penetrating gaze. There were enough for two hundred people, but only thirty or so were occupied.

"I see we have some new faces among us," he said in a tone suggesting he wasn't happy about this. "Perhaps the chairs should introduce them before we begin."

He nodded to a stylish Hispanic woman wearing a designer pantsuit and silk scarf. She stood and gestured to a short, rather stocky, blonde woman smiling enthusiastically next to her.

"I'd like to introduce Dr. Wendy Maddon. She comes to us from Bowling Green University and will be teaching our feminist theory and women in history courses."

Everybody clapped politely.

Then a nerdish older man with black-rimmed glasses and a red bowtie stood. He motioned to a young man sitting next to him. "This is Dr. Siddharth..." He paused and examined something written on an index card. "Bhat... Bhat..."

The new faculty member stood. "Bhattacharyya. But please, call me Sid."

"That's certainly a lot easier. I almost ran out of ink writing your name," the department chair with the bowtie said. "Anyway, Sid is from California State University, Northridge, and will be teaching our Introduction to Information Sciences course. Once he gets his feet wet, he will also be advising our undergraduates."

More polite applause.

It died away, leaving an uncomfortable silence.

"Don't you have somebody new, Grubber?" the Dean asked.

Craig grumbled something, then got to his feet. Hitching a thumb in Rob's direction, he announced, "That's Rod... something. We didn't hire him. He's an idiot."

Craig sat, his arms folded tightly across his chest.

"Well then," the Dean said. "I'm sure Rod will be appointed Provost before we know it."

The faculty chuckled.

The Dean consulted his notes, then looked up. To Rob, it seemed as though he was glaring directly at him.

"Perhaps I should introduce myself to the new recruits. I'm Captain Luther Hammer, USMC retired. I believe in two things. Doing your damned job and the chain of command. So let me be frank with you—do what you're told and don't bother me. If you do these two things, you'll be fine."

The Dean crumpled a scrap of paper and threw it into the trash.

"The next order of business involves the budget. The moron civilians in Madison have cut our funding by 10.3%. Our enrollment is down 19.8%. And we are carrying forward a $27.6 million deficit from last year. As a result, there will be a hiring freeze until further notice."

Somebody in the front row muttered, "Jesus Christ." It might've been Craig.

"Consequently," the Dean said sternly, "we will be decommissioning non-productive programs. I suggest you all consolidate sections to maximize profit margins. Moreover, all courses must cover their costs. That means none of this four or five student-per-class garbage. If the section doesn't have enough students to pay for the instructor of record, it doesn't run. Understand?"

Nobody said anything.

"Also, we will be relying more and more on adjunct faculty, so I encourage the chairs to maintain a list of available bodies to fill next year's openings. Remember, they must have at least a high school diploma and can pass the state's criminal background check."

A woman to Rob's left whispered to a colleague, "That eliminates everybody we currently use."

Her colleague nodded.

"And do not think for a moment that it is merely our esteemed university hearing the death knell," the Dean continued. "It's every goddamned university in this great country of ours. We're all in the same foxhole. So be thankful you have jobs. God knows you pampered, candy-assed, liberal intellectuals will never find any work in the real world. So, I suggest you do your part to keep us from going tits-up. Otherwise, you'll find out how worthless your pretentious degrees actually are."

The faculty shifted irritably as the Dean threw another wad of paper into the trash.

The professor directly in front of Rob whispered to the person sitting next to him, "Here it comes." They both produced pieces of cardboard with three-by-three grids.

"People," the Dean said solemnly, "in these dark financial times, we have to be proactive. We have to synergize. We have to pull together. Remember, there is no 'I' in 'team.' We're all in this together. Understand? We either sink or swim together. We must operate as a cohesive, well-oiled machine..."

The person kitty-corner from Rob muttered, "Bingo."

The other slid his card into his briefcase. "I'll pay you later."

"...All oars must be in the water and pulling in the same direction. We've got to buckle down and seize the opportunities presented to us with both hands. So," the Dean faltered, then added, "let's be careful out there!" He saluted. "Dismissed."

At this, Craig sprang to his feet. "Excuse me, um, sir!"

The Dean groaned. "What is it, Grubber?"

"It may not have come to your attention yet, sir, so I'd like to inform you that the pranks have started again. And I want them to stop! In addition to concocting some sort of explosive device using a bag of flour, somebody has destroyed my beautiful desk!" He shot a glance at a Berkinstocker who freakishly resembled Sigmund Freud. "And I want the culprits prosecuted to the fullest extent of the law!"

The Sigmund Freud-look alike leaped up. "Don't you narrow your eyes at me, Craig!" he said in a vaguely British accent. "I arrived on campus yesterday. And do you know what I found in my filing cabinets? Cow excrement! My drawers are full of it. It'll take me weeks to get the stench out of my office!"

Somebody behind Rob snickered.

"And how do you know it is cow excrement, hmm?" Craig retorted as if scoring a point. "Maybe you put it there!"

"Any imbecile can tell it's from a cow. First of all, there's the immense size. Even you couldn't produce that much crap!"

The Birkenstockers laughed and clapped.

"Lieberman..." the Dean said. "Grubber..."

"Perhaps it isn't excrement at all," Craig yelled across the room. "Perhaps it's a by-product of your program!"

"That's just like a behavioralist, only looking at the by-products rather than the input."

"People…" the Dean said.

"Outcomes are the only things that matter," Craig declared. "You constructivist bastard!"

"How can you possibly change anything if you don't address the underlying cause?" Dr. Lieberman countered.

"People…" the Dean said again, louder.

Craig spluttered, then shouted, "Your accent is fake! We all know you're from Iowa!"

"I'll have you know I was born in Little Ilmarsh!" Dr. Lieberman replied, offended.

Bert and Les joined the fray, as did the faculty around Dr. Lieberman. Bert called Dr. Lieberman "Mary Poppins," while a woman next to Dr. Lieberman told Bert to go wash his toupee.

"People…" The Dean hollered, "People!"

Everybody went rigid.

The Dean leaned over the lectern, his muscular frame threatening to crush it into kindling. "Allow me to be perfectly clear. If I catch the person or persons responsible for any of these pranks—I will have them discharged from the university. And don't think that any of this socialist, tenured bullshit is going to help you keep your cushy jobs. Some of these pranks involve the destruction of university property. Read your contracts. You'll find that's a fireable offense, regardless of your tenure status. So, God better have mercy on the assholes who are doing this because I won't show them any. Understood? I said—understood?"

A series of 'understood's percolated throughout the conference room.

"Good!" The Dean marched to the door. "See you next September."

Chapter 8

Rob sat on the rug in his office, putting together his new chair. With a high back and lumbar support, it was similar to the one stolen the week before—but less expensive. If it was so easy to take things from the faculty, he didn't want to spend any more than he had to. Besides, his first student loan bill had arrived. He had to watch every penny.

He tightened the last bolt, then admired his work.

"Nice!" somebody behind him said. Turning, he found the stocky blonde from the Dean's meeting standing in the doorway. "Mine is covered in duct tape and has one leg shorter than the other. It's like riding a teeter-totter."

Rob nodded at his old chair by the garbage can. "That's what they gave me. I figure if I wanted to sit for more than two minutes at a time, I'd have to buy my own. Please, come in. You're…?"

"Wendy. Wendy Maddon. And you're Rod, right?"

Rob wiped his greasy palm across his khakis and shook her hand.

"Actually," he said, painfully aware of the dark smudge he'd made along his pant leg, "it's Rob."

"Really?" She pointed to his door. "This says something different."

Sure enough, somebody had replaced his brass nameplate with a cardboard sign. In big red letters, it read: 'Pollyanna.'

Rob chuckled awkwardly. "The guys in my program… they're real kidders!"

"Yeah, I've heard about the guys in your program." She wagged her head. "Anyway, since we're both new, I thought we'd, you know, kind of hang out. Form a mutual admiration society or support group. After what your department chair said this morning, I figured you could use it."

"You know," Rob said, "I could! Thank you! I've been here since July and haven't had a positive interaction with anybody. It'd be terrific to have somebody to talk to."

"Great! Want to go out with Sid and me after work? Grab a pizza? Maybe a beer or two?"

"Sid?"

"The other new guy? He's in Information Science."

"Oh, yeah. Right," Rob said, disappointed he wasn't going to be alone with her. He'd hoped she was asking him on a date.

"Interested?" she prodded.

Craig pushed into the crowded office. "Out of my way!"

Wendy flattened herself against the wall, careful not to step on the new chair's discarded box and packing materials.

Craig stopped and narrowed his eyes at her. "You aren't in Teaching and Learning, are you?"

"No. Women Studies."

"Really?" He chortled. "Honestly, I have no idea how that even became a major. It's as useless as a degree in French literature or communications. Where do your students become employed— McDonald's?"

Gasping, Wendy started to reply, but Craig turned and shoved a folder thick with papers at Rob. "Since you didn't deem it necessary to attend our special education faculty meeting, we selected your committee assignments for you."

"What?" Rob checked his day planner. "I didn't miss it. It's in half an hour."

"Yes, well…" Craig smirked. "It got moved up a tad. And in case you didn't read your contract thoroughly — active participation in department, school, and university committees is required for reappointment. So, you best not miss any more meetings. You hear me, Polly?"

Laughing, he strutted out of the office.

Rob looked at the overflowing folder in his hands and then at Wendy.

"Oh, yeah," he told her. "I'll definitely need a few beers after work."

"I'll buy!"

Chapter 9

"You won a research award?" Wendy asked, amazed.

Around them, people talked, and music blared. Vino's was small and dark and had tables covered with decades of graffiti, but it was the only bar they could find near campus that didn't have a line out its front door.

Taking a sip from his beer, Rob lifted two fingers.

"Two awards?" Wendy cried.

"Holy cow!" Sid said. "And I can say that. I'm Hindu!"

They laughed.

A perky waitress in her mid-twenties came to their table. "Do you need anything? Anything at all?"

They shook their heads. Their pitcher was still a quarter full, and half of the cheese pizza remained uneaten.

"We're good," Rob told her. "But thank you."

"No problem." The waitress turned to the neighboring table. "How about you?" She readied her pen and paper. "Another round?"

"Are you from Tennessee?" one of the drunk college students asked, his head teetering slightly. "Because... you're the only... *ten-I-see.*" Blinking slowly, he leered at her.

"I'll come back later."

Walking away, she made a face suggesting she was going to vomit. The table of college students cheered and clapped.

Rob returned his attention to his fellow assistant professors. "What about you two? I know Wendy is in Women's Studies, but what's Information Sciences?"

"It involves the storage, retrieval, and display of information in useful ways." Seeing their confusion, Sid added, "It used to be called Library Sciences."

"You prepare librarians?"

"Not only librarians, but anybody working with information. For example, museums often hire our students to create exhibits and educational programs for the public."

"Cool. What made you go into that field?"

"I've always liked books," Sid said, almost apologetically. "When I was three, my mother found me sitting in a corner with a copy of The Hobbit. She thought I was some sort of protege. Boy, was she disappointed!"

He took a drink.

"At any rate, since I'm Indian, my academic advisor in college always assumed I liked computers. She kept encouraging me to go into programming. But I knew it wasn't for me. One day I was in the library, watching the librarians help people, and something kind of clicked. I changed my major and kept avoiding reality by getting more degrees. And—" He lifted his hands, palms up. "—the rest is history."

Rob nodded to Wendy. "What about you? Why Women's Studies?"

Wendy swallowed the pizza she'd been eating. "When I was a seven, I tried out for a little league baseball team. I was too heavy to run fast, but I could hit and throw and field as well as anybody. However, when the coaches found out I was a girl, they told me I couldn't play. They told me to try out for softball instead. After that, I became obsessed about how the lack of a penis impacted my life."

"Did you ever play softball?" Rob asked.

"Sure did. Including three years at Wright State."

"What position?"

"You kidding?" Wendy slapped her legs. "With thighs like these, I was a born catcher." She emptied her glass in one long pull, then filled it with more beer. "A pretty good one, if I say so myself. Batted .342 in my career. Made All-Conference all four years in high school." She motioned to Rob. "Your turn. Why special education?"

"To tell you the truth," Rob said, embarrassed, "I kind of fell into it. Originally, I wanted to teach social studies. I like history, and teaching seemed to be the only thing you could do with a history degree. During my undergrad, I student taught at a middle school. One day, the principal stopped me in the hall and asked how things were going. I told him I was finding it difficult to teach all the different kids in my classes."

"Different kids?"

"Yeah. I had a student who was gifted and taking college-level courses on the weekends. I had another one who stole a car, drove across state lines, and robbed a convenience store."

"Geez!" Sid said. "Did he go to jail?"

"No. He was back at school a few days later with a tracking device around his ankle. He used to pull it off to see how long it'd take the police to find him."

Wendy took a bite of pizza. "Funny."

"It wasn't at the time, believe me," Rob said, recalling all the occasions the police burst into his classroom. "Anyway, I told the principal about the problems I was having. I told him about how I had kids who were so smart I couldn't challenge them. And how I had kids who couldn't read or write."

"What did he say?"

"He said that I should always teach to the A and B students because…" Rob made quotation marks in the air. "'Those special education brats are always going to fail. We're fooling ourselves if we believe otherwise.'"

"Asshole."

"That's what I thought. So, I spent the rest of my student teaching trying to help the kids who wanted to learn but struggled. I ended up getting my master's and Ph.D. in special education. And—here I am."

A freckled-face college student who barely looked old enough to be out of high school gestured to their extra chair. "Mind if we take this?"

"Knock yourself out," Rob told him.

"Thanks!" He dragged it to a table filled with equally young-looking students.

Sid refilled his glass with warm beer. "If you don't mind me asking, how many publications do you two have?"

"Just one." Wendy chewed. "And I'm third author. But I'm hoping to get a couple studies out soon."

Sid and Wendy turned to Rob. He took an extra-long pull on his beer, giving himself time to think. He didn't want to brag, but their praise felt fantastic, especially after being called an idiot in front of everybody at the Dean's meeting.

"Six referred articles," Rob said. "And two chapters."

"Six!" Sid gasped. "Shit! I only have three. And one is a book review!"

"Rob!" Wendy said incredulously. "What the hell are you doing here? This is a teaching university."

Rob set his beer next to his plate of pizza crusts. He wasn't a big drinker and needed to pace himself. The last thing he wanted to do was get drunk and start acting like the college students sitting next to them.

"I believe there should be a connection between research and teaching. Think about it this way—" He reached for his beer, then forced himself to leave it alone. "You conduct a study. Write it up. Get it published in a top-tier journal and, what—? Perhaps fifteen people read it. Maybe twenty. If you're lucky, one of them will use your findings to guide their practices. But if I have a hundred students in an academic year, maybe ten will use what I teach them. That's every year. By the end of my career, I will have trained a small army of exceptional educators. And each of them will have hundreds of children passing through their classrooms." He took a drink. "Teaching is the most effective way to make the world a better place."

"Okay, I get that," Wendy said, "but—Christ, eight publications and two research awards? You should be at a research-intensive university. Harvard or Princeton or someplace like that."

"I'm not that good."

"Sounds like you are," Sid said.

Rob bit into a slightly burnt pizza crust, crumbs going everywhere.

"Thanks, but my focus is on severe disabilities." He swept the crumbs onto his plate. "It's a fairly specialized field. There weren't many schools looking to hire in my area, so I took the first tenure-track position I could. Also, I wanted to stay close to home."

"Where's home?" Sid asked.

"Chicago area. Westside."

Wendy nearly choked as she ate. "Don't tell anybody around here that. You're in Packer country!"

"I'll keep my Mike Ditka poster hidden in its shrine where it belongs."

"You better! I told somebody the Bengals were going to win their division this year and practically had my head handed to me."

That's Amore began playing on an old-fashioned jukebox by the door. The table of drunk college students next to them sang along.

"What kind of college bar plays Dean Martin?" Sid asked.

"I'm guessing the owner is Italian." Rob nodded to the pictures lining the walls. Half of them were of the Rat Pack.

Sid filled his glass. "Did you say you bought a house?" He caught the waitress's eye, then pointed to their empty pitcher. She indicated she'd be right there.

"Yeah. It's not much. Just a two-bedroom bungalow."

"Man, between my student loans and waiting to be tenured, I think I'll be living in my studio apartment for another thirty years."

"It's actually cheaper than renting," Rob told him. "Plus, you build a little equity. You might want to look into it. It's a real buyer's market. You could get a great deal."

The waitress set another pitcher of Budweiser in front of them.

"Thank you," they all said.

"No problem." She cleared away the dirty napkins. "Let me know when you want another."

"I'm sure this will be the last one," Wendy said. "We have class tomorrow."

The waitress laughed. "So does everybody here!"

Looking around, Rob realized they were the only non-college students in the place. He felt oddly like a spy in an enemy camp.

Wendy eyed the remaining pizza. "Where's your house?"

"Right by the lake. It's not too bad, considering the price. It was built in the 1920s and has tons of stained wood throughout. Not to mention a nice little yard with a colorful rose garden in front. You two will have to come over sometime. I'll cook dinner."

"Sounds marvelous." Giving in to temptation, she took the last slice. "How are the flies? I heard they're horrible that side of town."

Nonplussed, Rob shrugged. "I haven't seen any. Well, maybe a few, but they're not bad."

They nursed their beers and watched the television mounted in the corner by the ceiling. Sports Center was on. Somebody in a suit was talking about the Yankee's latest pitching sensation.

"What's up with your chair?" Sid asked Rob. "I can't believe how rude he was this morning."

"That was him being nice."

"Really?"

"He's a pompous buffoon." Wendy took another bite of pizza. "You can't imagine the stories I've heard about him."

"Oh yes, I can!" Rob told her. "I have yet to meet anybody who likes him."

Wendy swallowed. "How many committees did he put you on?"

"Twenty-four."

"Twenty-four!" Wendy exclaimed. "I'm only on two."

"Two?" Sid repeated. "I'm not going to be on any committees until my second year!"

"The worst part is that some of them meet at the same time," Rob said, pleased they thought his committee assignment was excessive as well. "I don't know what I'm going to do. Craig is going to have my ass if I miss any of them."

"Oh, you'll be fine." Finishing the pizza, Wendy wiped a grease-stained napkin across her lips. "You heard the Dean today. There's a hiring freeze on. They'll do everything they can to keep us here. If they don't, they'd never get our positions filled again."

"You think?"

"Absolutely. And if we left, who'd do all the grunt work? They would! I can't imagine your department chair wants to be on twenty-four committees! It sounds like he's trying to put you in your place. Ignore him."

"Yeah…" Rob wasn't sure if it was the company, the beer, or Wendy's perspective, but he felt much better about his situation. "You're probably right."

"Of course, I am. So don't worry." Wendy raised her glass. "And good luck on your first day tomorrow, everybody. Here's to being tenure-track professors."

They clinked glasses.

"Tenure-track professors!"

Chapter 10

Rob stood apprehensively behind the classroom podium. The clock on the far wall indicated it was 12:44, but his phone said it was 8:57 am. He gazed upon the sea of empty seats. According to his roster, two hundred and ninety-three students had registered for his pit class. But only thirty-nine bodies were sitting before him—and some of them were homeless people getting out of the rain.

He went through his notes, then set them aside. He'd been rehearsing for the better part of a week. He couldn't stand the sight of them anymore. Besides, he knew the lecture by heart.

He rechecked his phone. It was 9:01. The class should've started already.

Counting the students slumped in their seats, he found there were now forty-two. He wondered how he was going to get the other two hundred and fifty-one up-to-speed.

A student came to the stage. "Excuse me."

Rob bent down. "Yes? Can I help?"

"Yeah, you see. I wasn't in class last week and I was wondering if I missed anything."

"Actually," Rob said, trying not to make him feel stupid, "we didn't have class last week. This is the first session of the semester."

"Oh! Great. Thanks!"

Rob watched in disbelief as the student grabbed his backpack and left.

A few more people trickled in.

Taking a deep breath, Rob straightened his tie and hoped the sweat puddles spreading under his armpits weren't too noticeable.

At 9:05, he decided to begin.

"Okay, everybody—!"

An ear-splitting squeal sliced through the auditorium. Even the sleeping homeless people sat up with a lurch. Rob backed away from the microphone.

"Sorry about that. Anyway, I'm Dr. Chudinski. And this is Introduction to Abnormal Children. However, I'm going to call this class Introduction to Exceptionalities." He pushed the spacebar on his laptop. A new slide appeared on the giant screen behind him, changing the name of the course. "As we will discuss throughout the semester, people with disabilities aren't abnormal. In fact—"

"Wait!" a girl from the second row called out. "Isn't this Introduction to Abnormal Children?"

"Yes, it is," Rob replied. "I was saying that a better title for this course is Introduction to Exceptionalities because having a disability doesn't make you abnormal. In fact, when you consider the range of abilities within the typical population—"

"Where's the syllabus?" a guy toward the rear of the lecture hall asked. He had his feet propped on the vacant seat in front of him.

Rob tried not to show his irritation. "It's online. But before we—"

The students headed to the doors.

"Wait! Where are you going? We have a lot to cover before I let you go. And we still have..." Rob checked his phone. "...more than two and a half hours."

"It's the first day!" several of them cried.

"I know it's the first day. I want to give you an overview of the course, then go into the history of—"

"You can't cover stuff the first day! The first day is for reading the syllabus!"

"I'm sure you're all capable of reading the syllabus on your own," Rob told them. "I shouldn't have to read it to you."

The grumbling grew more violent.

"Look!" Rob shouted over the rising voices. "We have sixteen weeks in the semester. One week is for the midterm—another the final. A third is Thanksgiving Break. That leaves only thirteen weeks to cover everything you need to know about special education. I can't give up an entire week to—"

"But I'm not in special ed!" There was a chorus of agreement. "I'm not going to teach those kids."

"That's what you think," Rob countered.

"I'm in elementary education!" somebody else said. "I don't even know why this stupid class is required for my major."

"Same here!"

"Trust me," Rob said. "You will all be teaching kids with disabilities. If you'll take your seats and let me—"

"Man, this sucks!"

"How do you know we'll be teaching those kids? You don't know what our majors are!"

"Yeah!"

"All right!" Rob hollered. They quieted somewhat. "I'll tell you what. Give me ten minutes, and then you can run out of here as fast as you can. Okay? Give me just ten minutes."

A few people threw themselves into their chairs, but most remained standing by the doors.

Rob thought for a moment, then said, "Think about it this way. You're all going to be regular educators, right? Many of you think you'll be teaching elementary school. Some of you think you'll be teaching social studies or math or biology or honors English." He paused for effect. "But you're not! You're going to be teaching children—and some of those children will learn differently than their peers, or they have strange behaviors, such as screaming profanity."

"I'd like to scream some myself," muttered a husky student wearing a high school letterman jacket. According to the patches on his sleeves, he played football, baseball, and wrestled.

Rob called to him. "What do you want to teach when you graduate?"

"Me?" The student sat up.

"Yes, you. What do you want to teach?"

"I want to coach baseball."

"But you need a teaching license to get a job?"

"Yeah."

"Let me guess. You're in the history program."

The student in the letterman jacket looked at his friends sitting around him. They seemed as curious as he was about where this line of questioning was going. "Yeah."

"You know it's tough getting a job as a history teacher, right?" Rob asked. "I mean, there isn't a big demand for them. Plus, we're graduating— what? Fifty history majors each year? Maybe sixty? The competition for the few jobs available is going to be fierce. And, frankly, every former high school athlete wants to coach. You need to have something on your resume that will get you the job you want. That's where this class comes in. If you know something about special education, I guarantee you'll be more appealing to principals than all the other applicants."

The want-to-be coach appeared to consider this.

"One last question for you," Rob said. "What are you going to do if you can't get a coaching job?"

The student wavered. "I don't know."

"I can help you get a job. I'll teach you what IEPs and manifest determination are. I'll give you the ability to answer questions I know principals will ask in your interviews."

"But," a young woman standing by the want-to-be coach said timidly, "I don't want to teach crippled kids. I want to teach kids who are normal."

Rob smiled, then said into the microphone, "Tough shit."

The students blinked at him, shocked.

"Look, despite what you may think, people with disabilities are everywhere. They're in every classroom, from kindergarten to high school AP calculus. Some are even standing on a stage in front of you." He bowed. "You see, I have something called ADHD."

Somebody mumbled, "So do I."

More than a few heads nodded.

"Do me a favor," Rob said. "Give me two more minutes to tell you a story. If you want to leave after that, I won't try to stop you. But give me two minutes. Okay?"

Nobody left.

"When I was twenty-one," Rob began, "I graduated with a bachelor's degree from Purdue University. I wanted to teach social studies. I knew it would be tough getting a teaching job, so I took extra courses during the summers. In addition to U.S. and World History, I could teach sociology, psychology, government, economics, and even anthropology. Don't ask me why. I just thought anthropology sounded cool. You might say, I… *dug…* it."

They groaned.

Rob went on. "I graduated top in my class. Honor roll. Dean's list. Distinguished student awards. I was willing to move to any part of the country, so I sent out five hundred resumes—and didn't get a job. I ended up living in my parents' basement. Believe me. It's difficult to pick up women when you're twenty-one and living with your folks."

A few students chuckled.

"My father was so upset that I wasn't using my degree, he nailed a bill for $63,000 to my bedroom door. That's how much he paid to send me to Purdue. Anyhow, one day, I was looking through the help wanted ads, and I found an advertisement that said: 'Teachers wanted.' I thought, 'Hell, I'm a teacher! I have a license.' So, I applied."

Rob took a drink from his water bottle. The students waited.

"It turned out the ad was for a teaching position at a residential lockdown facility for juvenile offenders. I got the job and started teaching kids with disabilities who committed serious crimes. I worked with students who were arsonists. I worked with kids who molested other kids. I even worked with murderers."

"Bullshit," somebody said.

"No, I'm serious. One of my students killed his family with a hatchet." Rob pointed heavenward. "Hand to God. I even worked with a kid who set fire to his grandmother's house while she was inside."

"Did she get out?" a young woman asked.

"Nope." Rob hopped off the stage and approached the students clustered by the doors. "My point is this—every single one of my students was in a regular education classroom before they committed their crimes. From ADHD to autism to cerebral palsy to learning disabilities to quadriplegia to paranoid schizophrenia… you *will* work with kids with disabilities no matter what grade or subject you teach."

The students stood, thinking.

"One final comment. What I will teach you in this class will help you *get* a job. As I said, principals will ask you about special education in your interviews. That's simply how things are nowadays. You can't avoid it.

"But I will also teach you things that will help you *keep* your job. There's an extremely high burnout rate in education. The national average for teaching careers is a little more than three years. If you want to be a teacher and stay a teacher, you have to learn about students who act and think differently than what is typical."

He checked his phone.

"I've gone over my two minutes. Feel free to leave."

Rob climbed on the stage and shoved his notes into his briefcase.

"What happened to the kid who killed his family with a hatchet?" somebody asked.

"I'll make you a deal," Rob told them. "Let me cover the material I need to cover. Then I'll tell you all about him."

Chapter 11

Rob strolled along Agnew Hall's sixth-floor hallway, still high from teaching his first college course as a tenure-track assistant professor. Sure, the period got off to a rocky start. But, once he began engaging his students, most of them stayed. Hell, some even remained afterward to ask questions.

He shook his head.

Forty-two out of nearly three hundred students…

Still, he did reach some of them. And a few would go on to use what he'd taught in their classrooms. He was one step closer to producing his army of exceptional educators.

Up ahead, Craig's door came into view. It was open.

Rob slowed, trying to decide if he should approach him. Sometimes letting things die naturally was best. He passed the office. Craig was sitting at a card table, pounding on a computer keyboard with his two chubby index fingers.

Then again, perhaps not addressing them makes things fester. The sooner Rob cleared the air, the better. Besides, nothing could ruin his day, not even Walrus.

Rob knocked on the door. "Hey, Craig?"

"Out!" Craig shouted, not looking up from his keyboard. He continued thumping away on the keys like he was playing whack-a-mole. "What the hell is wrong with you?"

Rob checked his feet. "I'm not in your office. I haven't crossed the line."

"Don't get smart with me, Polly! I'm on to you. You hear me? I'm on to you!"

"Look, about that…" Rob tried to find the right words. "I'm… I'm sorry about how we started off. It's completely my fault."

Craig stopped typing.

Hoping he was making headway, Rob pushed on. "I'd like to begin again. You know, put the past behind us." Searching for something to say, he noted the paper awards covering the walls. "I know I have a lot to learn from you. Working alongside you will make me a better teacher and researcher… and person! I'm sure we'll become friends."

"Friends?" Craig repeated scornfully.

"Good friends!"

"Good friends?" Craig leaned over the card table. It buckled under his considerable girth. "Now you listen to me, Polly. We will never be friends. Do you understand? There's absolutely nothing I like about you. And if you think for a moment, we're going to be buddies and I'm going to buy you drinks at your favorite watering hole—you're delusional. Hear me? Delusional."

Rob tried to interject, but Craig cut him off.

"And I know what you're trying to do. *Learn from me?*" he mocked. "There's nothing you think you can learn from anybody. You think you're so smart. So very clever. Come here from your fancy school with your research articles and awards and all of your highfalutin ideas. You're right and everybody else is wrong. You know everything!"

"I never said—"

"I don't know how you got hired—" Craig's face turned an explosive shade of red, his veins throbbed. "—but rest assured, you will never get reappointed. Never! You have a one-year contract. That's it. Come next September, you'll be a forgotten memory. And I'll never see you again. Are we clear? You will never, under any circumstances, or in any sense of the word, be reappointed in the spring. Got it? Never! And Polly—I'm the one who decides whether or not you stay. Me. The department chair. So start looking for another job, because you're done here! Now…" Craig pointed at the hallway. "Get out!"

Shaken, Rob made his way to his office, opened the door, and sat behind his green metal desk. Almost immediately, the chair listed violently to one side, throwing him to the floor. Somebody had stolen his new chair again.

Chapter 12

"Rob!" Frank Russo gasped. "You can't leave after only one year!"

Rob sat on his living room sofa, his laptop balanced on his knees.

"I wasn't thinking of staying the entire year," he said. "I was hoping you'd know of something coming available in January. Maybe a post-doc or grant-funded position or something. Anything! I could even return as a student. I could take out more loans and, I don't know, get a degree in, in… economics or something. That could be useful, right?"

Frank massaged his neck in exasperation. "Rob, leaving this soon wouldn't be good."

"Why?"

"You have to understand. Academia is a very small, tightly knit community, especially those of us in special education. Everybody knows everybody. If you leave after one semester or even one year, people will hear about it and think something's wrong with you."

"Nothing is wrong with me! I… I have two research awards. I have eight publications. People will know I'm good!"

"First of all, those research awards are old news. You competed against other doctoral students, not actual researchers. And in all but one of your pubs, you're a co-author. Your professional name is basically et al."

Rob tossed his hands. His laptop wobbled. He caught it before it tumbled to the ground. "I can't stay here, Frank. I can't!"

"You'll have to. Oh, don't look at me like that. It won't be forever. Just for three or four years. Get some experience. Show people what you can do. Then go to a bigger university with more resources. That's how things are done. It's like you're in the minor leagues now. You have to pay your dues before you reach the majors."

"Frank! I'm not going to be able to make it three or four years."

"You'll do fine. Keep your head down and focus on your research. Get four or five single-authored pubs each year, maybe submit a grant application, and you'll be golden. You could go anywhere that has an opening. Maybe even get something at the associate professor rank."

"You don't understand!" Rob fought to keep his voice from going shrill. "They're not going to renew my contract. My chair won't allow it!"

"You're always so emotional about things. Seriously, you need to detach a bit. Otherwise, life is going to grind you to dust."

Rob slumped into the sofa cushion. "Easier said than done."

Frank studied Rob's face. "Wasn't today your first day teaching? I'm sure you weren't that awful. Besides, it takes a few weeks to get into a groove. You have to be able to read your students and keep their interest. Change the pitch and inflection of your voice. And don't lecture the entire time! Show videos. The more shocking, the better. Show a video of a kid having a seizure. That always grabs their attention."

"This isn't about my teaching. My classes today went pretty well."

"Then what's the issue?"

Rob tried to sound reasonable. "My chair hates me."

"I'm sure he doesn't *hate* you. He's merely showing you who's king. Alpha dog, remember? He's making you earn your respect."

"Frank, he told me in no uncertain terms that he will not be renewing my contract for next year."

"Come on. Everybody gets renewed. It's when you reach the tenure stage, they'll weed people out. I'm serious. In my thirty-two years in academia, I've only heard of one person who didn't get renewed after their first year—and he slept with a student."

Rob stared at his muted television. Rachel and Ross were kissing on *Friends.*

"Everybody gets renewed," Frank said calmly. "I'm not exaggerating, or blowing smoke up your ass, or telling you what you want to hear. At the very least, they'll want to keep you, if only so they don't have to go through the hassle of interviewing a group of new candidates. Trust me. Teach well. Go to the committee meetings. Be pleasant. And you'll be fine."

Chapter 13

Panting, Rob hurried along a dirt track cutting through the grassy area enclosed by a rectangle of identical brick buildings. Around him, hundreds of students milled about, staring at their phones. A few were even sunbathing in the bright September sun.

According to the papers Craig had given him, the Faulty Recruitment and Retention Committee met at noon halfway across campus from where Rob had just finished teaching, which meant he was going to be at least fifteen minutes late for the meeting. He hoped Craig would understand. After all, surely teaching came first.

Dappled with sweat, Rob ran to the room indicated on his committee assignment form, took a second to compose himself, and then opened the door. The room was dark and empty, chairs neatly arranged around a conference table.

He stepped into an office across the hall.

"Excuse me," he said to a receptionist sitting at the front desk.

"Yes, dear?"

Rob motioned to the room behind him. "Did the Faculty Recruitment and Retention Committee meet already?"

Leaning back, the secretary looked around a cubical wall. "Shelby, did the FRR Committee meet today?"

The tat-tat-tat of typing answered her.

"They were supposed to," another woman said.

"Damn it." Rob checked his phone. He was seventeen minutes late. "I guess it was a short meeting."

"I don't think so," the receptionist said. "I haven't seen anybody go in there this morning. Maybe it's been postponed."

"I hope so." Rob mopped his sleeve across his sweaty forehead. "I don't suppose you know if there's any way to have the meetings scheduled for a different time. I have a class that overlaps with it and another meeting scheduled in forty minutes."

"Ask the chair. Usually they use the first meeting to see when everybody can get together."

"I will, thank you," Rob said. "Do you know who the chair is?"

The receptionist peered around the wall again. "Shelby?"

There was more typing. Then a pause.

"This is interesting," the unseen woman said. "Didn't Dr. Webb-Callaway leave the university?"

"Yeah," the receptionist replied. "Went to Florida where it's warm. I wish I went with her."

"And Dr. Hensley?"

"He went somewhere in Ohio."

"And Dr. Ashabanulla?"

"I have no idea where he went, but he's gone as well."

The woman in the cubical chuckled. "You realize the entire Retention Committee from last year has left the university? The only person listed on the committee roster is somebody named Robert Chudinski."

"That's me!" Rob said.

"Well, there you go," the receptionist told him. "Looks like you're the chair. Schedule the meetings whenever you like."

"Great! That'll be a big help. Thanks!" Then something occurred to him. "Wait. Everybody who was on the Faculty Retention Committee left the university?"

"Honey—" The receptionist gave him a knowing look. "—if that doesn't say something about this place, nothing will."

Chapter 14

Rob jogged up the Administration Building's wide marble steps and opened a gilded door. Roaming around the palatial corridors, he eventually found the room he was looking for.

"Parking Appeals Committee?" he asked several people talking around a table.

An immensely overweight man choked on a donut. The word "maintenance" was written across his filthy overalls.

"Righty-o!" He brushed powdered sugar from his lap.

"Great. Thanks!"

The other committee members watched as Rob sat at the far end of the table, took out his laptop, and waited for it to connect to the internet.

"I don't mean to pry," said an older woman with curly salt and pepper hair, "but who are you representing?"

Rob accessed the lecture notes for his next class. "Representing?"

"Yes, we each represent people from across the university. I'm Beth. I represent the classified staff. Harold and Perry represent the custodial staff." Two men wearing matching maroon shirts with EWU's logo on the breast pocket inclined their heads. "Larry is from maintenance." The heavy-set man covered in powdered sugar saluted. "Tasha and Jeff are students." Two young people gazed intently at their cell phones as their thumbs frantically tapped buttons. "And Jack is from ground's keeping." A short man with white hair and a neatly trimmed mustache lifted a coffee cup in greeting.

"Oh." Rob noticed he was the only one wearing a jacket and tie. He felt over-dressed. "I'm from Special Education."

"Faculty?"

This sounded more like an accusation than a question.

Rob glanced nervously around. Everybody except the students was staring at him. "That's right."

Their eyes widened.

"Something wrong?" he asked, fearing he'd done something stupid.

"Well," Beth said, "not wrong. Just… odd. I've been on this committee for thirteen years, and in that time, we've never had a faculty member here."

"I've been on for eighteen," Larry announced authoritatively, "and we've never had a faculty member so much as step foot in this room. Not unless they were upset we didn't overturn their parking tickets." He slapped Harold across the chest. "Remember the professor who came here, threatening to get us all fired?"

They laughed.

"Are you saying faculty don't serve on this committee?" Rob asked, his hope rising.

"They're supposed to," Perry replied. "But nobody ever shows."

"Why?"

"First of all, we meet every week."

"Every week!" Rob exclaimed. "For how long?"

"Two, sometimes three hours." Perry grinned. "Starting to see why faculty don't come? We're only here because we're hourly employees, and we get paid to sit on our asses."

"And we get lunch!" Beth indicated a table in the corner with trays of donuts and bagels.

"Every week for two or three hours?" His shoulders sagging, Rob wondered whether Craig would check to make sure he was attending, then guessed he would.

Larry wobbled to the lunch table. "Best part of my job!" He returned with a stack of donuts.

"If you don't mind me asking," Rob said, "what do we do that takes eight to twelve hours per month?"

"Whenever somebody's issued a parking ticket on campus," Beth explained, "they get a chance to appeal. Here, let me show you." She selected a letter from a box on her right. A yellow ticket was stapled to its upper left-hand corner. "This one is from somebody who got a citation for failure to display the proper permit. He was in lot fifteen, spot thirty-seven. Here's the picture." She showed Rob a Xerox copy of a grainy photograph of a light-colored Honda Civic parked in front of one of the residence halls.

"His appeal is…" She cleared her throat and read: "'I was parked for less than a minute. It isn't fair I got a $15.00 ticket.'" She set the paper in a box to her left.

"That's it?" Rob asked. "That's his appeal? 'It wasn't fair'?"

"A few years back," Larry said, "we had this drinking game where we took a shot of booze whenever an appeal said *isn't fair*." He wagged his head. "It nearly killed poor Gus. I don't think he's had a drink since."

"Out of curiosity," Rob said, "under what circumstances are appeals upheld?"

"Upheld?" they repeated.

"Yeah, how do you decide when to rescind a ticket?"

"Oh, we never rescind a ticket!" Beth said in dismay. "The university wouldn't like that."

"That's why they give us lunch." Larry bit into a donut. Red jelly squirted out its end and splattered across the table. "We make them a ton of money."

"Wait a second," Rob said, trying to make sure he understood what was going on. "You sit here for two or three hours each week reading appeals that you know will never be approved?"

Attempting to clean the table, Larry smeared the jelly around with a napkin. "It beats working!"

Chapter 15

"You sat there for two hours, denying every appeal?" Sid asked.

It was the end of the first week of classes, and Vino's was packed. People could barely move without bumping into each other. Rob lifted a finger and got their waitress's attention. She nodded at him, indicating she'd be there as soon as she took somebody's order.

"I left a little early," he said. "I had to get to my afternoon class. But yeah. That's all they do every week."

"Man, remind me never to appeal a parking ticket! What a waste of time."

"Most of the appeals deserve to be rejected anyway." Rob went to take a drink, then remembered his glass was empty. "Some of them were kind of funny. One of the appeals was from a student who parked in a handicapped spot because he wanted to run up and have sex with his girlfriend while her roommate was out. He said he was only gone a few minutes and that he shouldn't have gotten a ticket because there was another handicapped spot open next to him."

"Only gone a few minutes," Wendy said, appalled. "That's reason to deny the appeal right there. Poor girl. He probably didn't even break a sweat."

"That's what somebody on the committee said!" Rob laughed. "Then there was this appeal because somebody lost his car."

"Lost his car?" Sid repeated. "How do you lose your car?"

"He got drunk and couldn't remember where he parked it. He found it days later in some field with dozens of tickets covering the windshield. He owes more than a thousand dollars."

"Wow! Expensive lesson to learn."

"My thoughts exactly."

A frazzled-looking waitress came to their table. She brushed away the strands of auburn hair falling into her eyes and readied her pen and paper. "What can I get for you?"

"Another pitcher, please," Rob said.

"Budweiser?" she asked, writing.

"Yes, please."

"Actually—" Wendy squinted at a sign on the far wall. "You have something called the Round the World Program?"

"Right." The waitress recited from memory, "The Round the World Club has imported beers from ninety-nine countries. We keep track of each country you visit. If you visit all ninety-nine countries within a school year, you get a free stein." She pointed her pen at a row of black porcelain steins lining a shelf behind the bar. "You also get your name added to the Traveler's Hall of Fame." She indicated a plaque over the antique jukebox.

Wendy arched an eyebrow at Rob and Sid. "Wanta try?"

"Ninety-nine beers in roughly thirty-two weeks? That's what—?" Sid's face tensed as he did the calculations in his head. "About three beers per week? Seems doable."

"I'm game," Rob said. "It could be kind of fun. We can take notes and compare the different beers. Maybe construct some sort of rating rubric to determine which are the best."

"Oh, my god!" Wendy gaped. "You're such a researcher!"

"So?"

Rolling her eyes, Wendy turned to the waitress. "Please bring us whatever's first on the list."

The waitress crossed something out on her pad. "I'll bring you each a bottle of Antares Kölsch from Argentina. It's a pilsner."

"Sounds great. Thanks!"

They listened to Frank Sinatra sing *The Way You Look Tonight*, barely audible above the commotion around them. Rob glanced at one of the televisions mounted on the far wall. ESPN commentators were analyzing the week's college football matchups. He predicted that both Purdue and the University of Illinois would lose.

"Tell us more about the donut committee," Sid said.

"There's not much else to tell," Rob replied. "We sit around the table while somebody reads the appeal. We then spend ten minutes laughing at it. Of course, not all the complaints are invalid. Do you know that the university sells an unlimited number of parking permits every year?

Anybody can get one! In fact, there are currently twenty-seven permits issued for every parking spot available on campus."

"Geez! No wonder I have to drive around a half-hour looking for a place."

"A half-hour?" Wendy said. "I drove around for more than an hour this morning. I almost ran out of gas."

"Parking is such a problem some homeowners around campus rent out their front lawns," Rob told them. "I'm sure they make a small fortune."

"I still don't understand why they don't prioritize permits." Sid drank his remaining beer in one swallow. "Give them to only faculty, staff, and upperclassmen."

"Upperclasspeople," Wendy corrected him.

"Sorry."

"Are you kidding?" Rob asked. "With the state freezing tuition, parking is one of the university's primary sources of revenue, both from permits and tickets. I bet the tickets we reviewed today totaled twenty-thousand dollars, if not more. And those are only from people who took the time to appeal. Imagine all the others."

A woman weaving her way through the crowd knocked into Wendy. Wendy shot her an aggravated glance. "Well, I, for one, will be showing up early Monday to get a spot right behind our building. It's a shame my classes aren't until afternoon. I was going to sleep in."

The waitress plopped three brown bottles with white labels in front of them. "Here you go." She rushed off to another table.

"Thanks!" Rob called after her.

Wendy lifted her bottle. "Congratulations again on surviving your first week, everybody."

"Three hundred and eleven more until tenure," Sid said.

They clinked bottles and drank.

"Not bad." Rob took another sip.

"Yeah, it's a lot richer than Budweiser." Wendy inspected the bottle's label. "How did your classes go, by the way?"

Rob exhaled wearily. "You wouldn't believe me if I told you."

"Sure, we would."

"My first class was supposed to have nearly three hundred students, and less than a quarter showed up. Then, when I started teaching, they all got upset. They practically stormed the stage with pitchforks and torches."

"You taught your first day? That's ballsy."

"Why? Didn't either of you?"

They both shook their head as they drank.

"The first week is considered optional," Sid said. "Students are still moving into their dorms."

"Really?"

"It's kind of a thing here. My chair told me to hand out the syllabus and thank them for paying my salary."

"Says something about the quality of education we're giving."

A college student bumped into their table as he passed, rattling their bottles.

"Speaking of chairs—" Wendy scooched a little to her right, trying to give the people walking by more room. "How are you getting on with Walrus?"

"I didn't see him today," Rob said. "He only teaches one class and, from what I hear, he cancels most of the lectures."

"You still thinking about moving?"

Rob sighed. "I don't know. My doctoral advisor says it's vocational suicide to leave so soon."

Much to his disappointment, they didn't disagree.

"What are you going to do?" Wendy asked.

"I don't know what I can do," Rob replied. "Craig told me flat-out I wouldn't get reappointed next year. I don't think I can get him to change his mind."

Draining her beer with satisfaction, Wendy set the bottle aside. "I have to call bullshit on that. I can't imagine one person controlling who gets reappointed and who doesn't."

"He's the department chair. He runs the program."

"Come on!" Wendy said. "One person having that kind of power? No business is like that nowadays. There're always checks and balances. I bet there're ten different committees whose sole job is to look at reappointment."

"Think so?"

"Of course. Hell, in our school alone, we have nine different associate deans and thirteen assistant deans. Nothing is as simple as one person making a decision."

"You know," Rob said, feeling relieved, "you're probably right. When I interviewed, somebody gave me an organizational chart for the university. There were so many boxes and crisscrossing lines, it looked like a maze scribbled by a child."

"There you go! Say what you will about how inefficient bureaucracies are, but at least they always provide countless safeguards."

"What does your department handbook say?" Sid asked.

"Department handbook?" Rob replied, feeling stupid.

"The handbook with all the rules and regulations governing the operation of the department? Didn't you get one when you were hired?"

Rob thought back to the stack of information he received during his orientation. The people in human resources gave him tons of paperwork on health care and retirement plans, as well as schedules for all the university sports teams, but he didn't get anything about the special education department.

"I don't think so. I still don't have a key to my office. I have to ask our departmental stripper to open the door each morning."

"Departmental stripper," Sid snickered. "Good one!"

Wendy narrowed her eyes at them. "That's not funny."

"I'm not being demeaning to women or anything," Rob insisted. "Our new assistant is actually a stripper. She even e-mailed me links to some of her videos in case I was interested in hiring her for… something."

"Yes, well, I'm sure things aren't easy for her."

Rob didn't dare disagree.

"You really should get a copy of your handbook," Sid said, returning to a safer subject. "How else would you know how you'll be evaluated?"

Finishing his beer, Rob set the bottle on the table with a decisive thud. "I think you're right. I mean, he's only the chair. And we're not living in a dictatorship. There has to be some sort of review process based upon a set criterion. After all, if there's an appeal process for parking tickets, there's got to be something similar for something as important at reappointment and tenure."

"Exactly."

The waitress returned to their booth, looking exhausted. She gave them a strained smile. "Ready for the second beer on the list?"

"Absolutely," Rob told her. "And I'm buying!"

Chapter 16

Rob gathered his notes and shoved them into his briefcase as complaining students filed out of his Characteristics of the Severely Crippled class. The lecture hadn't gone particularly well. As with his Introduction to Abnormal Children course the previous week, students were less than happy that he kept them the entire three hours. However, since only ten out of the fifty-eight students showed, he felt less threatened and pushed on with his lecture, ignoring their vehement protests.

A female student who looked to be about fourteen years old lingered by his podium. "Mr. Chudinski…"

"Actually—" Rob unplugged his laptop and wound the cord into a tight bundle. "—I prefer to be called doctor. At least until I pay off my student loans."

She blinked at him.

"The second part was a joke," he told her. "It's Hilde, right?"

"Right."

He slid his laptop and cord into his briefcase. "How may I help?"

She handed him a yellow document. "I have a disability and get accommodations."

"Sure. That's not a problem." He read the form from the university's Student Accessibility Services office. It didn't give any information other than the student's name and that she was supposed to receive time and a half on assessments.

"I need extra time for the final project," she told him.

"I don't understand." Rob flipped the form over but found that the other side was blank. "The final project isn't due until the end of the semester."

"I get extra time." She pointed to the paper. "See."

"Yes. I see that. But I'm still confused. The project will only take you fifteen or twenty hours of work. Why don't you start now and get it done?"

"I get extra time on all my assignments."

"Again, I see that. But what I'm saying is, you probably don't need it. The assignment isn't due for another fifteen weeks, and it should only take people twenty hours at the most to complete. Even if it took you thirty or forty hours, you'd still have plenty of time to finish the final project by the end of the semester."

She pointed to the form again. "I get—"

"Extra time," Rob said, annoyed. "Yes, I know. But I think this accommodation is for tests and quizzes. For example, most people will have three hours to complete the midterm exam. You can have four and a half hours. Same with the quizzes. The other students get an hour. You can have an hour and a half."

"Right."

They stared at each other for a few uncomfortable seconds.

"Let me see if I understand what you are requesting," Rob said, trying not to be snippy. He was tired and still had two more classes to go, but he thought this could be a teachable moment for the student. "Since you get time and a half, and the assignment is due at the end of the semester, are you suggesting you are going to turn the project in during the middle of next semester?"

"Right. I get extra time on—"

"Please stop saying that! I understand accommodations. I'm in special education. Remember?" Rob took a deep breath, then slowly released it through his nose. He put on a smile. "I don't believe this applies to the final project. Again, it'll only take you twenty hours or so to complete. Start now, and you'll be fine."

She pointed to the form. "But—"

"Let me ask you this," Rob said sharply. He softened his tone. "Why do you need the extra time?"

"I have a disability."

"I know you have a disability. We've covered that already. What I'm asking is… what difficulties do you anticipate you'll have completing the project? Perhaps I can help you overcome them."

The student shrugged. "I don't know. I haven't looked at the instructions you gave us. You just handed them out today."

Rob lifted a victorious eyebrow. "Then why do you think you'll need extra time to complete it?"

She pointed at the form again. "I get—"

"Allow me to rephrase!" Rob sat on the edge of a desk, trying to think of a way to explain things better. "If you don't mind me asking, what disability do you have?"

The student shrugged again. "I don't know."

"You don't—?" Rob clenched his jaw. Sensing his frustration, the student clutched her bookbag and retreated a step. "Okay. That's a shame. You need to know what disability you have so you can get the support you need. But maybe I can be of assistance. What challenges do you have in school? For example, do you have difficulty seeing the board?"

"No."

"Do you have problems hearing me?"

"No. My hearing is fine."

"Do you have difficulty reading or writing?"

"No. But I am really bad at math. I think that's why I get extra time."

As if hungover, the instructor for the next class staggered into the room. He noted the yellow form in Rob's hand and then rolled his bloodshot eyes.

"Hilde…" Rob rubbed his face. "There isn't any math in this class. You should be fine."

"But—" She gestured to the paper.

"I'll tell you what." Rob struggled not to shout. "I'll call Student Accessibility Services and get this all straightened out. Okay?"

"So, I'll get extra time?" she asked hopefully.

Gritting his teeth, Rob grabbed his briefcase and made for the door. "I suggest you start the project this weekend."

Chapter 17

"Her last name is Hagman," Rob said into his cell phone as he headed to his next class. He was trying to get clarification regarding the accommodations his student was entitled to. Unfortunately, the Student Accessibility Services office was being less than helpful. He'd been forwarded to four different people and was now speaking to the person who initially answered. "H-a-g-m-a-n. The form she gave me says she gets time and a half on assessments."

"Yes. That's right," the woman on the other end of the line replied. "She has a documented disability. According to the Americans with Disabilities Act, she is entitled to—"

"I understand," Rob interrupted as he wove his way through a noisy corridor crammed with students. "I'm in special education. I know all about the ADA. My question is—when it says she gets time and a half on assessments, that doesn't mean projects, correct?"

"Are the projects graded?"

Trying to hear her better, Rob plugged his right ear with his finger. "Yes."

"Then she gets time and a half."

A pudgy faculty member shouted for everybody to make room as he pushed a heavily laden AV cart through the crowd. Hoping to use the rattling cart like an offensive lineman blocking for a running back, Rob got behind the faculty member as he rolled down the hallway.

"But the project I'm talking about," Rob explained to the woman on the phone, "isn't due until the end of the semester, and she could easily finish it over a single weekend. Maybe even sooner. She doesn't need extra time."

"She has a disability and is afforded accommodations to level the playing field," she replied. "The law guarantees—"

"I understand that ADA enables students with qualifying disabilities to obtain reasonable accommodations. But I'm not sure how *reasonable* these accommodations are."

A young man passing in the hallway waved. Thinking that he waved at him, Rob waved back.

"Let me ask you this," he said, hoping the woman on the phone would see reason. "If a project is due at the end of the semester and a student gets time and a half to complete it. When is the assignment due for the student who has accommodations?"

"The middle of the following semester."

Rob tossed his free hand, nearly smacking somebody in the side of the head. "How is that possibly right?" He mouthed an apology to the person next to him.

"She has a disability."

"In math!" Rob cried. "There is no math in my class! Why would she need a semester and a half to complete a project she could do in a weekend?"

"All students with disabilities get time and a half to complete their assignments."

Rob stopped abruptly. Students scooted around him.

"Let me get this straight," he said. "All students with disabilities get the same accommodations?"

"Correct."

"Regardless of whether or not they need them?"

"It makes things much easier that way," the woman told him. "You must understand. We're a big university. We have a lot of students with disabilities attending Eastern Wisconsin and—"

"I'm sorry," Rob said, realizing he was fighting a losing battle, "but I have one more question. Let's suppose I move the deadline for the assignment to the middle of this semester. When would the student have to turn it in?"

"If you required the assignment to be completed by week eight..." There was the sound of tapping as if she were entering numbers into a calculator. "She would have until week twelve to turn it in."

"But it's the same assignment!" Rob exclaimed. "If she can complete it by week twelve, why can't she get it done by week sixteen?"

"She gets extra time because she has a documented—"

"Fine! I'll move the deadline. Thanks for your help." Rob hung up and shoved the phone into his pocket. "Idiots!"

Chapter 18

Rob stepped into Thelma's old office. The stench of cigarette smoke was so thick, it coated his tongue and burned his eyes.

"Hey, Ms. Miller?"

He stopped short. His new administrative assistant was wearing an outfit resembling the dress-whites worn by U.S. Navy officers; however, instead of pants, she had a form-fitting miniskirt. Further, the front of her blouse dipped so low it revealed her pierced navel—and that she wasn't wearing a bra.

Tiffani looked up from a sketch she was making of rabbits frolicking around a minefield. One of them lay in a pool of blood, blown to bits. "Yes?"

Fighting to focus his attention, Rob dragged his gaze from the mutilated rabbit to her breasts and then to the ceiling.

"I was looking for… something."

"A good time?" she suggested.

"You're a student, aren't you?" Rob asked, desperately trying to recall Frank's story about the only faculty member in history not to get his contract renewed after his first year.

"Yup. I'm a senior! Actually, I've been a senior for three years now." Then she added thoughtfully, "I think I'll go on for a master's degree. I've always wanted to be a master."

"Good idea. Hey, any progress on getting a new nameplate for my door?"

"What's wrong with the one you have?"

"First of all, somebody stole it. Second, my name was misspelled, remember?"

"I don't think so. I double-checked that before I ordered it."

Rob struggled to keep his expression amiable. "How about getting me one that says 'Dr. Chudinski'?"

"Oh, sure!" she said. "I can do that."

"Great!"

Rob examined the pot from the coffeemaker. It was so badly stained, it appeared as though somebody had been boiling oil. "Also, do you have my keys yet?"

"Keys?"

"To my office and the building?"

"Let's see." She opened a filing cabinet. There were little hooks with room numbers, but all of the keys were jumbled together at the bottom of the drawer. "I'm sure I can find them somewhere." Bending forward, she shifted through the pile.

Rob averted his eyes so as not to look down her blouse. "If you could get them to me within a few days, that'd be terrific. No rush, though."

"Sure thing. I'll put them in your mailbox before I leave today. Anything else?"

"Not right now." Then he remembered why he wanted to talk with her. "Oh, yeah! Do you know where I could find a copy of the departmental handbook?"

"What does it look like?"

"I have no idea. But it lists all the policies and procedures for the..." She appeared confused. "Never mind."

"It could be in one of those." Tiffani surveyed a row of dusty boxes lining a shelf. Each box had dates written on it. The most recent was fourteen years ago. "Let me check."

She climbed a stepladder and reached for a box. She wasn't wearing any underwear either.

"Okay!" Finding it difficult to breathe, Rob turned away. "Um. If you find it, could you put it in my mailbox with my keys?"

"Sure thing."

Rob stopped in the doorway and snuck a peek at her bare ass as she dug through a box labeled 1963-1964. "Thanks again."

She winked at him. "My pleasure."

Heart pounding, Rob went into the men's room and splashed cold water on his face.

"Sleeping with a student would definitely lessen my chances of staying," he told his reflection. His reflection seemed to think it might be worth the risk.

Stepping up to the urinal, he unzipped his pants and tried to think about something other than his assistant. He'd just started urinating when somebody walked in behind him.

"Hey," a female voice said. "You're Rod, right?"

Tensing, Rob suddenly thought he'd gone into the wrong restroom. He looked around wildly. He was standing at a urinal. He was relatively certain women's restrooms didn't have urinals.

The woman entered a stall. "I'm Becky, by the way. I'm in Sociology. My office is around the corner."

"I'm… I'm sorry." Rob looked around again. He was definitely in a men's room. "You shouldn't be in here."

From her stall came the sound of tinkling water.

"Oh, please. We're all grown-ups. Besides, the women's bathroom is one floor down. I'm not walking all that way every time I have to pee."

"But… it's the men's room!"

He heard her tear toilet paper from the roll, then pull up her pants. The toilet flushed.

"Don't be such a prude."

She came out of the stall and washed her hands.

Still standing at the urinal, Rob turned slightly, using his body to shield himself from her view. "I'm not a prude."

"Anyway—" Becky checked her hair in the mirror. "Welcome to EW-U. I hope you stay longer than most people. We need new blood around here. Know what I mean?"

"I suppose," Rob replied, not knowing what to say.

"Well, I'll see you around." She made for the door, then stopped. "Oh, hey. Do you smoke pot?"

"What? What kind of question is that?" Rob realized he hadn't urinated since she came in. Turning his back on her, he zipped his pants.

"I thought I'd ask. You seem like you'd appreciate the mellow stuff. Anyhow, if you need to be hooked up, I grow some Indica by my cabin in the north woods. It'll make the semester more pleasant, if you know what I mean."

"You sell pot?"

"No, of course not! At least not to faculty." She checked her hair in the mirror again. "Have a good term. Don't let the bastards get to you."

Rob stood in the middle of the men's room. First, a stripper for an administrative assistant and now a faculty member openly giving out pot. What bothered him most was that he was tempted to partake in both.

Chapter 19

Rob stood in Agnew Hall's main office, riffling through the scores of fliers and advertisements he'd found in his mailbox. Some of the takeout menus were interesting. However, most of the university announcements were for events that had already occurred the previous semester.

"Oh, hey there," the school director, Dr. Mary Jorgensen, said as she came in. "How are things going up there on the sixth floor? Good, I hope."

"Yes, they're—" Rob considered telling her the truth, but didn't want to sound like a complainer. "They're fine. Thanks. How are things on the first floor?"

"Never a dull moment! But that's how I like it. Keeps you going, you know?"

"I'm sure."

"Anyhoo—" She extracted the mail from her box and, without looking at it, dumped everything into the recycling bin next to the garbage can. "—if there's anything I can do, anything at all, ask. Okay?"

"Since you mentioned it," Rob said before she could leave, "there are a couple of things I'd like to ask you. Do you have a minute?"

"Absolutely!" Mary smiled at him. "Shoot."

"Well…" Rob considered which issue he should address first. "A few minutes ago, I was upstairs in the men's room, and a woman entered. She walked right in—like she belonged there or something."

"Curly black hair? Perky nose?"

Rob shrugged. He'd spent most of their encounter with his back turned. "Yeah, I suppose."

"That's Dr. Marshall. She's in Sociology."

"Yes, that's her. Anyway, like I said, she came right in while I was, well, using the facilities. When I asked her to leave, she said she didn't want to walk to wherever the woman's room was."

Chuckling, Mary put her hands on her hips. "Isn't she a hoot?"

"A hoot?" Rob repeated. "To be honest, it's rather awkward. I mean, after all—it *is* the men's room. Can you please ask her to stop?"

Mary's face turned serious, her eyes growing behind her thick glasses. "Yeah, no. I couldn't do that. She's a full professor, don't you know? With tenure and all." She leaned forward and whispered, "She's also sleeping with one of the Vice Provosts." She touched the side of her nose with her forefinger and nodded sagely.

"So—" Rob tried to repress his annoyance. "She can walk right in any time she likes?"

Mary thought about this.

"I can ask her to knock," she suggested.

Rob opened his mouth, then closed it. If the School Director wasn't looking so jovial, he would've guessed she was pulling his leg.

"That'd be terrific," he forced himself to say. "Thanks."

"No problem. Anything else?"

Rob remembered the main reason why he wanted to speak with her. "Yeah. There's one more thing."

"Sure! What is it?"

"Well, I'm starting to think about reappointment."

"Good for you! You know, my father always told me that it's never too early to start preparing for the future."

Next to them, the fax machine rattled and beeped as a page appeared in its tray.

"Yes, my mother says the same thing." Rob attempted to get back on topic. "You see, I don't know anything about the reappointment process, so I don't know how to prepare."

"Oh, gotcha!" Mary said. "Perhaps I can help you out there. You see, there's this four-step process designed to give everybody a fair hearing."

Rob exhaled with relief. "That sounds great. What's the process?"

"First, you submit your papers to your unit."

"Papers?" Rob patted his pockets, wishing he had something with which to write. There were several golf pencils by the fax machine, but none of them had a point.

"Exactly. They outline all of your accomplishments over the past academic year. Although, it's not really the full academic year. Your papers are due in February, so it's more like a semester and a month."

"Okay." Rob committed that to memory. "Got it. Then what?"

"Then the unit makes a recommendation to me as to whether you should get a one, two, or three-year contract extension."

"Wait!" He stopped her. "Not getting reappointed isn't an option?"

"Oh!" Laughing, she waved a hand. "You'd really have to upset somebody pretty badly for something like that to happen!"

Rob's heart sank. "What happens after you get the recommendation from the unit?"

"Then I make a recommendation to the Dean, who makes a recommendation to the Provost. He makes the final decision."

"That's good to know," Rob said, happy to hear that Craig didn't have the final say after all. "How are the reappointment papers evaluated? By what criteria?"

"That depends on what's written in your unit's handbook," she told him. "You see, every unit customizes its criteria to the unique needs of its specific field. For instance, you couldn't hold the art education folks to the same standards as the science people. That wouldn't do at all."

"That makes sense. I don't suppose you have copies of them—the handbooks, that is."

"No, I don't. But I'm sure Craig has one. Ask him!"

"I'll do that. Thanks." Rob thought for a moment, wondering how else he could get his hands on a handbook. "One last question, if you don't mind."

"Not at all. That's what I'm here for. Ask away!"

"Do you…?" He hesitated, a sense of foreboding suddenly descending on him. "Do you ever overturn the unit's recommendation?"

"Oofta, no! To be honest with you—" Mary leaned forward conspiratorially. "—I don't even read them."

Rob groaned, "Of course not."

"I mean, who knows your work better than the people in your unit? Am I right?"

"Right," Rob agreed weakly. "I suppose the Dean and Provost think the same thing."

"I'd be pretty surprised if they took the time to read all those reappointment papers. I mean, each one is a good two or three pages. And there're dozens of them!"

"I understand."

Glancing at the fax machine, Rob found the page that printed was an advertisement for the local community college. Its heading read: "Looking for a rewarding career in the heating and cooling industry?" He debated taking it.

"Is there anything else?" Mary asked.

"Nope." Rob tried to smile. "Unfortunately, that's it."

"Okey-dokey, then. Enjoy your term!" She wiggled her fingers at him as she left the mailroom.

"I'll certainly try."

Chapter 20

Pondering what Mary had told him about the reappointment process, Rob scaled Agnew Hall's stairs. Reeking of pot and urine and littered with debris, they reminded him of a New York City subway station. The only thing missing was a wino sleeping on each landing.

When he'd reached the fourth floor, he heard the voice he'd been dreading.

"Well, well, well," Craig said, coming down the stairs toward him, Bert and Les by his side. "If it isn't His Holiness, the Hypocrite. Off to ruin another student's life?"

Not liking being alone with Craig and his henchman, Rob trotted past. "What are you talking about? I'm going to my office to get ready for my next class."

"What about Hilde Hagman?"

Rob stopped on the flight above them. "What about her?"

Leaning haughtily on the railing, Craig said to Bert and Les, "Here he always says he wants to improve the lives of the crippled, yet he denies the accommodations a poor, disabled student needs to succeed in his class!"

Bert and Les tutted.

"She doesn't need accommodations," Rob replied, exasperated. "Her disability is in math!"

Craig gasped in feigned shock. "Did you hear that, lads? He violated confidentiality. The Holy Roller doesn't think laws apply to him!"

"Sounds like he's full of shit, Big Guy." Bert hitched up his pants. "Just like I've always said."

Les puffed out his meager chest. "Yeah! Holy Roller is full of it!"

"You're privy to her accommodations," Rob said, wondering why he was bothering to defend himself. "She's your student too. Remember?"

"You're still violating ADA," Craig told him. "We should call the accommodations police or somebody."

"Yeah, the accommodations—"

"Shut up, Les."

"ADA," Rob explained patiently, "provides students with *reasonable* accommodations. And for your information, I ended up giving her the deadline extension she requested."

"No, you didn't!" Craig cried. "You changed the due date so she had to finish the assignment this semester!"

"Which Student Accessibility Services said was fine," Rob retorted.

"Boy, you really take the cake, don't you? You talk endlessly about helping the crippled and being a caring educator. But when push comes to shove, you don't practice what you preach."

"Craig! Giving students accommodations when they don't need them only creates learned helplessness. She's perfectly capable of completing the assignment without the extra time!"

"You're always right, aren't you?" Craig's booming voice bounced off the grey concrete around them. "You know everything! Your interpretation of the law is always correct!"

"I never said that!" Rob shouted back.

"Have you ever been wrong, Polly? Ever? No! You're young and from an expensive school and know absolutely everything!"

"I'm not going to argue with you, Craig." Rob headed up the stairs. "Now, if you all excuse me. I have to get ready for my Assessing Students with Disabilities class. Have a good day."

"You're an elitist hypocrite!" Craig hollered after him. "And it's Assessing Disabled Students! Stop changing the course names without authorization! Do you hear me? Stop it—or you'll be sorry!"

Chapter 21

Rob sat in a stall in the men's room, going over what Craig had said. Was he a hypocrite? Yes, he'd always claimed he championed the rights of people with disabilities. And, yes, he did technically refuse to give Hilde accommodations. But she didn't need them. Her disability was in math. There was no math in his class! What she needed was to learn how to budget her time and complete assignments when they were due. After all, she couldn't be an effective educator without good time-management skills. He was doing her a favor. Wasn't he?

"Is everything okay in there?" a woman's voice asked.

"Ms. Miller?" Instinctively, Rob felt the urge to cover up. "What the hell are you doing in here?"

"I have something for you."

"And it couldn't wait until I finished?"

"I waited, but you didn't come out." She added, "Sounds like you need to eat more fruit or something."

"Ms. Miller!"

"What?"

"Can you please go outside?"

"Why? Becky comes in here all the time."

"Fine!" Standing, Rob pulled up his pants and flushed the toilet. Opening the stall door, he found his secretary leaning against the bathroom wall. She was wearing a black leather bodysuit; her hair dyed an electric blue. "Nice outfit."

"Like it?" Posing, she inspected herself in the mirror. "Is the hair too much?"

"Believe me." Rob washed his hands. "I don't think anybody notices your hair."

"Oh! That's sweet. Thanks!"

"You have something for me?" Rob prodded.

"Yeah." She shouted over the noise of the hand dryer, "You said you wanted a handbook!"

"You found it?" He took a packet from her. It was as yellow and stiff as the university's one-ply toilet paper. "Great! Thank you so much."

"No problem. Good assistants always help!"

Flipping through the brittle pages, Rob tried to read the faded print.

Tiffani leaned in closer, her breasts pressed against his arm. "Is there anything else you want?"

"What?" Suddenly realizing how close Tiffani was, he took a step away. "No, this is terrific. Thank you again. I appreciate it! You're a lifesaver."

"Well, I do know CPR!"

The door to the men's room swung open as Becky walked in. When she saw Rob standing by the sink, she said sarcastically, "Oh—I'm sorry." She stepped out and knocked three times, then re-entered. "Better?"

"Much," Rob said. "Thanks."

Entering the stall Rob had vacated, Becky stood on the toilet and pushed aside one of the white ceiling tiles. Reaching into the dark cavity, she extracted a sizable bag of pot.

"Is that my order?" Tiffani asked hopefully.

"No. This is for Pete. I'll bring yours next week." Becky made to leave, then looked at them. "You know the storage closet in the basement is available."

Tiffani laughed. "We aren't having sex. We're in a professional conversation!"

"Make sure you wear a condom." Tucking the bag of pot into her purse, Becky left.

Rob read the packet's table of contents, then turned to a random page. "Where did you find this?"

"It was in one of the boxes on the top shelf. There's all kinds of old stuff in there."

"I bet." Rob reached the end of the handbook. "Thanks again, Ms. Miller. I appreciate your help."

"If there's anything else I can do for you…" She bit her lip seductively. "Just ask."

Chapter 22

"Mary doesn't even look at the reappointment papers?" Wendy asked, aghast. "She admitted that?"

They were sitting in a corner booth at Vino's. It was early evening, and the Wednesday night crowd was starting to get rowdy.

"Yup," Rob replied. "She told me the department knows best. She doesn't even have the criteria for reappointment. Which reminds me…" He reached into his briefcase and pulled out the information Tiffani had given him. He tossed it onto the graffiti-riddled table next to the remains of their pineapple and onion pizza. "Here's our departmental handbook."

Sid and Wendy hunched over it.

"Blue ink?" Wendy turned the fragile pages. "Is this a mimeograph?"

"It sure is." Sid squinted in the dim light. "How old is this?"

Drinking his Brazilian beer, Rob pointed to the faded date on the cover.

"August 1972? Geez! There has to be something more recent than this."

"Tiffani couldn't find anything," Rob told them. "But she's going to keep looking."

"I hope she finds it. This won't help you much." Wendy flipped through the handbook. "And thanks for not calling her the departmental stripper."

"Yeah, that was mean of me. She's a good kid. Very eager to please."

"I'm sure she is!" Sid laughed.

Rob and Wendy glared at him.

"Oh, come on," Sid said. "That was begging for a comment."

Wendy turned another page. "According to this, what are the reappointment criteria?"

"That's just it." Rob took a bite of cold pizza. "There aren't any. There are sections discussing the department's mission statement and structure.

There are also descriptions of the courses. But there's nothing that talks about the evaluation of faculty."

"I'm sure it's in the updated version." Wendy handed the handbook back. Rob returned it to his briefcase. "The trick will be finding it."

Two drunk women climbed onto the bar and began dancing to the theme of *Footloose* blaring from the jukebox. The crowd cheered as the women race back and forth, evading the grasps of the bartenders.

"What are you guys doing tomorrow?" Sid asked as he nursed his beer.

Wendy picked at the pizza crusts littering her plate. "I don't teach or have any meetings. So I'm staying home and working on a study I'm trying to publish from my dissertation."

"What's it on?"

"The portrayal of women in movies when men direct versus when women direct."

"Sounds interesting. What did you find?"

"What you'd expect," Wendy said matter-of-factly. "Female leads are far more dependent on their male costars when a man directs. They also have fewer lines and scenes with their clothes on."

Rob watched the bartenders escort the dancing girls outside. One of the women was blowing everybody kisses. "I envy that you have time to write. Tomorrow, I teach three classes, have four committee meetings, and then at night, I have to go to someplace called Elwin Holme. Walrus is making me take his spot on their board of directors."

"Board of directors?" Wendy said, impressed. "Wow. That'll look terrific on your reappointment papers!"

"Not that anybody will read them," Rob snorted.

Sid took a drink. "What's Elwin Holme?"

"It's a residential school for kids with severe disabilities outside of town," Rob explained. "Autism spectrum. Intellectual disabilities. That kind of thing."

"Sounds right up your alley."

"It is. I'm looking forward to getting back into the field and helping out. I just don't have much time. Whatever comes across Walrus's desk lands on mine. I honestly don't know how I'm going to manage all the work he's giving me, let alone write up my research."

"Do what you can." Wendy ate the remains of a pizza crust. "That's all you can do."

"I know." Taking a sip of beer, Rob watched a commercial on one of the televisions mounted by the ceiling. A lawyer was shouting about how unfair the legal system was and that law-abiding, hard-working Americans needed a tenacious lawyer on their side. "But I have this strange feeling that if I don't publish more, Walrus will say I'm neglecting my 'scholarly responsibilities.' I don't want to give him any reasons for not renewing my contract."

Chapter 23

Exhausted from a day full of teaching and pointless meetings, Rob entered Elwin Holme's main lobby. Like most facilities for people with disabilities, it was tastefully decorated with new furniture, bright yellow paint, and motivational pictures that had words like "Inspire" and "Conquer" and "Dignity." As he wandered further into the building, however, the freshly painted walls gave way to peeling wallpaper smudged by hundreds of dirty hands. The tiled floor was chipped and cracked. And the stench of hospital disinfectant made it difficult for him to breathe.

The receptionist at the front desk had indicated the boardroom was easy to find, but after ten minutes of searching, Rob had no clue where he was or how to return to the lobby. He checked his phone and saw he only had six minutes before the start of the meeting. Above him, a surveillance camera monitored the hallway. Rob half-heartedly wondered whether he should hold up a sign asking for help. Maybe the security guards would send a search party to save him.

He turned down another corridor and passed several classrooms. He peered through the narrow glass window in one of the heavy steel doors. Inside, young children with disabilities were sitting in bean bag chairs, staring at Barney, the purple dinosaur, as he capered around a television screen. Their mouths open, the kids looked nearly comatose. They reminded Rob of his college students watching mindless videos on their cellphones.

He passed another room and looked inside. This one had a group of teenagers with disabilities. They were also watching a Barney video. However, these students appeared less interested in it. Several were rocking in their chairs or roaming aimlessly, flapping their hands in front of their faces.

Hating to interrupt but needing to find the boardroom, Rob tried the doorknob. It was locked. He knocked. One of the adolescents ambled to the door. He ogled Rob through the narrow window.

"Can you get your teacher?" Rob asked through the thick glass.

The boy made a gurgling sound and pounded on the door.

"Teacher." Rob pointed in the classroom. "Get your teacher, please."

The boy pounded harder. The door shook as though being hammered by a battering ram.

Putting his cheek against the tiny window, Rob tried to see around the boy. But the boy smooshed his drool-covered face to the window opposite him as if trying to see around Rob.

Guessing the teacher was somewhere in the back of the room, helping another student, Rob returned to the classroom with the younger children. He tried the knob. It was locked as well. He knocked. Nobody came to the door. He knocked again. A couple of the children glanced vacantly at him but didn't leave their beanbag chairs.

"Where the hell is everybody?"

His phone vibrated. A message appeared on its screen indicating it was time for the meeting.

"Shit."

Phone in hand, Rob jogged along another corridor, looking frantically at each door he passed. None of them appeared to lead to the boardroom.

Up ahead, he heard laughing. He ran to a door with a sign that read: Aquatic's Center. He reached for the knob, then stopped.

Inside he could see adults playing in a swimming pool.

"What the—?"

Rob looked closer.

They were all naked.

A flabby middle-aged guy did a cannonball as a woman lounging on the edge of the pool kicked water into the air. Two other people appeared to be having sex, their intertwined bodies gyrating together as though they were a load of unbalanced laundry in a washing machine. White uniforms lay scattered about the physical therapy equipment.

"Holy crap!" Rob gasped. "They're staff!"

His phone buzzed again. He was now two minutes late for his meeting.

As he attempted to process everything that was going on, footsteps thundered down the hallway. Turning, Rob found two burly men in white coats sprinting in his direction.

"Finally!"

He called to them as they approached, "Excuse me! Could you tell me where the board of directors—?"

Suddenly, one of the men lowered his muscular shoulder and tackled Rob, throwing him to the floor.

"Fucker!" He clutched the back of his head as it bounced off the tile. "What are you doing? Get off of me!"

He tried to hit the man who'd fallen across his chest, but the second man seized his wrist.

"Stop it!" Rob kicked and thrashed with little effect. "Stop it! I belong here! I'm on the board! I'm on the board!"

The man holding his wrist pried the phone from his grasp.

"Hey!" Rob shouted. "That's mine. Give it—!"

The man dropped the phone and stepped on it, grinding his boot heel into the cracking screen.

"Hey! God damn it! What the fuck are you doing? Get off me!"

The first man got to his feet. Breathing hard, he jabbed a finger at Rob's nose. "No photography!"

"What the hell are you talking about?" Rob replied, still lying on the floor. "I wasn't taking pictures. I was checking the time!" Next to him, the fragmented remains of his phone vibrated feebly. He was five minutes late for his meeting. "I'm on the god-damned board of directors!"

Chapter 24

The following morning, Rob sat in his office, deep in thought. After being physically dragged from Elwin Holme and tossed into the parking lot with the remains of his vibrating iPhone, he'd driven to the Appleton police department. When he told the officer at the front desk what had happened, the officer simply shrugged and repeated what the school staff had said — "Photography isn't allowed." Recalling the students' bored faces as they sat unattended in their locked classrooms, Rob was beginning to guess why.

He peered at the black and white photo Thelma had given him. The child between her and her husband seemed to grow larger and larger.

Craig burst in, red-faced.

"What the hell happened last night? What did you do?" He shook a fist. "If you lost us Elwin Holme, you'll be sorry. You hear me? Sorry!"

"Lost?" Rob tore his gaze from the picture. "What does that mean?"

"We need them to place our student teachers!"

"You're joking! Our students see what they do there?"

"Of course, they do. Where else can they find out how to deal with the droolers?"

Standing, Rob glowered at Craig. "You call them that again, and you'll be the one who's sorry. Do you hear *me*? I don't care if you are my chair."

Craig huffed through his walrus mustache, his face getting even redder. "Now you listen here—"

"I can't believe our students go there," Rob shouted. "The kids just sit around. There's no teaching going on. There's no learning. It's like an insane asylum in some third-world country!"

"I'll have you know," Craig shouted back, "Elwin Holme is a top-notch institution. They take all the hopeless cases nobody else is willing to touch with a ten-foot pole!"

"Hopeless—?" Rob repeated, horrified. "Craig, we're talking about people. Living, breathing people! They're not hopeless. They merely need specialized instruction to help them learn!"

Craig rolled his eyes. "There you go again! Everything is all rosy in your world. Isn't it, Polly? *Everybody can learn!*" he mocked. *"Everybody can succeed!"*

"Everybody *can* learn!"

Les poked his head into the office but immediately scampered back the way he'd come.

"I'll have you know," Craig said, "parents from all over the country have been sending their crippled kids there for almost a hundred years! Elwin Holme keeps their children safe and protected!"

"Protected from what?" Rob retorted.

"From…" Craig sputtered. "From the outside world! They feed and clothe them and keep them safe!"

"Those children don't get out into their communities?" Rob asked, flabbergasted. "They aren't integrated with their peers—at all?"

"No! They're a danger to themselves and others." Craig folded his arms across his chest. "They're better off where they are. As are we!"

For a moment, Rob was speechless. He could barely breathe.

"You actually believe that—don't you?" he managed to say. "That's what you're teaching our students? They all come through our program and leave thinking that kids with disabilities should be locked away and, and… not taught anything?"

"Not all disabled kids," Craig countered, "just the cripples. The droolers. The ones who are cognitively damaged."

"Oh my god!" Rob staggered, the implications of what Craig was saying crushing his soul. Eastern Wisconsin University produced hundreds of teachers every year. They'd go out into the world and impact generations of families. And their beliefs would spread to other teachers. It was like a black cloud, slowly corrupting everything in its path. "Only an idiot would think something like that."

Craig sucked in air. "How dare you!"

"Things change, Craig. We don't treat people with disabilities like that anymore. We've grown as a society!"

"Grown as a society?" Craig scoffed. "You know all the answers even though you have no information about—"

"You're a moron."

"Now," Craig snarled, "you listen here! I've taken about as much as I—"

Rob took a step forward. They were nose to nose. "Get out of my office."

The veins in Craig's forehead pulsated. His lips quivered. "That's it! That's—it! You're gone! This is insubordination. That's what it is. Threats! And, and… insubordination!"

Rob pointed to the hallway. "Out!"

"I'm going to talk to Mary! I'm going to talk to the Dean! You're gone, Polly. Do you hear me? Mark my words! You're fired. Then see if anybody else will hire you. I know people! People at every university offering special education licensure in the country. A year from now, you'll be working at a community college teaching foreigners how to speak English!"

Craig stomped out of the office, slamming the door behind him.

His heart skittering, Rob fell into his squeaking chair. He stared at Thelma's picture.

"Nothing has changed since the 1950s. Nothing."

The phone rang.

Rob wasn't going to answer it. He could barely unclench his jaw. But then he saw the call was from Urbana-Champaign, Illinois.

"Hey, Frank."

"Rob?" Frank Russo asked. "You okay?"

Rob ran his trembling fingers through his hair. "I'm not sure."

"Well, I have something that'll cheer you up." There was a pregnant pause. "I have a post-doc position for you! I was awarded a five-year research and training grant. It won't pay tenure-track money, but it'll get you out of your situation, and you'll be able to focus on your research. Publish your ass off and, in five years, you can go wherever you want."

Rob gazed at Thelma's faded photo.

"Rob?"

Don't give up, she'd said. *Don't ever give up.*

"You there?"

Rob took a deep, uneven breath. "Thanks, Frank. But—I'm staying."

"You sure?"

He stared at the little girl's laughing face. "Yeah. I'm sure. I have things to do here."

Chapter 25

"You turned down a post-doc position?" Wendy asked, surprised. "I would've guessed you'd jump at it."

Rob paced her immaculate office on Agnew Hall's second floor. Books and journal articles were everywhere; however, unlike his office, they were all in neat rows or piles. Without asking, he snatched a pink rubber stress ball from a table and throttled it.

"I have to stay!" he said, although privately he was beginning to have misgivings about rejecting Frank's offer. "You should've seen that boy staring at me through the door. It was like he was in prison or something, waiting to be executed." His voice cracked. "I have to do something, Wendy. I have to stop it."

Wendy leaned against her bookcase. "How? It sounds like a lot of people in the community support what they do."

"That's because they don't know any better!" Rob replied. "All they hear is what idiots like Craig tell them."

"Speaking of whom. Did he talk to Mary and the Dean?"

"Yeah. Mary offered to have a meeting in February. The Dean told him to get the hell out of his office."

"Sounds like you dodged a bullet."

"How so?"

"Look, Rob—" Wendy straightened a row of books on a shelf. "Like it or not, Craig's your boss. You can't go off on him every time you disagree." She added quickly, "I'm not saying I agree with his position or anything. I'm merely saying we're employees of this university. There're rules and expectations."

Rob stopped pacing and stared out the window at the parking lot below. He watched twenty cars slowly circling like sharks, waiting for a victim to leave their spot. "I know. I should've been more professional. It's just—you should've seen the boy's face! You should've seen his eyes." He attempted to push the image from his mind. "But you're right. I need to watch my temper."

The cars continued going round and round.

"What are you going to do?" Wendy asked.

"I'll tell you what I'm going to do," Rob said. "I'm going to stay and teach every student who goes through our program that what they're doing at Elwin Holme is wrong. Horribly, horribly wrong! People with disabilities should be included in their communities! They can learn! They need to be taught, not babysat!"

"You realize you can train all the teachers you want, but it'll take decades to change things that way. You need to go to the source."

Below, a white Ford Focus left its parking spot. Two SUVs converged onto the scene, both blocking the other's access to the open space. Horns blared.

"Have you thought about going to the school and talking to them?" Wendy asked. "Maybe present a better option?"

"That's a good idea," Rob said, trying to sound optimistic. "I could show them my research and help them develop a more inclusive curriculum."

"That sounds like an appropriate plan."

Still staring out the window, Rob brushed the tears from his eyes. "I can't believe things are this bad here. Never in my wildest dreams—"

Feeling a warm hand on his shoulder, he turned. Wendy kissed and hugged him.

For a moment, Rob stood there, blinking stupidly.

"Would you," he said, "would you like to go out sometime? Maybe get dinner and a movie?"

She gave him a meaningful look. "I'm in Women's Studies, remember?"

"So?"

"I'm a lesbian."

"Oh. Then why did you—?"

She shrugged. "You looked like you needed it. Besides, I'm always a sucker for a Don Quixote."

"You think I'm fighting windmills?"

"Everybody's gotta fight something."

Rob frowned, not sure which disappointed him more—the fact she wasn't interested in him romantically or that she thought he was fighting a losing battle. Looking for inspiration, he gazed out her window again. A student talking on a cell phone walked through the parking lot, a line of cars trailing close behind.

"I'll make an appointment to speak with Elwin Holme's superintendent," he said, more to himself than her. "He'll see reason. He'll have to."

Chapter 26

"Thank you very much for seeing me, Mr. Stanford," Rob said as he entered a spacious office off Elwin Holme's main lobby. "I greatly appreciate it."

He sat in a plush red leather armchair in front of a desk so enormous it rivaled the one Craig had. Behind it, a distinguished-looking gentleman with a neatly trimmed Vandyke, short grey hair, and a tweed jacket stared at him over steeped fingers.

"As I said on the phone," Rob went on, uneasily, "I want to clear up any misunderstanding that might have occurred a few days ago."

Mr. Stanford continued inspecting him as though he was a curious insect.

"First of all—" Rob shifted uncomfortably in his seat. "—I want to assure you; I wasn't taking pictures. I was late for our meeting and using my phone to check the time."

No response.

"Also…" Rob went on, "I was lost. That's why I was where I was. I couldn't find the boardroom. I must've taken a wrong turn somewhere." He gave a forced laugh. "After all, you have a huge facility here!"

Still no response.

"With that being said—" Clearing his throat, Rob glanced at the glass awards filling a curio cabinet behind Mr. Stanford's desk. Light shimmered through them, causing rainbows to arc across the ceiling. "I'd like you to reconsider your position on inclusion."

"Reconsider?" Mr. Stanford repeated doubtfully.

"Yes!" Rob said, relieved that the ice had finally been cracked, if not broken. "Exactly. You see, it's come to my attention that Elwin Holme's residences aren't integrated into their communities. They live here. They go to school here. And they rarely leave to go out to restaurants or the movies or whatever."

"I'll have you know," Mr. Stanford replied irritably, "we have recently obtained a half-million-dollar grant to renovate our entertainment center. It has closed captioning and volume-controlled earphones. It can accommodate fifty motorized wheelchairs. It even has snacks that meet our resident's strict dietary needs. No other theatre in the state is so equipped, Mr. Chudinski."

"Yes, sir." Rob considered telling Mr. Stanford that he was, in fact, a doctor and wanted to be addressed as such, but decided to focus on the task at hand. "I'm sure it's wonderful. However, being in the community is more than seeing a movie or eating in a restaurant. It's about feeling part of—"

"Let me tell you what happens in *the community*." Mr. Stanford leaned forward disdainfully. "People get hurt in the community. They get robbed. And assaulted. And raped."

"Yes," Rob said quickly. "I understand. That's why a curriculum focusing on teaching adaptive skills—"

"Mr. Chudinski," Mr. Stanford said, his patience clearly stretched thin. "I understand how things must look from the view of the ivory tower. I've read the romantic propaganda that you and your compatriots put out in ever-increasing volumes. But our students have severe and numerous challenges. They don't have the skills required to be included safely within the community."

"Ah!" Reaching into his briefcase, Rob pulled out a binder he'd filled with specially designed curricula for teaching individuals with disabilities. "I'm glad you brought that up. You see, I have here—"

"Do you see that young man over there?" Mr. Stanford motioned to a framed portrait of an affable-looking adolescent with Down's syndrome hanging on the far wall. "That's Donald Cribbs. He was one of our residents many years ago. Late one night, he snuck out of our facility and was hit by a car as he ran across State Road 45. He lay in a pool of blood all night— and could've died."

"That horrific," Rob said. "It is. However,…"

"There is no 'however,' Mr. Chudinski," Mr. Stanford said with a great deal of finality. "You see, I display Donald's picture to remind myself that, while it may be your job as an academic to postulate and theorize and discuss what might be, it is my job to manage what is."

Rob attempted to interject, but Mr. Stanford talked over him.

"I live in the real world," he said. "Not academia. You can write your theoretical papers and go to conferences and drink imported brandy and pat your academic friends on the back. But I actually care about people with disabilities. And I can assure you I will continue dedicating my life to keeping them safe from harm for as long as I have the strength to come to work every day."

Chapter 27

"Okay, everybody." Closing the door, Rob surveyed his Characteristics of the Severely Crippled class. Only seventeen out of the forty-nine students were present. He groaned inwardly. "Let's get started."

He put his briefcase on the lectern and wondered where to begin.

"I want to talk about something really important," he said. "I want to talk a little bit about the purpose of education. Not only for people with disabilities, but for everybody. You. Me. Everybody."

The door opened. An undergraduate student came in. She mouthed *sorry*, then took a seat by the windows.

"As I was saying," Rob went on, pacing in front of the whiteboard. "I want to talk to you about something very important. It's critical you all understand that—"

The door swung opened again as two talking students entered.

"Are we starting already?" one of them asked, checking his phone.

"I started a few minutes ago," Rob replied, irritated. "I don't know about you."

Dropping their book bags with a clatter, the students sat next to each other.

Rob began again. "I want to talk to you about something extremely—"

The door opened.

"God damn it!" Rob ushered the fourth student in, then locked the door. "Look. Class starts at nine o'clock. Not nine o' five. Not nine ten. Show up on time!"

The door rattled. Then a confused face appeared in its window. "Can you let me in? I'm in this class."

Rob pointed down the hallway. "Go!"

The student shrugged and disappeared from view. Against his better judgment, Rob ran to the door and opened it.

"Hurry up," he told him. "Take your seat."

The student sat in the front row.

"You have to show up on time," Rob told the class again. "How else are you going to learn? You can't learn if you're not here!"

A handful of students muttered their apologies.

"Today," Rob said, fully expecting the door to open at any moment. "I want to talk about the purpose of education. Before we begin to consider developing our lesson plans, we have to first understand why we are teaching at all."

A hand shot in the air.

"Yes, Rhonda. You have a question?"

"Why are we talking about lesson plans? I thought we were focusing on what the severely cripple—" She corrected herself. "I mean, what people with severe disabilities are like."

"We are. But I want to talk a little bit about—"

"Yeah," another student chimed in, "we talk about lesson plans in Training Abnormal Children."

There was a groundswell of agreement.

"Forget about lesson plans, okay?" Rob rubbed his forehead in frustration. He was getting a headache. "Let me explain. Okay? We have a lot to cover today."

He resumed pacing.

"Let me ask you this… Why are you all here?"

The students exchanged bewildered expressions.

"Because," one of the students sitting in the last row said slowly, "we have class."

Rob waved a hand as if batting away the answer. "Besides that. Why are you learning?"

Again, the students looked at each other.

"Because you're teaching?" a female student offered.

Rob rubbed his forehead again. This was going nowhere.

"You're here," he said, trying to sound pleasant, "so you can get a job, right?"

A few students nodded.

"And why do you want to get a job?" Rob asked. Several seconds went by, but nobody answered. "So, you can live on your own and buy good food and clothes and have money to go out and have fun!"

More nodding.

"That's—"

"Wait a second!" a student cut Rob off. She recited as she wrote, "…buy good food and clothes and have money to go out and have fun." She looked up from her notebook. "Got it!"

"Kendra." Rob sighed. "This isn't on the test. You don't need to take notes."

"It isn't?"

Most of the students took out their cellphones.

"Look," Rob said, feeling as though he was wading against a strong current. "What I'm trying to explain is… the reason why you are learning is the same reason why your students need to learn—so that they can have a better life. To get a job and make money and live on their own!"

"You mean," one of the few students paying attention said, "kids with milder disabilities, right? Learning disabilities. ADHD. That kind of thing?"

"No!" Rob exclaimed, happy for the question. "I'm talking about all kids with disabilities! Everybody can live and learn in their communities. We just have to teach them!"

Even the students fiddling with their phones looked doubtfully up at him.

"Here…" Rob wheeled an old television and DVD player in front of the class. "Let me show you some videos of students with significant disabilities living and working in their communities. While you're watching, ask yourself two questions. First, what skills do these students need to be successful? And second, how can we teach them what they need to know?"

Chapter 28

"Everybody can live and learn in their community?" Craig taunted.

He and Rob were standing in the middle of the sixth-floor hallway. Characteristics of the Severely Crippled had ended no more than ten minutes earlier and, like a gunfighter wanting to shoot it out in the streets of the Old West, Craig was already waiting by Rob's office.

"Absolutely. I'm glad we agree on something." Rob tried to scoot around him.

Craig stepped in front of Rob's door. "I'm not agreeing! What you're teaching is absolute poppycock! All students can live and learn in their community?" He grunted contemptuously. "That's rubbish. Some of these kids can't even feed or toilet themselves!"

"That's where we come in. We have to teach them. Now, if you'll excuse me—"

Craig blocked Rob's path again. "These kids can't learn. Everybody knows that! It's common sense." He chortled, "Or didn't they give you any at that fancy school of yours?"

"Any what?"

"Common sense!"

Remembering what Wendy had said about being professional, Rob checked his tone.

"I'm not saying that every child with a disability can become a CEO or live alone in their own house—"

"Ah-ha!"

"But they *can* learn," Rob insisted. "And it's our job to teach them to be as independent as possible. That's the purpose of education."

"Oh, come on!" Craig cried. "Most of these droolers can't even dress themselves. Why, I once worked with one who could barely put on a hat!"

"But he could, right?" Rob asked.

"Could what?"

"Put on a hat. Don't you see? He learned that. And he could learn to do other things as well. We simply have to produce educators who are willing to teach him."

Craig quivered with rage. "Don't twist my words!"

"I'm not twisting anything!" Rob lowered his voice. "I admit it's a challenge teaching students with intensive needs. But they *can* learn. Their root problem isn't their lack of ability. It's the lack of education they're being given."

Craig's face contorted as though he was about to explode.

"Do you know what the root cause of all the problems we have in this field is?" he asked. "It's because young egomaniacs like you always want to change things. You have to come up with some new theory or strategy so you can make a name for yourself. That's why you are so quick to dismiss everything your betters developed before you!"

"I'm not—!" Rob lowered his voice again. "I'm sorry you think I'm an egomaniac. I hope that I'm not. But what you're describing—the need to produce new theories and strategies—is how our field advances. It's how we make progress."

"Progress?" Craig's fingers flexed. Rob half expected him to lunge for his throat. "You listen to me. Teach what I tell you to teach. Nothing else! Do you hear me? Otherwise, your hippy ideas will be the *root cause* of why I kick you out of here!"

Chapter 29

"There he is!" Pete Mullins cheered as he entered Rob's office. He was either wearing the same black Grateful Dead t-shirt he had on when they first met or an identical one. He also reeked of marijuana and whiskey. "I heard you almost gave Craig a heart attack this morning. Good going! I saw him stewing in his office a few minutes ago. It looked like he needed oxygen or something."

"Hey, Pete." Rob kept typing. He had his third class of the day in twenty minutes, and he was still working on the PowerPoint slides for the lecture. "How've you been? I haven't seen you in a while."

"Full professor, remember?"

"Oh, that's right."

Trying not to spill his coffee, Pete sat and propped his cowboy boots on Rob's desk. "How was your first month at EW-U, kid?"

"Great. In addition to not killing Craig with a heart attack, I returned a quiz in my pit class. A hundred students bitched at me for an hour. They kept saying my questions were 'too hard' and 'tricky.' I wouldn't be surprised if my car bursts into flames when I start it."

"I'll tell you, the secret to a good life here is to make things easy on yourself. Easy on you. Easy on your students. Know what I mean?" Pete sipped his coffee with satisfaction. "You'll always get good course evaluations if you're easy on them. That, or buy them pizza the day they fill them out. If you're too much of a hard ass, they'll rip you a new one."

"If I bought all my students pizza, I'd have to take out a second mortgage."

Pete laughed.

Rob suddenly remembered something. He stopped typing. "Hey. Do you have a copy of the current department handbook?"

"The handbook? No. Why?"

"I'm trying to figure out what I need to do to get reappointed. I have an old handbook, but it's from the 1970s. And it doesn't say anything about reappointment. Mary told me I have to write a paper describing all the things I've done since being hired, but I don't know what matters. Nobody's given me any criteria."

"Oh, that." Pete reached down the back of his dirty jeans. "It's all very subjective."

Attempting not to watch Pete scratch himself, Rob resumed working on his lecture. "Unfortunately, that doesn't help."

"Maybe I can demystify things a bit." Pete drained his coffee in one long swallow, then threw the paper cup across the office. It hit the wall, leaving a dark splatter on the white paint, then fell into the trash can. "Two points. I should play for the Bucks."

"They need you. They suck this year."

"They suck every year." Pete settled into his chair. "Okay! Reappointment. You've got these three areas: teaching, service, and scholarship."

"Hold on." Using a screwdriver, Rob pried open a desk drawer, then extracted a pen and notepad. He wrote teaching, service, and scholarship. "Okay. Got it. Go ahead."

"Your papers should focus on the things you did in each area. You don't have to write a lot. As a matter of fact, it'll probably help your case if you don't. Put an introductory paragraph and some bullet points highlighting what you've accomplished. Then end with a paragraph summarizing everything."

Rob wrote that down.

"Wait—" he said. "Won't the introductory paragraph and summary paragraph say the same thing?"

"Yup."

Nonplussed, Rob put an equal sign between 'introduction' and 'summary.' "Okay."

"Make it quick and easy for us. That's the name of the game here. If you make us read a bunch of crap, you'll piss people off."

"Good to know." Rob wrote, 'make it easy.' "So, I should have six paragraphs? An introduction and a summary for each of the three areas?"

"Right. Keep them short."

"How many bullet points?"

"You don't need a lot. Four or five. And no fluff. Fluff will piss people off too."

Rob scribble 'no fluff' and underlined it twice.

"This is great! Thanks. What else do I need to know?"

Pete put his hands behind his head and examined the brown water spots staining the ceiling tiles. "You need to do well in at least two out of the three areas. If you excel in one area, you can be average in the others, but you can't suck at anything. Know what I mean?"

"Yes, but what's 'well'? How's that defined?"

Pete lifted a shoulder. "It's like pornography. We know it when we see it."

"That's really helpful for new faculty," Rob said sarcastically. "We have no clue what we're supposed to do. There's no guidance at all!"

"Think of this process like dating. By the time you get to the tenure stage, we have to ask ourselves whether we want to be married to you for the rest of our vocational lives. 'Cause, despite what the Dean says, once you're tenured here, you can't get fired unless you kill somebody." He considered this, then added, "Or threaten to."

"But how do I prepare for a date when I don't know where we're going? What should I wear?"

"That all depends on the individual reviewer," Pete told him. "Some people value teaching more than research. Some research over teaching. Nobody values service."

"Wonderful!" Rob groaned. "Craig keeps giving me more and more committee assignments. I'm on twenty-seven now! And they don't matter?"

"I'm not saying blow them off. But don't give them much of your energy. Hell, when I had to go to meetings, I used to sit in the corner and watch movies on my computer. Never said a word. When people raised their hands to vote, I always went with the majority. Had no clue what I was voting on."

Tapping his pen on the paper, Rob reviewed what he'd written. "What about teaching? How's that evaluated?"

"Course evaluations."

"From the students?"

"Yup."

"That's it?" Rob asked, amazed. "How the hell do my students know whether I'm a good teacher until they've been a teacher themselves? I mean, I could stand in front of them and talk gibberish the entire time. Or teach them things that are fifty years out-of-date. They wouldn't know!"

"I'm not saying I disagree," Pete said. "It's all screwy. But that's how it's done."

Rob circled 'student evals,' then put three exclamation marks by it. "So, you're saying I need to kiss my students' asses?"

"Just until you get tenured. Then you don't have to even look at their evaluations again. Hell, I haven't given mine out this century."

"I can see why there's no incentive to hold students accountable or to challenge them academically."

"The course evals are way better than what we used to do," Pete said. "The university used to require that tenured faculty attend classes taught by non-tenured folks and write assessments of their teaching. But none of the tenured faculty did it."

Rob stared at the words: teaching, service, and scholarship. He thought he could do well with research. A couple publications in mid-tier journals would probably be impressive. If service didn't matter, that only left teaching—and given the ferocity of his students' protests regarding his numerous quizzes, he didn't think they'd rate him very highly. He wondered how he could get his students to like him without compromising the quality of his instruction.

"Anything else?"

Pete yawned. "It all comes down to how many votes you get."

"Votes?"

"Sure. If you get the majority of votes in the department, you're good. And don't worry. You have mine."

"Wait a second." Rob leaned forward excitedly. "Craig made it sound like it was his decision and his alone."

"Craig's a fuctard. He'll chair the meeting where we discuss your papers. And he'll try to sway people to his side. But he has only one vote." Pete stood and stretched. "But I'm mainly talking out my ass. I can't recall the last time we voted on reappointment. We haven't had a pre-tenured faculty member in decades. If you really want to know more about the process, talk to Jim."

"Jim?"

"Jim McFee. He's the other full professor in special education."

"There's another professor in our program?" Rob asked, astonished. "I don't remember him at my interview. Why haven't I heard of him?"

"Like I said, he's a full professor," Pete replied. "He rarely comes in. I haven't seen him in years."

Rob readied his pen. "When does he teach?"

"He doesn't."

"What do you mean he doesn't? I thought we had to teach as part of our contract."

"He has some sort of reoccurring grant with the state. Something about the changing demographics of school-age populations. He's had it since the late-1980s. It buys him out of teaching."

"He doesn't teach at all?" Rob asked.

"Nope. Not even an online class. I tell you, he has the life. Anyway, he's been here longer than anybody. E-mail him and see what he has to say."

Chapter 30

For the better part of a week, Rob attempted to get ahold of Dr. McFee, but the most senior member of the special education faculty hadn't returned any of his calls or e-mails. Throwing courtesy to the wind, he thought he'd visit his mysterious colleague. The problem was finding his office. According to the directory posted in Agnew Hall's front entrance, Dr. McFee was in B-12. However, few of the basement rooms were marked, and the ones that were appeared to be misnumbered. For instance, room B-25 was next to B-48. B-16 was across the hall from B-192. The odd thing was there couldn't have been a hundred and ninety-two rooms in the entire building. None of it made any sense.

Expecting Freddy Krueger to leap out of the musty shadows at any moment, Rob wandered the labyrinth of dark subterranean passageways. He knocked on a door hoping somebody could help him—but nobody answered. Backtracking, he found a cavernous room filled with giant rattling and hissing machines he guessed were furnaces or boilers. He stopped, taking stock of his situation.

Above him, the fluorescent lights flickered. Somewhere water dripped. Then he heard faint snatches of a conversation—a conversation he'd heard before.

Leaning closer to an unmarked door, he heard somebody say in a southern accent, "I'm your Huckleberry."

Rob knocked.

The conversation stopped.

He knocked louder. He thought he heard footsteps.

"Could you help me? I'm a bit lost." Rob hammered on the door. "I know you're in there. You're watching *Tombstone*. I love that movie. It's much better than Costner's *Wyatt Earp*, though Costner's film was more factually accurate."

He listened.

"Please?"

The door creaked open, revealing half the face of a scruffy, twenty-something-year-old graduate student.

"What're you looking for?" he asked through the crack.

In the room behind him, Val Kilmer in a black cowboy hat remained frozen on a large screen television. In front of the television was a grey recliner and a coffee table with a half-eaten foot-long sandwich from Subway. Food wrappers and pizza boxes lay scattered around an overflowing garbage can.

"I'm looking for B-12," Rob explained. "Do you know where—?"

"Never heard of it."

The door started to close.

"But—!" Rob thrust his foot in between the door and the jamb. "This is B-12, isn't it!"

"Look, man, I don't know anything about—?"

"I need to speak to Dr. McFee." Then Rob said, hoping it'd help, "It's urgent!"

At the word *urgent*, the young man wavered. "What is it?"

"You know him? This is his office?"

The graduate student exhaled wearily. "It's one of his offices. I'm his research assistant."

"Is he in?" Rob asked, trying to peek through the narrow crack. "I need to speak with him."

"Why?"

"Why?" Rob was about to say it was none of his damned business but decided against it. Being argumentative wouldn't get him anywhere. "You see, I'm a new faculty member in special education. And, well, Dr. Grubber isn't going to let me get reappointed. I need to talk to Dr. McFee so I can stay. The staff at Elwin Holme aren't teaching kids with disabilities or integrating them into the community. The kids are basically treated like prisoners. I want to change things around here but, but…" Rob ran out of breath. He looked desperately at the half-face blinking at him. "I need help!"

The pressure on his foot eased somewhat.

"Grubber is a fat asshole," the research assistant said.

"He is. But he's the department chair, and he isn't going to renew my contract. He told me so." Rob tried to appear as pathetic as possible. "I can't lose this job. I have a mortgage and car payments. Not to mention eighty-thousand dollars in student loans."

The student loans seemed to hit the mark. The door opened a little wider, revealing an unmade cot in the corner. "What do you need from Dr. McFee?"

"I need information about the reappointment process. What evaluation criteria are used. What I can do to be reappointed." Rob shrugged. "Mostly, I need him to vote for me next semester. Like I said… I can't lose this job because of Walrus!"

"Walrus." The research assistant snickered. "All right. I'll talk with Dr. McFee. He's out collecting data around the state, but I'm sure he'll get back to you as soon as he can."

Rob pulled his foot from the doorway.

"Thank you so much! And please tell Dr. McFee I'd love to buy him a drink or lunch or something. It'd be nice to have a friendly colleague in the department."

"I'll do that. But, as I said, he's very busy with the grant. He's not on campus much."

"I understand. When he returns, send him up to the sixth floor. I'm always in my office."

"Will do."

"Oh, wait! One more thing," Rob said before the door could close. "Can you tell me how to get out of here? I'm completely lost."

Chapter 31

Another week passed, and Rob had yet to hear from Dr. McFee. Sid thought he should call him at home.

"Clearly, he isn't getting his messages," he'd said when they had dinner at Rob's house earlier that evening. "I bet his research assistant never bothered telling him you stopped by."

Wendy, however, thought Rob should give Dr. McFee more time.

"The last thing you want to do is alienate him," she'd said. "Like his graduate student told you, he's busy collecting data. Give him until the end of the month before you e-mail him again."

Stretched out on the sofa in his living room, his laptop balanced on his thighs, Rob wrestled with his options. Wendy was probably right. He couldn't afford to make any more enemies. However, he wished he had some idea who this Jim McFee was. Maybe if he could learn something about him, find some shared interests, they could become friends. That's what he needed most of all—somebody who could be his champion and stand up to Craig for him.

On a lark, Rob typed "Jim McFee" into Google's search engine. Hundreds of hits appeared.

He tried "James McFee" and "Wisconsin." This narrowed the results substantially.

The first twenty or so links were from the university. Most were minutes from old meetings Dr. McFee had attended or information about classes he'd taught in the 1980s. Rob clicked on his faculty web page.

A dated picture of a jolly, middle-aged man with thinning hair appeared. Reading his bio, Rob found that he and Dr. McFee had a lot in common. Both worked with kids with severe disabilities. Both were Chicago Cubs fans. Both liked 1960's rock and roll.

Feeling as though his future was getting brighter, Rob looked at some of the other web pages his search pulled up. One included the value of Dr. McFee's house. Curious as to where a full professor would live, Rob clicked on the link. He found that James L. McFee and Audrey M. McFee lived in a beautiful two-story colonial in Neenah, Wisconsin, worth $212,950.

"Wait a second…"

Rob looked closer.

That's not what the site indicated. It indicated that the McFees *sold* their house for $212,950 twelve years earlier.

Rob typed "James L. McFee" and "Audrey M. McFee."

A similar real estate website came up, but this one from Florida. It revealed the McFees

purchased a three-bedroom condo in Pensacola the same month they sold their Wisconsin home.

"Huh?"

Rob searched the White Pages for James L. McFee in Neenah. Nothing came up. He tried J. McFee, J. L. McFee, Audrey McFee, A. McFee. There was no record of him or his wife living anywhere in Wisconsin.

He searched Pensacola. Immediately their address and phone number appeared.

"Collecting data around the state, my ass!"

Living in Florida would certainly explain why nobody had seen him for so long.

Something about this struck a faint chord. During his orientation, Rob vaguely recalled somebody in Human Resources telling him that university employees had to reside in the state. Was that right?

He clicked on the link to the university's rules and regulations handbook he'd bookmarked, then searched for "residency requirements." Sure enough, it plainly stated that university employees must maintain their primary residence in Wisconsin.

"Interesting…"

Rob opened his e-mail, then withdrew his hands. Maybe he should let sleeping dogs lie. After all, he didn't want to provoke Dr. McFee. Then again, he needed to get Dr. McFee's vote. And since he hadn't returned any of his previous e-mails…

Rob began typing:

Dr. McFee,

I'm sorry for bothering you again; however, I was hoping we could get together to discuss my reappointment situation. As your grad assistant probably told you, Craig is threatening not to reappoint me, and I could use your thoughts on how I can stay. I recently bought a house, and I don't want to leave.

Please let me know when you're taking a break from collecting data. I'd love to buy you a cup of coffee.

-Rob Chudinski

Rob added: *P.S. I hope you are enjoying Pensacola. I'm sure it's a lot warmer there in the winters than in Wisconsin.*

He clicked send before he could chicken out.

For many moments, he stared at the computer screen, wondering if he'd made a fool out of himself. Then, as he started closing the various websites he'd visited, the computer beeped. An e-mail from Dr. James L. McFee appeared in his inbox. It read:

Rob.

Don't let Craig get to you. I'll vote in favor of your reappointment, as will Pete, I'm sure. You'll be fine.

Regards,

Jim

P.S. If you could keep Florida to yourself, I'd be grateful.

Chapter 32

"I had no idea homecoming was this popular," Wendy said as she walked through campus with Rob and Sid. They, and thousands of others, were headed to the football stadium where the Eastern Wisconsin Cheesemongers were preparing to battle their despised archrivals, the Western Wisconsin Rivermen.

"They just like the opportunity to get drunk and party," Sid said. "Without alcohol, football is pretty boring."

"Think so?"

"Yeah, it's thirty seconds of action followed by three minutes of standing around. The only sport worse is baseball."

"I suppose you like soccer or something."

"No. Basketball. I used to dream about playing in the NBA. And, believe me, I know how odd that is for a five-foot, seven-inch Indian-American to say."

A pickup truck filled with drinking students sped by. One of the women in the truck bed screamed and flashed her breasts. The guys lining the road cheered.

"Can you believe kids nowadays?" Sid asked, trying to be heard over the stereos blaring from every rental property encircling campus. Throngs of students dressed in Eastern Wisconsin's colors of light blue and burnt orange stood in the front yards, plastic cups in hand, kegs protruding from trashcans filled with ice.

"Hey, if I had tits like that," Wendy said, "I'd show them off too."

Sid shot her a look.

"What?" she asked. "She should be proud of her body."

"If Rob or I would've said that, you would've smacked us across the head."

"Being a woman does have its privileges," Wendy admitted.

They continued up the hill toward the stadium.

Wendy nudged Rob's elbow. "What's wrong? You've been uncharacteristically quiet today."

"I got ahold of the other professor in special education—Dr. McFee," Rob said. "He told me he'd vote for my reappointment."

"You're kidding!" Sid exclaimed. "That's great! Way to go!"

"So what's the problem?" Wendy asked. "Why aren't you happier?"

"The problem is," Rob said as people jostled around him, "it's still two votes to three. I need either Les or Bert to switch sides."

"Bribe them," Sid suggested.

"I thought about that. But I'm not sure my bank account would allow it."

"You can kiss up and do nice things for them. Or make them feel sorry for you. After all, this is your livelihood we're talking about. I'm sure they don't want to see you get fired."

Rob raised an eyebrow. "You haven't met them, have you?"

"I still say," Wendy said, "you're making a big deal about nothing. Craig is an ass. But he likes having you around to bully. He'll vote yes if only to keep you under his thumb. Think about how miserable he can make your life while you're going up for tenure. He won't want to miss that!"

Rob shook his head. "You weren't there. When he told me I wasn't getting reappointed, he left no room for doubt or ambiguity."

"Don't worry. Things will work out. You'll see."

More people pushed by them, eager to get to the stadium.

Sid surveyed the slowly moving mob. "Why does everybody have an umbrella? We aren't expecting rain, are we?" He inspected the bright blue autumn sky.

"Beats me," Wendy replied.

They passed rows of tables promoting various university organizations. Student workers pressed fliers into everybody's hands. A young woman with EW-U painted on one cheek and three Greek letters on the other gave Rob a pamphlet that read: *Safe Sex Week. Be a Winner! Wrap that Weiner!*

Rob stopped and stared at it, dumbfounded.

"You can't give these out!" he told her.

"Hey!" The student worker's expression changed from drunken merriment to drunken puzzlement. "Why not? It's part of our sorority's service project."

"Look at this!" He showed her the pamphlet.

"What? We want to promote safe sex!" A guy in a car honked. She pointed to the table's bunting and yelled, "Wrap that wiener! Woohoo!"

She handed out more literature.

Rob snatched them. "Stop giving these out!"

"What's wrong?" Wendy asked. "What's going on?"

"They're giving these away." Rob showed her the pamphlet.

Wendy covered her mouth. "Oh, god!" Whether she was laughing or not, Rob couldn't tell.

"Is there a typo?" the student asked.

Rob snarled, "Look at this!" He tapped the condom stapled to the corner.

"What? Condoms are an important tool in the prevention of unwanted pregnancies and sexually transmitted diseases!" she said as if reading her own material.

"These aren't!"

Rob pulled the condom off the pamphlet, plucked out the staple, then ripped the packet open. The student watched in confusion as he unrolled the condom and then took a cup of beer from her table.

"Now watch." He poured beer into the condom. Two streams arced out from the staple holes. "Kind of defeats the purpose, doesn't it?"

The sorority girl's face turned scarlet. "Oops!"

"Oops! That's what you have to say?"

"We ran out of tape!"

"Just stop giving them out! Okay?" Then, against his better judgment, Rob asked, "What's your major?"

She brightened. "Special education! I'm in your Introduction to Retarded People class."

"My what?" Rob roared.

"Come on!" Wendy pulled him away. "We're not changing the world today. Besides, we're going to miss kickoff."

Grumbling, Rob followed her. "She'll probably be our program's valedictorian. Honestly, we accept everybody. We actually have a student who got a three on the ACT. I didn't even think a score that low was possible."

"I have a student who failed the class I'm teaching four times," Sid said. "I asked him how he managed to stay enrolled in the university. Know what he told me?"

"What?"

"Nobody has asked me to leave."

"Terrific."

"Why are you two surprised?" Wendy asked as they walked along with the crowds. "The university needs money. They're not kicking people out, and they're accepting anybody with a pulse."

"Everybody who's check clears, you mean." Rob snorted.

"Exactly. It's a business."

"It's a business with a shoddy product. And nobody realizes it!" Rob wadded the safe sex pamphlet and threw it into an overflowing garbage can by the side of the road. "We're taking tens of thousands of dollars from these students, and we can't even challenge them intellectually. If we do, they'll give us bad reviews on our teaching evaluations, and then we don't get our contracts renewed. They leave here as ignorant as they were when they arrived."

"The system's broken," Sid agreed.

Wendy shook Rob's shoulders playfully. "No work stuff! Okay? We're not going to fix anything right now. Let's enjoy the day."

"Fine."

They came to the chain-link fence surrounding the football stadium. Half the people trickled to the left; the other half went to the right.

"Which gate do we go in?" Sid asked.

"This one." Wendy led them to a gate with a big blue "5" over it, handed her ticket to the elderly ticket-taker, then lead them up a tunnel with an orange arrow saying, 'Faculty Section.'

"What exactly is a Cheesemonger, anyway?"

"They sell cheese." She looked at him over her shoulder. "How long have you been in Wisconsin? There's a cheese shop on nearly every street in town."

"Right between the bars and tattoo parlors," Rob said.

"And the churches." Climbing the bleachers, Wendy searched the numbers stenciled on the concrete steps. She pointed. "This is us."

They skootched along the row.

"How would I know what a cheesemonger is?" Sid asked, finding his spot. "The only places I've been are my apartment and work." He sat on the aluminum bench next to Rob. "I haven't become acquainted with the local nuances yet."

"You haven't missed much." Rob tried to get comfortable in the tight space. If anybody sat in front of him, they would have his knees jammed into their spine.

"I don't know." Wendy perused the crowd. "I think there're a lot of nice places in town—our bar for one. I like the dark, 1950's Italian feel to it. And all the black and white photos of the Rat Pack and everybody. It has charm."

"And?" Rob asked. "What else do you like about this crap hole?"

"And…" Wendy went on, "there're some hiking trails north of the lake. I hear they're pretty."

"I do love the lake," Rob admitted. "I sit in my living room watching the waves more than my television."

"Wait until spring."

The crowd filed in around them. Several people accidentally knocked into Rob as they passed.

"Seriously," Sid whispered. "Why the hell does everybody have an umbrella?"

Wendy shrugged. "Beats me. Another local nuance, maybe? Perhaps it's an affectation. You know, kind of like how English gentlemen stroll along, an umbrella dangling from the crook of their arm."

A vendor carrying a rack of plastic cups with Eastern Wisconsin University's logo descended the bleachers. "Beer! I've got nice, cold beer here! Beer!"

Standing, Rob pulled out his wallet. "Either of you want something to drink?"

"You kidding?" Sid replied. "I'm saving all of my alcohol intake for those around-the-world steins."

Rob returned his wallet to his pocket. "I suppose you're right." He sat. "This place is turning me into an alcoholic. I've never drunk so much in my life."

"Welcome to Wisconsin."

Over the public address system, the announcer rattled off a bunch of information about the pending game, glossing over the fact the Cheesemongers had yet to win all season.

Wendy flicked her chin at the field where the Cheesemonger mascot waved a giant wedge of cheddar cheese. "I wonder what that's about."

"Who knows," Rob said. "I feel sorry for the guy wearing the costume. It must get incredibly hot in there."

"The *person* wearing the costume," Wendy corrected him. "We can't see if he has a penis from here."

They watched the mascot rally the fans.

"That head looks like it weighs a ton," Sid said.

"I'm sure it's paper mâché or something like that," Rob told him. "I wonder how he—or she—sees."

"Thank you," Wendy said. "And there're probably holes in the mouth or nostrils."

The mascot lifted five fingers and then pointed the wedge of cheese at the faculty section, dropping a finger each time he pointed.

"I'm not sure I like the looks of this," Rob muttered to Wendy.

"It's probably only a—"

When the mascot's final finger fell, a sea of umbrellas suddenly unfurled around them as a deluge of egg-sized objects flew from the student sections and rained down upon the faculty.

"What the—?" Wendy cried as white globs pelted her. "Ugh! What the hell is this?"

Attempting to shield her from the onslaught, Rob pulled a wad of half-melted gunk from her hair. "They're cheese curds!"

A cheese curd smacked Sid's forehead. Another slammed into his ear. He huddled next to Rob. "Geez! Good thing we aren't the fishmongers!"

Chapter 33

"Hey, Les!" Rob knocked on Les's half-open office door.

It was the Monday after homecoming, and Rob had spent all Sunday baking as well as trying to get the smell of beer-soaked cheese curds from his hair.

"What do you want?" Les asked sharply. He jerked a file from an overflowing filing cabinet.

"Nothing. I thought I'd see if you wanted a brownie." Rob held out a plate of dark, moist brownies, the scent of chocolate wafting out as he pulled back the cellophane wrapping.

Les recoiled. "Are those Becky's *funny* brownies?"

"What? No. I made them."

"You?"

"I like to bake."

Les guffawed. "What a surprise. Polly likes to bake!" He resumed rearranging files. "I bet you have a frilly pink apron and everything."

Rob ignored the comment.

"Hey," he said as casually as he could. "I'd love to get together with you sometime and discuss what you teach in your classes."

Les flinched. "I'm not gay!"

"I never said you were."

"I'm not! My students are just mean. All of them. None of what they put on rateyourprofessor.com is true!"

"Anyway," Rob continued, "I'd like to see where we can make some improvements in our program."

"Improvements?" Les repeated doubtfully.

"Yeah, you know—update our curriculum. Streamline the content. Make everything more cutting edge and all that."

"The edges of my classes cut fine. Thank you very much!"

"Okay. Sorry I brought it up." Rob watched him yank files out of his filing cabinet and then slam them someplace else. "What are you doing?"

"I had everything arranged perfectly, but somebody keeps coming in here and messing with it. I think it's those constructivists in the Teaching and Learning Department. First, the exploding flour, now this." Like a battle-hardened soldier who'd seen more than his share of bloody combat, Les's smoldering gaze drifted off into the distance. "Oh, how I'd like to fix their wagons!"

Rob tried not to laugh. "Are they the ones who cut Craig's desk in half?"

"Exactly. We need to punish them for that as well."

An idea germinated in Rob's mind.

"You know," he said, thinking. "Maybe we could join forces."

"What the hell does that mean?" Les asked.

"I bet between the two of us, we could come up with some sort of epic prank."

"Epic prank?"

"Absolutely. You know, avenge your files and Craig's beautiful desk." Rob shook his fist in the direction of the courtyard around which Agnew Hall was built. "We'll make those constructivist assholes pay!"

Les stopped filing. "Have an idea? Something really good?"

"Well…" Rob searched for a suggestion. He noted the brownies in his hand, then smiled mischievously. "We could ask Becky for some of her herbs and bake a special batch of brownies. We could leave them in the TL's breakroom before their next birthday party!"

"Herbs?"

"Pot, Les. We can make them funny brownies like you said."

Les stuck out his chin. "Marijuana is illegal in this state, mister!"

"Okay. How about laxatives? They'll eat the brownies and spend the entire day in the bathroom. We can even put out-of-order signs on all the bathrooms in the building."

Les considered this. "No. That sounds childish. What else do you got?"

Rob thought. He motioned to Les' office. "Do they have offices as small as ours?"

"Yeah. Why?"

Rob laughed. "You know that expanding foam they use to insulate the walls of old houses? We could slide a hose under their doors and fill them to the ceiling."

"What would that do?"

"Think about it. They'd open their doors and find their offices filled with insulation. It's funny. Trust me."

"I don't know. That could damage something."

Down the hallway, Craig emerged from the stairwell, winded from his climb. He took a step toward his office, looked up, and glared at Rob leaning against Les' door.

"At any rate—" Rob put the plate of brownies on Les' desk. "Let me know if you come up with anything. We can't allow those bastards to push us around, you know? We have to show them who's boss!"

Chapter 34

Mid-October meant two things at Eastern Wisconsin University—the weather turning wet and cold, and midterm examinations. Rob was from Chicago and was used to northern winters; however, he couldn't understand why the air conditioning remained on. Every room in the university was freezing. No matter how many layers he wore, he couldn't keep warm.

He also couldn't understand his students' reactions to midterms. Even students who hadn't taken them were complaining about their grades. Wendy called it "pre-emptive bitching."

Sitting at his desk, a newly purchased space heater warming his numb feet, Rob opened his e-mail and groaned. There were forty-four messages, all from students.

He read the first one.

Stacey Edens asked: "Dr. C. Is the cumulative midterm over everything covered in class so far? Or only what you talked about last week?"

Rob typed, "Please look up the definition of 'cumulative.'" Then, thinking he was being an asshole, he deleted this and wrote. "It's over everything we covered since day one. Good luck!"

Danielle Reed wrote: "When is our midterm again?"

Rob reviewed his rosters, found Danielle's name, then checked his calendar. He wrote, "It was yesterday. Hope you did well."

Tonja Sorgasen had an exceedingly emotional e-mail saying she wasn't in a "good place" to take the midterm because her grandmother died earlier in the month. She asked if she could take it in a couple of weeks.

Rob replied, "Sorry for your loss, Tonja. Unfortunately, you'll still have to take the exam. My thoughts go out to you and your family in your time of need. Hopefully, your grandmother is in a good place." He read this over and then, thinking the student would believe he was making light of her situation, deleted the last sentence.

Chloe M. Slutz wrote, "I was wondering if you were going to grade on a curve."

Rob typed a detailed response explaining that a "curve" meant a "C" was determined by the average test score, thereby forcing a significant proportion of the class to get low grades regardless of how well they did. Consequently, most students would do better without the curve. Then he deleted everything and simply replied, "No."

Marcie Wallace sent an angry and capital-ridden e-mail that ended with the statement, "I showed up for class! I took notes!! I DESERVE NOTHING LESS THAN AN A!!!"

Rob typed, "Please listen to the song *Can't Always Get What You Want* by the Rolling Stones." He was about to push send then decided not responding would probably be best.

Buddy Barbour sent a convoluted e-mail that went on for four screens but contained only three rambling sentences—none of which ended in a question mark. Rob read the entire treatise twice. Finally, he replied, "I'm sorry, Buddy. I'm not sure what you're talking about." He considered this for a moment and then changed it to, "I'm not sure what you're asking. Could you either rephrase your e-mail or make an appointment to talk with me directly?"

Andrew "Andy" Wilson wanted to know what he needed to get on the midterm to get his grade up to an "A." Rob checked his grade book and found that Andy had missed five out of six quizzes. He wrote back, "An act of god." He pushed send before he could change his mind.

Brittany K. wrote, "Dear Mr. Chudinski. I've done some calculating and I've found I'm only six percentage points away from getting a B- and I was wondering whether you rounded up or gave extra credit because I've worked really hard in this class and would really like to get above a C. Thanks for your consideration."

Staring at the screen, Rob tried to push away his annoyance. He wanted to explain that there was a vast difference between percentage points and points on an exam. Also, her "calculating" was a bit off since she was currently failing the course. But he couldn't bring himself to type all of that. So he simply wrote, "No extra credit. I round up to the nearest hundredth decimal." Then he added, "That's the second digit to the right of the little period." He pushed send.

Clare Fergusson indicated she missed the midterm and asked if she could make it up when she wasn't so busy. Rob replied, "Absolutely. You can take it next semester when you're retaking the course—if your schedule permits."

Lyndsey Burgeon sent an e-mail explaining she was getting a "low A." There was no question. It was merely a statement of fact. Rob tossed his hands, then typed, "Thanks for letting me know."

Cailey Marie Simon's e-mail indicated that she was doing poorly in the class and needed to pass so she could student teach in the spring. She then said, "I'll do anything for a C-." She ended with two emojis—one of hands clasped together in prayer, the other of a winking smiley face kissing a heart.

Laughing, Rob imagined the student doing 'anything' for a C- only to realize later she needed a 'C' to student teach. He wrote, "You might want to consider studying." He pushed send.

Another Cailey asked, "What's on the midterm?"

Rob quickly typed, "The War of 1812. Non-linear geometry. And the mating habits of the blast-ended skrewt." He pushed send.

Amanda Horwitz sent a three-screen e-mail whining about how "tricky" and "unfair" his midterm was.

Rob replied, "Perhaps you should wait until you get your score back before complaining."

James T. Martin asked, "How important is the midterm?"

Rob responded, "People have died for less."

Somebody with the username Sexykitty09 wrote, "Is there a book for this class? I can't remember. And do we need to read it for the midterm?"

Clenching his teeth, Rob typed, "Please consult the syllabus."

As he took a sip of cold coffee, the computer beeped. There was a new e-mail from the second Cailey. She asked, "When did we cover the War of 1812????"

Chapter 35

"Thank you for seeing us, Dr. Chudinski," said a woman standing in the hall. She clutched her purse to her chest as though somebody might rip it from her grasp. Five other parents stood behind her, looking equally uncomfortable. "We greatly appreciate it."

"Please, call me Rob." He ushered them inside the first-floor conference room, then checked the corridor. Other than a few students milling about, waiting to see their academic advisor, it was empty. "Where are your children?"

"Our children?"

"You said you wanted to learn more about special education. I assumed your children were interested in enrolling in our program once they graduate high school."

"Actually—" She slipped a guilty glance at her companions. "—our children have disabilities. They go to Elwin Holme."

Rob's stomach tightened. None of the parents appeared particularly happy, and he was starting to sense he'd fallen into some sort of trap.

"I'm sorry." He raised his hands placatively. "I don't want another confrontation. Perhaps you should—"

"Give us a minute and we'll explain," one of the men interrupted. He had curly black hair and an expression that suggested he'd been the loser of a prolonged and heated argument. "It's not what you think."

"Okay…" Rob set aside the brochures on the special education department he'd planned on giving them. "Please, have a seat."

The six grim parents sat around the conference table. Dressed in an expensive three-piece suit, one of the men appeared to be an angry divorce attorney.

Rob sat closest to the door. "What can I do for you all?"

The parents exchanged glances again. Finally, the woman directly across from him spoke.

"We understand you were at the school a few weeks ago."

"I was," Rob said, not wanting to say anything that could be used against him in court.

More pained expressions passed between the parents.

"What *exactly* happened?"

"Look…" Rob stood. "I'm not sure where this is going, but I think I might need university council present." He made for the door. "Thanks for coming. I'm sorry I can't help you."

"It's not like that," she said quickly. "We're not trying to make trouble."

"Yes, we are," retorted a stony-faced woman sitting to Rob's right. She chewed her gum as though it had personally wronged her. "I think it's high time we made all the trouble we can."

"Let's get the facts first," the woman in front of Rob told her. "We don't know anything."

"We know enough."

"Maybe we should start with some introductions," muttered a middle-aged man sitting in the corner. With short red hair and broad shoulders on a straight spine, he appeared to be former military, or perhaps a police officer. He looked everywhere but at Rob.

"That's a good idea." The woman across the table said, "We're the Morrisons. I'm June. This is my husband, Randy."

The man Rob thought was a lawyer stood and extended his hand. Rob shook it.

"These are the Harroffs," June went on, looking to her left.

"Daniel and Alyse," the husband said.

They shook Rob's hand.

"And we're the Codners," the last woman said. "I'm Madeline. Call me Maddie. My husband is Tom."

The man with the short hair at the far end of the table looked away.

"Nice to meet you all." Rob took his seat, still wondering what the hell was going on. "How may I help?"

"We understand they dragged you out of Elwin Holme and smashed your phone," June said. "We'd like to know why."

Rob peered about the table. Nobody was making eye contact with him. Everybody was either staring at the floor or out the windows.

"I believe the phone was probably a misunderstanding," Rob replied. "They thought I was taking pictures."

"That probably terrified them," Alyse Harroff grunted.

"The rest…" Rob lifted a shoulder, not knowing what to say. "Well, we had a bit of a disagreement. Different professional philosophies, you might say. I believe students with disabilities should be integrated within their communities. They think—"

"Students like our children?" Maddie interrupted. They were all looking at Rob now. Some of the men appeared doubtful, but curious. "Have you seen the students at Elwin Holme?"

"Yes." Then Rob corrected himself. "That is, I've seen some."

"And you think they can learn?"

"Oh, absolutely!" Rob watched them digest this. "Perhaps you should tell me what's troubling you and how I can help."

Nobody said anything. Eventually, Maddie went on, "As I mentioned before, our children are taught at Elwin Holme."

Gritting her teeth, Alyse swore under her breath.

"Perhaps *taught* isn't the correct word," Maddie admitted.

"Dr. Chudinski," Alyse said angrily, "how many years would it take you to teach somebody to tie their shoes? Because my son has been in Elwin Holme for nine years. And for nine years, that's what they've claimed to have been teaching him. Nine years—and he has yet to do it once." Her husband, Daniel, tried to calm her, but she swatted him away. "I don't know what the hell they're doing there, but learning plainly isn't involved."

"It's like that with all of our kids," Maddie explained. "None of them are making any progress. In fact, some of their behaviors are getting worse."

As if a dam had burst, Tom blurted, "And we're not allowed to go into the school to see our son! They always bring him out to us. It's as if they are hiding something."

The parents murmured in agreement.

"Well," Rob said, wondering which problem to address first and how much he should say. Talking ill of Elwin Holme would only get Craig angrier. He needed to start smoothing things over, not riling them up. "Why don't you get your son penny loafers or shoes with those Velcro straps," he suggested to Alyse. "Then you can change his IEP goals to something more useful."

"IEP?" Alyse repeated.

"Yes, their Individualized Education Program." Then Rob added, "It's the document you and teachers draw up when you meet with them every year."

The parents appeared confused.

"You don't know what an IEP is?" Rob asked, trying not to sound negative.

"Dr. Chudinski," Randy Morrison said bitterly, "let me tell you how things are from our perspectives. You see, one day you find out your wife is pregnant—and everything is wonderful. Then you go to the doctor's office for some routine tests and are told your unborn baby has something called Down's Syndrome. Then everybody starts telling all kinds of conflicting information. One person says we should put him in an institution where he'll be safe for the rest of his life. Another person—" He choked on his words and turned away.

"My doctor told us our boy would never do anything for himself," his wife, June, said teary-eyed. "That he'd be a vegetable. He told us it would be best to abort him."

"Honestly—" Tom stared out the window. "I don't think we know half of what we need to know to be decent parents."

"Less than half," Randy agreed.

The other parents nodded.

"We need help, Dr. Chudinski." Maddie took her husband's hand. "Any honest and straightforward information you can give us will be greatly appreciated."

Rob thought he saw an opportunity.

"How about if I do this," he said, "what if I put together a workshop. We can go over some of the basics of special education and, if you like, we can talk about how we help your children live the lives they want. Are you free tomorrow night?"

"That would be fantastic." Maddie dabbed a tissue under her eyes. "Could we bring some friends?"

"Of course," Rob told them. "Let me know how many will be coming, and I'll make sure there are enough snacks."

Chapter 36

Rob arrived at campus later than usual. He'd spent the previous night putting on a workshop for parents of children with disabilities and was mentally and physically exhausted. Seventeen people attended and, although the initial presentation lasted only thirty minutes, they kept him there another two hours, asking a continuous stream of questions. In the end, he agreed to put on another workshop the following week.

As Rob entered the department's main office, he found a now blonde Tiffani dressed in a provocative version of a Star Trek uniform.

"Boy!" She handed him the stack of quizzes she'd photocopied. "You look bad. Hungover?"

"What? No. I'm tired." He thumbed through the quizzes, trying to recall which class they were for. "Nice outfit, by the way. I didn't realize the Federation issued fishnet stockings to their science officers."

"I had to make some adjustments." Tiffani tugged at her black, knee-high boots. "The skirt was too long, so I took it up a bit."

Rob snuck a peek at her shapely thighs. "A bit?"

"Think I should've gone higher?" she asked.

"I think you're perfect the way you are."

"Thanks!"

He regarded her again and gave in to his growing curiosity. "If you don't mind me asking, why are you wearing that? You don't strike me as a Trekker."

"It's Halloween!"

"Friday's Halloween."

"Craig wanted me to come in each day with a new costume. I think he really likes Halloween!"

"I bet." For a moment, Rob lost himself imagining what his administrative assistant might wear next. He pulled himself back to reality. "Did you manage to find a more recent copy of the handbook?"

She scanned the boxes lining the shelves. "No. But I'm still looking. I've only gotten through about half of them." She crinkled her nose. "They're all dusty."

"I appreciate your effort."

"No problem. And, speaking of Craig—he told me to tell him the second you arrived." She bit her bottom lip nervously. "He wasn't very happy."

"He's never happy." Rob tucked the quizzes into his briefcase. "I'll see what he wants. Thanks for letting me know."

"Anything for you!"

When Rob exited the main office, Bert and Les were huddled outside Craig's open door.

Les saw Rob and shouted, "There he is!" Rob half expected him to add, "Get him!"

"Where?" Craig appeared into the hallway, looked around, then hurried at Rob, a crumpled piece of paper clasped in his fat fist.

Bert raced after Craig. "Now you're in for it, Polly!"

Les brought up the rear. "In for it good!"

"What's wrong?" Rob asked, resigned to the fact that his day was going to get worse.

"What's wrong?" Craig huffed. "What's wrong? I'll tell you what's wrong!" He shook the paper. "Do you know what this is?"

"Takeout menu for Chuck E. Cheese?"

"No!"

"The bill for your weight loss program?"

"Don't get smart!"

"Yeah!" Les said from a safe distance. "Watch your tone!"

"What do you want me to do, Craig?" Rob asked calmly. "You wave something in my face and ask me to guess what it is. How the hell would I know?"

"It'll tell you what it is!" Craig said. "Mr. Stanford sent it to me!"

The name rang a bell. Then Rob recalled the superintendent of Elwin Holme. "I'm sorry, but that still doesn't tell me what it is."

"It is an advertisement!" He shoved the paper at Rob. "About you!"

Rob smoothed the paper and found it was a flier advertising the previous night's special education workshop. "Cool!"

"Cool?" Craig repeated scornfully. "It is most certainly not cool! Mr. Stanford is pissed! He's threatening to refuse to take any of our student teachers next year!"

"Good. Now, if you excuse me, I have a Curriculum Committee meeting to get to."

Rob tried to get past them, but Craig stepped in front of him.

"You listen to me, Polly," he said. "You will not put on any more unauthorized presentations. Do I make myself clear?"

"Craig," Rob said with an effort, "if there's some sort of screwy rule here saying I need permission to host a free workshop, then I'll get a room at the public library. I'm sorry, but I have a meeting…"

"You will cease and desist!" Craig shouted.

"Cease and desist?" Rob smiled. "Gee, Officer Fife, I think I'll have to take this up with Officer Taylor."

"That's not funny!"

"What's he talking about?" Les whispered to Bert as they stood watching the exchange. "Who's Officer Taylor?"

"He's referring to the Andy Griffith Show," Bert whispered back. "He's making fun of the Big Guy."

"Look—" Rob tried to defuse the tension. "I don't know why you're upset. Maybe you can explain it to me so I can see what I did wrong."

"Why I'm upset? I'll tell you why I'm upset!" Craig hesitated as if attempting to recall what the conversation was about. Then he remembered. "You're filling these parents' heads with all kinds of hippy malarkey!"

"No I'm not," Rob replied defensively. "I'm teaching them about special education. We talked about IEPs and BIPs and what their rights are!"

"They don't need to know any of that! That's what we are for." Craig waved a hand at Bert, Les, and himself. "We're the professionals. They're the parents. They do what we say. That's how things work!"

Rob debated whether he should respond. It wasn't as though he was ever going to change Craig's mind about anything. In the end, he couldn't help himself.

"The Individuals with Disabilities Education Improvement Act mandates that parents be informed of their rights every year." Then he added because he memorized it for his preliminary doctoral exams, "It's in the Due Process clause. Section 300.511, part A. If you'd like to know."

The white-collar around Craig's ample neck seemed to shrink. Veins bulged in his forehead. "Don't give me any of that legal mumbo-jumbo. If parents could make decisions about their crippled children's education, why would we need to prepare highly trained teachers? Eh? Answer me that!"

"I'm not saying parents will replace special educators," Rob said. "I'm saying they need to know their rights so they can work *with* school officials and so they will understand what's going on."

Craig snatched the flier and brandished it in Rob's face. "I want this to stop! You understand. Stop!"

Rob checked his watch. He had another twenty minutes before his next meeting, but he didn't want to spend them standing in the hallway arguing.

"I'll tell you what," he said reasonably. "How about if we do the next workshop together. I'll tell everybody what the law says, and you can tell them why I'm wrong. We can be partners!"

"Partners?" Craig sputtered. "Oh, very funny! Very funny, indeed!"

"I'm not trying to be funny, Craig. I'm being serious. If you can't make it, maybe Bert or Les could present your side."

"Hey!" Bert retreated, hands raised. "Keep us out of this. Nothing good ever comes from being around a group of educated parents."

"Exactly!" Craig thumped a finger into Rob's chest. "You are *not* going to do any more of these, these—performances! Understand? My foot is down!"

Chapter 37

"That's incredible!" Maddie Codner exclaimed as her husband, Tom, looked on. "How did you get him to listen to you? He never does what I say!"

Rob sat on the living room floor of the Codner's double-wide trailer next to their twelve-year-old son, Jamie—the same boy he'd seen gazing longingly through the narrow glass window at Elwin Holme. Three days earlier, Maddie had quit her job as a cashier at a grocery store and was now homeschooling him. She'd called Rob and asked for his help.

"I'm not saying it'll be easy," Rob told them. "But you have to be consistent and systematic. Don't think autism means stupid. Jamie wants to learn. He wants to communicate. It's easier for him as well as for you. But he needs to know what you expect, and your expectations have to be consistent."

"Okay." Maddie knelt by her son and stroked his unkempt hair. He knocked her hand away. "Show me what to do."

"First, you have to give very clear instructions. Use his name. Also, be brief. Nobody wants to listen to somebody who can't get to the point."

"Got it." Feeling her pockets, Maddie looked around. "I really should be writing all of this down."

"I'm on it." Tom typed on his phone. "Clear, concise, and consistent. The three C's. What else?"

Rob went on, "In the beginning, you're going to use immediate and continuous reinforcement. As soon as Jamie does something appropriate, praise him and give him a small reinforcer. Let him choose what he gets. That's important. He needs to have a say in what's going on."

"Let him choose the reinforcer," Tom repeated, typing. "Won't he get sick of the reward if we give it to him too frequently?"

"Yes. That's why giving him a choice is so important. He might find something reinforcing one day but then hate it the next. It also encourages him to communicate."

Rocking, Jamie clapped. Then he pointed to a picture of an M&M candy on the rug in front of him.

"Hold on, Jamie," Rob told him. "You'll get a chance to earn a reward soon. I promise." He turned back to Tom and Maddie. "Also, that's why you'll want to fade the frequency of the reward over time. But you're going to do so systematically. For the first week, reward him every time he does what you tell him to do. Then every two times. Then every four and so on. However, praise him whenever he does what you ask, regardless of whether you give him anything."

"Did you get that?" Maddie asked her husband.

Tom finished typing. "Yup."

Jamie's rocking intensified. He clapped louder.

"Let me show you again." Rob faced their son. "Hey, Jamie! If you put this block—" He tapped a wooden block with letters painted on each side. "—in this box—" He tapped a tattered shoebox. "—you will get another reward. Okay?"

Jamie picked up the block and tossed it at the box. It missed and bounced along the floor. Maddie reached for it, but Rob shook his head. Not making eye contact, Jamie held out his hand.

"Oh!" Rob said enthusiastically. "That was a good try, Jamie! But the block is not *in* the box. It has to be *in* the box for you to get the reward. Try again!"

Jamie stopped rocking, crawled over to the block, then dropped it in the box.

Maddie and Tom traded astonished looks.

"Great job, Jamie!" Rob arranged four pictures in a line. One had an image of a television, another of a grape, the third had a computer, and the last had an M&M. "Now, show me what you want as a reward."

Jamie thumped the picture of an M&M.

"You want an M&M?" Rob asked him.

The boy gave a curt nod.

"Good job telling us what you want, Jamie. Here's your M&M." Rob dropped a green M&M in Jamie's outstretched hand. The boy gobbled it up, then resumed rocking.

"Notice what I'm doing," Rob said to Jamie's parents. "First, I'm using his name. Also, I'm using very direct statements. A lot of people are verbose and moralize."

"Moralize?" Maddie asked.

"Yeah. Imagine Jamie hits somebody and you say, 'Hitting is wrong! How would you feel if he hit you? Would you like that?'"

"Oh, god! I do that all the time."

"Why's that bad?" Tom asked.

"First of all," Rob said, "the concepts of right and wrong are pretty nebulous. Leave them to the philosophers and theologians. Stick to stating exactly what you want and don't want. Say, 'Don't hit.' It's direct and to the point."

"Write that down!" Maddie told her husband.

Tom's thumbs flailed about his phone. "Got it."

"Also," Rob continued, "kids with autism often have difficulty understanding other people's perspectives. When you ask them to imagine somebody doing something that hasn't occurred, it tends to mystify them. They're very literal thinkers. Like I said, keep everything concrete."

Jamie pounded the picture of the M&M.

"Want another M&M, Jamie?" Rob asked. "Tell you what. If you pick up all the blocks and put them in this box—" Rob tapped the shoebox again. "You can have another M&M. Okay?"

Jamie got up and began gathering the blocks strewn throughout the living room.

Maddie covered her mouth. "Oh, my god! He's doing it! He's listening to you!"

"For now," Rob said. "Remember, he's an adolescent. He'll test your boundaries and have good and bad days. Sometimes he won't do what you want no matter what you offer him. Also, he'll still throw tantrums from time to time. But hopefully, we can reduce how often they occur."

"What do we do when he has a tantrum?" Tom asked, ready to type.

"Clearly state what you want him to do. Make sure it's concrete. Don't say 'calm down,' that means nothing to him."

"Jesus!" Maddie cried. "I say that a hundred times a day!"

"Rather than saying 'calm down,' say something like, 'sit in this chair.' Direct and concrete. That's your mantra from now on—direct and concrete, direct and concrete."

Rob got to his feet. He'd been sitting for over an hour and his legs and butt were tingling. He tried to get the blood flowing to them again.

"This is what I want you to do. Consider it your homework assignment for the week. I want you to make three lists. The first will be things Jamie likes, such as M&M's, arranging his blocks, and so forth. The second will be his triggers—"

"Triggers?" Tom asked.

"The things that tend to set him off," Rob explained. "For example, I noticed Jamie didn't like it when Maddie touched his hair. Try to ascertain what makes him act out. Maybe it's a smell or a noise or change to his routine or something you've done. Keep a list."

"That's going to be a long list," Tom said, typing.

"Good. It'll give us things to work on. Finally, I want you to watch for patterns of behavior. For example, when touched, Jamie tensed and quickened his rocking. If you were to continue touching him, I bet he would show other signs of displeasure."

"He rubs his head like this!" Maddie dug her knuckles into her temple.

"Great. You see, he's trying to communicate that he's unhappy. If you can identify his pattern, you can then cut off his aggressive behaviors before they escalate into a tantrum."

"Oh, god, that'd be marvelous!"

"Also," Rob said, "you need to start thinking about Jamie's future— where is he going to live when he gets older? Is he going to work in the community or a sheltered setting? Those kinds of things."

"Work?" Maddie gasped. "His teachers at Elwin Holme told us he'd never have a normal life. That he'll always need to be looked after and protected."

Rob put on his jacket. "I'm not sure what a *normal* life is. But our goal should be to prepare him for a life that'll make him happy. And plenty of people with disabilities work and live in their communities."

Maddie and Tom looked at each other.

"We should've been doing this years ago," she told him.

He hugged her. "I was thinking the same thing."

"Again, it's not going to be easy," Rob said. "That's why we'll focus on achieving small victories, such as getting him to use pictures to communicate more effectively. Next time, I'll show you how to collect and chart data and use them to evaluate your progress. Remember, he's teaching you as you teach him."

"This is incredible!" Crying, Maddie threw her arms around Rob. Much like Jamie, Rob stiffened, not knowing what to do. "Thank you so much!"

"Yes. We greatly appreciate all your help." Tom pulled out his wallet.

"Oh." Rob eyed the twenties in Tom's hand. The money could certainly come in handy, but given that Maddie had quit her job, he figured they could use it more than he could. "That won't be necessary."

"Are you sure? Your time is valuable."

"I'm happy to help." Rob headed to the door. "If you need anything, feel free to e-mail me. Okay?"

"Actually," Maddie said earnestly. "There is something else. You see… we can't find a decent babysitter. We run through them like water. Do you know anybody capable of staying with Jamie for a couple of hours here and there while I run errands?"

"Or we have a date night?" Tom asked. "We haven't been out together in, well—forever."

"You know," Rob said, thinking. "I believe I have just the people you're looking for."

Chapter 38

"One final thing," Rob announced as his students shoved their books and notes into their backpacks. He waited for them to quiet down. They still had four minutes left in his Curriculum for the Educable Child class, but he doubted he could keep their attention that long. "Some of you have asked for opportunities for extra credit."

Suddenly most of the students stopped moving.

Rob held up a stack of handouts. "This is a list of parents in the area who have kids with disabilities and need support."

"Support?" a junior in the second row repeated.

"Exactly! They need help with their children, and they're willing to pay for it."

Now the entire class was listening.

"If you're interested, this is what I want you to do. First, take one of these." Rob set the papers on the table next to him. Two students in the front row reached for them. "Hold on! Let me tell you everything! Then you can decide if you want to participate."

The students retreated to their seats.

"On these forms, you will find names of parents, their contact information, and what they're looking for. For example—" Rob selected a family from the list. "The Pelleck's are looking for somebody to help teach their seven-year-old daughter, Rayna, how to count. They're willing to pay qualified applicants fifteen dollars an hour."

The class sucked in air.

Rob selected another family from the list. "The Daczo's have an eighteen-year-old son with Angelman's syndrome." He lowered the paper. "If you don't recall what that is, please consult your notes from week three."

Several people flipped through their binders.

"Their son would like to learn how to get around the community," Rob continued. "He needs to know how to get to the grocery store, shop, and so forth. His parents will pay sixteen-fifty an hour."

This gasp was even louder.

"Debbie Mahon has a sixteen-year-old son with an intellectual disability who wants to learn how to cook and use money. She is willing to pay twenty dollars an hour."

"You're kidding!" somebody cried.

"Not at all," Rob told them. "They're willing to pay people to provide effective, high-quality instruction to their children. So treat this like an actual job."

"This is going to be great!" somebody whispered.

"I hope so. For you and the families." Rob returned the handout to the table next to him. "This is what you have to do. Find a family or two on the list you think you can help. Then, being as professional as possible, contact them. Tell them you're one of my students. They're expecting your calls."

Everybody started taking notes.

"Then—" Rob waited for them to look up. "I want you to use everything we've covered in this class to help the family who hires you. You will need to write measurable objectives." They resumed writing. "You will need to collect and chart data on the target behavior. And you will need to develop a reinforcement plan based upon what motivates your child."

"Reinforcement plan?" one of the students asked.

A classmate leaned across the aisle and said, "Chapter nine."

The student opened his textbook. "Thanks!"

"Finally," Rob said, "you will write a one-page essay on what you learned from this experience. Turn all of this in—the measurable objectives, the data charts, reinforcement plan, and essay—and you shall receive…"

The students held their breaths.

"…thirty extra points added to your final exam grade."

They gave the loudest gasp yet.

Rob called over the growing commotion, "Any questions?" A hand shot into the air directly in front of him. He pointed. "Yes, Ms. Schultz?"

"Do our students have to accomplish their goals for us to get credit?" she asked.

"Excellent question. The answer is no. However—" Rob waited for the din to subside again. "If the family fires you, you will receive no points. In fact, you will incur my fiery wrath! So do a good job. I mean it. These people need your help. Not only can you get extra credit and some spending money, but you can get something even more valuable—glowing letters of recommendation for when you apply for teaching positions."

People in the next class started trickling into the room. Rob's students got to their feet.

"And—" Rob shouted over the turmoil. "Don't try to bullshit me. I *will* be speaking with each of your families to make sure you did what you claim you did! Dismissed!"

Every student snatched a handout as they hurried to the door.

Chapter 39

Later that day, Rob found Bert sitting on the edge of Tiffani's desk, leering at her breasts as they bulged out of the skin-tight flight suit she was wearing. He leaped to his feet as Rob entered the office.

"Oh, it's you." Bert sat again. "What do you want? Putting on a workshop to save the world 'one child at a time'?"

"That's next week. Want to come?"

"No."

Rob handed Tiffani a folder fat with papers. "Thanks again for grading these, Ms. Miller. The key is on top. Circle the questions they get wrong in red and write the correct answers in the margin. Add up the questions they got correct and put it at the upper right-hand corner."

Tiffani whipped off her aviation sunglasses and saluted. "Absolutely, Captain Chudinski! I'll get them to you by the end of the day, sir!"

"Thank you, cadet." Rob returned the salute. "I appreciate your assistance."

"What the hell are you two going on about?" Bert asked, watching.

Tiffani pointed to the wings insignia on her chest. "I'm in the Air Force today! You know, like Top Gun?"

"Well—" Bert leaned closer. "—I'd love to show you my top gun!" He winked.

Rob mimed putting a finger down his throat. Tiffani giggled. Bert seemed to think he'd scored a point with her.

"Thank you again, Ms. Miller," Rob said. "You're a big help. But there're nearly two hundred quizzes there. If you can't finish them today, tomorrow will be fine too." He headed for the door.

"Anything for you, Dr. Chudinski." She called after him, "Oh! I asked Craig about the handbook."

Rob stopped. "And?"

Her face contorted apologetically. "He told me not to waste my time."

"Of course, he did." Rob sighed. "Oh well. It was worth a try." Then, noting Bert ogling Tiffani's breasts, he remembered he still needed one more vote to get reappointed. "Hey, Bert?"

"What?" Bert attempted to trace Tiffani's cheek with a seductive finger, but Tiffani pushed his hand away.

"I was wondering if you'd help me. You see, I'm working on this research article from my dissertation. I thought you could give it a quick once over and tell me what you think. I'll put you on as the second author."

Bert grunted, "What would I care about research?"

"Don't you have to publish to be reappointed?" Seeing the disgust wash over Bert's face, Rob said, "I'm sorry. Are you tenured already?"

"I'm not tenured, idiot. I'm NTT."

"You're an NTT?" Rob asked, not sure why he didn't know that.

"What's an NTT?" Tiffani asked.

"It stands for Non-Tenure Track," Bert told her proudly. "We run this place. They couldn't do a thing without us."

"How often do you go up for renewal?" Rob butted in.

"Renewal? I don't know. I come here and they pay me. That's all I care about."

"Is Les NTT as well?" Rob persisted, his heart quickening. Non-tenure track faculty usually only taught courses. They didn't participate in governing academic units.

"Of course! You think that imbecile has a Ph.D.?" Then he said to Tiffani, "I'm the senior NTT. I'm the head honcho of the entire department. That's why they pay me the big bucks!"

Chapter 40

Chuckling to himself, Rob walked past Agnew Hall's main office. He'd just attended another two-hour Parking Appeals Committee meeting. Since they automatically denied all the appeals, it was a colossal waste of time; however, the reasoning behind the requests always brightened his mood.

Today, a student appealed a ticket he received for parking in the president's spot. The student's appeal was five single-spaced, profanity-laden pages. He concluded with a statement that it was worth the twelve-dollar fine to make the university president drive around the campus looking for someplace to park "her fucking Beemer."

Of course, the president didn't drive around campus. When she found her spot taken, she jumped the curb and parked on the grass in front of the Administration Building. Since the parking police refrained from giving the president a ticket, scores of other frustrated drivers did the same, blocking her in. It took the tow truck four hours to have all the cars cleared away so she could leave.

Rob passed the school director in the hallway.

"Oh, hey there, Rob," Mary said cheerfully. "How's it going?"

"Great! A bunch of students barricaded the president's car so she couldn't leave for the airport. She missed her flight to the Bahamas."

"Didn't she recently get back from the Bahamas?"

"Yeah. Apparently, she's going again. Recruiting trip or something."

"She's always going on a—" Mary made quotation marks with her fingers. "—*recruiting trip*. And it's never to any place like Cleveland or Newark. It's always someplace warm with beautiful beaches."

"Must be nice to be the president."

"I'd imagine."

"Oh!" Rob remembered something that had been bothering him all day. He flattened himself against the wall and let a group of students go by. "I have a question for you if you don't mind."

Mary brightened as though answering questions was her sole purpose in life. "Sure. Shoot!"

"Earlier today, I was talking to Bert. And he told me both he and Les are NTTs."

"Right you are! They started as adjunct lecturers. Somewhere along the line they became permanent staff." She scrunched her face, trying to think. "I believe Bert became full-time ten years ago or so. Les probably six or seven. But don't quote me on that. I'm guessing. Why?"

"No real reason," Rob said coyly. "However, I was wondering… what role do NTTs play in faculty governance?"

Mary considered the question, then shrugged. "They don't. They only teach."

Rob's briefcase nearly slipped out of his hand.

"Are you telling me NTTs don't vote on reappointment or tenure?"

"Oh, no!" Mary hooted. "We couldn't allow that! Only people who've been tenured can vote for tenure. Same thing with reappointment. NTTs aren't even voting members on university or school committees."

For the first time since Craig told him he wasn't going to get his contract renewed, Rob suddenly felt he had an answer to all of his problems. But he wanted to be sure he wasn't missing anything.

"So… the only tenure-track faculty in special education are—?"

Mary ticked off on her fingers. "You, Craig, Pete, and Jim."

"And…" Rob held his breath, his hands shaking with anticipation. "How many votes do I need to be reappointed?"

"A simple majority. In your situation, you'd need two out of the three votes."

Barely able to restrain himself, Rob inched toward Mary. "Are you sure? Absolutely sure?"

"Absolutely positively!"

Down the hallway, Sid stepped out of the stairwell. Seeing Rob, he lifted his hand in greeting and then headed in the opposite direction.

"There isn't…" Rob asked the school director, worried she'd suddenly recollect something to the contrary. "There isn't some sort of hidden clause somewhere requiring that the chair vote for me?"

"Nope!" Mary said. "His vote counts the same as everybody else's."

Rob forced himself to take a deep breath. "Let me get this straight. If I get two tenure-track faculty members to vote for renewing my contract—"

"You'll be reappointed for at least one year. Probably more."

Feeling light as a feather, Rob exhaled in triumph. "Thank you!" He came close to hugging the petite woman. "Thank you so much! You've made my day!"

Mary beamed. "Glad to hear it. If you have any other questions, let me know. After all, that's what I'm here for!"

Chapter 41

Not wanting to wait for the elevator that rarely worked, Rob sprinted up the stairs to the sixth floor, taking two at a time. As expected, Craig's office door was open. He was inside with Bert and Les, grunting and gasping as they tried to turn an enormous cherry wood desk so that it faced the hallway.

"Got a new desk?" Rob asked, still winded from his climb.

"Very good, Polly," Craig said sarcastically. "Did it take all of your fancy research skills for you to figure that out?"

Bert and Les laughed as they strained under the desk's weight.

"You're never going to fit that in there." Rob nodded to the row of filing cabinets lining the left-hand wall. "You need to get rid of those."

"If I wanted your opinion," Craig snapped, "I'd ask for it. Idiot!"

Rob watched them struggle.

"Maybe," Bert panted. Sweat saturated the collar of his olive-green shirt. "Maybe if we move the cabinets to the rear wall—"

"Don't touch those!" Craig cried. "There are priceless mementos in there, and I don't want you messing with them! Besides, if I moved the filing cabinets, I wouldn't have room to sit."

"We can try to get the desk closer to the door," Les offered. Doubled over and wheezing, he appeared as spent at Bert.

"The door swings inward, moron. If we put it too far forward, I won't be able to get in or out, nullifying the need for a desk in the first place. Think!"

"You could get a smaller desk," Rob suggested.

Craig's beady eyes narrowed at him. "Don't you have a committee meeting to go to? Or a class? Honestly, I can't wait until we get rid of you!"

"About that," Rob said pointedly. "How many votes do I need for my contract to be renewed?"

"Three! And trust me, you aren't going to get them."

Breathing hard, Bert and Les attempted to turn the desk.

"Come May, you're out of here, Polly." Bert puffed. "You're gone!"

"Yeah. You and your crappy brownies," Les added.

Rob put on an overly perplexed expression. "I'm sorry. Aren't you two non-tenure-track faculty?"

"What of it?" Trying to lift his end of the desk, Bert banged into the row of filing cabinets. They rang like a gong.

"Careful!" Craig hollered. "Get over on this side. We'll all lift together. On three. Ready? One. Two. Three!"

Again, the desk banged into the filing cabinets.

Cursing, Craig leaned against his chair, trying to catch his breath.

"From what I understand," Rob said, watching from the hallway, "only tenure-track faculty vote on reappointment. So… I only need… *two*… votes."

"Who told you that nonsense?" Craig gestured for Bert and Les to take their places. "This time, let's tilt it upward a bit and then turn it. On three."

"Mary told me."

Craig's sneer gave way slightly. "She said you needed two votes?"

"Yep."

"Yeah, well—" Craig chuckled. "—you won't get those either. You can buddy up to Pete as much as you want. I'm still voting no. So pack your bags, hippy." He said to Les and Bert, "On three. One. Two. Three!"

They tried to tilt the desk upward.

"Actually," Rob said with slow relish, "Dr. McFee told me he'd vote for my reappointment as well."

Craig dropped his end of the desk with a crash. "You spoke to Jim? When?"

"He sent me an e-mail a few weeks ago." Rob's smile turned into a mischievous grin. "I have the two votes I need to stay." He stepped over the tape dividing Craig's office from the hallway. "So why don't you get off my fucking back, you fat ass, and let me do my goddamned job?"

Chapter 42

"And what did he do?" Wendy exclaimed. It was Halloween night, and she was dressed as Wonder Woman, though in a much less salacious outfit than what Tiffani had worn earlier in the week.

Rob wore a full-bodied white rabbit suit. Initially, he thought it would keep him warm in the cold Wisconsin rain pouring outside. But now, as Vino's filled with singing college students, he regretted his choice of costume. Sweat dribbled down his temple.

"He didn't say anything," Rob yelled over the pounding music. "He simply stood there, his face all purple and trembling! God—" He took a drink. "—that was the greatest moment of my life. Seriously! I've never felt so free and relaxed."

"That's the beer talking," Sid said, blurry-eyed. "And next time, make sure you tell me you two are going to dress up. I feel like a loser."

Wendy wrapped her arm around his shoulders and shook him playfully. "Oh, don't be that way! And Rob and I didn't plan on dressing up together. We just did it!"

"I still feel like a loser." Rearranging the bottles littering their table, Sid cleared a space in front of him. "By the way, what country are we on?"

"Czechoslovakia."

"Ninety-nine beers by May." Moaning, he lay his head down. "What were we thinking?"

"Wait until we get to Scotland," Wendy told him. "Their beers have the highest alcohol content in the world."

"Terrific."

Next to them, three slutty cheerleaders danced.

"You know," Rob went on, trying to keep his attention focused on Wendy, "as soon as I walked away from them screwing with that stupid desk, I felt like a new man. Like I had a future or something." He took another drink. "Not only am I going to teach every student who comes into our program that kids with disabilities can learn, but I'm going to put on more workshops for families. I may not be able to change things at Elwin Holme, but I can change things here."

Head still on the table, Sid lifted his beer. "Here's to that."

They clinked bottles.

A woman in black stilettos and dressed as a Playboy bunny wobbled up to them.

"Hey!" She fell laughing into Rob's lap, spilling much of her sangria on him.

Rob brushed the wine from his shoulder. Grimacing at the red splotch spreading over the white fur, he doubted if he'd get his rental deposit back now.

"I'm a rabbit too!" She pulled off her bunny ears and showed him. "See?"

"Very nice." Ordinarily, Rob would've loved to have a pretty woman in his lap, but he guessed she was an undergraduate student, and he didn't like the temptation building within him. "I'm sure it runs in the family!"

"What's your name?" the Playboy bunny shouted over the music.

"What name do you like?" Rob replied, quoting the line from the movie *Harvey*.

"You're funny!" Stroking Rob's wet fur, she leaned in closer. "We should go somewhere and fuck like bunnies!"

She tried to kiss him but ended up banging her forehead against his.

"That's enough." Wendy shooed her away. "He's with me."

"That's okay," the Playboy bunny said. "You can watch."

"All right! We're done." Standing, Rob set the woman on her unsteady feet. "Look!" He pointed across the bar. "There's a guy dressed as Hugh Hefner!"

"Where?"

"By the bathrooms. Go see if he remembers you."

"Okay!"

As she staggered across the dance floor, people bumped her one way and then the other. She fell and disappeared among the gyrating bodies. Then somebody lifted her above the crowd.

She yelled, "Fucking bunnies!"

Everybody cheered.

Rob returned to his seat. Wendy smirked at him.

"What?" he asked.

"You should see your face. When was the last time you got laid?"

"It's been a while."

"You should change that."

"What we need to change is the subject." Rob pulled his rabbit-eared hood down and fanned himself with a plastic menu. He wasn't sure what made him perspire more, the heat in the hairy rabbit suit or his frustrations.

"Fine." Wendy eyed the cheerleaders dancing next to them as she drank. "What's going to be the first move in your rebellion?"

Rob flagged down a passing waitress and asked for a glass of ice.

"First," he said when the waitress had gone, "I need to change the names of the courses. They're all horrid. Crippled this. Abnormal that. They give the students the wrong ideas. Then I need to go through the syllabi and see what's being taught where. Once I do that, I can figure out what topics need to be added or taken out."

"Sounds like a lot of work."

"It will be. But it'll be meaningful, you know? Not like all these damn committees I'm on. They're a titanic waste of time. I can feel myself aging as I sit there, listening to everybody debating every little piece of minutia."

"I bet!"

"This week," Rob said, his throat getting sore from shouting, "during a curriculum committee meeting, somebody noticed a typo in the description of a course. It wasn't anything important. Two words ran together and needed a space between them. That's it. The person who pointed it out said, 'It doesn't matter, but there's a typo here.' We then discussed how it didn't matter for twenty-seven minutes. I actually timed the discussion! Every damned person said, 'It doesn't matter…' But they still had to talk about it. I wanted to scream."

"That's the problem with us academics." Wendy shook her beer bottle, found it was empty, then took a drink from the one in front of Sid. "We can't discuss anything in under two hours. We have to debate about all sides of an issue, even if it's pointless."

"We're a strange breed," Rob agreed.

They watched the movie *Halloween* on one of the televisions mounted on the wall. Jamie Lee Curtis was sneaking through a dark house, peeking around each corner. The closed captioning was too small to read, but Rob had seen it enough to know what was about to happen.

"Do you think Walrus is compensating for something with those desks of his?" Wendy asked.

"I wouldn't be surprised!" Rob laughed. "Do you know what he drives?"

"What?"

"A red Mazda Miata convertible. He can barely fit in it. He has to lift his stomach and twist his way in."

"Sounds like the poor guy's going through a midlife crisis. It's not exactly the kind of car to have in Wisconsin during winter."

"He's probably sleeping with your secretary," Sid said, his face still affixed to the table.

"I hope not," Rob replied thoughtfully. "That'd make me sad. I'd hate for her to be in that kind of position—feeling obligated to put out so she could keep her job."

Wendy patted his hand. "There's hope for you yet."

"Maybe."

"Any of you teaching early tomorrow?" Sid asked sleepily. "'Cause I think I'm going to sleep in."

"Tomorrow is Saturday," Rob reminded him.

"Oh, right." He closed his eyes. "Good!"

The waitress came with Rob's glass of ice.

"Can we have the next beer on the list?" Wendy asked her.

Sid groaned.

"Absolutely," the waitress said. "Be right back."

For the tenth time that evening, the song, *Monster Mash*, blared from the jukebox. Students sang along.

"You were in the office early this morning," Wendy said to Rob as they watched the television. "I got there at seven-thirty, and your car was already in the parking lot."

"I had a committee meeting that started at seven."

"Seven? Crap! Which one was that?"

"The Committee on Committees."

"You're making that up!"

"No, seriously!" Rob said. "It's the committee that decides whether or not something should have its own committee."

"You're kidding!" Wendy looked sidelong at him. "You have to be."

"I wish I were. Believe me."

The waitress returned with three bottles.

"These are from Denmark." She set one in front of each of them. "It's brewed with coffee, so he—" She indicated Sid sprawled across the table. "—might appreciate it."

"I'm sure we all will. Thanks." Rob read the label. "Fanø Red Wedding." He lifted his beer. "Here's to the Danes."

He and Wendy clinked bottles, then drank.

"What else does the Committee on Committees do?" Wendy asked.

Rob filled his glass of ice with dark red beer.

"Today, we reviewed the mission statements of committees to see if they matched the tasks they were doing. The problem was that none of the committees had mission statements. So I spent the entire time creating my quizzes."

"You're still giving them each week?" She took a drink. "I thought you were going to kiss student ass until you get tenured."

"The quizzes are back on, baby!" Rob cried. "If I'm going to teach a class, I want it to be meaningful. I want them to learn something worth knowing." He sipped his cold beer. "Do you know Bert has his students watch videos of somebody else lecturing? Seriously! The whole course is him playing forty-year-old VHS tapes of somebody talking about things that no longer apply to special education! The lecturer on the tapes refers to a chalkboard that isn't even visible. Bert's students have no clue what the hell is going on."

"Is Bert the short one with the shifty eyes?"

"That's Les. Bert is the guy with the greasy combover and the slimy grin on his face. He's always in the office hitting on Tiffani."

Wendy took a pull on her beer. "He looked at me the other day in the hallway. I felt like I needed a shower."

"Yeah, well, I never have to worry about them again. I can focus on my research and teaching and making a difference in the lives of people with disabilities."

Wendy lifted her bottle. "Here's to your revolution." She took another drink. "May it be mostly bloodless."

Chapter 43

After Halloween, campus was a disaster area. Condoms hung from trees like Christmas ornaments. Beer bottles and plastic cups rattled about the streets. In a scene reminiscent of *Monty Python's Quest for the Holy Grail*, university groundskeepers went around with wheelbarrows, carting away drunk students who'd passed out in doorways or behind bushes. It took the better part of a week to clean everything up.

Despite this, Rob was in high spirits. He'd found a few hours to work on his research. More people were attending his classes. And he'd even been getting reports from parents that his students were doing excellent jobs working with their children. Everything was going well. It felt as though he'd finally found his rhythm.

That Thursday morning, Rob stepped out of the sixth-floor stairwell and noticed two figures at the far end of the hall—a well-dressed woman with a microphone standing in front of Pete Mullins's door and a man pointing a television camera at her. Puzzled, Rob continued to his office. Then the camera swung in his direction.

"Excuse me!" the woman called to him. "May we have a word with you?"

Seized by an unnatural sense of terror, Rob fumbled with his keys.

"Wait!" the woman sprinted toward him, the cameraman close behind.

Thrusting his key into the lock, Rob opened the door, jerked out the key, and then darted into his office. Breathing hard, he slammed and locked the door behind him.

"Dr..." There was a pause as the reporter read his nameplate. Thankfully, it said *Dipshit* rather than his actual name. She knocked. "Excuse me!"

"What do you want?" Rob yelled.

"I want to ask you a few questions about what happened last night."

"I don't know anything. Go away!"

"You don't have to appear on camera. You could give a quote. It could be anything you like."

"Go away or I'll call the police! I mean it! I have work to do."

The hammering stopped. Then Rob heard the reporter say in a dignified tone, "Repeated attempts to contact Eastern Wisconsin University faculty have gone unanswered. It appears nobody wants to comment on last night's unfortunate events. This is Michelle Riviera for Channel Six news. Back to you in the studio."

Heart thumping, Rob lowered himself into his chair. With a shaking hand, he turned on his laptop and logged into his e-mail. There were seventeen messages. Most were from students asking what was going to be on that week's quiz; however, two were from the university president. Rob clicked on the first one. Dated the evening before at 11:24 pm, it read:

Dear Eastern Wisconsin University community,

By now, many of you are aware of what occurred last night with special education faculty member Dr. Peter Mullins. As University President, I'd like to state categorically that we in no way condone his alleged actions. Further, we are making every effort to investigate the incident and to ascertain the facts. We ask that all university personnel refrain from interacting with the press or making public comments at this time. I'll keep you informed as we gather more information.

Sincerely,

President Beaker

Rob was about to click on the President's second e-mail when his phone rang. The name, Wendy Maddon, appeared on its screen.

"Wendy?" he said into the receiver.

"Jesus Christ, Rob! You okay?"

"Me? I'm fine," he told her. "But I have no idea what's going on. A reporter was pounding on my door, asking me to comment about something. I'm trapped in my office. It's like I'm in a scene from *The Walking Dead*!"

"You don't know what happened?" Wendy asked.

"No! Do you?"

There was a pause, then Wendy said, "One of your coworkers had some sort of episode in class last night. He announced that if anybody else came in late, he'd kill them."

"Oh, god."

"It gets worse."

"Oh, no."

"Evidently, he insisted his pen was a gun, and he threatened to shoot a student with it."

"Oh, no!"

"He then started talking about government conspiracies to take over the university and men in black suits implanting devices into people's brains."

Rob leaned back into his squealing chair, hand clasped to his forehead. "You're kidding me!"

"I'm not!" Wendy exclaimed. "Then he started going off on how squirrels were behind it all."

"You're joking. You have to be! This can't be real."

"It is! He ranted for the full three-hour class period saying all kinds of crazy things."

"Is he all right?"

"Nobody knows. The last I heard, he was running naked through campus screaming about parking. You should see the videos. They're all going viral!"

"There are videos?" Rob groaned. "The poor guy."

"Yeah."

They sat in silence for a moment. Rob tried to remember what he knew about Pete's family. If he recalled correctly, he and his wife were getting a divorce, and his son was in jail for selling crystal meth.

"You know what stuns me the most?" Wendy asked. "His students actually stayed the entire time and listened to him! I can't get my students to stay for more than an hour. They all sneak out or disappear during the break."

"Maybe they were too afraid to leave."

"Maybe."

Rob looked out his window. A squadron of news trucks blocked the road. Mobs of students swarmed around them; many stood in front of television cameras, talking to reporters.

"Hey, thanks for calling, Wendy."

"No problem," she said. "Let's get together tonight. No drinks, though. I need to give my liver a break."

In the street below, police cars pulled up, their red lights flashing. Officers got out and tried to disperse the crowd, but nobody was going anywhere.

"Sure," Rob said. "Perhaps we could go to a new restaurant. But it'll have to be late. I have classes until nine-thirty."

"Great. I'll call Sid."

Hanging up, Rob clicked on the president's most recent e-mail. She'd sent it shortly after three o'clock that morning.

Dear Eastern Wisconsin University community,

I'm writing to inform you that Dr. Peter M. Mullins has been terminated, and a restraining order is in place. He is not to get within five hundred feet of campus or any off-campus university events. If you see him violating this order, please contact the city police immediately.

Sincerely,

President Beaker

Embedded at the bottom of the e-mail was a photo of Pete taken in the early-1990s. Ironically, he had a crazy glint in his eyes.

Sighing, Rob wondered what to send Pete's family. Were flowers appropriate? He was pretty sure Hallmark didn't make cards saying, "Sorry your loved one went bat-shit crazy."

People congregated outside his door, talking about what'd happened. Rob checked his phone. It was 8:24. The Teaching and Technology Committee meeting was supposed to start in six minutes, but he had no desire to attend. He joined everybody standing around the hallway.

"Can you believe it?" Tiffani exclaimed. "Did you see the videos of him running down the street? It looked like he was drunk or stoned or something."

"Hey!" Becky from sociology raised her hands defensively. "Don't blame me. My stuff mellows people out, not hypes them up."

"Does anybody know if Pete is okay?" Rob asked.

"Who cares?" Bert replied. "He was good for nothing anyhow."

"Who cares?" Rob repeated. "We're in special education. *We* should care! Clearly, he's had some sort of psychotic break. He needs help, not ridicule."

"Is Polly going to cry because he couldn't save a colleague?"

"Yeah!" Les chimed in. "Wah. Wah. Wah. I say good riddance. And dibs on his office."

"Dibs?" Bert cried. "You can't call dibs."

"Why not?"

"Because I already did!"

"When?"

"As soon as I heard about him going nutzo. Besides, I have seniority. I get the office." Bert rubbed his hands together. "Finally, a window!"

"That's what you're concerned about?" Rob shot back. "Offices and windows? You two should be ashamed of yourselves. He has a family!" He shook his head. "I can only imagine what they're going through. Has anybody called his wife?"

"I think she changed their phone number after she kicked him out," Tiffani said. "They're about to finalize the divorce, and it didn't sound like it was going good for him. She was getting the house and boat."

"Poor guy."

They stood in a circle, everybody but Bert and Les staring sadly at the floor. Then a booming voice echoed along the hallway.

"Well, well, well…" Craig strode up to the group. "Looks like the vote will be one to one, Polly. Who's the fat ass now?"

Chapter 44

Rob leaned against a dry erase board, waiting for Teaching Retarded Kids to Read to begin. He'd never taught the course before. But since the university president had permanently banned Pete from campus, Rob had to cover his three classes. It was probably against the rules to have faculty teach so much without receiving extra pay; however, he thought it would give him more opportunities to make a positive impact while he still could.

As Rob thought about his future at Eastern Wisconsin, a student with a beat-up skateboard tucked under his arm bounded into the classroom.

"Dr. C!" the student said. "You teaching us now?"

"I'm afraid so, Justin," Rob told him. "Think you can stand me for yet another class? I'll try to tell different stories."

"Naw, man. You're the best! You're the only professor here who tries to get us to learn stuff. I was worried Les was going to take over and read to us all night."

More people filed in and took their seats as Rob considered how he could get another job.

"Hey, Dr. C?" Justin asked, still standing there. "I have a problem with my kid. You know, the one I'm working with for the curriculum class?" He gave a knowing wink.

"Yeah, I know who you mean," Rob said. "And good job keeping confidentiality. What's the problem?"

"It's that, well—he's really crippled."

Rob blenched. "Is there a better way you can say that?"

"I'm sorry. I mean—" Justin thought for a moment. "—he has a lot of challenges."

"Better. Go on."

"Like, you know, he has a profound intellectual disability."

"Excellent use of correct terminology. So what's the problem?"

"Like I said," Justin continued, "he has a lot of challenges. He can't talk. He isn't toilet trained. He grabs and bites. I don't think he's capable of learning."

Taking a deep breath, Rob reminded himself that Justin was only nineteen and had to unlearn everything Craig had already taught him. "Notice how you're focusing on the negative, such as saying he can't do this, or he can't do that."

"But he can't," Justin insisted. "He's basically a violent vegetable!"

Rob silently counted to ten as more students came in and took their seats. A few waved to him. "How about saying he's non-verbal. Or he communicates using non-traditional methods?"

"But that's it! The little monster doesn't communicate at all. He just screams and grabs and bites. He bit me twice yesterday. Look!" Justin pushed up the sleeve of his tattered EW-U sweatshirt to reveal two oval-shaped bruises.

"But don't you see? That's how he communicates. Think of it this way. Suppose you didn't speak English and I couldn't understand what you wanted. You're hungry or in pain or frustrated that nobody is helping you. Wouldn't grabbing and biting be a pretty effective way of getting somebody's attention?"

"Yeah… I suppose."

"So the child *does* communicate. You simply need to teach him a better way to express himself."

Justin appeared doubtful.

"Trust me," Rob told him. "He wants to communicate better so he can get what he wants. You need to teach him a method that works for both of you."

"But he's seven and can't talk! If he hasn't gotten it by now, the dude isn't going to."

"What's another method of communicating that doesn't involve verbal speech?"

Justin scratched his peach-fuzz beard. "You mean like sign language? How can I teach him that when I don't know it myself?"

"I was thinking about using PECS." Seeing Justin's confusion, Rob added, "Look it up in the book for this class. I believe it's chapter eight."

"Okay. I'll give anything a shot. I'm tired of being bitten."

"The big thing is to find out what he likes and to use it to systematically reinforce the desired behavior. Start small and build. Okay? Don't expect big changes right off the bat. Also, if one way doesn't work, try another. And above all—" Rob pat Justin's shoulder. "—don't give up. Okay?"

"I won't. Thanks, man."

Watching Justin take his seat, Rob recalled Thelma's post-it note, then muttered to himself, "Don't give up…"

Chapter 45

"Well, you've certainly had an eventful day," Wendy said as Rob collapsed into a chair across from her and Sid.

They were at a small, hole-in-the-wall restaurant located in a strip mall a few blocks from campus. Even though it was close to ten o'clock, the place was still bustling with college students and professors grabbing a late dinner after their last evening class.

"You can say that again," Rob groaned.

"Well, you've certainly had an eventful day."

"Very funny."

Wendy grinned. "I thought so."

"You know what bothers me the most about the whole thing?" Rob told them. "A coworker has a mental breakdown, changing his life forever—and all I can think about is how to convince Walrus to let me stay."

Wendy tossed a menu into his lap. "How about you figure out what you want to eat. I'm starving, and I'm not waiting for you to make up your mind."

Sid perused their options. "The pad thai is good here. But you'll have to ask for extra spices if you want a kick."

Rob ignored the menu. He didn't feel like eating anyway.

"Do either of you have any ideas how I can get Craig to vote for me?" he asked. "Any ideas at all?"

Wendy got the waitress's attention and indicated that they were ready. "I'm sure things will work out. You'll see."

"Think so?"

"Absolutely. Rob, you're an immensely talented teacher and researcher. I've read your articles. And I've heard your students talking about you in the hallways. You're really good."

"Thanks," Rob said. "I appreciate that."

"It's true. And I told you—deep down, I'm sure Walrus wants to keep you around, if only to make your life miserable for a few more years. Plus, with that other guy getting fired, your department is one faculty member short. Imagine how things would be for Walrus if he let you go too. He'd have to do everything himself!"

"I hadn't thought about that."

A cook in a dirty white apron hustled past, carrying two armloads of take-out orders to the front register.

"My students talk about me?" Rob lifted an eyebrow. "What do they say?"

"That you're an asshole who tells funny stories," Wendy said.

Rob laughed. "That's better than what I thought they'd say."

An elderly waitress filled their water glasses. She appeared as exhausted as Rob felt. "Ready to order?"

"Yes!" Wendy said enthusiastically. "I would like pad thai, medium spicy, with chicken. Please."

"Very good." She turned to Sid, still looking at the menu.

With a sigh, he set it on top of Wendy's. "I'll have pad thai as well, spicy, with tofu. No fish sauce, please."

"And you, sir?" she asked Rob.

"Same as her. Thank you."

"That'll be three pad thais, two with chicken. Medium spice. And one with tofu, no fish sauce. Spicy."

"Yes, thank you very much." Rob watched her disappear into the noisy kitchen. Overhead, cheerful Asian music played. "I don't know, Wendy. I still don't think Craig is going to let me stay. He couldn't have been any clearer earlier in the semester."

"You can try kissing ass," Sid offered. "I know it's distasteful, but Walrus seems like the type of guy who wants to have a bunch of sycophants around him. Fawning over his every breath. Start doing that and maybe he'd vote for you."

"The problem is, he isn't stupid. He knows what I think of him. He isn't going to believe I've suddenly changed." Rob wagged his bowed head. "I shouldn't have taunted him with that fat ass comment."

Sid took a sip of water. "Like Bilbo said, 'Never laugh at live dragons.'"

Wendy gaped at him. "Oh my god! You are such a nerd!"

"What? I work with books and computers. It kind of goes with the territory."

Next to them, a busboy rushed to clean a vacated table. Dirty dishes and silverware rattled as he tossed them into a tub.

"Look," Wendy told Rob, "you have two choices. Stay or get another job someplace else. If you want to stay, you have to make yourself useful. Be the kind of colleague Walrus can't live without. Otherwise, publish your brains out and see what positions come available next year. Pick an option. Make a plan. And follow through."

Rob watched the busboy hurry to another table.

"You think there's a chance he'd let me keep my job?"

"Of course. Like the dork said, Walrus likes having his little posse around him. But don't beg. He won't respect you. You have to show him he needs you. The trick will be to find out what he values and then do that."

Leaning forward, Rob put his elbows on the table. "What he values…"

Chapter 46

Rob stood in Agnew Hall's mailroom, reading a letter he'd received from the editor of *The Journal of Cognitive Disabilities*. Six months earlier, he'd submitted his paper, *The Impact of Self-Identified Reinforcers on the Vocational Outcomes Achieved by Individuals with Autism Spectrum Disorders*. According to the letter, the paper wasn't rejected, but it wasn't accepted either. The editor encouraged him to revise and resubmit. He even provided four single-spaced pages of suggested changes.

Not knowing whether to feel good or bad, Rob reread the letter. The Journal of Cognitive Disabilities was a top-tier journal, and getting a solo-authored paper published in it would be a major feather in his academic cap. However, the analyses the editor requested would take time. Moreover, his new results may not be statistically significant, which would make all of his work pointless.

Rob mulled over the idea of sending the original paper to a lower-tier journal. They might accept it as is, allowing him to focus his energies on another study. But the editor's suggestions were extremely insightful. If more rigorous data analyses supported his hypotheses, he could have something impressive enough to get him an interview at another university.

Shouts from the Dean's office interrupted his internal debate. Rob wondered who was brave enough to yell at the Dean. Then he recognized the British accent.

"We were in the loo the entire bloody day!" the chair of the Teaching and Learning Department, Dr. Lieberman, screamed. "We had to cancel our classes! I missed meetings!"

There was a pause.

Somebody must've said something Rob couldn't hear because Dr. Lieberman responded, "As you indicated at the beginning of the term, these pranks have got to stop! They have become dangerous not only to university property but also to our health as well!"

Another pause.

Rob peered around the corner. The administrative assistants had stopped working.

"Who else would've done it?" Dr. Lieberman asked. "Who? Grubber has been pulling pranks on us for years—and I want him sacked!"

The Dean's door flew open. Rob ducked into the mailroom as the assistants suddenly started typing.

"Get out!" Captain Hammer roared. "Idiot, faculty! If you're so God-damned smart, then why can't you figure out who's pulling these pranks?"

Dr. Lieberman protested weakly as he, Craig, Les, and Bert scampered out of the Dean's office.

"Bring me evidence!" the Dean hollered. "Cold, hard, evidence! Do you understand? Use those massive brains in your swollen heads for a change. And if you ever bother me again—I'll bust you so far down you'll be scrubbing out the latrines!"

The door slammed, shaking the ceiling tiles.

Dr. Lieberman stood outside the Dean's office trembling while Craig, Bert, and Les strutted past the mailroom. Craig was so giddy it appeared as though he was about to pee himself. He slapped Les on the back.

"Lester, my boy!" he whispered. "You're brilliant. Fucking brilliant. Laxatives in their brownies." He snickered. "I'm buying you dinner tonight! And I'm going to give you a course release next semester. You've earned it!"

"The key was to leave the brownies in their breakroom when I knew somebody had a birthday," Les said. "That way, they wouldn't suspect a thing!"

"It was my idea!" Bert hurried after them. "All mine!"

"Was not!" Les snapped. "I thought of it all by myself. You had nothing to do with it. It was me! All me!"

"You know, Bert," Craig said as they entered the stairwell, "if you had half the initiative and creativity as Les does, you'd be useful around here."

Chapter 47

That Sunday, Rob arrived at campus shortly after dawn. He wanted to spend the entire day revising his manuscript and couldn't do it at home. Things like his refrigerator, television, and nice, warm bed kept distracting him. He also thought an empty Agnew Hall would be more conducive to productivity; however, as he walked down the dimly lit sixth-floor corridor, he realized the building wasn't completely deserted. A bright light shone from under Craig's closed door.

For a moment, Rob considered leaving. He didn't want to be alone with the ass. If they came to blows, he could kiss both his job and his career goodbye. But he told himself he was being stupid and continued to his office.

Suddenly, there was a tremendous, crashing bang.

"Son-of-a-goddamned-bitch!" Craig hollered.

Thinking his department chair had fallen and hurt himself, Rob burst into Craig's office. Craig was leaning against his filing cabinets, holding his side.

"What's wrong? You okay?" Rob asked all at once.

"You!" Craig panted. "You did this! Didn't you? Don't try to lie to me, Polly! I swear to all that's good and holy—"

"What are you talking about?"

"I'm talking about this!" Craig heaved his considerable bulk against his throne-like chair. It didn't move. Its wheels were encased in a block of rubber cement. "It's glued to the god-damned floor! And I can't reach my desk!"

"Can't you push your desk closer to your chair?"

"Idiot! Don't you think I thought of that? It's glued to the floor as well!"

Craig drove his shoulder into the chair again. It remained where it was. He stared at the rubber cement, trying to catch his breath.

"You know," Rob said, not sure why he was trying, "I'd like to stay here next year. If there's anything I can do to get you to change your mind—"

"Nothing doing! You called me a fat ass!"

"Yeah, I'm sorry about that. It won't happen again. I promise."

Craig put his back to the wall and feet against his monstrous desk. Shrieking like a bodybuilder trying to lift a heavy barbell, he pushed—but the desk didn't budge. He collapsed to the floor, gasping. "And you ruined our relationship with… with one of the few schools who… who will take our student teachers! Don't forget that!"

"But—" Rob bit his tongue. "Yeah. That was stupid of me. I'm very sorry about that as well."

"Sorry doesn't put the cat out!" Glaring at his desk, Craig mopped a handkerchief across his brow. "Those bastards. Those fucking bastards. I'll get them if it's the last thing I do!"

Remembering how Craig praised Les for the laxatives in the brownies, Rob decided to take a different approach.

"I'll make a deal with you," he said, frankly. "If you let me stay—I'll pull an epic prank on the Teaching and Learning faculty."

"What the hell are you blathering on about?"

Rob flashed a devilish grin. "I'll pull something they'll never forget. Something so humiliating, they'll never live it down. By the time I get through with them, they'll fear special education!"

"I'll tell you what, Polly." A glint flickered in Craig's beady eyes. "If you punish those constructivist bastards, and I mean really punish them… something that'll be, as you say, *epic*... I'll let you stay. But you have to do it a week from today."

"Why?"

"Because that Monday, the TLs are being visited by their accreditation agency, and I want them seen for the fools they are."

"I don't know if I could pull off anything that soon," Rob said, wondering what he'd gotten himself into. "Certainly not anything epic. I need time to plan and prepare."

Craig fought his way to his feet. "Next Monday or no deal! And it better be the best prank ever pulled, Polly. I mean it! I want to make sure their goddamned Birkenstocks never step on my floor again!"

Chapter 48

Rob lumbered along at a steady five miles per hour, his skinny pale legs pounding the treadmill beneath him. Sweat dripped from his nose and soaked dark circles under his armpits. He regretted coming to the university's recreation center with every forced step, but he didn't want Wendy to think he was a wimp.

Jogging on the treadmill next to him, she nodded toward a young couple standing a few machines away. The woman wore a grey sports bra and tight black shorts reminiscent of something Tiffani would wear. What appeared to be sweat glistened on her cleavage, yet her hair and makeup remained perfectly done. As she talked, the guy standing with her had an expression anybody could read. He was practically salivating.

"What a meat market, eh?" Wendy was as sweaty as Rob. But rather than looking haggard and spent, she seemed to glow with renewed energy.

"Yeah." Rob tried to think of something to say. "I don't remember Purdue's rec center being like this. People came to workout."

"Oh, I'm sure the teenage Rob Chudinski did his fair share of wolfing after pretty co-eds."

"I suppose." Rob watched the couple flirt. "It seems like such a long time ago."

Below them, the treadmill belts whirled as the timers on the consoles gradually ticked down. They had a little more than six minutes left. Rob wasn't sure he was going to make it that long.

"You okay?" Wendy asked.

Rob tried not to look at her. He wasn't terribly coordinated and was liable to trip and break his neck if he didn't concentrate. He also didn't want to keep staring at Wendy's bouncing breasts as she jogged along. He already made a fool out of himself once with her. He didn't want to do it again.

"I think I've found a way to make myself valuable to Walrus."

"Really? How?"

Rob wrestled with the urge to tell her. He knew what she'd say. Unfortunately, it wouldn't help him keep his job.

"By pulling a prank on the regular education faculty. Something so brilliant, they'll never forget it."

Wendy laughed. "Nothing will top the laxative brownies and the out-of-order sign on the bathroom. That's a classic!" She decreased her treadmill's incline. "Of course, I thought the filing cabinets full of manure was funny too. So I suppose I have a sophomoric sense of humor."

"Do any of your faculty get pranked?" Rob asked. "I only hear what happens to the people in Teaching and Learning or us."

"No. Not really. We keep to ourselves and everybody leaves us alone. Besides, nobody wants to incur the wrath of a bunch of empowered lesbians."

She slowed her speed to a brisk walk. Relieved, Rob followed suit.

"But it's not just you guys." She dabbed a white workout towel across her face and neck. "The chair in Sid's program had the wheels stolen from his car. But that might've been an actual crime. Nobody knows. Then there was Dr. Walters. A few weeks ago, he returned from a conference and found a dead sturgeon in his desk. It stunk up the entire floor."

"What department is he in?" Rob asked.

"Math."

"Oh, right."

Wendy eyed him. "You thinking about pulling a prank to get on Walrus's good side?"

Rob prepared himself for the argument he knew was coming. "Maybe... I don't know."

"Rob!"

"I have to do something! Craig said if the prank is epic enough, he'll let me stay. But I have to do it next Monday when the TLs are getting reviewed by their accreditation agency."

She slid him an expression of displeasure.

"What?" he asked. "I've been through it over and over in my head. The only way to be reappointed is to get Craig to vote for me. The only other option is trying to find another job. You know how the job market is. Not many universities are going to be looking for somebody with an emphasis on severe disabilities."

She decreased her pace to a slow walk and draped the towel around her shoulders. "There's always another way."

"If you think of one, let me know; because I'm all out of ideas." Rob slowed his treadmill. "Like I said, my only two choices are to kiss up and stay or pray I can find another job. And, well—I don't want to leave. I'd miss you and Sid."

"Aw! That's sweet. I'd miss you too. But I still say there's another option. We simply haven't found it yet."

In the free-weight section, somebody gave a screaming grunt and then dropped two clattering dumbbells to the matted floor.

"How's your research coming?" Wendy asked.

Rob brushed away the sweat cascading into his eyes. "I resubmitted the manuscript I wrote when I was a doctoral student. And I'm trying to work on two more, but I don't have the time. Now that I'm teaching Pete's classes, I'm barely able to prep, let alone go to all the committee meetings I'm supposed to attend. I've even stopped giving weekly quizzes because I'm not able to make them fast enough."

"Bet your students appreciate that!"

"I'm sure they do." Then Rob said, "Not that many of them show regularly. Any given week, a quarter of my class is missing."

"You teach big pit classes," Wendy reminded him. "They think you won't notice. Besides, having three-quarters show up is really good! That's certainly better than how many came at the beginning of the year."

"True. The funny thing is I e-mail them and say, *Hey! You haven't taken any of the quizzes or attended a single class all semester. Are you okay?* And they reply, *Oh yeah. Sorry. I forgot about class. I'll be there next week.* And then they still don't show."

"I think it's great how much you care."

"That's always been my problem. I'm a Don Quixote, remember?"

"That's not a bad thing, Rob." She touched his arm. "I think you're an incredible guy. If I weren't gay…"

Rob rolled his eyes. "Yeah, yeah. If I had a nickel for every time a woman told me that!"

They laughed.

Wendy pushed the stop button and stepped off her treadmill. Rob did likewise.

"You're not seriously considering pulling a prank to make Walrus happy, are you?" she asked.

Rob took a cloth and spray bottle from a nearby stand. "What else can I do?" He cleaned his machine, then handed everything to Wendy. "If you have another idea. I'm all ears."

"You can't get involved in these stupid practical jokes." Wendy sprayed her treadmill. "Do you remember what the Dean said at the beginning of the semester? If you get caught, you'll get fired—regardless of how epic the prank is."

She put the spray bottle and cloth back where Rob had gotten them.

"As a matter of fact," she went on more emphatically, "I bet you that's what Walrus wants. He wants you to get caught. Think about it! That's probably why he wants you to do it Monday! He's setting you up!"

"You sound like Hermione Granger."

"Who?" She followed him past the basketball courts. Every court was jammed with running men shouting for the ball.

"You know, Harry Potter?" Rob explained. "When Malfoy challenges Harry to a wizard's duel in the trophy room at midnight, Hermione tells him it's a trap."

She stopped, dumbfounded.

"Hey," Rob said. "I'm not as big of a nerd as Sid!"

"He's in Information Sciences! What's your excuse?" They headed to the locker rooms. "Trust the system. Okay? Do your work. Make yourself useful. Everything will be okay."

Rob didn't dare disagree. There was no arguing with Wendy's optimism. They stood in front of the women's locker room, students filing passing them.

"So," she said begrudgingly, "what was your prank going to be?"

"I was going to slide a hose under their doors and fill their offices with that expanding foam insulation."

Wendy chuckled. "Can you imagine opening your door and finding it filled with that stuff? And it hardens, so they'd have to tunnel their way in!"

"I'd need a hose that could reach the third floor," Rob said, wondering if Home Depot had them that long.

"You'd get caught. And it'd get into the computers and radiators and cause a bunch of damage." She folded her arms in front of her. "You're not going to do it, are you?"

Rob considered his options. "No."

"You promise?"

"Yes, Hermione!"

Wendy smiled. "It would've been epic," she conceded. "I'll give you that. But don't worry. We'll find some way for you to stay. Trust me."

Chapter 49

Holding his breath, Rob slowly poked his head out of the third-floor stairwell. Down the darkened hallway, rows of closed doors extended as far as he could see. It was nearly midnight on a Sunday. Nobody was around.

He knew this was stupid. Not only was caulking office doors shut far from epic, but even if it were, there was no guarantee Craig would let him stay. He could simply laugh and call Rob a naïve Pollyanna as he voted him out of the university. Then again, maybe if Rob showed that he was willing to follow orders and fit in, he'd have a chance. After all, there was a great deal at stake. He had to do something, and he didn't have any other ideas.

Rob shot one last glance up and down the deserted stairs. Then, bathed in the ghostly red glow of the emergency exit sign, he crept into the corridor. Behind him, the stairwell's heavy fire door banged closed. It echoed around him like a cannon blast.

Heart pounding, he checked the numbers he'd written on his palm. Lieberman's office was Room 333. Or, as Craig often said, *"Half the number of the Beast."* The office directly across from him was 301.

Hefting his backpack, Rob stalked further into darkness.

Passing Room 311, he wondered whether campus police patrolled the interior of buildings. He hoped not. The last thing he needed was to get arrested for vandalism. Then he really could kiss getting reappointed goodbye.

He passed Room 329.

Room 333 came into view. On its door, a brass plaque read: "Dr. Royce T. Lieberman." A plaque below it said: "Department Chair." The plaque below that said: "Baird Foundation English History Fellow." Various fliers and announcements for regular education majors adorned the neighboring bulletin board.

"Okay…" Rob took a deep breath. "Let's get this over with."

Setting his pack down, he extracted a caulk gun and a canister. He cut off the canister's pointy end, loaded it into the gun, and pushed the plunger as far as it would go. Squeezing the trigger, he was about to trace the edge of Dr. Lieberman's door when he heard a faint metallic click.

At first, Rob thought there was something wrong with his caulk gun. He squeezed the trigger again and found everything was in order. A string of clear caulk oozed out of the canister. Then, toward the far end of the hallway, a door opened. A beam of light pierced the dimness as a hulking figure stepped into the corridor.

"Shit!"

Fumbling, Rob looked around, desperately trying to find someplace to hide. Then, snatching his pack, he sprinted in the opposite direction, caulk spurting out the end of his gun.

Behind him, the Dean's voice boomed, "Who's there? Show yourself!"

The light swung in Rob's direction, illuminating his back as he jerked open the stairwell door. He dove inside.

"I'll catch you!" the Dean bellowed. "You can't escape me!"

Chapter 50

Rob awoke, his head affixed to his desk with dried salvia. Too afraid to make a run for it, he'd spent the entire night hiding in his office. He wiped the drool from his cheek and checked his phone. It was 8:03 am. His Monday morning class would start in less than an hour. He dragged his fingers through his matted hair. Then, hoping to get rid of the slimy film coating his mouth, he drank what water was left in a bottle by his elbow.

Realizing he had to pee, he made for the door, then stopped. Outside, Bert and Les were talking, and it didn't sound as though they were going anywhere anytime soon. Unfortunately, his urine was about to.

"Polly!" Bert cried when Rob stepped out into the hallway. He looked in disgust at the ratty sweatpants and faded Purdue shirt Rob was wearing. "What the hell is wrong with you? You drunk?"

Rob tried to flatten his hair. "No. I was working late and fell asleep."

Bert glanced knowingly into Rob's office. "Who was she?"

"What? Nobody. I was working on—"

"You know, I think it's sickening how you treat our female students!" Les said. "I hope you get caught and fired."

"Me? I don't—!"

Down the hall, Craig's door opened.

"Well, Polly!" Craig called. "It's Monday, and I'm waiting to hear about this epic prank you pulled. You know, the one that would avenge my desks and strike fear into their hearts? All I've heard is that somebody went into Tuckerman's office and rigged his chair to collapse when he sat on it. Not exactly the type of thing to make them quake in their boots if you ask me."

"I tried to caulk their doors shut, but Dean Hammer was patrolling around." Rob eyed Craig suspiciously. "It was almost as though he was looking for somebody pulling a prank."

"I'm sure he was," Craig told him. "He's always roaming the building at night. Shame he didn't catch you. That would've solved all of my problems."

Rob's bladder tightened. "Excuse me. I have to go to the bathroom."

"Too bad we don't have a shower in there. You stink!"

As he hurried to the men's room, Rob sniffed his armpit. Crap. He did stink. Perhaps he could run to the recreation center and grab a quick shower. He might even have some clean underwear in his locker.

"You know," Bert said as Rob reached for the bathroom door, "instead of caulk, maybe we should try gluing their doors shut."

Slowing his pace, Rob listened, his bladder straining.

"We could use that super glue!" Les said. "You know, the kind where they glue the guy's helmet to an iron beam and dangle him a hundred feet above the ground? They'll never get their offices open!"

"That stuff comes in small tubes, doesn't it?" Craig asked, thinking. "We'd have to get a ton of it."

"How expensive could it be?" Bert asked. "And those little tubes go a long way!"

"Maybe." Then Craig said, "I wonder if we could do it while they're inside."

"Or how about while they're in a faculty meeting?" Les said excitedly. "You know, seal all the rats in one trap! Then we could pull the fire alarm!"

Laughing, Craig slapped Les's shoulder. "Lester! You're rapidly becoming this program's most valuable faculty member—after me, that is."

The door to the men's room swung open, nearly startling the piss out of Rob.

"Oh," Becky said, coming out. "Sorry. All yours!"

Rob hurried inside, his bladder about to burst as Craig, Bert, and Les whispered excitedly in the hallway.

Chapter 51

"I told you!" Wendy's voice said through Rob's cell phone.

It was the afternoon after he attempted to seal Lieberman's door closed. Rob had called Wendy and admitted he almost got caught by the Dean.

"I know you did." He set his briefcase outside his office and fished keys from his coat pocket. "You were right. I was wrong."

"What? You're breaking up."

"You were right," Rob said louder. "I was wrong."

"What?"

"Oh, shut up!"

Wendy laughed. "Well, I'm glad you didn't get caught. That would've made matters worse."

Rob opened his office door and threw his stuff onto the guest chair. "Yeah, I know. Hey, I think I have another idea. Hold on."

He checked the hallway. It was empty. He closed his door.

"It seems," Rob whispered gleefully, "Craig is interested in following my example and gluing the regular education faculty into their conference room while they're in a meeting. Wouldn't it be incredible if the Dean were there to nab him?"

"Don't get involved, Rob."

Rob let himself fall into his rickety chair. It squealed. "Why not? What can I lose?"

"I don't know," Wendy said. "But these pranks seem beneath you. I think you'll fare better if you were the responsible adult in your program."

"Maybe. Still, I'd love to see Craig try to explain why he was carrying a bunch of tubes of superglue while lurking outside the Teaching and Learning conference room."

"Don't get involved. Okay?"

"Fine!" Rob sighed. "You're probably right as usual."

"What?"

"Shut up!"

Wendy laughed again.

"I still need to figure out a way to stay," Rob said.

"Want to go to Vino's tonight and talk about it?" Wendy asked. "Maybe grab a pizza?"

"I'd love to." He booted up his computer. "Can you make it around ten? Since I had to run home, take a shower, and change before my morning class, I'm a bit behind."

"Sure. I'll call Sid."

"Great." Rob checked the time. "Hey, I gotta let you go. I have an Alumni Appreciation Committee meeting in twenty minutes, and I still have to prepare for my Intro to Exceptionalities class."

"Alumni Appreciation Committee? What the hell do they do?"

"We try to figure out ways to show alumni how much we appreciate them so they will donate to the university. Unfortunately, we spend more money wining and dining them than they donate. So it's a losing proposition."

"Typical!" Wendy said. "Okay, then. See you tonight. And don't do anything stupid, all right? We'll figure out how you can stay. I promise."

"I'll hold you to that. Enjoy your day off doing research."

"Enjoy your afternoon of pointless meetings and half-filled classes."

Hanging up, Rob wished once again that Wendy wasn't gay.

He opened his e-mail and then blinked at the screen. There were four hundred and twenty-seven unread messages.

"Crap!"

Thinking his account had been hacked or he'd downloaded a virus, he changed his password and began running a full McAfee scan. Then, dreading the idea of having to sort through and delete over four hundred e-mails, he opened his inbox.

The subject lines filling the first page contained the words: *My food!* The addresses were all from the university.

"What the hell?"

Fearing that another professor had gone crazy and threatened to kill a student, Rob scrolled down and came to the first unread message. It was from somebody named Lyle Barten and read:

Dear thoughtless colleagues.

Once again, somebody has eaten my lunch. Silly me! I should've brought enough for everybody! Seriously, whoever keeps stealing my food from the faculty refrigerator better stop, or they'll regret it! Next time you may find rat poison in my wife's meatloaf.

Dr. Lyle Barten

Professor

Psychology Department

Rob opened the next message.

Hey idiot. Do you realize you sent this to everybody on campus?

Then the next.

Who's the idiot? You sent it to everybody on campus as well!

Then the next.

You're both idiots.

Then the next.

STOP REPLYING TO ALL! You're filling our inboxes with garbage!

Then the next.

You should follow your own advice, moran!

Then the next.

What kind of "moran" misspells MORON, you moron?

Rob randomly selected an e-mail a little higher on the screen.

For the love of the gods! Please, STOP replying to all! What the hell wrong with all of you?

The one after that read: *Gods? Plural? What are we—Ancient Romans?*

The next: *"Ancient" shouldn't be capitalized. Trust me. I'm in the English department.*

The next: *If you're in the English Department, you'd know that "department" should be capitalized.*

The subsequent twenty e-mails debated the rules of capitalization.

Stop the god damn replying to all! This is ridiculous!

Don't you mean "gods damn"? We are Ancient Romans, aren't we?

There's only one true God and Jesus Christ…

This e-mail went on for three pages, so Rob skipped the rest of it.

The following fifty e-mails debated the merits of Christianity versus the ancient Roman gods. The overwhelming consensus was that there were no gods because nobody would stop replying to all.

Jesus fucking Christ! STOP! JUST STOP!

I don't appreciate you taking our Lord and Savior's name... This one went on for four pages.

Soon, students started getting in on the action. One asked: *Is this going to be on the test?* Another started several lengthy rants by suggesting that food left in a public refrigerator was legally up for grabs. She cited a dozen court cases that faculty in the Criminology Department vigorously insisted were fake.

Seriously! I'm going to kill the NEXT person who posts to everybody!

Starting when?

How do you know we're people? We could be rats from the Psychology Department exacting our revenge!

Isn't it the Department of Psychology?

What EXACTLY is the definition of people?

Rob laughed out loud when one of the e-mails had a meme of a gun pointed at a slice of meatloaf. The caption read: "I want a hundred tater tots or Meaty gets it!"

PLEASE! PLEASE! Stop! I'm begging all of you! Walk away from your computers! Walk away!

Another meme had a slice of meatloaf with a bite out of it, ketchup dripping like blood from a wound. Its caption read: *"I want my hundred tater tots! I'm not fucking around!"*

There was an e-mail from the Provost telling everybody to get back to work.

Then the University President wrote, "I will fire the next person who sends a message to the entire university community!"

The e-mail after that simply read—*Tenured.*

The ensuing sixty e-mails included a copy of the President's threat followed by various emojis, including many with rolling eyes, Bart Simpson's bare butt wiggling back and forth, and the French knight from Monty Python's Quest for the Holy Grail sticking out his tongue and hitting the top of his pointy helmet.

Rob knew he should get to work. He had a meeting to go to and a class to prepare for. He kept saying he'd only read one more e-mail, but he couldn't stop himself. He hadn't laughed so hard in his life. When the University President threatened to call the National Guard, he nearly wet himself.

Rob skipped ahead to an e-mail from the original poster, Dr. Lyle Barten. It read: *Sorry, everybody. I left my lunch in the car. My mistake.*

His computer beeped as the number of unread e-mails in his inbox suddenly leaped to seven hundred and eighty-two.

Five minutes later, Rob no longer had access to the internet. Whether the server was taken offline on purpose, or it crashed, he didn't know.

Headed across campus to his meeting, he found almost every telephone pole, streetlamp, and stop sign had posters reading: "Save Meaty!" or "Have you seen this meatloaf?"

Chapter 52

"Honestly!" Rob attempted to catch his breath. He, Sid, and Wendy were in a corner booth at Vino's, empty bottles scattered about their cluttered table. It was past eleven o'clock, and they were still laughing over the day's events. "It was the funniest thing I've ever seen!"

"I'm still getting e-mails," Wendy said. "I'm never going to get rid of all of them. I'm surprised the server hasn't crashed."

"It'd take a lot to crash the server." Sid lifted his beer from the Dominican Republic. Then shouted, "Free Meaty!"

"Free Meaty!" the drunks at the bar replied.

Everybody took a drink.

Rob erupted into another fit of giggles.

"God!" He was grinning so much that his cheeks were hurting. "That was exactly what I needed."

"Don't you mean gods?" Sid asked.

"Don't you start!" Wendy scolded.

"What? I'm Hindu."

"Oh, that's right. Sorry."

A waiter who looked remarkably like a skinny Michael B. Jordan checked on them. They indicated they were fine. He went to the neighboring booth.

"So," Wendy said, changing the subject, "do you think Walrus is going to glue the other department's doors shut?"

"Hey!" Sid sat up. "You should tell the Dean what he's up to and get *him* fired!"

"I already thought about that." Rob flipped an overly exacerbated glance at Wendy. "But *Hermione* won't let me."

"Why not?" Sid asked. "It's both brilliant and satisfying, you know? Turning the tables by using his own trick against him. Come on, Hermione! Let us duel Malfoy in the trophy room!"

"I used the same literary reference!" Rob lifted a hand.

Sid gave him a high-five. "Sweet!"

"First of all…" Wendy took a drink, probably to hide the fact that she was smiling. "I'm not a Hermione. Although I think it would've served the story better had she been gay."

"Dumbledore was gay!"

"No, he wasn't! Rowling can't say a character is gay and make it so! There has to be some sort of indication he was gay in the books. It's like saying, 'Harry was a cross-dressing alien. You just didn't see him wearing women's clothes or his antenna!' It makes no sense!"

"Okay, you too!" Rob said in a stern, fatherly voice. "Don't make me send you to your rooms."

"I'm sorry," Wendy said irritably, "but it pisses me off." She took another drink, then muttered, "Dumbledore gay." She harrumphed.

"Anyway," Rob said. "You were saying?"

Wendy set her beer aside. "If you want to get involved with what Walrus is planning, be my guest. But you're going to get into a lot of trouble."

"And lose points for Gryffindor!" Sid blurted.

Wendy lifted her middle finger.

"I appreciate both of your perspectives," Rob said diplomatically. "But I'm guessing Craig's going to have Ferret or Toady do it. He isn't stupid. He won't risk his own neck. So telling the Dean wouldn't help me even if I knew what their plan was."

"Then get one of them fired!" Sid said.

"No. They're assholes, but they're only doing what Craig tells them to do. Can you imagine how miserable he can make their lives? They're on year-to-year contracts as well. Plus, they need their jobs. With their skills, they probably couldn't get hired digging ditches."

They nursed their beers.

"I'm going to be sorry to see you go," Sid said.

"Me too," Rob replied sadly. "I've enjoyed hanging around with you two. I hope we can all stay in touch."

"Oh, come on!" Wendy exclaimed. The conversations around them faltered. "Let's not give up yet. I still think there's a way you can get reappointed. Let's look at the facts. Okay?"

Rob waved for her to go ahead.

"Fact number one." She touched her thumb. "To get reappointed, you need the majority of tenured faculty to vote yes."

"Yeah, and there are only two tenured faculty left in the department. I need both to vote for me. One won't cut it."

"Has the other guy said anything?" Sid asked. "The one living in Florida?"

"Jim? The last e-mail I got said, if Craig wasn't going to vote yes, he couldn't change his mind." Rob nodded to Wendy. "What's fact two?"

Taking a drink, Wendy shrugged. "I'm not sure I have a second one."

"It seems to me—" Sid's head teetered drunkenly. "—you have two options. One is to get Walrus to vote for you willingly. The second is to make him fear voting no."

"Fear voting no?" Rob repeated. "Are you suggesting I should threaten him? Leave a horse head in his bed or something?"

"Oh! Now, that would be an epic prank!"

"No," Rob replied. "I like horses."

The waiter returned to their table. "Want another beer?"

"Yes, thank you," Wendy told him. "The next on the list."

"Sure thing."

"I'm stopping after this one," Sid told them. "I can't keep drinking like this."

Wendy muttered, "Lightweight."

"What? I'm a hundred and forty pounds. I can't pack it away as well as—"

Wendy turned slowly in Sid's direction. "I suggest—" She narrowed her blue eyes at him. "—you chose your next words very carefully."

"You know," Sid said, "that's a beautiful dress you're wearing. It's very becoming on you."

"Nice save."

The waiter set three brown bottles in front of them. He read from a card. "This is Doggerlander Belgian Dark Ale. Despite having Belgian in its name, it is from Ecuador. It's a strong ale with medium malt and a complex and fruity aroma and flavor. As you sample it, see if you can deduce what fruits it contains." He bowed. "Enjoy!"

"I like him," Wendy said when he'd gone. "I feel like I've learned something. We'll have to give him a good tip."

"I like that he used the word 'deduce,'" Rob said.

They all tasted the beer.

"It is good," Sid said. "It's probably my favorite so far."

Rob nodded as he drank. "Me too."

"There's a hint of chocolate or something." Wendy inspected the label. "Do you taste it?"

"I taste caramel."

"Yes, exactly!" Then Wendy tossed her hands into the air. "Damn! We should've been savoring all the beers like this. Now we'll have to start over!"

"No, we won't!" Sid told her. "We have seventy-three beers left. Eye on the prize!"

They sat drinking and watching the Tonight Show, Starring Jimmy Fallon on the television above the bar. Tom Hanks was Jimmy's first guest.

"What about your departmental assistant?" Wendy said abruptly.

"What about her?" Rob asked. "Want me to fix you two up? She'd probably be interested."

"Please! She's too young for me." Then Wendy added, "But she is a hottie."

Rob took another drink. "I wouldn't know."

"Yeah," Sid laughed. "Right!"

"I meant your first one," Wendy went on. "The lady who passed away. What was her name?"

"Thelma." Rob groaned. "And don't remind me. She practically made me promise on her deathbed that I'd change things around here. I feel like I'm letting her down. Her chain-smoking ghost will probably haunt me for the rest of my miserable life."

Wendy tapped her beer bottle. "Didn't she say something about knowing where Craig's bodies were buried?"

"She was speaking metaphorically."

"Of course, she was speaking metaphorically. I don't believe Craig literally killed people!"

"If he did," Sid said, "he'd probably eat them." He looked at Wendy and Rob. "Sorry. Bad taste. Go on. You were saying?"

"She brought you here against Craig's orders. Right? And, she'd have to know he wouldn't want you sticking around. Why bring you if Craig could merely get rid of you a year later?" Wendy jabbed her bottle at Rob. "She had to have some sort of plan to keep him out of your way."

"And for me to get reappointed…" Rob said, thinking.

"Exactly."

They peered in different directions.

"Free Meaty!" somebody shouted.

A chorus of "Free Meaty!" filled the bar. Everybody took a drink.

"Where the bodies are…" Rob muttered.

"What do you think she meant?" Sid asked.

"I don't know. But I think you're right."

"Me?"

"Both of you. There are only two ways Thelma could've controlled Craig. Either he respected her and did what she wanted, or he feared her. And since he didn't show for her funeral…"

"She had to have something on him. I bet a guy like him has tons of secrets."

Rob set his beer aside. He was already feeling a bit light-headed and didn't want his thoughts clouding any further. "Okay. We're researchers. We can figure this out. Think. If she had something on Craig, what would it be?"

Sid shrugged. "Maybe he slept with your departmental stripper."

"Her name is Tiffani," Wendy said, annoyed.

Rob considered this. "No. I don't think that would be it. She might give him private dances, but I don't think she'd stoop to sleeping with him. Besides, Craig isn't that stupid. He knows if he got caught, he'd be in hot water."

"What else can it be, though?" Sid asked.

"I don't—" Rob stopped.

"What?"

"It has to be something tangible, right?" Rob said, trying to think things through.

"What do you mean?"

"It has to be something physical. Something Thelma had. For example, if he slept with a student, she'd need proof. Something to show the Dean or whomever."

"Like a video of him doing it with her?"

"Exactly."

"His rolling mass of sweaty flab heaving as he—"

"Enough!" Rob and Wendy both cried, covering their ears.

"Don't put that image in my head!" Wendy said. "I'll never sleep tonight."

Drumming his fingers on the table, Rob felt he was getting close to something significant. "Something tangible. Something he doesn't want people to know about. Something possibly illegal. What would that be? What would cause a tenured faculty member to lose his job?"

"According to the Dean," Sid said, "that could be anything. Tenure is merely an obstacle to be stepped over."

"What would piss off the Dean enough to fire somebody?"

The waiter asked if they needed anything. They indicated that they didn't.

"Rob!" Wendy seized his arm. "Whatever it is would probably be in her office! But there's a problem. If Craig knew she had something on him, he wouldn't wait for somebody to find it."

"He'd get rid of it."

"Right!"

"I have to get in that office and look around!" Rob said.

Sid took a pull from his bottle. "I just hope a giant three-headed dog isn't in there, standing guard!"

Chapter 53

The next day, Rob sat in his office with the lights off, waiting for everybody to go home. Craig had been shut up in the special education conference room with Bert and Les for hours, talking in hushed tones. What they were plotting, he couldn't guess. He just hoped it didn't involve him.

By ten o'clock, the last of the night classes were over, and everybody headed to their cars. At a quarter past ten, Rob cautiously peeped out into the hallway. Dim emergency lights illuminated the rows of closed doors. Nobody seemed to be around.

Carefully, he crept across the hallway. He didn't know why he was sneaking. After all, if anybody caught him, he could say he was working late. Still, Rob had a lingering feeling that Craig had been watching him, and he didn't want his department chair to know he was looking for a way to stay.

Unlocking the main office, he slipped inside and closed the door quietly behind him.

The place was a mess. Under Tiffani's reign, Thelma's organized chaos had deteriorated to merely chaos. Piles of paper covered her desk and parts of the floor. Office supplies were heaped on top of the cabinets. Cabinet drawers hung open.

"Where to begin?"

Climbing a footstool, he pulled down a dusty box from the top shelf. The faded date on its lid said: 1974-1975. Inside he found carefully labeled files. Some contained the minutes of staff meetings. Others had syllabi for courses. All had turned yellow and stank of cigarettes.

He pulled down another box—this one labeled 1997-1998.

Inside were more files. One caught his eye. It said: "Faculty Curriculum Vitae." Sliding it out, he rifled through the CVs, not recognizing most of the names. He came to Pete Mullins's.

Apparently, Pete had graduated with his bachelor's from the University of Wisconsin at Steven's Point, had gotten his master's from Eastern Wisconsin University, and his Ph.D. from the University of Wisconsin at Milwaukee. He had three publications, all on teaching kids with mental illnesses. Rob shook his head at the irony.

Flipping through the folder, he found Craig's vitae. According to the two-page document, Craig had gotten his bachelor's and master's in special education from Eastern Wisconsin University. No doctoral degree was listed.

How could he not have a doctorate? Was this one of the bodies Thelma had alluded to?

Rob regarded the date on the box. Craig looked to be about fifty. Maybe fifty-five. If he got his Ph.D. in his late twenties, he probably wouldn't have had it by 1998. He must've obtained his doctoral degree later.

Rob inspected the most recent box, this one dated 2006-2007. Searching through it, he didn't find any meeting minutes, curriculum paperwork, or handbooks. All he found was a green knit hat, a stack of old school newspapers, and several empty files—one of which was labeled "State Standards."

He slid the boxes back where he'd gotten them and stepped off the stool.

This was getting him nowhere.

Bored, he took a three-ring binder from a bookcase. It contained teaching evaluations for the academic year 2009 to 2010. He flicked through them and found Craig's. All of his students rated him as excellent.

"That can't be right."

The other day, Rob had walked by Craig's classroom and listened to him read the textbook to his comatose students. Several had their heads down, saliva connecting their faces to their desks. How could that be considered "excellent"?

As he examined the student evaluations more closely, the answer occurred to him. On every form, the tiny scantron bubbles were filled in with the same dark decisive mark.

"He did these himself."

Well, that was something. But was it damning enough to push Craig out of his way? Probably not. Nobody at the university seemed to care about the quality of instruction. As Pete had said, tenured faculty didn't even have to give out course evaluations.

From down the hallway, a door clicked closed. Quickly, Rob returned the binder to the bookshelf. He stood listening.

Everything was quiet.

He waited.

Still, nothing moved.

Cautiously, Rob opened the door and peeked out.

Captain Hammer stood in the hallway, silhouetted against the red emergency lights. He held a khaki duffle bag and was wearing camouflage. Even his face was painted various shades of dark green.

"You!" The Dean shoved his way into the office. "What are you doing here? So help me if you're pulling some sort of idiotic prank—!"

"I'm not!" Rob squeaked. "Honest!"

The Dean's eyes narrowed. "What program are you in? Are you in Teaching and Learning? You shouldn't be on this side of the building."

"What? No! I'm in special education!" He held up his office key as proof. "I, I was…" He tried to think of a plausible explanation for being there. "I'm working late!"

The Dean stalked closer. "Doing what?"

Rob swallowed.

"I'm…" He remembered an article on the Chronicle of Higher Education's website. "I'm working on a grant application to NIDR." Then, thinking he needed to include some details, he added, "It's for a research and training center. If I got it, it could bring in nearly three million dollars to the College!"

The Dean straightened. "Three million?"

"Well, I'm not sure what the indirect costs would be, but the request for proposal says it's a five-year grant with a three-million-dollar cap. I'll probably bid a little lower. You know, try to undercut the competition."

"Good." The Dean almost smiled. "Good! That's what I want to hear. Get that grant proposal to my secretary by the end of the week!"

"End of the week, sir?"

"I'll need to approve it before it goes out."

"Oh, right!" Rob moaned inside. The last thing he needed was more pointless work. "Right. I'll have it to you Friday morning."

"Splendid!" The Dean headed toward the stairs. "Carry on!"

"Sir?" Rob said. The Dean turned, annoyed. "A grant application would certainly help my chances of being reappointed, wouldn't it?"

"Only if you get it. We don't reward losers here, soldier."

With that, the Dean disappeared into the dimly lit stairwell as if hunting elusive prey.

Chapter 54

Pulling his knee-length winter coat tighter around himself, Rob jogged across campus. He couldn't find a spot near Agnew Hall, so he had to park by the Recreation Building a half-mile away. To make matters worse, Wisconsin's famed winter had arrived early.

As he hastened along, trying not to think about his cheeks freezing stiff, he noticed a woman crossing to his side of the street. At first, he thought she was a prostitute. Then he realized it was his assistant. She was wearing a provocative version of a Catholic girl's school uniform—complete with black heels, a plaid miniskirt barely covering her ass, and a white halter top so tight he could tell she was freezing.

"Miss Miller!" Rob called to her. He quickened his pace. "Tiffani!"

She turned.

"Oh hi, Dr. Chudinski. How're you doing?"

"Never mind that." He took off his coat and draped it around her shoulders. "What's wrong with you? You're going to freeze to death!"

"I left my jacket somewhere."

"Miss Miller…" Rob's breath appeared as grey vapor before him as he hastened her along. "I enjoy your outfits as much as any heterosexual man."

"You do?"

The glimmer of hope in her eyes both pleased and unnerved him.

"Maybe I shouldn't have said that." He started over. "What I'm trying to say is, you really shouldn't dress like this. It isn't professional. Besides, people will respect you more if they see less. Know what I mean?"

Either she was embarrassed, or the cutting wind was freezing her cheeks as well.

"I have to work at my other job tonight, and I don't have time to go home. Also, Craig told me he'd give me a raise if I dressed 'creatively.'"

"Don't listen to him. Craig's a giant dick."

"No, he isn't."

Rob looked at her, surprised she'd defend him.

"Believe me." She tried to smile. "He's a tiny dick!"

They burst out laughing. A student wearing a parka rushed past them, snuck a glance at Tiffani, then dashed into a neighboring building.

"Why do you..." Rob changed what he was going to say. "...put up with him and the others?"

"I can handle them. I deal with bigger creeps at the club. Besides, I need to keep my job. It has insurance. I have asthma and the medicine and allergy shots are expensive without it." She added quickly, "I don't have sex with them! I only dance. They keep their hands to themselves—if you know what I mean."

Unfortunately, Rob thought he knew exactly what she meant, and the image made him ill.

They continued through campus as fast as Tiffani's heels and skirt would allow. Rob wondered whether she'd report everything he said to Craig. In the end, he thought he'd take the chance.

"Do you know Craig well?" he asked.

"Not well. I mean, he talks about stuff—afterward, that is." Tiffani trotted along, clutching his coat around her. "But none of it is very interesting."

"What does he talk about?"

"His dogs, mainly. Sometimes his wife."

"You know," Rob said, fighting the urge to get involved. "If you ever wanted to stop dancing for him, he wouldn't fire you. After all, you could always tell his wife what's been going on."

"Oh, she knows."

"She knows?"

"Sure. If you were her, would you care what he did? I do things so she doesn't have to. She even sends me Christmas cards every year."

"You're kidding!"

"No. They're really pretty. They're like little paintings. I hang them in my apartment during the holidays."

Agnew Hall came into view.

"Let me ask you," Rob said, shivering. "How did Craig get along with Thelma?"

"Craig hated her!" Tiffani said. "Called her 'the old bat.' He worshipped her dead husband. But hated her. Why?"

"I'm trying to keep my mind off the temperature."

"I'm sorry. Here." Wrapping her arm around him, she attempted to share the coat.

Rob pulled away. "No. You… you should probably keep it on yourself. You have more exposed skin."

They hurried along. His body trembling, Rob was tempted to pick Tiffani up and run with her to the warmth of the nearest building. But he thought that would appear even stranger than having a student wrap her arms around his waist.

"I appreciate how n, n, nice you are to me," she said, teeth chattering.

"I want to help. So, if there's anything I can do for you, let me know. Okay?"

Her head twitched in the cold. "You too. And I don't m, mean…" She gestured to her outfit. "Unless—" She raised a questioning eyebrow.

"Oh," Rob said, embarrassed. "I'm fine in that department."

"You are? I thought that blonde professor was a dyke."

They ran up the steps to Agnew Hall.

"I believe they prefer to be called lesbians. Or gay. Or queer. Actually, I'm not sure what they prefer anymore. But I think 'dyke' is definitely not their top choice."

"Right. Sorry."

Rob opened the door. Warm air billowed out to greet them.

"Hey," he said as they scurried into the foyer. He looked around. Students were going here and there, but nobody was paying any attention to them. He lowered his voice. "Could you do me a favor?"

"Sure." Tiffani blew into her blue hands, then slid them under her armpits. "Name it."

"Craig is going to make sure I can't keep my job next year. If you overhear or see anything that could help me stay…"

She gave him back his coat. "I'll see what I can find out."

Chapter 55

It took several sleepless nights, but Rob finally finished the grant application he told the Dean he was working on. Despite the mad rush to complete it, he felt he did a fairly decent job. However, he had no delusions about it getting funded. With federal grants, school reputation and resources meant a great deal, and Eastern Wisconsin University couldn't compete with the larger research-intensive schools like the University of Illinois or Purdue. Still, he'd gotten it done and hoped to use it as an opportunity to speak with the Dean about his situation.

Lingering in the mailroom, Rob pretended to read a notice about how the price of parking permits would increase twenty percent the following school year. When the receptionist went to make copies, he quickly snuck past her desk and knocked on the Dean's door.

"What?" Captain Hammer shouted.

Rob entered the sprawling office. It had a bank of impressive floor-to-ceiling windows looking into the weed-infested courtyard, a leather sofa and matching wing chairs, wall-to-wall built-in cabinets with beveled glass, and a private bathroom. Scattered about were various military pictures and totems, including a two-foot-long dagger displayed on the Dean's desk. Its keen edges gleamed menacingly in the sunlight.

"Dr. Chudinski reporting as requested, sir." He was tempted to salute but thought it might be overkill.

"Requested?" the Dean repeated.

"You asked me to bring this to you first thing today."

The Dean squinted suspiciously at him.

"The grant application?" Rob prodded. "I'm applying for a three-million-dollar grant from NIDR."

"Right! Right!" The Dean took the offered papers and set them next to the dagger. "Thank you. I'll inspect them asap." He turned to his computer screen.

"Yes, sir. Thank you."

"Anything else?"

"Only a question, if you don't mind. I know you're busy. But I was wondering if you had any advice for new faculty going up for reappointment. I'd like to do everything I can to stay here."

"Really?" the Dean asked, surprised. "Why?"

The question caught Rob off-guard. Struggling, he considered telling the Dean how teachers at Elwin Holme thought kids with disabilities couldn't learn and that he'd promised a dying woman he'd do something about it—but he guessed the former Marine wouldn't care. Indicating the deer's head mounted on the wall, Rob finally said, "Hunting's good."

The Dean thought about this. Then, nodding, he turned back to a webpage on fly fishing.

"So," Rob went on, "any suggestions?"

"Do your job and do it well. And don't make enemies you can't kill. That's how you succeed in life. Also—" He gave Rob a strange look. "—don't think your smarter than you are." He gritted his teeth. "God Almighty, how I hate arrogant phonies!"

"Yes, sir. That's good advice. Thank you. One final question. Do you ever vote against the recommendations made by the department chairs or school director?"

The Dean faced him again. "I'll tell you the key to good company cohesion," he said as if revealing a trusted family secret. "Make sure your subordinates have clear orders and that they carry them out. Then you don't need to worry about frivolous details."

"That's a no, isn't it?" Rob asked, his heart sinking.

"Affirmative." The Dean scrolled through the article he was reading. "Dismissed."

Chapter 56

Rob sat in his office late Sunday night, his lamp illuminating mountains of quizzes strewn across his desk.

For most of the semester, Tiffani graded his assignments for him. Since Rob had over four hundred students, it saved a tremendous amount of time. However, when Craig found out, he forbade her from helping any further. So, in addition to teaching eight courses and attending an endless slew of meetings, Rob now had to grade everything.

Leaning back in his squealing chair, he yawned and stretched. He couldn't keep doing this. His bloodshot eyes wouldn't focus anymore.

He sipped cold coffee, then blinked at his door.

Maybe he should take another look around the department office. After all, there were still twenty or thirty boxes he hadn't searched. Perhaps he'd find the bodies Thelma mentioned in one of them.

He regarded his stack of ungraded quizzes with disdain, then shrugged. He needed a break. He might as well do something productive.

Crossing the shadow-filled hallway, Rob found the department office even messier than it had been the week before. Sighing, he peered into a dusty box. It was filled with yellowing paper, some of which had carbon copies behind them. He looked in another. It contained research articles from the 1960s.

Retreating a step, he surveyed the disorder around him.

This was stupid. He couldn't go through everything. He didn't even know what he was looking for. He had to think. If he were a chain-smoking elderly secretary who had a secret, where would he hide it?

He noted the filing cabinets and began opening random drawers.

The first contained three tampons, a lacy black bra, a carton of condoms, and several fashion magazines.

The second had a sketchbook, a heap of colored pencils, pens, a tape dispenser, hundreds of paperclips linked together into a tangled necklace, and at least twenty staplers—all labeled 'The Property of the Department of Teaching and Learning.' Bored, Rob flipped through the sketchbook.

There were drawings of hands and eyes and ears and breasts and more than a few penises at various stages of erection. Several pages included pictures of women pole and lap dancing while hideous men leered at them like ghouls.

Turning the sketchbook sideways, Rob examined a picture of a forlorn woman sitting naked on the edge of a bed while an overweight, middle-aged man got dressed in the background. Twenty-dollar bills lay crumpled on the table next to her.

"Holy shit. She's good!"

He looked at another picture of a sobbing woman sitting in a corner, her head in her hands.

"Really good!"

Rob returned to the picture of the woman sitting on the edge of a bed, then reluctantly put the sketchbook where he found it. He'd talk to Tiffani about her art tomorrow. Right now, he had to concentrate.

Opening the remaining cabinets, he found nothing of consequence.

Disappointed, he scanned the office, wondering if he was wasting his time.

His gaze came to rest on an open drawer filled with keys. Then he remembered what Sid had said—if there had been something here, Craig would've taken it after Thelma died.

Where would he have put it?

A chart taped to the wall listed everybody's office number. Craig was in Room 602.

Should he?

No. He had every right to be in the department's main office. Sure, milling through the boxes and cabinets might appear strange, but he could always say he was looking for something, such as an extra pen or condom. What would his excuse be for being in Craig's office? Besides, going in there was probably illegal.

Rob peered into the drawer. Key 602 was sitting on top of the pile. It practically had a big flashing arrow pointing at it.

He weighed the pros and cons.

Pro: He might find what he needed to stay.

Con: He might get arrested.

Pro: He didn't know any other way to get reappointed. Craig wasn't going to change his mind. If Rob didn't do something, he'd be out of a job. And he might not find another one for a very long time.

Con: He might get fired on the spot. Moreover, this was the kind of thing that would make it impossible for him to get hired elsewhere. Nobody would employ somebody fired for breaking into a colleague's office.

Rob thought about this. He could always say he found the door open and that he went inside to make sure Craig wasn't on the floor, dead of a heart attack. Given his colossal girth, people would probably believe that.

"Fuck it."

Seizing the key, Rob headed to Craig's office, his determined footsteps echoing in the darkened hallway around him. He knocked. There was no answer. He opened the door. It banged into the massive cherry wood desk like an alarm. He slipped inside.

"Okay. Stay calm."

With a sweaty hand, he turned on the fluorescent lights. They shone out into the hallway like a beacon.

"Where to look?"

To fit his new desk, Craig had moved the row of filing cabinets to the far wall, partially obstructing his window. They were as good of a place to start as any.

Rob snuck another peek into the hallway. The coast was still clear. Then he scooted through the narrow gap between the desk and the wall and hurried over to the filing cabinets. He opened the first drawer. It was empty.

He opened the second. It was empty too.

He checked the third and fourth drawers. They were empty as well.

"What the—?"

He checked the other cabinets. They were all empty.

Why would somebody have six empty filing cabinets in their tiny office? It didn't make any sense.

He looked around.

On the shelves next to him were rows of pristine special education textbooks. Rob took one down and opened it to the copyright page. It had been published in 1989, yet its binding was so stiff and musty, it probably had never been opened.

He returned the book and inspected the certificates taped neatly to the walls. One was from Elwin Holme, thanking Craig for his years of dedication. It was dated 2002. The newer awards, however, were from someplace called "OFM." He read the smaller print.

"Organization for the Feeble-Minded?"

According to what Rob was seeing, OFM had given Craig an award for "Outstanding Service to Abnormal Children" twelve years running.

"Abnormal…? Feeble-Minded…?"

Nobody would use those terms. Maybe fifty years ago. But not now.

He stared at the photos perched on the gigantic desk. In one, Craig held a plump, rosy-cheeked middle-aged woman. In another, he knelt beside two beautiful golden retrievers, their tongues lolling out of their mouths as if exhausted from a day of chasing balls. In the third, he wore a black cap and gown and pointed to a diploma. An older version of Thelma's husband stood next to him; his arm draped around Craig's shoulder. In all the photos, Craig appeared deliriously happy.

"Something's wrong."

Chapter 57

Back in his office, Rob typed "OFM" into Google's search engine. Numerous web pages appeared—some for a chemical company, others for the Office of Financial Management. None of them had anything to do with kids with special needs.

He tried "Organization for the Feeble-Minded." A web page came up concerning American institutions for the disabled from 1876 to 1916, but nothing else.

"Organization for the Feeble-Minded…"

Were all those awards fake?

And those empty filing cabinets—were they for show?

Somehow that made sense. As Frank had said, people like Craig wanted to be the alpha dog. They wanted to impress everybody. A hand-carved desk, a row of filing cabinets, and a wall full of awards might do that.

How could this help him stay? Craig was a liar. But that wouldn't surprise anybody. And it certainly wouldn't get him fired.

Rob searched the internet for Craig's name.

The typical links appeared—where he lived, a few old newspaper articles, his university webpage—but nothing more substantial.

Rob accessed Google Scholar and typed "Craig Grubber." There were two research articles, but they were in molecular biology. He tried "C. Grubber" and got three pages of hits. None of them were in any disability-related field.

He opened Craig's university web page.

The picture was at least twenty years old and showed a thinner, younger Craig with a neatly trimmed black mustache. The blurb described him as an "award-winning scholar" and "champion of the crippled" and a "noted authority."

Opening another browser, Rob searched PubMed.com for "Craig Grubber." Then "C. Grubber." Then just "Grubber." The last produced several items, but nothing had been published within the past three decades. He tried Education Research Complete, PsychINFO, Education Research Clearinghouse, and Researchgate.com. There was nothing on any of them.

Rob made sure he was spelling the last name correctly. He was.

He returned to Craig's university web page and clicked on the link to his curriculum vita. According to this version, Craig had received his Ph.D. from the University of Northern Montana. His dissertation was entitled: *Teaching mathematics to young adults with sub-average intelligence.*

That didn't sound like anything Craig would be interested in.

Going back to Google Scholar, Rob entered the title of Craig's dissertation. There were no matches.

What was he missing?

Picking up his cell phone, Rob called Sid. Sid answered on the second ring.

"Hey, Rob. What's up?"

"I'm not sure," Rob said. "But I was wondering if you could do something for me. You busy?"

"Not at all. I'm just grading papers while I binge-watch Breaking Bad. What do you need?"

"Are you by a computer?"

"Yeah. I have my laptop right here. Why?"

"I've been searching for information on Walrus, specifically any research studies or articles he might have published. I was wondering if you came up with the same results I did."

"Sure. Give me a second." There was the sound of tapping. Then Sid asked, "It's Craig, right?"

"Right. And his last name is spelled G-r-u-b-b-e-r."

"Isn't that the terrorist from Die Hard?" Sid asked.

"You're thinking of Hans Grüber. One 'b.'"

"Oh, right."

More typing.

"Huh," Sid muttered.

"Find something?" Rob asked.

"Hold on."

The typing grew more insistent.

"Just to confirm," Sid said, "his last name is G-r-u-b-b-e-r? Two 'b's."

Rob checked the university web page. "Correct."

"I'm not finding anything under Craig Grubber. Do you know his middle initial?"

Rob went to the top of Craig's vita. "It's R. And he'd be publishing things involving special education or people with disabilities. Maybe mathematics."

"There's nothing on a C. R. Grubber. Let me try something else." There was a pause. "I'm getting hits on a C. Grubber. But nothing related to disability or mathematics. Let me try one more thing."

The typing lasted many minutes.

"There's nothing here," Sid said eventually. "He hasn't done anything."

"We must be missing something."

"Rob, I'm in Information Sciences. Searching for stuff like this is what I do. I can guarantee you Craig hasn't published anything. Not a research article, white paper, book chapter… he hasn't even published meeting proceedings. There's literally no reference to him in any of the databases. As a matter of fact, nobody has even cited anything he's done. How the hell did he get promoted to a full professor?"

"That's what I was wondering."

"Do you think this was what your secretary was talking about?" Sid asked.

The picture on Craig's university website smiled condescendingly at him. "Maybe."

"Need anything else?"

"No. I'm good. Thanks."

"Sorry I couldn't help."

"Actually, you've helped plenty. Thanks again."

"No problem. Keep me posted. Okay?"

"I will. See you tomorrow."

"See you."

They hung up.

Rob sat for a moment, thinking. Then he reread Craig's vita. There wasn't anything too informative, just where he got his degrees, a list of a handful of local presentations he'd made in the 1990s, and the classes he taught.

On a hunch, he typed "University of Northern Montana" into his search engine. Eight pages of hits appeared. Reading the first one, Rob grinned. It was about how the University of Northern Montana was shut down because it wasn't accredited. In fact, according to a newspaper article dated March 13th, 2002, it had no campus or faculty. For five thousand dollars, people received fake degrees and transcripts. It was a diploma mill.

"Bingo!"

Chapter 58

Craig stepped into Rob's office, a big smirk across his round face.

"Hey, Craig," Rob said as he typed an e-mail. "Have a good weekend?"

He was tempted to ask him where he'd gotten his Ph.D., but he didn't want to blow his advantage. After all, the last time he thought he had the upper hand, things didn't go too well. He wanted to be absolutely sure he had Craig before he confronted him.

"Like you'd care." Leaning against the doorframe, Craig watched Rob type. "Applying for jobs? You'll be lucky to work in some community college teaching—"

"Teaching English to foreign exchange students. Yeah, you said that before." Rob went on typing. "You want something?"

"Do I want something? I'll tell you what I want, Polly. I want you to know that I'm on to you. Nothing goes on in this program that I don't know about. You hear me? Nothing."

"Not only can I hear you, but I can also smell you. Maybe put the Old Spice on *before* you take a shower."

"You little—" Craig's mustache twitched. "I will not stand for this insubordination!"

Rob gestured to the chair on the other side of his desk. "Would you like to sit?"

Craig huffed, his veins bulging. "I'm going to—!"

"What? Fire me? Make sure I don't get reappointed? Tell all of your many friends in the field not to hire me?"

"Exactly! All of those! Mark my words, Polly, I'm—"

"You know, Craig." Rob stopped typing. "I'm getting sick of your attitude."

"*My* attitude?"

"I understand I was hired by accident. I get you're pissed about that. But from day one, you've been busting my balls, and I'm tired of it."

"Oh, are you now?" Craig mocked. "Is little Polly upset? Is the holy roller sensitive?"

"And another thing, my name is Robert Chudinski. Call me Rob if you like. Or Dr. Chudinski. You can even call me Chud. But I'm sick of all the insults."

Craig opened his mouth, but Rob cut him off.

"And if you steal another of my nameplates—" He pointed to his open door. A piece of paper with the word "Imbecile" was where his name should've been. "—I'll report it to the police. I've paid for the last three of them. I'm not going to pay for a fourth."

Craig laughed, his belly shaking. "Do you honestly believe the police are going to give a rat's ass about your stupid nameplate? My desk cost over two thousand dollars, and they did nothing when those TLs cut it in half. So, spare me your empty threats." He gloated. "I'm the chair of the department. There's absolutely nothing you can do to me."

Then Rob heard it slip out. "Tell me, Craig. Where did you get your Ph.D.?"

Craig sucked in air. "Why?"

"I hear they don't have many professors. Perhaps, if I don't get reappointed here, they'd hire me. After all—" Rob winked. "—*I have* a Ph.D."

Craig pointed a shaking finger at him. "You watch yourself!"

"Or what?"

"Or I'll make sure nobody ever hires you again. I mean it, Polly! I know people! I have influence! You tangle with me, and I'll not only get you fired from here, but I'll ruin your career. Do you hear me? You'll never work in academia again!"

Chapter 59

As Craig stormed away, Rob searched Google for Northern Montana University and printed the articles describing it as a diploma mill. He then hurried to the main office before anybody could get to them. Tiffani was at her desk, dressed in an appropriate skirt and blazer, drawing a picture of a young girl staring longingly out the window.

Rob peered over her shoulder as he snatched the papers from the printer. "That's incredibly good."

"Really?"

"Absolutely. In fact, I'd like to see anything else you might have drawn. Maybe you can sell me a few sketches."

She studied the picture and then looked skeptically at him over her horned-rimmed glasses.

"I'm not bullshitting you," Rob told her. "Or trying to get in your pants."

"I'm not wearing pants."

"You know what I mean. Hey, I have to get going. But I think you should consider transferring to the art program."

"I'd love to, but—" Her shoulders sagged. "Craig said that wouldn't be very smart. He said I could never make a living as an artist."

"I'm not saying you'll get rich or anything, but—honestly—you're extremely talented. If you want to be an artist, then be an artist! You can do it. When I get back, I want to see anything else you've done. And I'm going to buy what I like. Okay? So think about how much you'd want for each picture."

Rob made to leave.

"Dr. Chudinski?"

"Yeah?"

Tiffani kissed him hard on the lips. He was about to drop the articles he'd printed and grab her ass when Bert walked in.

"Hey darl—" He stopped short. "What the hell?"

Pulling away, Rob wiped the lipstick from his lips. "Ms. Miller!" His heart and other parts of his body pounded.

"I'm sorry." She giggled. "I… I kind of slipped."

"As much as I enjoyed it, please don't let that happen again. Okay?" He took a deep, quavering breath. "And I meant what I said. You're a gifted artist. Don't let anybody convince you otherwise."

Rob stepped toward the door, but Bert blocked his way. "Now you've done it, Polly! You can't sleep with a student!"

"Out of my way, Bert."

Rob pushed past him.

"I'm going to tell the Big Guy!" Bert called.

"Go wash your hair and leave me alone."

"That's it! You're through here! Pack your bags!"

Rob dashed to the elevator, repeatedly tapped the button, and then decided he didn't want to wait. Articles in hand, he bounded down the six flights of stairs to the first-floor hallway. A student called to him, asking if he'd missed anything when he wasn't in class the previous week, but Rob didn't answer. Hurrying into the administrative suite, he poked his head into the School Director's office.

"Mind if I talk with you?" he asked out of breath. "It'll only take a minute."

"Sure!" Mary set aside her sudoku puzzle. "How are you doing? Doing okay there?"

"What? Yeah, yeah, I'm fine. Thanks. Look, there's something important I need to discuss with you. It's about Craig."

"Is he okay?" she asked, concerned.

"It's not about his health or anything. I've learned something rather disturbing, and I thought you should know."

"Goodness. What is it?"

Rob handed her the copies of the websites he'd printed. "This is where he got his Ph.D."

Confused, Mary shuffled through the papers.

"You see, it says here Northern Montana University wasn't a real university." Rob pointed to the top article. "They didn't have a campus or any staff. They gave people diplomas for a fee." He said triumphantly, "Craig doesn't have a Ph.D. He's been lying!"

Mary's brow furrowed. "Oh, dear." She skimmed the rest of the articles, then handed them back.

"That's all you're going to say? Oh, dear? Mary, he's a fake! He doesn't have a doctorate. He should be fired!"

"Well…" Mary said vaguely. "Maybe."

"What do you mean—maybe?"

"You see—" She put her elbows on her desk and steepled her fingers contemplatively. "—things change over time."

Rob looked wildly about her office, trying to find somebody to explain what was going on. The hundreds of cat figurines lining the shelves offered him no help.

"What are you saying?"

"It could be they didn't require a terminal degree when he was hired. It was a long time ago, don't you know? I'll have to check."

"Check?" Rob repeated. "On his vita, he says he has a Ph.D. He insists students call him doctor. He isn't a doctor. He doesn't have a Ph.D. He's a fraud!"

"I hear what you're saying," Mary said calmly, "and I can see this is something that interests you a good deal."

"It does!"

"Then let's do this." She searched her desk and found her appointment book. "How about we set up a meeting to discuss it? We can rope everybody into the same conversation. What do you say there?"

"Why would we need to meet? Here's the proof!"

Rob shook the web pages in front of her.

Mary inspected her empty calendar. "How about March fourth at seven in the morning? It's a Friday."

"March fourth? That's five months away!"

"I should have some answers for you by then."

Rob glanced around again in disbelief. "Is Captain Hammer in?"

The pleasantness drained from Mary's face. "You don't want to go bothering him about something like this. That's for sure."

Rob stomped out of her office.

"You don't want to meet then?" she called after him.

The Dean's door was closed, but light illuminated its frosted window. Rob ran past his receptionist.

"You can't go in there!" she told him.

"He'll want to see me."

Rob knocked and burst in. The Dean was reading a hunting magazine, his feet propped on his desk.

"What in blazes?" Captain Hammer shouted. "You? You better have a damn good explanation for—" Then he appeared to understand. "You got the grant?"

"No. They won't announce the winners until early spring." Rob closed the door behind him. "I'm sorry to barge in like this, sir, but there's something very unethical going on, if not illegal, and I—"

"Hey!" The Dean stood and waved his hands. "I don't want to know."

"What do you mean you don't want to know?"

"Go tell your superior."

"But it's about my superior!"

"Then tell his superior!"

"I did," Rob said. "But she won't do anything other than schedule a meeting! It's really important! You see, Craig doesn't have—"

"I don't want to hear it! Understand? Follow the chain of command. Now leave!"

The Dean guided Rob out of his office and slammed the door behind him.

Rob stood there, still clutching the papers he'd printed. He blinked at the receptionist.

"You're lucky he didn't fire you," she said. "Or worse!"

Chapter 60

"What do you mean, '*It happens*'?" Rob asked, outraged.

He paced his kitchen, his laptop perched on a counter littered with ingredients for a mushroom lasagna.

On the screen, his dissertation advisor, Frank Russo, shrugged. "I mean, it happens. There are tons of diploma mills. Hell, I think we graduate too many undeserving doctoral students here. Present company excluded. And for the love of God, stop moving! You're making me ill. Sit down."

Rob stood in front of his computer, struggling to suppress the frustration building inside him.

"I understand it happens. I'm even willing to concede that it happens far more than I realize. But what I don't understand is why nobody cares. My Dean literally said — I don't want to know! How can he say that? He's the damned Dean!"

"And he's a smart one. Not knowing things is the best way to get promoted when you're in administration."

"You're not helping, Frank!"

"I'm not sure what you want me to help with. I keep telling you—this is the real world. Academia isn't this wondrous realm of pure intellect and thoughtful discourse among rational adults over steaming cups of Earl Grey tea. It's a dark and seedy sewer riddled with assholes and backroom politics."

"I don't believe that," Rob said. "Sure, maybe here. But most people who go into academia do so to make a difference in their chosen field. They don't spend half their lives in school, getting expensive degrees, so that they can sit in pointless meetings every day."

"You're naïve."

"I'm not naïve!"

"Yes, you are. And hyper-emotional as always. Stop pacing!"

Rob stood still again.

"The reason why most people get Ph.D.'s," Frank said, "isn't because they want to acquire knowledge or save the world. It's so they can go to their favorite restaurant and say, 'Table for two for Dr. Buttlicker.' For most people, it's a status thing. They don't care about their impact on their field or the world. It's a job."

Rob wagged his head, trying to restrain himself.

"Don't believe me?" Frank asked. "Then tell me—why has every study found rates of scholarship drop drastically after people get tenured?"

"I don't know."

"It's because most people aren't in this business to make a difference. They're in it for a cushy, life-long job, where you get summers off, and you don't have to worry about accountability."

"No accountability," Rob muttered. "That's for sure."

"Look, you're a brilliant researcher. And you're writing is impeccable. It's clear, direct, and you're able to present complex ideas in a way that makes sense to people who don't have your academic background. That's also going to make you a terrific teacher."

"Thanks, but—"

"Listen for a change. Okay?"

Rob motioned for him to go on.

"All of that," Frank said, "the teaching, research, and writing—it's only a small fraction of what it means to be an academic. There're tons of politics. And, despite what it seems like when you're sitting alone in your office, it's as much of a team sport as football or basketball. You have to get along with everybody, or your life will be miserable."

Rob gritted his teeth.

"Remember what I said about how there should be a television show like Survivor, but with higher education?" Frank asked.

"Yeah."

"I wasn't kidding. It'd be fantastic. A bunch of boorish intellectuals trying to sabotage each other—fighting over who teaches what or who gets the offices with windows. Who wouldn't watch that?"

Rob snatched a dish towel, then threw it on the counter. "Then explain to me why nobody cares about Craig? If it's as cut-throat and underhanded as you say, why aren't people pouncing on the fact he lied about his credentials?"

"Think about it from the university's perspective," Frank told him. "They don't want to look bad."

"They'll let somebody who's not qualified teach future educators simply to protect their asses?"

"I'm not sure having a Ph.D. qualifies anybody for anything. Hell, I bet half the academics in our field haven't seen a kid with a disability in the past decade, if not longer. Some have never even taught in special education at all. How does that make any sense?"

Steam rose from a pot of boiling water on the stove.

"I can't believe this," Rob said.

"Believe it," Frank replied. "It's the state of higher education."

Rob seized the dish towel again and throttled it. "God damn it! I thought I had him. I do have him! But nobody cares."

"Maybe you're focusing on the wrong things." Frank adjusted his camera so that he was in the center of the screen. "How's your research coming?"

"I resubmitted that paper to the Journal of Cognitive Disabilities," Rob said bitterly. "The results were the same, but the statistical significance was less than it was."

"But still statistically significant?"

"Yeah, barely."

"That doesn't matter. Significant is significant," Frank told him. "What about the new stuff?"

"I'm working on it."

"Work harder. Your data are getting stale. You need to get everything published by the end of next year, which means getting everything accepted by spring."

"What about my chair?"

"Don't worry about your chair. Get your research published in top-tier journals, and things will work out. You'll see."

"Frank." Rob sighed. "I think I need to face the fact that I'm not going to get my contract renewed here. I think I need to start looking around for another position for next fall."

"You can't do that," Frank said.

"I don't want to. I have a wonderful house and friends here—but my chair is never going to vote to keep me. Never."

"You can't leave after one year."

"Why not?"

"If you leave a tenure-track position after only one year—" Frank struggled to convey the seriousness of the situation. "—people are going to wonder what's wrong with you."

"Nothing's wrong with me," Rob replied. "It's this place that has something wrong with it!"

"Job hopping is never a good thing. Look, I'm telling you, keep your job for a few years. Do whatever you can to appease your chair. But don't start sending out applications. Word will get around that you're a malcontent or something."

"Malcontent?" Rob stared at Frank. "Is it really *that* bad if I leave after one year?"

"Rob," Frank said firmly, "if you can't keep a job at a place like Eastern Wisconsin, I doubt anybody would be willing to hire you."

Chapter 61

The doorbell jingled as Rob slid his mushroom lasagna into the oven. Curious to see who was stopping by at eight o'clock on a weeknight, he hurried to the foyer. The distorted image of a woman standing on his front step appeared in the beveled glass. He opened the door.

"Hi. May I—?" Surprised, he retreated a step. "Ms. Miller?"

Wearing faded jeans, a baggy Eastern Wisconsin University sweatshirt, and a ski jacket, she was barely recognizable.

"Sorry for bothering you at home," she said. "I hope you don't mind."

"No, of course not. Come in." He showed her inside. "You look…" He attempted to find the right words without sounding like he was hitting on her.

"Normal?"

"I was going to say different. But in the best possible way."

"Thanks." She strolled around his living room. "This is pretty. I love all the wood. Older homes have so much more character than what they build today."

"I think so too."

"How are the flies this close to the lake?"

"You know," Rob said, "you're the second person to ask me that. They're fine as far as I can tell. A few here and there, but no complaints. Have a seat. Can I get you anything? Something to drink?"

"No, but thanks." She examined the photos on the wall. She pointed to one of a five-year-old Rob holding a baseball bat and smiling at the camera. His four brothers were standing away from him, watching warily as though he might bash their kneecaps. "Cute."

"Thanks. Sadly, that was the extent of my baseball career."

They sat on the sofa, Rob making sure he didn't sit too close.

"Everything okay?"

"Yeah. Fine. Well, that is. I'm fine, but…" Anxiety grew in her brown eyes. "Craig is going to get you fired."

"He's told me… several times."

"He means it. He wanted me to tell the Dean you slid your hand up my skirt and tried to force yourself on me." She added, "I told him I wouldn't lie. So don't worry."

"Is he upset with you?" Rob asked. "For not doing what he said?"

She lowered her head. "Yeah. He's threatening to fire me too."

"I see." Rob watched Tiffani twist a cheap ring around her finger. In her regular clothing, she seemed so young and vulnerable. "What are you going to do?"

"I'll be okay," she said unconvincingly. "When Craig gets angry at me, it usually blows over in a few days. I'm more worried about you."

"Don't worry about me. I'll be okay too."

"I don't think you understand. Craig is mean and spiteful. Whatever you did, he's taking it personally. There's no telling what he'll do. You need to watch yourself."

"Did he say anything in particular?" Rob asked.

"No. But he had this crazy look in his eyes. And he kept saying, *'I'm going to get him! I'm going to get him! I'm going to get him if it's the last thing I do!'* He was scary. I don't even think he realized I was in the room. He kept talking to himself, his hands clenching and unclenching." She frowned at him. "Be careful. Okay?"

"I will."

"Well…" She got up. "That's what I wanted to tell you. I'll let you know if he says anything else. You might want to watch out for Bert and Les as well. They'll do whatever Craig says."

"I'll keep my eyes open." He walked her to the door. "Thanks for letting me know, Ms. Miller. And thanks for being on my side. I didn't mean to drag you into all of this."

Chapter 62

Craig burst into Rob's office, out of breath. "What did you do? What did you do?"

Sitting in front of his computer, Rob enlarged the font on the slides for his next lecture. "I don't know. Can you be more specific?"

Bert appeared suddenly in the hallway. Then Les. Both looked as terrified as Craig.

"Did you give it to him good, Big Guy?" Bert asked. "Did you finally toss him out?"

"Yeah!" Les said. "Toss him out!"

"Will somebody please tell me what's wrong?" Rob asked, annoyed. "I don't have time for your games."

"Games?" Craig attempted to master his emotions. It appeared as though his head was about to rupture. "Did you complete an early-warning grade form on a Mr. Rock Fitz?"

Rob thought for a moment, then remembered the name. "Yeah, I think so."

"You *think* so?" Craig's entire body quivered. "You *think* so?"

Pulling up his class roster, Rob found the student.

"Here he is. He's in my Introduction to Exceptionalities course."

"You're what?"

"He means Introduction to Abnormal Children!" Les said. "He's been changing the names of all of his courses. He didn't even go through the curriculum process!"

"I'll deal with that later." Craig turned back to Rob. "Now—did you or did you not complete an early warning grade form on Mr. Fitz?"

"Yeah," Rob said. "He's failing."

"Oh, Jesus Christ!" Bert covered his head as he turned in a circle. "Jesus fucking Christ!"

"Now you've done it, Polly!" Les said. "Now you've really done it! Toss him out of here, Big Guy! Toss him out!"

Craig loomed over Rob's desk, his face practically glowing scarlet. "Do you know what the hell you've done?"

"He hasn't attended a single class since the start of the semester," Rob told him. "He's literally getting a zero percent."

"And?"

Rob set his lecture notes aside. "I don't understand why you're upset. The e-mail we got from the Dean of Students said we were supposed to complete the form on any students who were at risk of failing our courses."

"She didn't mean it!" Craig cried. "What's wrong with you?"

"You know, Craig," Rob said calmly. "Something just occurred to me."

Craig's jaw tightened. "And what is that, pray tell?"

"You keep telling me I'm not going to get reappointed next year." Rob crossed his arms in front of him. "It that's the case, it doesn't matter what I do. Does it? I can piss you off as much as I want."

"Now, you listen here, Polly—!"

Down the hallway, the stairwell door thudded closed. Les peered out of the office, his face going ashen. "He's coming!"

"Dear God, help us!" Bert gasped. "What do we do? What do we do?"

Craig pointed at Rob. "You! You!" Then, pulsating with rage, he bolted out of the office, Bert and Les on his heels. Three doors slammed.

Seconds later, a figure filled the doorway. For a moment, Rob thought it was Captain Hammer but found that it was an obese white man with a belly to rival Craig's. Despite the chilly autumn weather, he was wearing shorts and a windbreaker. He looked at the nameplate on the door, then at the office number.

"You Chudinski?" he snarled at Rob.

Given the EWU football logo adorning every article of his clothing, Rob guessed what he'd done.

"Aye! That I am, matie," he replied in a pirate voice. "And you must be our esteemed football coach. Ar!"

Taken aback, the coach asked, "Why are you talking like that?"

"I thought it was funny."

The coach blinked at him. "Well, it isn't."

Rob reclined in his chair, making it squeal. The coach flinched. "Let me guess. Rock Fitz is one of your players. And you're upset because he's failing my class. Is that it?"

"He's my star running back." The coach glowered, trying to regain the malice he had when he entered the office. "And he's going to play this week. Got me?"

The chair squealed again. The coach cringed.

"Let's be honest," Rob said. "If he's playing for this university, he can't be that good. He was probably the best player at some crappy division five high school, making him the best player here. Am I right?"

The coach blustered. "You miserable—"

"Look, Dauber. There's not a shot in hell any of your mediocre players are ever going to play in the NFL. Consequently, they need an education. And if they don't show up for class, they can't get it. They fail. Do you understand me?"

"You little... Do you know who I am? I'm—" The chair let loose a long, ear-piercing squeal. "Stop doing that!"

"I know exactly who you are," Rob said. "You're some crappy football player who faked an injury so you could tell people how great you could've been. Now you're coaching at a university whose mascot is a cheesemonger. Please spare me the stories about how you scored four touchdowns in the big high school game back in Buttcrack, Indiana."

"You're not tenured! I checked. I'll have you out of here so fast it'll—"

"Blah. Blah. Blah. Believe me, Bundy, I'm already on the way out." Rob flicked his chin toward the hallway. "See the fat asshole who ran away? That's my chair. He's already told me I'm not getting reappointed." Rob stood up. He was at least six inches shorter and seventy pounds lighter than the coach, but there was something in his expression that made the coach give way. "There's absolutely nothing you can do to me. Got it? Nothing."

The coach gnashed his teeth. Then he relaxed. "I appreciate a man with intestinal fortitude. How about you and me make a deal. You pass my boy, and I'll make sure you get reappointed."

And there it was—his ticket to salvation.

Judging by how quickly Craig scampered to his office, Rob had no doubt the coach could compel him to do anything he wanted. University coaches wielded the power of the gods. But then again, Rob would have to compromise his most deeply held belief that education mattered.

"Rock hasn't shown up for any of the classes," he said, buying himself time to think.

"I'll make sure he attends here on out."

"He hasn't taken a single quiz or the midterm," Rob added, the temptation to take the lifeline dying within him. "Even if he got perfect scores on everything for the rest of the semester—"

"I'll get him a tutor. Hell, I'll pay you to do it. You could use the extra cash, couldn't you? Pay back some of your student loans?" He noted Rob's rickety chair. "Maybe buy some decent office furniture?"

"No. I couldn't do that. I'll certainly help him, but not for money."

"You sure? We have an account in the athletic department's budget especially for things like this."

Somehow, that wasn't surprising.

"No," Rob said with an effort. "I wouldn't feel comfortable taking money to help a student. It's my job."

The coach sized Rob up, then put his enormous foot on the guest chair.

"Very admirable of you." He leaned forward as if haggling on a used car. "Would you offer him extra credit? Maybe he could do a project for you? Rake your yard or clean your gutters."

"Sorry," Rob said. "I like raking my yard. It makes me feel manly."

"How about allowing him to do makeup work?" the coach suggested. "It wouldn't have to be for full credit, just enough so he can pass—if he does well, of course."

Rob considered this. The goal of teaching was to get students to learn the material. Sure, he would be giving this student a little extra help, but perhaps he could offer other students the same opportunity. That way, there wouldn't be any ethical dilemmas. Maybe...

"I'll tell you what..." he said, wondering if he was joining the dark side. "I'll allow your player to re-take the quizzes—in my office with me supervising." This stipulation seemed to deflate the coach a bit. "But he'll also have to show up for the remaining classes. No excuses. If his entire family dies in a horrible plane crash, he skips their funerals and comes to class, even if he has the flu or terrorists take over his dorm."

The coach extended a beefy hand. Rob shook it.

"Done! I'll have him here first thing tomorrow."

"Fine. Have him come at seven o'clock. We have class at eight. You might want to remind him of that."

"I will. And I'll talk with your dean about having you stay."

"I hope he'll listen."

"Oh, he'll listen. The Captain and I go way back." The coach winked. "I'll take care of everything. You'll see."

Chapter 63

The next day, Rob got to work early. With November turning even more fridge than October, finding a parking spot close to Agnew Hall was becoming a matter of life and death. Earlier that week, he thought he'd gotten frostbite running the five blocks from his car to the office. Even after he finally got inside, his face was so stiff he had difficulty blinking. He couldn't move his lips until he had his second cup of scalding coffee. Of course, with the air conditioning still on, it was nearly as cold inside. His office was like a meat locker.

Seven o'clock came and went. Then quarter after. Then half past. Still, the football star didn't show.

Waiting in his office, Rob checked his e-mail. There was nothing from the student saying he was going to be late. Perhaps he went to the classroom by mistake. Gathering his things together, Rob headed to class. By eight o'clock, two hundred and twenty-six of the two hundred and ninety-three students were there; Rock wasn't one of them.

Deep down, Rob was relieved. He'd tossed and turned all night, unable to sleep because he was kowtowing to a student-athlete. Now, with the student electing to blow off his course yet again, he didn't have to worry about violating his ethics. He just needed to find another way to keep his job.

Chapter 64

Another week of argumentative students and pointless meetings slowly crawled by. As Rob entered his office, his phone rang. The green screen indicated that Coach Dingle was calling. Snickering at the name, Rob answered.

"Hello?"

"Bob! Coach D here. Listen, we have a big game this weekend and Rock still has that academic warning on his record. I need you to take it off so he can play."

Rob girded himself for the coach's imminent tirade, then realized it didn't matter. There was nothing he could do.

"Rock didn't show up for his first makeup quiz. Or for class."

"Yeah, I heard about that. He overslept."

"It's Thursday," Rob said. "He overslept for three days?"

"He'll be in your office first thing Monday morning."

"About that. Clearly, Rock doesn't have much desire to learn. I'd like to help him. But he seems unwilling even to try. He's going to fail the course. He can retake it next semester."

"What about the academic warning?"

"It stands."

The coach hollered, "But he has to play this weekend!"

"Then he should've set his alarm or e-mailed me. He needs to learn to be responsible for his actions."

"You listen here, you little snot-nosed academic! If you don't take that warning off his record, he's off the team. Do you understand me? That's it for him and his scholarship! He won't have any other opportunity to get an education or to—"

"Sorry, Coach." Rob checked his watch. "I have to get to a meeting. Good luck this weekend. I hope you win."

He hung up, wondering how many more enemies he could handle.

Chapter 65

Grumbling students filed out of Rob's final class for the week. After three lectures and four soul-crushing committee meetings, he was as exhausted as they were. He was looking forward to having a nice, relaxing dinner with Wendy and Sid, then a productive weekend of grading papers and writing up his research.

"Mr. Chudinski?" A young, powerfully built black man in a pinstriped suit and wingtip shoes stood awkwardly by the door.

"It's Dr. Chudinski." Rob gathered his papers and slid them into his briefcase. "What can I do for you?"

The student dithered. "I don't know if you'd remember me from the beginning of the semester, but—I'm Rock Fitz."

"Oh!" Rob said knowingly. He could see where this was going.

"Look, you have every right to be angry with me."

"I'm not angry with you, Rock. Maybe disappointed. But certainly not angry. After all, it's your education, not mine. I get paid the same whether you show up or not."

This apparently derailed Rock's prepared speech. He tried to find what he wanted to say. Eventually, he said, "I need to play tomorrow!"

Rob set his briefcase on the table next to him. "Why?"

"Why?" Rock repeated as if it were a trick question.

"Why do you *need to* play tomorrow?" Rob asked.

"I'm on the team."

"But that doesn't answer my question. Why do you *need to* play at all?"

Rock fumbled incoherently.

People for the next class gathered by the open door. Rob indicated he'd be done in a second.

"Let me ask you something," he said. "Do you think you'll make it to the NFL?"

"I don't know. Maybe if I work hard. My coach says—"

"Forget what all of your coaches have told you. Okay? They don't care about you off the field. They don't care about your future." Rock started to protest, but Rob went on. "I'm sorry, but they don't."

He sat on one of the desks. "I don't mean to be an asshole, okay? I only want to tell you the truth. You're, what—five-nine? A hundred and fifty pounds?"

"A hundred and fifty-five."

"Defensive linemen in the NFL are three hundred, three hundred and fifty pounds. If they hit you, they'd snap your spine in half. Hell, if they even landed on you, you'd be dead. I'm sorry, but the chances of you playing in the NFL are about as high as me playing with the Beatles."

Rock stared at the floor.

"Again, I'm sorry," Rob said sympathetically. "I don't mean to shit on your dreams. But the smartest thing for you to do is to get an education and make sure you don't end up working at Walmart for the rest of your life—talking about what a terrific football player you used to be."

Rock didn't look at him.

"Don't you want to make something of yourself?" Rob asked. "Isn't there something you want to do besides play football?"

Jamming his hands in his pockets, Rock shrugged. "I'd kind of like to coach. You know, work with little kids, and maybe teach them how to play the game and get in better shape. Maybe teach gym or something."

"That's a great goal! It really is. But you'll have to dedicate yourself to your education for that to happen. If you want to be a teacher, you'll need to get a teaching license, which means getting a degree."

"I'm not exactly the smart type."

"Start showing up for classes, and maybe you will be."

Not willing to wait any longer, students for the next class filed into the lecture hall.

"Are you going to let me play tomorrow?" Rock asked.

"No, Rock. I'm not."

"Please? If you don't, I'll be kicked off the team! I'll lose my scholarship!"

"I'm sorry." Rob grabbed his briefcase. "It's time you start taking your education seriously. Because nobody is going to do it for you."

Chapter 66

"Wow!" Wendy exclaimed as they entered the restaurant. "Fancy! I'm glad you told me to take a shower after I worked out."

Overhead, a crystal chandelier sparkled.

"Yeah," Sid said, "I should've worn clean underwear."

An attractive hostess in a black dress and pearls approached them as they stood by the door. "Name?"

"Chudinski," Rob said.

Her finger slid down the computer screen, then stopped. "Right this way, please."

She led them through the main room, the orange glow of flickering candlelight on the faces of the well-dressed diners.

"I think you're trying to upstage the place I picked last week," Sid said.

"Who can upstage Pizza Hut?" Rob asked.

"Hey! You said you love pizza!"

The hostess brought them to a table in front of a crackling fireplace. "Is this suitable?"

"Suitable?" Wendy rubbed her hands and placed them close to the fire. "It's marvelous. Thank you very much!"

"It's my pleasure. Your attendant will be with you, momentarily."

"Thank you."

They draped their heavy coats over the extra chair and sat. In the far corner, a pianist played classical music.

"Boy! Look at all this." Sid inspected the menu. "And a wine list! Wait! You're paying, right?"

Rob laughed. "Absolutely. It's my turn."

"You dying or something?" Wendy asked.

"What? No! Can't a guy take his friends to a nice restaurant once in a while?"

Wendy eyed him.

"I thought it'd be fun!" Rob told her. "You were both saying you wanted to get out of town and see what Appleton had to offer."

Wendy kept staring at him.

"Fine!" Rob said begrudgingly. "I wanted to do something special to thank you for being my friends. Okay? There. That's my nefarious motivation."

"Was that as pathetic as it sounded?" Sid whispered to Wendy.

"Bad day?" Wendy asked Rob.

Rob read the list of entries. "Not *bad*, exactly. Certainly not worse than usual. But that football player came in and begged me to let him play tomorrow. That wasn't particularly pleasant."

"What did you tell him?"

"I told him the truth." Rob surveyed the soup section. Having something hot could help thaw him out. But he didn't recognize anything being offered and wasn't feeling particularly adventurous. "He'll never make it in the NFL, and his only hope in life is to get an education."

"Ouch!" Sid said. "A bit harsh, isn't it?"

Rob lowered his menu. "Why? It's true."

"You believe it's true, you mean. Nobody can tell what's going to happen. Who knows? Maybe he'll get on a practice squad and end up fighting his way onto the starting team. Ever see the movie, Rudy?"

"Seriously? You think a five-foot-nine-inch, hundred and fifty-pound kid from EW-U is going to be in the NFL?"

"All I'm saying is I don't know." Sid set his menu aside. "And neither do you."

Feeling attacked, Rob regarded Wendy sitting next to him. "What about you?"

"What about me?" she asked.

"What do you think?"

"I think I'll have the steak and lobster."

"That's not what I mean. What do you think about my student?"

Wendy set her menu on top of Sid's.

"If you're talking about your decision not to let him play," she said, "I think you absolutely did the right thing, and I'm proud of you. I mean, even after you gave him the opportunity to retake the quizzes, he still didn't show up! If he gets kicked off the team, that's his fault. Not yours."

She took a drink of water.

"If you're talking about whether he could play in the pros—" She lifted a hand. "How the hell would I know? The only game of theirs I've seen, we lost by forty-eight points. It didn't look like they could play high school ball, let alone in the NFL."

A waiter with slicked-back gray hair and a black suit stopped by their table. "Are we ready to order?"

"Not yet." Rob turned his attention back to his menu. "Sorry. Two more minutes, please."

"Certainly, sir."

The waiter went to another table.

"But Sid is right," Wendy went on. "Who knows? It's probably a million-to-one shot for any kid. It's probably a two-million-to-one shot for anybody from our school. But he still has a chance."

"That's all I'm saying," Sid said. "I don't think it's our place to tell students what their future holds. Hell, if you told me last year I'd be working up here in the frozen tundra, I would've called you crazy. You simply never know."

Next to them, the fire snapped and popped.

"You're right," Rob said, deflated. "I should apologize to him."

"Don't go all morose, okay?" Wendy squeezed his hand. "You're a fantastic teacher. I love how much you try to help your students, both in and out of class."

"Me too," Sid said. "And I'm sorry about that crack about sounding pathetic. I was trying to make a joke."

Rob sighed. "I know."

Watching the flames dance over the shifting yellow coals, Rob wondered if he'd been too opinionated with all of his students. The last thing he wanted was to limit their future like was done to kids with disabilities.

"Any more ideas about staying here?" Wendy asked.

Rob shook himself out of his thoughts. "My advisor from U of I insists I have nothing to worry about. But he also indicated nobody would hire me if I left my job after only one year. He said everybody would think I'm a malcontent."

"How's your research going?" Sid asked.

Noticing they didn't contradict his advisor's opinion, Rob grimaced. "I haven't heard about the revisions I resubmitted. I'm working on two other papers but haven't made much progress. With everything going on, I don't have much time to work on them."

"You know," Wendy said tactfully, "if you ever need to bag our weekly get-togethers…"

"No." Rob put on a smile. "Being with you two is the best part of my week. I honestly don't know what I would do without you."

The waiter reappeared, "Ready?"

"As ready as I'll ever be," Rob told him. "You go first, Wendy."

Chapter 67

"Can you tell us another story?" somebody called from the darkness.

Standing on the stage in his pit class, Rob shielded his eyes from the bright can lights shining down on him. Of the two hundred and ninety-two students currently registered for his Introduction to Abnormal Children course, a record two hundred and eighty-one had shown—though perhaps twenty already snuck out while he wasn't looking.

"You want to hear a story?" Rob replied doubtfully.

There was a smattering of "yeah's."

"I know what you're doing," Rob said into the microphone. "You want to get me off-track so I don't cover what we need to cover for this week's quiz!"

Students laughed.

"Okay. I'll tell you a story." Rob strolled about the stage, trying to think of something that might educate them as well as keep their attention. "After I got my master's degree, I took a job at a high school transitioning students with intellectual disabilities into the community. We'll talk about intellectual disabilities next week. But what you need to know is that intellectual disabilities are what used to be called 'mental retardation.' But don't use that term. Say intellectual disabilities or ID."

He watched with satisfaction as several students wrote that down.

"Anyway, it was my job to teach students adaptive skills. For example, I taught them how to ride the public buses—how to read a bus schedule, where to wait, and so forth. Anyway, I had this student with Down's syndrome. Let's call him Doug."

"Name changed to protect his confidentiality," somebody in the second row said.

"Yes, exactly! So, I was teaching Doug how to ride the bus. I told him to yank the little cord to let the driver know we wanted to get off. He yanked the cord. The driver slows down, pulls over, and opens the door. I start getting off the bus. Doug was right behind me."

Rob chuckled to himself, recalling what happened. "However, when I stepped onto the sidewalk and the bus door closed, Doug was nowhere to be found. As the bus pulled away, I see him sitting by a window, waving at me."

Wearing a goofy smile, Rob waved vigorously at his students.

"What did you do?" somebody toward the rear of the auditorium asked.

"What could I do?" Rob replied. "I ran!"

He imitated himself frantically chasing a bus along the street.

"The bus kept getting farther and farther ahead. I sprinted after it, all the while thinking, 'Shit! I'm going to get fired! You can't lose a student and keep your job!'"

Rob took a drink from his water bottle.

"Fortunately, a few blocks later, the bus stopped, and I was able to catch it before it drove away."

"Did you beat his retarded ass?" somebody asked.

"Intellectual disability," Rob corrected him. "As I said, don't use the r-word. It's like the n-word in the disability community. But to answer your question, you might say he was already *beating* himself."

The students blinked at him.

"When I got to where he was sitting, I found him with his pants unzipped—masturbating."

The class gasped.

"Gross!"

"What did you do?"

"You have to understand," Rob explained, "I'd just ran three blocks, chasing a bus! I was winded and getting ready to yell at him. Then I saw what he was doing. I was speechless! I simply stood there."

"Did anybody else see?"

"No," Rob said. "It was the middle of the day, and the bus was practically empty. I'll be honest with you… I had no clue what to do. I never had a course that covered students masturbating in public. Was I supposed to stop him? And how? I mean, I wasn't exactly eager to get any closer."

"You said you wanted to teach him where to get off," a male student shouted from the left side of the lecture hall. "I guess he learned!"

The class laughed. Rob laughed with them.

"This is what I want you to understand…" Rob paused, hinting that they should take notes. "One! People with intellectual disabilities are like everybody else. They have the same biological needs and sexual urges as you do."

The students murmured in astonishment.

"If I had a dollar for every time one of my students whipped it out and began… you know, I'd be a wealthy man. And I'm being serious. That's why we have to teach them when and where to do such things. And how to do them appropriately."

"Appropriately?"

"Yes. I've had several students who…" Rob tried to think of a proper way to say what he wanted to say. "…they were, um, a little too *enthusiastic* in their endeavor."

Groaning, several guys instinctively lowered their hands to their groin. Most of the female students, however, didn't seem to get the point.

"They," Rob said, "well, they hurt themselves in the act—if you understand me."

"That's what you teach in special education?" a woman called out, appalled. "Masturbation?"

Rob drew closer to the edge of the stage, trying to see who had spoken. "We teach whatever the child needs to learn. And, believe me, if they are masturbating in public or hurting themselves, yes—we need to address it. That's the second thing I want you to remember. Special education focuses on the child's unique needs. Yes, we might teach reading, writing, and arithmetic. But we might also focus on riding the public bus and learning how to keep it in your pants. Everything depends on the individual. Every day is completely different."

Several students leaned forward enthusiastically.

"Okay!" Rob pushed the spacebar on his laptop. The slide on the giant screen behind him changed. "Back to what we were talking about—"

"Wait!" somebody said. "What happened to Doug?"

"What do you mean?"

"Did he get in trouble?"

"Ah!" Rob gave a knowing look. "You tell me. What did we learn last time about disciplining students with disabilities?"

Hands shot into the air. Rob called on a brunette sitting in the middle of the auditorium. "What do you think?"

"You couldn't punish him," she said, "because his disability contributed to the behavior."

"Right! Good job. Does anybody remember what that's called? It's one of the main principles of the Individuals with Disabilities Education Act."

Half the class consulted their notebooks.

"Manifest determination," somebody yelled.

"Exactly!" Rob said. "Manifest determination is the process by which we determine if we can discipline a special education student because of their behavior. Now, let's return to the—*climax*—of our lecture!"

An enormous groan rumbled through the darkness in front of him.

Chapter 68

"He's talking filth in his classes!" Craig bellowed. Within an hour after the lecture, he'd heard about the masturbation story and had dragged Rob down to Mary. "I want him removed from his position immediately!"

"I was telling a story about an actual child with disabilities," Rob protested, still holding the remains of a grilled cheese sandwich he'd been eating when Craig stormed into his office. "The story had educational value!"

"Where in the bloody course description does it say you should talk about… *that*… in class?" Craig asked. "Where?"

Rob searched for somewhere to set his sandwich but found no place appropriate. "The course description specifically says we will cover adaptive behaviors and life skills."

"And how is that relevant to this?"

"Are you kidding? Masturbating—"

"Stop using that word!" Craig hissed.

"Mary…" Rob turned to the school director, sitting calmly behind her desk. Despite the volume of the argument, she appeared rather amused. "People believe individuals with intellectual disabilities are eternal children, that they don't ever grow up or deal with adult issues. But they do. They have the same biological needs as everybody else, including masturbation."

"Stop!" Craig exclaimed. "For the love of God, stop with your filth!"

Rob went on. "Teachers need to be able to address these issues before they occur in their classrooms. Because they won't be able to wish them away by covering their ears and saying *Stop! Stop! Stop!*"

"Oh, very clever! Very clever, indeed." Craig faced Mary. "There are rules. There are regulations. The state and our accrediting body require that we cover certain material. And smut isn't on the list!"

"Actually—" Rob typed on his phone. "—it is."

"What the hell are you prattling on about, you degenerate? Mary, I've been more than patient. But he's gone too far! First, he ruins our relationship with our most valuable student teaching placement site. Then he changes the names of his courses—without going through the official curriculum process, I might add. Now, he's talking filth to our impressionable young students. We can't have him harming our program any more than he already has!"

"According to our accreditation body," Rob said, "our courses are supposed to be aligned with the professional standards outlined by the Council on Exceptionalities." He slid a glance at Craig. "Not that you have updated our courses this century."

"Our courses are top-notch!" Craig huffed. "They cover everything special education teachers need to know when working with these types of problem children."

"You were saying?" Mary prompted Rob.

"COE's Standard 1.2 states—" Rob read from his phone. "—*special education professionals must understand the physical, cognitive and emotional development of individuals with exceptionalities.* Masturbating on a bus is a pretty clear example of not only the sexual development of adolescents with intellectual disabilities, but also an illustration of the deficits in adaptive behavior they often display."

"He's making all that up!" Craig said.

Rob offered him his phone. "It's right here on the COE's website."

Craig waved the phone away. "I don't care what he says, Mary. This kind of lewd and vulgar behavior is not what they want us to teach. Think of the scandal! Think of the outrage parents will have if word gets out he's talking about, about—"

"Masturbation?" Rob offered.

"Stop it!" Craig shouted again. "You might think this is funny, Polly. But I don't! The brilliant Dr. Larsen and I created this program. We were the first in the country to train teachers to work with crippled children. People came from all over the country to learn from us. And now you're destroying decades of our hard work!"

"Is it only masturbation you object to?" Rob asked, feigning interest. "Or is it all sex acts? Where do you stand on fellatio?"

"I don't even know what that is!"

"It's oral sex," Mary told him.

"That's it!" Craig cried to the heavens. "I'm not going to stand here and listen to this smut. I want him gone, Mary. Gone! Do you hear me? If he doesn't vacate his office by tomorrow, I'll... I'll... I'll bring the matter up with the Dean! Or... I'll call the press! That's what I'll do! I'll call the press and have a bunch of reporters here asking embarrassing questions!"

"Oh!" Mary grew serious. "I don't think the Captain would like that. Do you?"

Craig considered this, then resumed his rant. "I want him gone, Mary! Gone!" Marching out of Mary's office, he slammed the door behind him.

"I guess he doesn't want to schedule a meeting to discuss the matter," Mary said wistfully.

"Am I fired?" Rob asked.

"Absolutely not. The fact you're getting so many students to show up for class is a testament to your ability to engage them on their level. Keep it up!"

"Thanks, Mary. And I'm sorry if I said something wrong."

"It's nothing. Our students hear worse things on late-night television. Or the news!" She wrinkled her nose. "Did the boy really do that? Right there in public and all?"

"Mary, it happens all the time! Adolescents get excited when a warm wind blows, and they masturbate. Adolescents with intellectual disabilities do too. But they don't understand the social constructs governing when and where it's appropriate."

"Boy!" She grinned. "Who would've thought that special education was so—*stimulating?*"

"Ah!" Rob laughed. "Good one."

Chapter 69

Rob sat at his desk, a pile of tests to his left, a hotpot full of dark roast coffee to his right, and a red pen in-between. Surveying the mountain of ungraded exams, he realized Pete had been correct—he should've made things easier for himself. It wasn't that he should make his courses less challenging. He still firmly believed he should hold his students to a high standard. But giving short-answer and essay exams to over four hundred students at the same time was utterly asinine.

He muttered, "Live and learn."

Taking his pen, he began reading the first exam.

"Excuse me." A woman in a blue business suit and teased blonde hair stood in his doorway. She checked the nameplate on his door, which now said *Filth Peddler*. "Professor…?"

"It's Chudinski." Rob inclined his head at the nameplate. "My coworkers have a strange sense of humor."

"Nice coworkers."

"Tell me about it. How may I help?"

"Actually—" She put on the air of a salesperson about to give Rob the deal of a lifetime. "—I am hoping you'll let me help you! I understand you are teaching—" She checked her clipboard. "—almost everything by the looks of it. You must be new."

"I am. And you are?"

"Oh, I'm sorry." Pulling a large suitcase on wheels, she entered his office and shook his hand. "Ann Taylor. Scribe Hall Publishing. I'm your book representative. I was wondering if I could take a few moments of your time and show you our new products."

Not waiting for an answer, she unzipped her suitcase and began pulling out textbooks.

"We have several recently updated editions suitable for your Introduction to Abnormal Children course." She banged four shiny new textbooks next to his ungraded exams. "And here are a couple for your Characteristics of the Severely Crippled course." She added two more. "And…" She rechecked her clipboard. "…three for Assessing Disabled Students. And these are for Controlling the Behavior of the Disturbed and Curriculum for the Educable Child."

"Thank you." Rob peered over the wall of books she'd created. "But—"

"All of these are available online and are supported by numerous videos, test banks, and supplemental resources available on our website," she continued. "Students can even rent texts, which saves them money!"

Rob moved some of the books so he could see her. "I'm sure that's true, but—"

"And, of course, I will offer you the same arrangement your colleagues have taken advantage of over the years."

"Arrangement?"

"I'll give you a hundred dollars per title you assign your students. That's per semester, of course."

"You pay us to use your product?" Rob asked. Somehow, that didn't sound right.

"Absolutely. Your students get high-quality educational materials from the leader in academic publishing. We sell books. And you get a little something for your efforts. It's all completely legal. The pharmaceutical industry sends doctors on trips and gives them all kinds of freebies." She chuckled. "I bet you wish you were a real doctor, don't you?"

"I am a real doctor," Rob replied stiffly.

"Of course, you are!" She handed him a card and a catalog. "Here's our portfolio. And this is where you can reach me. I'll settle up with you once you place your order for the spring semester. Cash, okay? That way, you don't have to worry about taxes and all that."

"And all that…" Rob found himself saying. He'd never heard of taking money for adopting a textbook, but he was realizing there was a great deal they didn't teach him in his doctoral program.

"Fabulous!" She shook his hand again. "Thank you so much for your time. I'm very excited to be working with you. I hope to hear from you soon."

Rob stood. "Thanks for the books. Do I need to return the ones I don't use?"

The question seemed to stun her.

"No," she said. "I'm not about to lug them down six flights of stairs. They're all yours."

"Okay. Thanks."

"My pleasure." She consulted her clipboard again. "Say, have you seen Dr. Mullins? I haven't been able to get a hold of him, and his name isn't on his door."

"He..." Rob hemmed, not knowing what to reveal. "He's not part of the program anymore. I'm teaching his courses for the remainder of the year."

"You're teaching eight courses? I didn't think that was allowed."

Rob grimaced. "They're making a special exception for me."

"Wow! On the bright side, that certainly allows you to rake it in next semester!" She unzipped her suitcase again and piled more books onto Rob's desk. "Pete usually assigned three or four texts for each of his classes."

"Unfortunately, his students never read them."

"Either way, we both win!" She emptied her suitcase with a happy sigh. "Well, you've certainly freed up my day!"

"Glad to help."

She shook his hand a third time. "Thank you so much. I'm looking forward to a profitable relationship."

"Thanks, Ann."

Rob watched her leave, then began clearing away the books. There must be forty of them—all brand new. He was wondering how he'd find time to read them all when a squirrelly man with a greasy combover appeared in the doorway.

"May I help you?" Rob asked. The last thing he needed was more unscheduled visitors.

The man handed him a battered business card that read: *Barry B. Balkins. Book Buyer.* "Give me a second."

The book buyer scanned the ISBN codes for each of the books with a hand-held electronic device, then entered numbers into a calculator.

"I'm sorry," Rob said irritably. "I'm a bit busy. Could you please—?"

"I can give you eight hundred and fifty dollars for the lot of them."

"Eight hundred and fifty dollars?" Rob repeated.

"Okay—" Barry pulled a wad of folded bills from his pocket. "An even nine hundred. But that's as high as I can go."

Craig poked his head into Rob's office.

"Berry!" he said gleefully. "When you're done with Filth Peddler here, come to me. I have a bunch of books for you. And bring your wagon. You'll need it! Cha-ching!"

Chapter 70

"Sorry I'm late." Sid took off his winter coat, shook off the flecks of snow that had accumulated on his hood, then draped it over the empty chair next to Wendy. He sat across from Rob. "I went to the Starbucks in the Student Center. I'd forgotten you wanted to meet at this one. What did I miss?"

"No worries." Wendy warmed her hands around her Caffè Americano. Like most of Starbucks' customers, she still had her hat and coat on. "I just got here as well. I went to the one across the street by mistake. Rob was talking about the textbook scam."

"Oh, I know!" Sid said. "I made five hundred bucks! Can you believe it? Good timing, too. I need the money to fix my car."

Rob sipped his hot chocolate, then licked the whipped cream from his upper lip. "What's wrong with your car?"

"Fuel pump. I also need a battery that can withstand these brutal northern winters." Sid settled into his seat. "Anyway, how's everybody's week so far?"

"I've been swamped with grading," Wendy said. "I've read so many term papers on feminism in modern media my eyes are going cross."

"Me too," Rob replied. "But it's my fault for assigning essays. Next year I'm using scantron forms and have the testing center grade everything for me."

Wendy lifted her cup. "Hear! Hear!"

The barista called out, "Ronald!"

Behind them, an elderly man in a fedora shuffled to the counter and picked up his order.

"Hey!" Wendy said to Sid as if recalling something she'd forgotten. "How was your date Tuesday?"

"You had a date?" Rob adjusted his tone so he didn't sound astonished. "With whom?"

The door to the coffee shop opened, letting in a blast of icy air. Instinctively, everybody hunched forward.

"Her name is Claudia." Sid pulled his coat over his shoulders. "I met her at a furniture store last week. She was looking for a sofa; I was looking for a computer desk for my apartment. We hit it off, and she offered to show me around town a bit."

"How did it go?"

"It was fine," Sid said. "Nothing special. You know what I mean? I doubt I'll see her again."

"Didn't get laid?"

"Not even close! I got the wave goodnight." Sid put on a big smile and waved like the Queen of England.

"The wave? Talk about cold." Wendy huddled over her coffee. "You can do better. Don't worry."

"It's always difficult dating white women. With them, I'm that 'Indian guy.' We spend the first ten dates talking about me being Indian—what religion I believe in, who the god with all the arms is, is India really that hot? Like I'd know! I'm fifth-generation American. I've never even been out of the country."

The barista called out, "Jenny! Megan!" Two undergraduate students bundled in long coats, hats, and scarves stepped to the counter.

"With Indian women," Sid went on. "I'm simply a guy trying to get them into bed. It's a refreshing change. We can talk about other stuff."

The door opened again. Another wintery gust swirled through the lobby.

"It's not a racial thing," Sid insisted. "Not that one woman is more attractive than the other. It's merely a different frame of reference. Oh—" He said to Wendy, "Speaking of dates, how was yours?"

"You met somebody too!" Rob had been in Wisconsin longer than either of them, and the closest he'd gotten to a date was being kissed by a stripper. He was beginning to think he'd die alone.

"I did," Wendy told him. "But it wasn't anything with a future. She was basically a cis wanting a new experience."

"Rothgar the Bloodthirsty!" the barista shouted.

Sid stood. "That's me." He darted through the mass of bodies gathered around the counter.

Clutching her coffee, Wendy looked at Rob with a hint of pity. He could tell she was going to inquire about his dating life, but then changed her mind.

"How're your classes going?" she asked. "Still talking smut to your students?"

"You kidding? After the masturbation story exploding in my face, I'm afraid to say anything remotely controversial."

"You might not want to say masturbation and exploding in your face in the same sentence."

"Ha! Ha! But I'm serious."

Holding a venti coffee, Sid returned to the table. Taking off the lid, he inhaled the steam rising for his paper cup.

"Speaking of masturbation—" Rob continued.

"That's what you were talking about?" Sid asked. "Geez, I miss all the good stuff. Go on."

"You wouldn't believe what happened in class today." Rob took a sip of his now-lukewarm hot chocolate. He leaned in confidentially. Wendy and Sid did the same. "This morning, I was on stage lecturing about epilepsy when I see a couple in the middle of the auditorium snuggling really close. I mean, they were practically on top of each other."

"What do you expect?" Sid asked. "It's damned cold out. And they say the worst has yet to come. Do you know it routinely gets to minus twenty degrees Fahrenheit here? Minus twenty! I didn't think that was possible."

"Yeah, they were keeping each other warm, all right," Rob replied. "The guy had his hand so far up the girl's skirt, I thought he'd crawl inside of her. It was like that scene in Star Wars where Han Solo shoves Luke into the dead Tauntaun."

"You're kidding!"

Wendy rolled her eyes.

"I'm not!" Rob said. "It was embarrassing. She was right there in front of me while I lectured, arching her spine and whimpering. I was tempted to use her as an example of what a tonic seizure looked like."

"You should've!" Sid laughed. "That would've been funny. And they'd never do that again. At least not in your class."

Behind them, the barista hollered, "Sherry!"

"That's the problem." Rob ignored a middle-aged woman jostling him as she pushed by their table. "I'm afraid to say anything now. I stood there and froze."

"You froze because you're a sexually repressed white male," Wendy told him.

"I am not!"

Wendy reached across their table, took his hand in hers, and said seductively, "Clitoris."

Rob jerked his hand back. "Okay! Enough."

"See!"

"At least I'm not cold anymore," Sid said. "Thanks!"

"You two are such prudes," Wendy told them. "Have you forgotten what it was like being a college student?"

"What does being a college student have to do with voyeurism?" Rob asked.

Wendy looked at him, astounded. "You never had sex in class before?"

"No!"

"I was lucky to have it in my dorm room," Sid admitted. "Or anywhere else, for that matter."

"Boy, you two missed out." Wendy smiled as though recalling pleasant memories. "There's nothing like classroom sex."

"Changing the subject!" Rob announced.

"Fine." Wendy grew more serious. "Walrus still on the warpath?"

"Unfortunately. I swear he's having Bert and Les lurk outside my classrooms, listening to every conversation I have. I wouldn't be surprised if he bugged my office."

"Tina!" The barista surveyed the crowd. Nobody came to the counter. "Tina?"

"What are you going to do?" Wendy asked.

"What can I do?" Rob drank the dregs of his hot chocolate. "I'll watch everything I say—and pray I can find a way to keep my job."

Chapter 71

"Okay!" Rob strolled around the classroom. He enjoyed teaching his Assessing Children with Disabilities course because it was the only one with fewer than fifty students. Also, they were all special education majors and had at least some interest in the subject. "Let's go over it one more time."

Students grumbled under their breaths.

"What are the main differences between somebody with LD versus ID?" he asked.

One of the few males in class appeared lost.

"Question, Mike?"

"Yeah…" The student shot a sheepish expression at the people sitting next to him. "Um. What's LD again?"

"Learning disabilities. Also called SLD or specific learning disabilities. Dyslexia, dysgraphia, and dysnomia are all examples of SLDs."

"Right!" Mike wrote something down. "And… ID?"

Rob took a deep breath, trying to hide his impatience.

"It stands for intellectual disabilities," he told him. "Some people prefer to use the term intellectual disability—singular. However, I believe the condition is caused by many different syndromes, hence the plural."

"Gotcha!"

"Good."

Rob resumed walking around the classroom, giving them time to check their notes. He also liked to see what people doodled during the lectures. One student had a series of stick figures in the margins of her notebook doing incredibly pornographic things.

"What's one difference?" he asked. "Think back to the videos we watched. What did you notice?"

A woman in the front row raised her hand.

"Yes, Samantha," Rob said. "Impress me."

"Well, I'm not sure how to say this, but people with mental retard—" She corrected herself. "People with intellectual disabilities seem to have problems with, well, everything."

"And people with learning disabilities?"

"Their problems are more with school stuff."

"Good start!" Rob wove his way down another aisle. "Kids with ID tend to have global deficits. That is, they may have problems processing abstract concepts, such as understanding math or people's emotions. They also have poor adaptive skills."

One of the students got up and stumbled out of class. This wasn't unusual. Students at Eastern Wisconsin seemed to have bladders the size of thimbles. They couldn't last ten minutes without going to the bathroom.

"Who can give me an example of an adaptive skill?" Rob asked, looking around. "Anybody?"

Another woman raised a tentative hand.

Rob called on her. "Claire! Give me one example."

"Oh, I'm not answering the question." Clare nodded to the empty desk the student who'd left had vacated. "I don't think Sanna's feeling well. She was all white and sweaty."

"Really? Hold on…" Rob made for the door. "Keep reviewing your notes about ID and LD. See if you can come up with three key differences between the two conditions. I'll be right back."

Stepping into the hallway, Rob found Sanna leaning against the wall, shaking.

"Hey, Sanna?" He approached her. "You feeling okay? Do you want me to call—?"

Eyes rolling upward, she collapsed into his arms.

At that moment, Craig turned the corner. He saw Rob and then the woman he was holding. He pointed at them. "Now I've got you! I've got you dead to rights!"

He sprinted away as fast as his bulk would allow.

Looking down, Rob suddenly realized he was clutching the student's breasts.

"Shit!"

He let go, the unconscious student slamming into the floor.

Chapter 72

"He was fondling her breasts," Craig bellowed. "Right there in the hallway! I saw him!"

Craig and Rob were back in Mary's office, but this time the school director didn't appear amused at all.

"Let me explain," Rob said earnestly.

"You can't explain your way out this," Craig told him. "Not this time. I saw you. And don't deny it!"

Mary motioned for Rob to continue. "Go on. What happened?"

Rob took a deep breath, trying to calm himself.

"I was teaching class, and Sanna got up—"

"Is that the student?" Mary asked.

"Yeah," Rob said, feeling a bit light-headed. "She got up and left. I went on teaching because I thought she was going to use the restroom. But then a student who was sitting next to her said she didn't appear well. She said Sanna was pale and sweating. So I went out into the hallway."

"Where he was alone with her!" Craig said.

Rob nodded reluctantly. "We were alone." Then he added, "But only for a minute. Not more. I swear to god!"

Craig made a dismissive sound.

"Then what?" Mary asked.

"Then—" Rob knew what he was about to say sounded crazy. He wondered whether Mary would believe him. "And then she fainted into my arms."

"Oh, nonsense!" Craig said. "He's making it sound like she swooned at his feet, falling in love with the dreamy young researcher. This isn't a black and white movie!"

"What happened after that?" Mary asked solemnly.

Rob wiped the sweat from his brow. He wanted to sit, but Mary's coat and purse were on the extra chair. He leaned against it, his legs trembling.

"Then Craig came around the corner and saw us. He yelled something and ran away."

"I ran to get help," Craig corrected him. "The poor girl was being molested, right there in our hallowed halls! Molested by him!" He pointed at Rob.

Mary watched Rob closely. "And?"

Rob dithered, wondering how much to reveal. He didn't like lying but telling the truth might dig him into a deeper hole. Then again, sooner or later, Mary would talk to the student and hear what had happened.

"I realized," Rob said, "that when I caught her, I was... I was holding on to her... her—chest."

"Oh, dear." Mary's face drained of color.

Craig sprang forward. "Ah-ha! There it is! He admitted it! He admitted it! You heard him, Mary. You heard him. Throw the scoundrel out on his child-molesting ass!"

Mary appeared as shaken as Rob felt. "Is there anything else I need to know?"

"No." Then Rob added, "Not really. But... seeing where my hands inadvertently were... I let go and Sanna fell to the floor. That's how she bruised her forehead."

"Oh!" Craig rubbed his hands together. "You're gone, Polly! Gone! You can't talk your way out of this. Molesting a student! Even you can't let him stay, Mary. Fire him!"

"I didn't molest her, Mary! Honest. She fell into my arms and I... well, I grabbed hold. It was all instinct." Rob said, hoping it'd help, "I'm sorry."

"He's sorry!" Craig cackled. "Did you hear that? He's sorry. Well, sorry doesn't pay the bills!"

"I'm sorry too, Rob," Mary told him. "But I'm going to have to refer this to legal counsel. This is out of my depth."

"Can they fire me for something like this?" Rob asked. "I was trying to catch her!"

"I'm afraid so. Also—" Mary frowned. "They may refer the matter to the city police department."

"Jail!" Craig cried triumphantly. "That's even better than firing. I told you I'd get you, Polly. I told you. Now I finally have!"

Chapter 73

Rob stood in the sixth-floor hallway, listening to Craig hum merrily to himself as he rummaged in his office. Taking a deep breath, he wiped his shaking hands onto his already damp pant legs, then tapped on Craig's open door.

"Hey… Craig?"

Craig recoiled in feigned horror. "Oh, no! The molester!"

"That's not funny."

"Do you see me laughing, Polly?" Craig pointed to his face. "No. I'm smiling. See!" He smiled broadly.

"This is serious!"

Craig sat in his chair; its wheels still encased in great globs of rubber cement. "You should've thought about that before you molested that poor defenseless girl."

"I didn't do anything!" Rob said. "And stop using that word!"

"What? Molested? Isn't that the term for when somebody forces themselves on an innocent child? You're a molester! That's what you are. A mo—lest—er!" Sitting on the edge of his immobilized seat, he reached forward and searched through papers spread across his enormous desk. "From the moment I set eyes on you, I knew you were no good. But nobody believed me. Everybody thought you were oh-so-smart and good-looking. The talented young researcher here to save us all! Now that you've shown your true colors, everybody will know what a fiend you truly are."

"Craig," Rob pleaded. "We're not talking about me losing my job here. We're talking about me going to jail."

"Yes, well—it serves you right. You thought you were so clever, didn't you? That you have all the answers. What you are is smug and arrogant. Look at you. How clever are you now, Polly?"

"Craig!" Tears rose in Rob's eyes. "This isn't funny. We're talking about my freedom! My career!"

Craig ignored him.

"You want me to apologize?" Rob asked, his voice cracking. "Fine! I apologize. You want me to say kids with disabilities can't learn? Fine! They can't learn. Just tell Mary what happened. Tell her that Sanna fainted and I caught her. Tell her I was holding her up!"

"Holding her up?" Craig repeated contemptuously. "That's not what I saw."

"This is my life! This is my career!"

Craig stopped sifting through his papers. "You should've never tangled with me, Polly. I'm going to make sure you never work in this field again. Do you understand? By the time I get done with you, not even a community college will give you an interview."

"Craig! Please!"

"I'll see you at the hearing tomorrow. Until then—" He pointed to the hallway. "—get out!"

Chapter 74

"Thanks for being with me," Rob told Wendy.

They were sitting on a bench outside the main conference room in the Administration Building. Inside, Craig was telling the Faculty Disciplinary Committee what he'd witnessed, probably in graphic and exaggerated detail.

"It's my pleasure." Wendy corrected herself. "I'm sorry. I didn't mean that. I meant—"

"I know what you meant." Rob smiled weakly at her. "Think Sid will make it?"

"He has class."

"That's right. I forgot."

In the conference room, Craig's voice reached a Hitler-like fervor. It echoed down the polished marble hallway.

"You okay?" Wendy asked.

Rob was about to say he was fine, but he couldn't. His heart pounded so hard, he thought he was having a heart attack.

"No," he said finally. "No, I'm not. Not being renewed because of a petty personality conflict is one thing. Being dismissed mid-semester for molesting a student is another." He struggled to breathe. "I could go to jail."

"Stop using that word! You didn't molest anybody. You touched her boobs. What's the big deal?"

"It's one of those things they frown upon if you're a male professor."

"It's still stupid! Everybody treats them like they're sacred relics or something. Honestly, they're just like elbows or earlobes."

Rob bent his head. He couldn't keep the tears away much longer. "I think they're a bit different than elbows or earlobes."

"Maybe." Wendy rubbed his back. "What did the student say? Didn't she tell them what'd happened?"

"She doesn't remember anything. One moment she was in class. The next, she was lying on the floor, a bunch of paramedics around her."

"You're going to be fine. You know that, right? They're reasonable people. Present your evidence and… everything will be fine."

Unable to speak, Rob nodded. Wendy had been saying 'everything will be fine' all day. It was becoming a vocal tic. Unfortunately, he wasn't sure she believed it any more than he did.

The door to the conference room opened as a dour-faced assistant stepped into the corridor.

"Dr. Chudinski?" she asked softly. It sounded as though she was about to escort him to the electric chair. "They're ready for you."

Wendy squeezed his hand. "Good luck."

Rob nodded. "Thanks."

Entering the conference room, Rob found a table long enough to seat forty people. Each chair contained somebody wearing an expensive suit and a bleak expression. The chairs lining the far wall were also filled. As soon as he entered, every head turned toward him.

"There he is," Craig said, sitting by the windows overlooking the quad. "The molester!"

"That's enough, Dr. Grubber." The Provost indicated the empty chair at the far end of the table. "Dr. Chudinski, if you could have a seat, we'd like to ask you a few questions."

"Allow me, Your Honor." Standing, Craig buttoned his jacket. Then, lunging forward, he stabbed his finger inches from Rob's nose. "Where were you on the night of November 13th?"

Flustered, Rob recoiled. "What? I— I—"

"Dr. Grubber," the Provost said. "We'll ask the questions. If you'll both please take your seats."

Craig sat with a satisfied grunt.

"Now, Dr. Chudinski—" The Provost folded his hands and looked sternly down the table at Rob. "—I'm sure you're aware how serious the accusations against you are."

"Yes, sir," Rob said, trying to speak clearly.

"We cannot, and will not, take any kind of sexual contact between faculty and a student lightly. Especially when the contact is uninvited and the student was unable to respond on her own accord."

"Yes, sir."

"Could you please tell us what occurred on the afternoon of November 13th?"

"Yes, sir." Trying to exude a sense of confidence that wasn't there, Rob sat as straight as possible. "I was teaching my class and a student staggered out of the room."

"I'm sorry." A woman at the far end of the table cupped her hand behind her ear. "Could you speak up, please?"

"Sure." Eyeing the pitcher of water just out of arm's reach, Rob cleared his dry throat. "I was teaching my class and a student staggered out of the room," he repeated louder. "I went into the hallway to check on her, and she fainted into my arms. I caught her and, well, in doing so, I inadvertently grabbed her… her—chest."

Craig leaped to his feet. "See! I told you!"

"Dr. Grubber…" The Provost said, annoyed.

Craig returned to his seat, his face split by a gloating grin.

"Why did she faint?" asked a woman with grey hair in a tight bun. "Do you have any idea?"

"According to the paramedics," Rob replied, trying to be as factual as possible, "she was dehydrated and had a fever. She also didn't have anything to eat that morning."

"I see."

Several people wrote on their yellow legal pads.

"How long were you alone with the student?" a gentleman sitting next to the Provost asked. He wore a shiny gold watch that probably cost more than Rob's new car.

Rob thought for a moment. "Maybe three seconds before Dr. Grubber arrived."

"Three seconds?" Craig scoffed. "That's highly unlikely!"

"Dr. Grubber, please." The Provost motioned for Rob to go on. "You were saying?"

"It all happened very fast. I was teaching and Sanna left the room. Then a student said she didn't look well. So, I went to check on her. I stepped into the hallway and found her leaning up against the wall. Then she fainted and I caught her. That's when Dr. Grubber came around the corner."

"Strange coincidence, I'd say," Craig muttered.

Everybody ignored him.

Rob went on, "After Dr. Grubber ran to get help, I was alone with Sanna another four or five seconds. That's when some of my students came out of the classroom to see what was going on. Oh!" Rob dug into his briefcase. "Here are their accounts. Once the paramedics left, I had them document everything they saw and heard. I'm sorry I didn't make copies for everybody."

Craig shot to his feet again. "Inadmissible!"

"Dr. Grubber!" the Provost shouted. Craig took his seat. "May I see those, Dr. Chudinski?"

"Yes, sir." Rob handed the papers to the assistant, who delivered them to the Provost. He put on a pair of wire-rimmed glasses and began reading.

"To be clear," the man sitting next to the Provost said, "you admit to grabbing the student's breasts."

"Yes, sir. Inadvertently. She fainted forward. That is, into my arms. And I tried to catch her. I'm sorry."

People around the table took more notes.

"And you say you were alone with her a combined total of seven to eight seconds?" the man next to the Provost asked.

"Yes, sir," Rob replied. "About that. If you read my students' accounts, many of them indicated that I was gone for less than a minute."

"This student," the Provost said, reading one of the papers, "says you were gone *a few minutes*. Minutes. Not seconds." He looked over his glasses at Rob.

Rob lifted a hand. Sweat prickled his forehead. "I don't think he meant that literally. If you read the rest of them, some clearly indicate—"

Craig vaulted to his feet again. "Oh, what does it matter? Is it so much better that he only molested her for a few seconds versus a few minutes? Are we the type of university that allows such deviants to teach our students? Do you think parents will send their precious children to us if they know somebody like him is a faculty member? I say, get rid of him before his presence stains our hallowed halls!"

"Dr. Grubber..." Provost gritted his teeth. "Sit down. Be quiet. And stop using the phrase 'hallowed halls'!"

Craig sat as the Provost returned to reading the students' accounts.

"I'm not sure what the issue is here," a diminutive man to Rob's left said. "He admits to touching the student's breasts. What more do we need to know?"

A rustle of agreement rippled around the table.

Craig bounced in his seat, struggling not to say anything.

"The issue we need to determine," the person next to the Provost said, "is the context of the contact. If you accidentally bumped into a woman's chest while walking through a crowded corridor, the implications would be significantly different than had you reached out and seized them with intent."

"Then the question is…" the woman who asked Rob to speak louder said, "does the evidence support Dr. Chudinski's claim that she fainted into his arms?"

The person immediately in front of Craig raised his hand. The Provost called on him.

"I have two questions." He consulted his notes. "First, what level of proof do we need to act? And second, does Dr. Chudinski need to prove his innocence, or do we need to prove his guilt?"

All eyes turned to the man sitting next to the Provost.

"We must remember," he said, "this is not a legal proceeding. We do not use terms like 'guilt' or 'innocence.' Your task is to determine whether Dr. Chudinski violated university policy and whether it is in the interest of the university and its students for him to retain his current position."

An uneasy silence descended upon the conference room, broken periodically by the Provost turning pages.

Somebody knocked on the door. It opened. Tiffani entered, dressed in a business suit almost identical to the one worn by the woman who'd retrieved Rob from the hallway.

"I'm sorry for being late," she said.

The Provost peered at her over the rims of his reading glasses. "And you are?"

"Tiffani Miller, secretary for the Special Education Department, sir."

"What are you doing here?" Craig growled under his breath.

"Yes," the Provost said, "I'd like to know that as well. Do you have any connection to this hearing?"

Tiffani appeared slightly confused. "I was told to be here. I was in the hallway when the incident occurred."

More murmurs filled the room.

"I told you not to—!" Craig said.

"Dr. Grubber," the Provost said. "Go wait outside."

"But… Your Honor!"

"Go wait outside! I'm not telling you again."

As Craig marched out, he made pointed eye contact with Tiffani. She didn't return his gaze.

"Would you like me to step outside as well?" Rob asked.

"You're fine where you are," the Provost said. "Provided you don't act like a jackass or call me 'Your Honor.'"

The Provost faced Tiffani, still standing by the door. "Could you shed some light on what you saw, Ms. Miller? We're particularly interested in the events leading immediately up to Dr. Chudinski's contact with the student."

"Yes, sir." She said loud enough for everybody to hear, "I was walking along Agnew Hall's first floor south hallway. A woman stumbled out of a room up ahead of me. I thought she had been drinking. Then Dr. Chudinski came out and she collapsed face-first into his arms. He caught her."

"And for how long did Dr. Chudinski hold onto the student?"

Tiffani thought. "A second or two. Then Dr. Grubber came around the corner and yelled, 'I've got you now!' Dr. Chudinski let go of the student and she fell to the floor."

Everybody began talking.

"As I told Dr. Grubber," Tiffani went on matter-of-factly, "Dr. Chudinski wasn't molesting the student. He was trying to help her."

The Provost took off his glasses. "You *told* Dr. Grubber you saw the student faint into Dr. Chudinski's arms?"

"Yes, sir. We discussed the incident several times. He's the one who indicated that I should come here at four-thirty." She looked at the clock on the wall behind her. It read quarter to four. "Good thing I arrived early."

"Yes." The Provost slammed the papers he'd been reading. "Good thing, indeed! Dr. Chudinski, you're dismissed with my thanks for aiding an obviously ill student. And for your honesty. Both are greatly appreciated. Please send Dr. Grubber in as you leave. I'd like to speak with him."

Chapter 75

"Here's to Rob, the breast-groping professor!" Wendy cheered as she lifted her sixth beer of the evening.

"Shhhh!" Rob hissed. He shot furtive glances around Vino's. It was a quiet Wednesday night, and more than half the tables were empty. A couple of guys at the bar looked in their direction, but then turned away. "That's not funny!"

Head wobbling, Wendy wrapped her arms around Rob's neck. "I'm sorry. But, honestly, they're only boobs. Why's everybody afraid of them? Here." She hefted her breasts at him. "Touch them! Go ahead. I won't sue."

Turning red, Rob pushed Wendy back. "Put those away! You're going to poke somebody's eye out."

Wendy peeked under her sweater. "I suppose it is cold outside."

Rob took Wendy's Guinness Draught. "I think you've had enough to drink. I don't want your students seeing you like this."

"Screw the students! They're the ones who got you into this mess. If she'd said nothing happened from the start, you wouldn't have gone through all of that." Wendy straightened as if suddenly realizing something. "You know… this job would be great if we didn't have any damned students!"

"It wasn't her fault." Rob started to take a drink, then realized it was Wendy's bottle. "It's Craig's. He knew I was holding her up. He made it sound like I had her pinned against the wall, fondling her."

"Asshole. We should do something about him."

Sid lifted his head from the table, his eyes straining to focus. "How many beers do we have left?"

"Sixty-two," Rob told him.

Groaning, Sid lay back down.

"Christ!" Wendy leaned against Rob. "We're never going to get those damned mugs."

Their waitress came to their table. "Another?"

"No!" Sid muffled voice said.

"I believe he means—*no, thank you.*" Rob opened his wallet. "And thanks for putting up with us all night."

"No problem." She took his credit card. "I hope you enjoyed your celebration."

"We did. Thanks."

"I'll be right back with your receipt."

"Take your time."

Watching their waitress go to the register, Rob wondered if he would get a reputation around campus for grabbing women. Then he realized it didn't matter what people at Eastern Wisconsin thought. He only had one more semester left there anyway.

Wendy nudged Rob's elbow. "Why aren't you happy? After what you've been through, you should be ecstatic!"

"I don't know," he said, wondering the same thing. "I suppose because nothing's changed. I mean, I'm still not going to get reappointed. I'm still going to have to leave. Students will still graduate thinking that kids with disabilities can't learn."

"Oh, come on! Don't be a buzzkill. Be happy!" She shook his arm playfully. "And things *have* changed! Now people know Walrus is after you. Important people like the Provost and that university lawyer guy. And all the people in that room! They all know he was being... you know, assholish. Now maybe he'll be too afraid to vote against you."

"Maybe..."

The waitress set a small black folder on the table. "Here you go!"

Adding a sizable tip to the total, Rob signed the receipt, then handed the folder back. "Thanks again."

"No problem. Enjoy your evening."

Rob pulled Wendy's coat around her. "Okay, you guys." He tapped Sid's head. Sid moaned. "Time for me to drive you two home."

"Hey!" Wendy slid her arm into her coat sleeve. "So, so what happened to the stripper?"

"Her name is Ms. Miller."

"Right. Her."

Rob guided Sid to his unsteady feet.

"I haven't seen her since the hearing. I'm sure Craig will fire her, if he hasn't already. Which is a shame. She needs the insurance."

"You know what she should do?" Wendy leaned against the table. "The stripper? She should sue him. Sue his fat ass off for wrongful something. You know?"

Rob pulled on his coat, hat, and gloves. He wasn't looking forward to stepping outside. It was damn cold, and nothing kept out the Wisconsin wind. Then again, it might sober his companions up.

He guided them to the door. "I'm sure she can't afford a lawyer."

"Hey!" Wendy bumped into him. "That's what you should do, too. Sue. Sue his fat ass off! I mean, he has no reason to deny you reappointment. There're no criteria, right?"

"Right." Rob zipped up her coat. "You two able to get to my car? Or should I pick you up at the door?"

Sid plopped down into an empty booth. "Door."

"Okay. Stay here."

Rob made to leave, but Wendy snatched his arm.

"Rob!" she said. "You're not listening. Sue! Sue him for everything he's got! I bet he's violet… violetted…"

"Violated?" Rob offered.

"Right! I bet he's violetted a bunch of laws. You can't fire somebody willy-nilly. You can't! And… and he, he didn't like you from the start. Right?"

Rob propped her up against the table. "Right."

"See!" she said as if her point was obvious. "You had no chance!"

"Stay here. Okay? Don't move. I'll be back in a second."

Wendy hugged him. "I mean it!" She rested her head against his chest, closed her eyes, and said dreamily, "Sue! Sic a lawyer on him. That'll show the fat walrus bastard!"

Chapter 76

Rob lifted his head from his nice, cool pillow. As if seen through a mostly empty beer bottle, his bedroom sloshed hazily around him. He listened to the still darkness.

The doorbell jingled again.

Groaning, he rolled over and checked his alarm clock. Its red lights glowed 2:11 am. He'd only been asleep for about twenty minutes.

"What the hell?"

Rob propped himself on his elbows, debating whether he should answer the door. As his grandmother used to say, visitors in the night were rarely friends. Of course, she was referring to the Russian and German soldiers who frequently visited her village in Poland. He had no clue who would stop by this late, but he guessed it was important.

Swinging his legs out of bed, he steadied himself against the nightstand, then pulled on the clothes that lay crumpled about the floor.

The doorbell rang again.

Stumbling downstairs, he could see somebody standing on the front step. He opened the door, fridge air slapping him in the face.

"Ms. Miller?" She was wearing a skin-tight police officer's uniform, black high-heeled boots, and fishnet stockings. Handcuffs dangled from her leather belt. For a very fuzzy moment, he thought she was going to arrest him. "Come in. What did I tell you about wearing stuff like that in this weather? You should have a coat."

He closed the door behind her.

"Sorry for coming so late." She shivered. "I came by after I got off work, and you weren't here. Then I drove by again and saw your car in the driveway. I took a chance that you might still be up."

"Is everything okay?"

She lifted a shoulder. "Craig fired me."

"Oh, god." Rob leaned in to hug her, but then thought better of it. In his drunken state, he might not be able to control where his hands went. "I'm sorry. You know, I think you could fight it. I mean, maybe get a lawyer and—"

"No. I don't want that job anymore. Performing on stage is one thing…" She trailed off.

"I understand." He motioned to the couch. "Come in. Sit down. Would you like to have a drink or something?"

"Are you having one?"

They sat on the sofa in the living room.

"No," Rob said, painfully aware his hair was going every which way. "I reached my limit a few hours ago."

She grinned faintly. "Looks like it."

He suddenly remembered why he'd been out all night. "Hey, I want to thank you for coming to the hearing and saying what you said."

"I was happy to do it."

"Well, you saved my ass today. Or yesterday, that is. And I appreciate it. Good thing you were walking along the hallway when you did. Believe me. Otherwise, I'd be out of a job. Not just my job—my career. Hell, I could be in jail right now!"

He caught something in her eyes.

"You weren't in the hallway at all, were you?" he asked.

Her grin became more genuine. "I told Craig I was. He told me to keep quiet. When he threatened me, I decided I didn't want to live like that anymore. Feeling afraid and guilty and everything. It's time for me to do something else anyway, so I thought I'd help you out."

"Thanks. I owe you, big time."

She shrugged. "It was the right thing to do."

The grandfather clock in the dining room chimed the quarter-hour.

"What are you going to do?" Rob asked.

"I interviewed for a job working at an art gallery up in Green Bay. It's really nice. I also enrolled in the art program. I don't think I'll ever earn a lot selling my stuff. But I can make good money at the club, at least while I'm still young and pretty enough to dance."

"What about insurance?"

"After six months, I'll get some through the gallery. It won't cover much, but it isn't too expensive."

"That's good." Rob tried to think of something supportive to say. "Look, I really want to thank you again for—"

She launched herself into his arms. For many minutes, they kissed. Then Rob pulled reluctantly away, his heart thumping.

"I have to stop."

"Is it because of…?" She tugged at her outfit.

Rob's gaze slipped to Tiffani's exposed cleavage, then down her long legs. He wrestled with his drunken urges. "You're a student."

She seemed relieved. "And when I graduate?"

"I'll take you out to celebrate."

She put her hand on his thigh. "You're the only one who's ever treated me like, like…" She started crying, mascara and glitter tumbling down her cheeks.

He held her hand.

"Things are going to be different," he said, attempting to sound inspirational. "But they'll be okay. Everything will be fine. You'll see."

She got a Kleenex from her purse and dabbed it at her eyes. "Craig is still going to get you. You know that, right?"

"I think he'll ease off a bit. The Provost yelled at him pretty good."

She shook her head. "That's not how he is."

"Don't worry about me. I'll be fine."

"You know—" She sniffled. "—if you want to stay here, you'll have to learn how to play their game."

"Game?"

"I mean, well, when Craig gets angry at me, I usually give him something else to think about. Something that will distract him. You should do the same."

"Unfortunately—" Rob gestured to his wrinkled clothes. His sweatshirt was inside out. "I don't think he'd get distracted by all of this."

Tiffani choked on a laugh. Then she touched the side of his unshaven face. "Be careful."

"I will. And if you ever need anything… If Craig or anybody bothers you, you let me know. Okay?"

"I will." She stood. "Oh, I almost forgot." She pulled a much-folded packet of papers from her purse. "I found this. I thought you might want it."

"What is it?"

"It's the most recent departmental handbook. Last week, I told Craig that Mary asked for a copy, and he gave me this."

Rob examined the front cover. It was dated August 1998.

She kissed his cheek. "I hope it helps."

Chapter 77

"So those are the primary principles of the Individuals with Disabilities Education Act, or IDEA," Rob said to his classroom full of parents.

This was the tenth workshop he'd put on, and each time more parents came. Some even attended multiple sessions. He was considering recording the presentations and putting them online. That would free up his time considerably; however, he'd miss interacting with his audience. They always made him feel useful and wanted.

He peered at the darkness outside the snow-flecked windows and then at his phone.

"They're going to start securing the building for the night, so I'm sorry to say our time is up. If you have any questions, feel free to contact me. My e-mail address is on the business card I included in your handouts. Also, I recommend you look at the resources I listed on the last page. You'll find some great videos on YouTube about things like IEPs and 504 Plans. Watch them at your leisure, and—thanks for coming!"

The parents clapped enthusiastically. Rob bowed.

Many people came forward and thanked him in person. A few called him 'wonderful.' A mother of a child with autism hugged him and said he was a 'godsend.' As they filed out into the dimly lit corridor, Rob said goodbye and asked them to drive safely.

"Excuse me," he called to an exiting parent who'd been sitting at the far end of the room. "Mr. Nguyen?"

Mr. Nguyen looked about the crowd, trying to determine who called his name. Rob waved him over.

"Thank you very much for an informative workshop, Dr. Chudinski." He shook Rob's hand. "We all appreciate it."

"I'm glad it was useful. Say… when everybody introduced themselves, you indicated that you were a lawyer."

A knowing expression crept across Mr. Nguyen's face. "DUI?"

"What? No. Not at all."

"Parking tickets?"

"Tons, but that's not what I wanted to ask you about." Suddenly feeling as though approaching Mr. Nguyen was a bad idea, Rob changed his mind. "I'm sorry. I'm guessing you get pestered about legal stuff all the time. How about if I schedule an appointment and come in when you're working?"

"It's no problem. Go ahead." Mr. Nguyen sat at one of the desks. "Consider it payback for what you're doing for us."

The last participant left, leaving them alone.

Rob sat. "Okay, this is the deal. Every year we have to go up for reappointment."

"You mean you're on a one-year contract that gets renewed annually?"

"Right."

"Okay. I'm with you."

"Anyway, I've had a bit of a personality conflict with my department chair, who has indicated he's not going to renew my contract. And, well, I hate to sound like my students, but—it seems kind of unfair."

"I'm sure the university has some sort of rules governing the renewal process," Mr. Nguyen said. "What do they say?"

"That's just it," Rob replied. "You see, the university guidelines say each unit's tenured faculty vote and that their recommendation goes to the School Director and then to the College Dean and then to the Provost. The university guidelines say the decision is supposed to be based upon the criteria in each unit's handbook. But the Special Education Department, my academic unit, our handbook doesn't talk about reappointment. There are no criteria at all."

"It doesn't say anything?"

"There's a brief section about how we're expected to remain current in our areas of expertise and that we are supposed to…" Rob recited from memory, *"adequately perform the essential job functions of our positions."*

"Have you ever been told what your position's essential job functions are?" Mr. Nguyen asked.

"No." Then, trying to be completely accurate, Rob added, "Not exactly. The only thing that comes close is the advertisement for the position, which stated I'm expected to teach, conduct scholarly activities, and provide service to the department, school, university, and community."

"Well," Mr. Nguyen said, thinking. "Keep in mind, I am an intellectual copyright attorney. Labor law isn't my specialty. But I think you have some grounds here, should you not be renewed. You can bring a suit saying it would be impossible to evaluate you fairly given there are no evaluation criteria."

"Exactly!"

"However, that may not be of any help to you."

"Why not?"

"You see, these things take time. With all the hearings and motions for discovery, you may not see a judgment for years."

"Years?"

"And the university lawyers will know you can't hang around waiting to get your contract reauthorized. They'll drag their feet and ask for continuances and so forth."

"While I rack up legal fees."

"You got it. And even when your case is brought before a judge, there's no guarantee you'll get the ruling, especially if the university can show you shouldn't be retained due to incompetence or insubordination. If you push them, they may push back."

Rob slumped in his chair. "Great."

"If you ask me," Mr. Nguyen continued, "it sounds like your best bet is to get some guidelines written into the handbook, and then you have something you can react to. You can show you met the stated criteria beyond a reasonable doubt."

"Get something in the handbook…" Rob repeated pensively.

"I think that's your best option."

Chapter 78

"Okay, that takes care of our old business," the chair of the Committees on Committees said. Around the table, faculty members stared at their phones and laptops. "Is there anything new we need to consider?"

Rob's raised his hand, but the chair called on an elderly gentleman from the Economics Department.

"I believe," the professor said with excruciating slowness, "we need to look into how much salt they put down when it snows. Last week, I was going into Elagabalus Hall and it was like walking on marbles. They put so much salt down it covered the entire sidewalk. I could've broken my neck!"

"Motion to consider the proposal?" the chair asked.

Somebody lifted a listless hand.

"Second?"

Another person inclined a finger.

"Discussion?"

Nobody said anything.

"The motion is to examine the salting practices used by grounds." The chair studied a list of committees. "Where should we send it?"

"We can send it to the Committee on Safety," somebody suggested.

"All in favor?"

'Aye's' rumbled dully throughout the room.

"Nays?"

No response.

"Abstentions?"

Still nothing.

"Motion carries." The chair scribbled something on a pad of paper, then thumbed through her notes. "Okay, it looks like our next meeting will be on—"

"Excuse me." Rob waved his hand.

"Yes?"

"Faculty in my department requested that I bring up an issue regarding reappointment criteria. It seems some academic units don't have any, which could lead to significant legal ramifications if somebody were to challenge a unit's decision. I'd recommend we send the issue to the Faculty Recruitment and Retention Committee."

"Units don't have reappointment criteria?" the chair asked. "How do they make reappointment decisions?"

"That's the issue," Rob replied, trying to sound knowledgeable without being invested in the problem. "Nobody knows. We can have the FRR committee investigate that as well."

"Very well. Motion to approve?"

Rob raised his hand again.

"Second?"

Somebody at the far end of the table nodded.

"Discussion?"

He held his breath.

"All in favor?"

"Aye!" Rob said.

"Nays? Abstentions? Motion carried."

Chapter 79

The next day, Rob was sitting in his office, creating the final examination for Pete's Teaching Retarded Kids to Read course, when Craig sauntered in.

"Here you go, Polly." Craig threw a thick file onto Rob's already cluttered desk. "As your direct supervisor, I am officially assigning you this work. And I've done some checking with the university lawyers. According to chapter twelve, section seven, paragraph three of our governing bylaws, failure to perform essential job functions is grounds for *immediate* dismissal. And these tasks I'm officially giving you…" He tapped the file. "…are essential functions of your job. Failure to carry them out will…"

He seemed to lose his train of thought.

"Result in my immediate dismissal?" Rob offered.

"Precisely! That's what I'm saying. Failure to perform these official essential job functions will result in your immediate dismissal!"

"Very well." Rob took the file. "I officially accept these tasks as essential functions of my job and will complete them with all due haste."

Attempting to determine whether Rob was being sarcastic, Craig scowled. "See that you do. And make sure you do them before the end of the semester. I want all of our work completed promptly!"

"No problem." Rob looked up from his keyboard. Craig was still standing there. "Anything else?"

"What? No. Not at the moment. But rest assured, there will be more where that came from. Good day!"

Rob leafed through the papers Craig had given him. As he anticipated, it included the mandate from the Faculty Recruitment and Retention Committee requiring that all department handbooks have criteria for reappointment.

"Uh-oh!" Rob said with exaggerated dismay. "I'm afraid I can't do some of this. Sorry."

Craig reappeared in the doorway. "And why not, pray tell?"

"Because some of this requires your signature." Rob shook his head regretfully. "Here." He attempted to hand the folder back. "You'll have to take care of it yourself. Sorry. I'd like it documented that I officially tried to perform these essential job functions but found that I was unable to do so due to my lowly status as a non-tenured assistant professor."

"What signature? Where?"

"Like this one from the FRR committee." He showed Craig the form. "It needs your signature right there, so I'm afraid I officially can't—"

Snatching a pen from a cracked Purdue cup on Rob's desk, Craig signed the blank form. "There! Now you can fill out all the paperwork they want. And if it is not done properly, you're gone! I mean it, Polly. I've cleared it with the Dean and University Counsel. One slip up in… in…"

"Essential job duties?"

"Exactly! One slip up in essential job duties is grounds for immediate dismissal!"

"In that case," Rob said, "I'll make sure I go over all my work with you in painstaking detail." He opened his day planner. "I'm spending most of the week creating my final exams, but I can squeeze you in Friday morning. Does that work for you?"

"What?" Craig said in disbelief. "You don't get it, do you? I don't want to see any of this. It's your responsibility. Do what needs to be done and then move it along. And if you don't—"

"Immediate dismissal?"

"Yes!"

Craig stomped out of the office, then hesitated. "I don't know what you're up to, but rest assured you will be out of my department as soon as I have cause!"

"Then," Rob replied, "I better adequately perform my essential job functions!"

Humphing, Craig disappeared down the hallway.

Rob pried open his bottom desk drawer and extracted the new reappointment guidelines for the Special Education Department. Humming to himself, he stapled them to the form Craig signed.

Chapter 80

Although winter break didn't officially begin until Monday, by eight o'clock the Friday night before, Eastern Wisconsin's campus appeared deserted. There were hardly any cars in the snow-covered parking lots, and the full moon cast an eerie blue stillness over the darkened buildings.

Heading to his office to enter his final grades, Rob noticed light seeping underneath Les's door. As he passed, he thought he heard a faint sob. He stopped. Whether it was the feeling of Christmas in the frosty air or the joy of having four weeks off, he didn't know, but Rob found himself knocking.

"Les?"

Inside, there was a mad scramble. "Polly? Polly, is that you?"

"You know my name is Rob, right?"

"Get me out of here!" Les pleaded. "Please! Get somebody to break the door down!"

"Break the door down? Why? What's wrong?"

The door rattled. "It's stuck! Go get help. Please!"

"Stuck?" Rob found the problem right away. Somebody had jammed several pennies between the door and the jamb. "Pull on the doorknob."

"What are you going to do?"

"I'm going to get you out of there. Are you pulling?"

"Yeah."

Rob pried the pennies out with his key. The door flew open as Les tumbled over his desk, papers scattering everywhere.

"You okay?" Rob asked.

"Yeah!" Les fought his way to his feet. "Thanks. I could've… I could've died!"

"Don't be dramatic." Stepping into Les's office, Rob sniffed, then looked in the wastebasket. There was a pile of feces at the bottom. "How long have you been in here?"

"All day."

"All day?"

"I've been grading since lunch and, when I went to use the restroom around four o'clock, I couldn't open the door! Somebody trapped me inside!"

"Why didn't you call campus police?" Rob asked, trying not to sound like Les was an idiot.

"Somebody cut my phone line!" He lifted his receiver and showed him the severed cord.

"Why didn't you use your cell phone? Or e-mail somebody?"

Les's face went as white as the snow fluttering by his window.

"Well, you're free now." Rob headed out of the stench. "You might want to wash out your garbage can. Or, better yet, switch it with Bert's."

"Yeah, yeah… I'll do that. And Rob?" Rob turned. "Thanks!"

Rob nodded. "No problem. And, for the record, let's say you left your cell phone in the car and the internet was down."

Les laughed uneasily. "Yeah. Let's, let's do that! Thanks again."

"Merry Christmas, Les."

Chapter 81

Rob raised his bottle of Nastro Azzurro. "Here's to the end of our first semester as tenure-track faculty!"

Wendy and Sid cheered as they clinked their beers together.

Other than an elderly man at the bar and two twenty-something-year-olds at a corner booth, they were the only ones in Vino's. All the students had headed home for winter break.

"I can't believe somebody trapped that guy in his office," Sid said. "Talk about dangerous. I bet the custodial staff are already on vacation. Who knows when he would've gotten out."

"Oh, he would've been fine," Rob said. On the television mounted above the bar, a commercial for *It's a Wonderful Life* showed George Bailey running through the snowy streets of Bedford Falls. "Sooner or later, he would've remembered to e-mail somebody."

"Still, it was a rather mean practical joke, especially given the holiday season. What if there was a fire?"

"The jokes are getting out of hand," Wendy agreed. "Did you hear what happen to Dr. Crawford?"

Rob and Sid shook their heads as they drank.

"Somebody rigged his doorknob to shock him when he touched it," Wendy said. "Apparently, he got a second-degree burn."

"Geez!" Sid exclaimed.

"Then a flour bomb exploded in Dr. Leseure's office," Wendy went on.

"He's in psychology, right? The one who walks with a cane, kind of hunched over?"

"That's him. He got a lung full of flour and had to go to the hospital."

"I hope the Dean catches the asshole who did it." Rob took another drink. "Fun is fun. But, at this rate, somebody's going to get killed."

Their waiter set a large onion and pineapple pizza in front of them. "Here you go."

"Thank you!" Wendy pulled a piece to her plate. She cut the strands of cheese connecting it to the rest of the pizza. "Has Walrus found out about the new reappointment guidelines?"

Rob took a slice. He was about to take a bite but then decided to let it cool. The pineapples were still sizzling. "Not yet. I didn't want to ruin his holiday."

"That's very kind of you." She licked her fingers. "I have to say, getting him to sign that form was pure genius! And sneaky!"

"It was kind of sneaky, wasn't it?" Rob said. "You know, I always try to play by the rules. But, working here, I've learned that sometimes you have to create the rules that suit you."

"Well said!" Sid chewed. "Hey, I wonder if you could get him to sign something else, like a form giving you a pay raise. Or maybe his resignation as chair!"

They laughed.

"By the way…" Wendy wiped a grease-stained napkin across her lips. "Did you make the reappointment guidelines incredibly easy?"

Rob checked the television again. The game was back on. Unfortunately, Indiana was up by seven points with eleven minutes left in the second quarter. He took a bite of pizza.

"Not incredibly easy," he said. "I still believe we need to have high standards for faculty. But I made sure they were very quantifiable. For example, to be reappointed to their second year, faculty must submit at least one article for publication and make at least one presentation. They also have to serve on two university committees."

"All of which you have."

"Yup! I also put in a clause saying that faculty could not be denied reappointment unless they failed to meet the criteria or were convicted of a felony."

"Convicted of a felony?" Sid repeated, impressed. He caught the bartender's eye and pointed to his empty bottle. He lifted three fingers. The bartender nodded. "I wouldn't have thought of that."

"Again, I think there should be some standards here. Otherwise, how are things going to change?"

"Well, regardless—" Wendy took another bite of pizza. "Congratulations again. I'm really proud of you. I know that sounds silly coming from me..."

"It's not silly at all," Rob told her. "You're the ones who kept encouraging me to find another way to stay. And I appreciate all the support you two have given me. I mean that! You're the only sources of comfort I have in this insane asylum. I couldn't have survived without you."

"Pre-tenured faculty have to stick together," Sid said.

They watched the game as they ate and drank. Indiana fumbled on their own three-yard line. Purdue recovered.

"Yes!" Rob shouted, "Go Purdue!"

The waiter came and set three brown bottles in front of them.

"This is Red Stripe. It's a pale lager from Jamaica." He gathered their discarded napkins and empty bottles. "It's one of my favorites. Hope you enjoy it."

"Thanks!" Rob told him. "I'm sure we will."

Sid sipped the new beer. "Mmmm. It's sweet."

"I taste apple," Wendy said.

"Me too." Rob took another pull. "It's faint, but nice."

They ate some more pizza.

"What are your plans now that we have a month free?" Wendy asked.

"I'm going home for a few days and put up with my mother asking why I didn't become a real doctor like my brother, Arjun," Sid replied bitterly. "I'll then subtly insert into as many conversations as possible how I don't have to worry about malpractice insurance or getting sued."

"Where's home again?" Rob asked, one eye still on the game. Purdue was second and goal and had three receivers spread wide. He bit into a pizza crust.

"Artesia, California. In a neighborhood called Little India. It's right by Los Angeles. How about you?"

"Downers Grove. It's a town a few miles west of Chicago."

"You going home for the holidays?" Wendy asked Rob.

Rob pried his attention from the television and focused on his friends. "I'll go for a few days around Christmas. But I'll be here the rest of the time. Now that I don't have to worry about losing my job, I think I might adopt a dog from the Humane Society."

"Really? That's quite a commitment."

"I know. But I always had a dog growing up, and I figure I could give one a good home." Then he admitted, hoping he didn't sound too pathetic, "And I get kind of lonely. The house seems so empty. I bought the grandfather clock so something would make noise once in a while. But the ticking and the chimes make me feel like I'm in an Edgar Allan Poe poem."

"That's sweet," Wendy said, chewing. "I was thinking about adopting a cat. But I don't want to have that responsibility until I know I'll be tenured."

Purdue settled for a field goal.

"Oh, come on," Rob told her. "You got two publications this year. Keep that up and you're more than a shoo-in for tenure. We all are! Go save a kitty."

"I'll think about it."

Rob took another bite of pizza crust, then washed it down with Jamaican beer. "You going home over break?"

Wendy watched Purdue kick-off. Indiana took the touchback. "No. I want to relax. Besides, I was there for Thanksgiving."

"Hey… I'll tell you what. I'll only be in Chicago for a few days. How about we celebrate New Year's together? Maybe you could help me pick out a dog."

"I'd like that. Maybe I can find myself a Crookshanks."

Sid tossed his hands. "If I would've said that, you would've called me a nerd!"

"You're not a beautiful blonde," Rob said.

Wendy shot Rob a mildly disapproving yet appreciative scowl. "Thanks."

"I'll give you a call when I get back," he told her. "Then we'll go to the shelter."

"Okay. But you have to promise you'll only let me adopt one, maybe two. The last thing I need is to become the university's crazy cat lady."

Sid drained his beer, wiped his mouth with a napkin, then stood. "Sorry, I have to split. My flight leaves at seven-forty in the morning, and it takes a good hour to get to the airport in Milwaukee. I need to get to bed."

Wendy hugged him. "Have a great break! See you next year!"

"You too." He shook Rob's hand. "And congratulations again. You've pulled a prank for the history books! I wonder how Walrus is going to react when he finds out."

Chapter 82

When he wasn't playing with his newly adopted seven-year-old basset hound, Guster, or having Wendy over for dinner, Rob had a very productive winter vacation. He'd submitted two studies to top-tier journals and received word that the paper he'd revised had been accepted for publication. He'd also put on three more workshops for parents of kids with disabilities—most of whom had pulled their children from Elwin Holme. Things were going so well he hated to see the break end.

When he returned to campus the week before the spring term, Rob found an attractive young woman sitting at Tiffani's desk. Thankfully, other than tight jeans with gaping holes in the knees and a sweatshirt that said, "Bite me!" she wasn't wearing anything too inappropriate.

"Hi!" she said as he entered. "I'm Karlee! I'm your new secretary."

She extended an eager hand. Rob shook it. "Dr. Chudinski."

Immediately, she yanked her hand back, the smile vanishing.

"Let me guess," Rob said. "Dr. Grubber told you some horror stories about me."

"Craig is a wonderful man," she replied defensively. "He's mentoring me!"

"Of course, he is. Just—" He was about to say, 'be careful' or maybe 'keep your clothes on,' but he didn't want to get into it. He was in too good of a mood. "Just let me know if you need anything."

Karlee's face contorted as though she wouldn't need anything from him even if he were the last academic on the planet.

Entering his office, Rob found the red light on his phone flashing. Tossing his briefcase on the guest chair, he sat behind his desk and pushed the message retrieval button.

"Message one…" the computerized voice said.

There was a click. Then a panicked student came over the speaker. "Mr. Chudinski! This is Alyssa. Somehow, I got a C- in your class and now I can't student teach this semester. I need a C! What can I do?"

Pulling a pen and pad of paper from a drawer, Rob jotted down the name "Alyssa" and the words "student teaching."

"Message two…"

"Hey, Dr. C.," a young man who sounded stoned said. "I'm in your Monday morning class. Anyway, there's something wrong with my grade. For some reason, it says I have a D. Can you fix that? Thanks, man!"

"You didn't tell me your name," Rob said to the phone. Then he grumbled, "No wonder you got a D."

The recording clicked.

"Message three…"

An angry male voice came on. "I can't believe I got a D- in your goddamned class! I did everything—"

Rob hit the skip button.

"Message four…"

An angry female voice came on. "How did I get—?"

Trying to determine how many messages there were, Rob hit the skip button several times.

"Message eleven…"

He tapped the button again.

"Message fourteen…"

He resumed tapping.

"Message nineteen…"

"Oh, screw this." He exited out of his voicemail.

The phone rang.

"Hello?" he said. "This is Dr. Chudinski."

"It's about time you answered!" a woman hollered. "I've been calling you for weeks!"

"Yes, well," Rob replied pleasantly, "there's this thing called holiday break. That's when our masters unchain our leg irons and allow us to spend time with our families."

"I don't care!"

"Obviously." Praying he didn't have hundreds of e-mails, Rob booted up his computer. "How can I help?"

"You gave my daughter a C-!"

Rob sighed. "Who is this?"

"I'm Alyssa Fletcher's mother. You gave her a C- and now she has to retake your stupid class!"

"I see." Balancing the receiver between his neck and shoulder, Rob typed the student's name into his laptop. His roster for Introduction to Exceptionalities appeared.

"Don't give me any of your condescending crap," she snapped. "Now Alyssa can't student teach until fall!"

"Uh-huh."

Rob accessed the student's grade. Alyssa had actually earned a D+, but he rounded up and gave her the C-. He must have been feeling charitable that day.

"Do you know how much another semester at your stupid university costs?" the mother ranted.

"I'm not sure." Rob typed the student's name into the advising menu. "But I believe we're having a sale next month. Everything is ten percent off."

"I don't care about next month! I want to know what you're going to do about this now. She will *not* go another semester simply because she had a lousy teacher. You *will* correct this situation. Do you understand? She will *not*—!"

"I'm sorry, Mrs. Fletcher," Rob interrupted. "But I'm looking at your daughter's advising file."

"And?"

"And she didn't sign the FERPA waiver."

There was a crackling silence. Then the mother asked, "What the hell is that? Is that for her to student teach? I know we filled out everything. If there's a mistake, it's your fault. Not hers."

"The FERPA waiver enables me to talk to people about her grades," Rob explained. "I'm sorry, but without it signed, I can't even acknowledge she's one of my students."

"She's my daughter! I pay for her tuition!"

"Maybe if your daughter paid her own tuition," Rob said, knowing he was going to regret it, "she would've shown up for class once in a while."

"I'll have you know—" She shouted so loud, Rob winced as he pulled the receiver from his ear. "—my daughter is brilliant! She's gifted! She was on the honor roll all four years in high school!"

"And now she's an adult. You might want to cut the umbilical cord."

"How dare you!"

"Look." Rob tried to sound reasonable. "What are you going to do when your daughter becomes a teacher? Are you going to attend her interviews too? Maybe call her principal if she has a bad day? If you treat her like a grown-up, maybe she'll learn to act like one."

"That's it! I want the name of your supervisor!"

"Oh, absolutely." Rob pried open a desk drawer and pulled out the building directory. "Do you have a pen ready? I'll give you his home phone number."

Chapter 83

Once the commotion about final grades finally died down, the first month of the spring semester was rather pleasant. Rob had taken Pete's advice and made things easier on himself. He still gave weekly quizzes, but they were all multiple choice and graded by computer. Further, he only had office hours once per week, rather than every day. Despite the bitterly cold Wisconsin weather, things were finally looking up.

Craig appeared in his doorway, mustache quivering.

"So help me!" He balled a fist. "If you give another one of your crackpot parents my phone number, I'll—!"

"But you're my direct supervisor," Rob said innocently.

"That's right!" Craig seemed to recall why he was there. "I am! And as your direct supervisor—" He noted Rob's new chair. It had a built-in footrest like a Lazyboy recliner and was nicer than what Craig had. "The department didn't pay for that, did it?"

"Nope! Santa gave it to me. I was a very good boy last year."

Craig harrumphed, then looked closer. "Why on earth is it chained to your desk?"

"So those constructivist bastards don't steal it."

"Yes, well—" Craig sniffed, evidently not liking that he agreed with something Rob said. "What was I saying?"

Rob swiveled back and forth in his comfy chair. "Not a clue. I wasn't listening."

Remembering, Craig snapped his fingers. "As your direct supervisor, I am here to officially inform you that your reappointment papers are due by four o'clock this afternoon. Not a second later! Do you understand? Failure to turn them in on time will result in an automatic rejection."

"Great. Thanks. I'll have them in your mailbox before my afternoon class."

Rob continued swiveling his chair.

"And you needn't put much effort into them," Craig went on. "Because I'm voting no!"

Rob spun in a circle. "If that's what you think is best."

"It is! You've been a thorn in my side long enough. After this semester, you're gone, Polly. Gone!"

Rob spun in the opposite direction. He was getting sick, but he knew his behavior was perplexing Craig. "We'll see."

"We will, indeed!"

Craig watched him spin.

"Shouldn't you be looking for a new job, eh? Maybe there's something available at McDonald's." He laughed.

"Judging by your weight, I'm sure you'd know."

Craig bristled.

Rob spun as fast as he could and counted how many times Craig's bewildered face came into view.

"You're awfully calm for somebody who is about to be unemployed," Craig said suspiciously. "Or do you think you'll be able to finagle your way into staying? Maybe sweet talk Mary? Well, don't count on it! The unit vote is the only one that matters. And you need a majority! That's two yes votes—and I can tell you right now you won't get them!"

Rob stopped spinning. He was about to puke. "All I can do is address the reappointment criteria in my papers as best as I can. The rest is up to fate."

"Reappointment criteria." Craig snorted. "Fat lot, you know. There is no reappointment criteria!"

"Are."

"What?"

"Criterion is singular. Criteria are plural. You'd say, 'There *are* no reappointment criteria.'"

"Yes, very funny! Either way, you're gone. Aren't you? Make a joke about that!"

Pulling the lever on his chair, Rob reclined, his feet on the elevated footrest.

"You think your oh-so-clever, don't you," Craig said. "So very high and mighty. Mr. Research Awards. Mr. Workshops. Well, I'll tell you again, the only reappointment criteria come from me. Me! The department chair. I decide if you stay or go. And, believe me, Polly, when I say you're gone— you're finally gone!"

"You've said that already."

"And now I'm saying it again!"

"Okay." Rob put his hands behind his head and closed his eyes. He prayed the room would stop spinning.

"Well, then…" Craig searched for something cutting to say. "Good luck at McDonald's!"

"Thank you. I'll make sure I give you a few extra fries with your Happy Meal."

Rob opened his eyes. Craig was still standing there.

"I don't know what your game is," Craig said. "But it's over! You are out of here! Come May, you will never step foot in this building or any other again!"

"I'm never going to step foot in any building again?" Rob asked doubtfully. "Ever?"

Craig's cheeks burned red. "You won't be on campus to step in— Oh, you know what I mean!"

Growing weary of the conversation, Rob pushed the lever on his chair forward and sat up. Reaching into his desk drawer, he extracted the updated version of the departmental handbook. He tossed it to Craig.

"What's this?" Craig asked.

"Look at page seven."

Craig flipped angrily to page seven, read the two paragraphs discussing the reappointment criteria, then turned to the front page. "What the hell is this?"

"The new special education handbook."

"You can't go changing the handbook!"

"I didn't." Rob smiled. "You did."

"What are you blathering about?"

Rob handed Craig another piece of paper. "A couple of months ago, you told me to do a bunch of work for the Faculty Recruitment and Retention committee. And I did it. You even signed the approval form."

"I did not!" Craig examined the signature, then shook the paper at Rob. "This isn't legal! I didn't know what I was signing. I signed this under duress!"

"Maybe you should talk to the chair of the Faculty Recruitment and Retention committee."

"Oh, I will! Believe me. This will not stand! This will… *not*… stand. Do you hear me?"

"Unfortunately, I hear you too often." Rob gathered his books together. "Now, if you'll excuse me, I have to get ready for my next class."

Craig made to leave, then stopped. He started chuckling, then cackled wildly.

"This—" He turned back to Rob. He was laughing so hard tears were welling in his eyes. "This… this doesn't take effect until next term! See!" He pointed to the date at the bottom of the first page. "It doesn't apply to you! You're gone! The oh-so-clever-research-award-winner is gone!" His laughter rolled along the hallway like a thunderclap. "Gone!"

Chapter 84

As soon as Craig left his office, Rob raced to the first floor and spoke with the school director. Unfortunately, Mary wasn't very helpful.

"What do you mean there's nothing you can do?" Rob waved the new handbook. "This is the official reappointment criteria for the special education department!"

"Yes, however—" She blinked at him like a sad owl. "—I'm sorry to say Craig is correct. The new criteria won't take effect until next academic year. That means you'll be evaluated by the criteria under which you were hired."

"But there aren't any criteria! None!"

"Well," Mary said diplomatically, "some units feel that having formal criteria is too limiting. They feel it is best to take a more holistic view of faculty."

"Holistic view? Mary, that's asinine! How can you evaluate people without criteria against which you're evaluating them?"

"That's a fair question." She reached for her appointment book. "Perhaps we should schedule a meeting to discuss this."

"No meetings!"

"Are you sure? Because I have an opening in July."

Rob collapsed into Mary's cushy guest chair. He put his head in his hands, hoping she'd pity him enough to help. "Craig isn't going to let me stay."

"You don't know that."

"Yes, I do! Believe me. And there's nothing I can do about it."

"As my father used to say, where there's life, there's hope!"

Glaring, Rob wanted to punch her elderly face.

He took a deep breath.

"In a department with only two tenured faculty members," he asked, trying to find some angle he hadn't considered before, "how many yes votes do I need to keep my job?"

"The regulations say you need a majority, which is one more than fifty percent."

"Then I need both faculty to vote yes? Both Jim and Craig?"

"Correct. And good for you for getting Jim to vote so early! I haven't seen him around in ages. He's a bear to get ahold of."

Rob was tempted to tell her that Jim hadn't been on campus for years but decided it wouldn't help his case any.

"After the unit votes," he said, "then it's your turn, right?"

"Correct. And then the Dean."

Rob leaned forward. "Will you vote for me, Mary? Please?"

She looked doubtful.

"I have a house," he went on. "I have friends here. I want to stay! I'm a good teacher. I do research. I've submitted two studies to top-tier journals! I'm on over thirty committees!"

"It sounds like you're doing a bang-up job," she told him. "Good for you!"

"You'll vote yes?"

"Oh…" Her joy faded. "I'm not sure I'm the person to overturn the wishes of an entire department. I mean, after all, what do I know about special education? I didn't even know those kids did, you know—that thing you said your student did on the bus."

"Mary!" Rob pleaded. "Please. I'm going to be unemployed! I won't be able to make my mortgage or car payments. I'll be homeless!"

"I'm sure it won't come to that."

"Mary! If you don't overturn the department vote, it *will* come to that! I promise you!"

Mary frowned.

"I have to stay!" Rob said. "There's this school, Elwin Holme, and they don't believe kids with disabilities can learn, so they don't bother teaching them. The staff makes them watch Barney videos all day!"

"Oh, dear!"

"I'm trying to stop it. I'm trying to educate parents about their rights and teach future teachers that it's wrong—but I need more time. I need your help! Please!"

She placed her folded hands on the desk between them. "I tell you what. I'll ask the Dean and Craig to get together so we can circle the wagons and hash things out."

"Circle the wagons?"

"It's the best I can do, I'm afraid."

Chapter 85

Rob had put his reappointment papers in Craig's box before his afternoon class. When he'd finished teaching, he found them taped to his office door—the word *REJECTED* written in red marker across the first page. Standing in the hallway, Rob stared at it.

"There he is!" Bert said as he and Les came out of the stairwell. "Polly want a job?" He laughed. "Get it? Instead of cracker, Polly wants a job!"

"Shut up, Bert," Les said.

"What the hell's wrong with you?" Bert asked him. "You feeling sorry for Mr. Holy Roller?"

"Who's going to teach his classes once he's gone?" Les shot back. "Us, that's who."

"Yeah, well, that means more money."

"And what if the person who replaces him is even worse? Some ball-busting lesbian or something? Once they're hired, they can't be fired! Ever think of that? We'd be stuck with her forever, talking about the home improvement projects she's doing with her—" He made quotation marks with his finger. "—partner."

"That's what the interview is for. We'll get some sweet little thing fresh out of her doctoral program. She'll be putty in our hands!"

"You know how the interviews go. You never know what you'll get."

"You sound like Forrest Gump, you idiot." Bert stared at him. "You're telling me you want Polly to stay?"

"He teaches the courses nobody else wants," Les replied. "With him gone, everything will fall on us again. That's all I'm saying."

"Oh, you're nuts!" Bert hefted his lime green pants, then said to Rob, "You should've never messed with the Big Guy. Nobody gets the best of him for long. So pack your bags!" He went to the bathroom and pushed open the door. "You in here, Becky?"

Taking his reappointment papers down, Rob nodded to Les. "Thanks."

"Don't mention it," Les said. "And Rob—good luck."

Chapter 86

Over the next three weeks, Rob hardly saw Craig. The only time he caught a glimpse of him was when Craig left his office door cracked open and Rob could see him pore intently over professional journals. Rob half-heartedly considered asking him what he was reading, but then decided it was best to leave him alone. Besides, Rob was too busy teaching, submitting studies, and sending his curriculum vita to anybody who would agree to read it. He couldn't care less about what his department chair was doing. As long as Craig kept his distance, they were both better off.

Early one morning, Rob sat at his computer, trying to rewrite the seventh draft of a cover letter he planned on sending to Ashland Community College in Ohio. He was so engrossed with his work he didn't notice Craig leaning against the door until he coughed.

"Not now, Craig." Rob reviewed what he'd written. "I'm busy."

"Working on your resume, eh?" Craig asked. "Trying to whitewash why you couldn't keep your job here?"

"Actually, I'm finishing up a study," Rob lied. "You know—research? I'm sure you heard of it when you were the valedictorian at the prestigious Northern Montana University."

"I'll have you know I read plenty of research!"

Rob continued typing. "Let me know if you want me to explain any of it to you."

"Oh, very funny! You think you're so smart. Well, I've read your research and found it hopelessly flawed!"

"Which study?"

"What?"

"What study of mine did you read? I've had six papers published. As a matter of fact—" Rob held up a letter he'd received the day before. "I got another one accepted earlier this week."

In truth, the letter said his paper was accepted "conditionally." But the changes the editor wanted were relatively minor and would only take a few hours to fix. Rob just wished the journal was more prominent. To get an interview in the spring, he'd needed all the clout he could get.

"I don't recall the bleeding title." Craig sniffed. "Honestly, the entire paper was hopelessly flawed. I can't imagine how you got it published. They probably needed to fill space and didn't have a good cartoon." He chuckled.

Rob re-read what he'd typed, then deleted it. "What was it about?"

"I told you, I don't remember. It was all rubbish. The methods were… they were…"

"Hopelessly flawed?" Rob offered.

"Yes! And the results. Well!" Craig wagged his head contemptuously. "They were…"

"Hopelessly flawed?"

"Shut it! I know research as well as anybody in the field. Better even!"

"I'm sure." Wondering whether Times Roman looked more confident and decisive than Calibri, Rob changed his cover letter's font. "Unfortunately, not many kids with intellectual disabilities have been taught statistics. So, I'm sure you're slightly more informed than they are."

Craig stomped his foot.

"That's it!" he shouted, spit flying. "That's it! You have pushed me too far! I'll show you about research!" He jabbed a finger at the ceiling. "I hereby challenge you to a duel!"

"A what?"

Flummoxed, Craig hesitated. "I mean—a debate! You and me. Mono e mono!"

"I believe you mean *mano a mano*."

"Whatever!"

"Craig," Rob said, somewhat amused. He had two more courses to teach and three meetings to attend. That didn't leave him much time to waste talking to his department chair. "Go away. I have work to do."

Craig announced loudly, "I challenge you to a debate on the dangers of including crippled kids in the community! And don't you dare chicken out!"

"What the hell are you talking about?"

"Elwin Holme's Board of Directors has asked me to educate the public about their program. Not you. *Me!* I'm the expert."

Rob stopped typing. "The board is considered revising its inclusion policy?"

"Not after they hear what I have to say!" Craig said smugly. "I've thoroughly researched the matter. Did you know crippled children are seventeen times more likely to be sexually assaulted than—"

"When?" Rob interrupted. "When is this debate?"

"Six o'clock. Tonight!"

"I'll be there."

Craig rubbed his hands together. "Oh, I'm going to show you up good. By the time I'm done with you, everybody will know what a fraud you are!"

Chapter 87

"This the place?" Sid surveyed the inspirational artwork, leather sofas, and flower-filled vases placed strategically throughout Elwin Holme's lobby. "It isn't too bad."

"You should see the rest of it." Rob flipped frantically through his index cards. He'd only had a couple of hours to prepare, and he didn't want to forget anything. "The hallways reek of urine and echo with the haunting moans of neglected children."

Wendy put a hand over his notes. "You're going to do fine. Try to relax."

"I need to do better than fine." Rob reluctantly put his cards away. He felt as though he was hyperventilating. "This is my last chance to make a difference here and to fulfill my promise to Thelma."

"Don't say that. You have your entire career ahead of you."

"Maybe."

They followed a slowly moving stream of people trickling along a corridor.

Somebody called, "Dr. Chudinski!"

A group hurried up to them.

"I'm so glad you could make it." Maddie Codner hugged him.

"Sorry I'm late," Rob said. "I only found out about this a little while ago."

"We all did," her husband, Tom, replied. "They're trying to keep it under wraps. The last thing they want is a mob of angry parents attending." He scanned the murmuring crowd with satisfaction. "But we managed to get the word out well enough. They won't be able to ignore us, that's for sure."

"If they don't want parents attending," Wendy said, "why are they having this at all?"

"I'm sorry." Rob gestured to Wendy and Sid. "I'd like you to meet my friends, Dr. Maddon." Wendy waved. "And Dr. Bhattacharyya."

"Call me Sid."

Rob indicated each couple in turn. "These are the Codners, Harroffs, and Morrisons. They suffered through my workshops."

"Suffered?" Alyse Harroff grabbed Wendy's arm. "Dr. Chudinski is an absolute lifesaver!"

"He's truly changed our lives," Randy Morrison agreed. "Before we met him, I didn't have much hope for our son."

Daniel Harroff said, "We didn't have any."

"And to answer your question," Maddie told Wendy. "Some of the board members are having doubts about the quality of their programs. Or the lack of quality, I should say."

"I think they're more worried about all the children being pulled from the school," Tom said. "I bet they're operating at half capacity."

Wendy nudged Rob. "See! You're making a big impact!"

"Not big enough." Rob took a deep breath. "Let's see if we can get them to start teaching something meaningful."

They entered a packed boardroom. Upon a raised dais, fifteen people in business attire sat behind a long table. His name written on a folded piece of paper perched in front of him, Craig was at the very end, flipping feverishly through index cards of his own.

The superintendent, Mr. Stanford, banged a gavel. "Could you take your seats?" He called over the surrounding conversations, "Please! We have a great deal to discuss today and not much time. Please take your seats."

"Good seeing you, Dr. Chudinski." Tom Codner shook Rob's hand. "We appreciate you coming."

"My pleasure," Rob replied. "I hope I can help."

Maddie hugged him again. "Good luck!"

"Thanks!"

They went to find someplace to sit.

Rob glanced about. Almost all of the two hundred folding chairs were taken. At least thirty spectators stood along the walls.

Mr. Stanford banged his gavel. "Please! We'd like to get started!"

Wendy motioned to three seats to their right. Rob and Sid trailed after her, trying not to bump into anybody as they slid along the row.

"Let's begin, shall we?" Mr. Stanford said as everybody quieted. "We have an exceedingly full schedule. And since most of you are here for our discussion on the proposed changes to our Safety-First Policy, perhaps we should reorder things a bit. Do I have a motion to alter the agenda and begin with item six?"

"I so move!" Craig declared.

"Thank you, Dr. Grubber. Do I have a second?" The woman sitting to Mr. Stanford's left lifted a finger. "Mrs. Kowalski seconds. Any discussions? All in favor?"

Everybody on the dais said, "Aye."

"Very good." Mr. Stanford faced the audience. "Now, in an effort to answer the growing number of questions I've received recently regarding the measures we take to ensure our residents' wellbeing, I have asked our esteemed board member, Dr. Grubber, to discuss the merits of our practices and how they are rooted firmly in scientific research."

"Rooted firmly in scientific research?" Sid said. "Sounds a tad biased, doesn't he?"

Rob didn't respond. He was getting nervous. The mood in the boardroom felt like the calm before the storm. Given the amount of support Elwin Holme had, he wondered how much of the lightning would be directed at him.

"For nearly three decades," Mr. Stanford went on, reading from a prepared script, "Dr. Grubber has been a stalwart force and advocate for people with disabilities in this state. In addition to chairing the special education department at Eastern Wisconsin University, he is also an award-winning researcher."

"What research?" Sid whispered. "I still haven't found a single thing he's published!"

"He has won the OFM Teaching and Research award an astounding twelve years in a row and is a renowned expert on the care for the disabled. Please welcome—Dr. Grubber."

There was a smattering of applause as Craig got to his feet. Rob, Wendy, and Sid clapped politely.

"Thank you, Superintendent Stanford." Craig buttoned his jacket and then wheeled an old overhead projector in front of a screen behind him.

Turning it on, he reeled, hands upraised to shield his eyes from the bright light.

Wendy and Sid snickered.

Rob jotted down a few more things he wanted to say.

Clearing his throat, Craig mopped a handkerchief across his glistening brow. "Mr. Superintendent." He bowed to Mr. Stanford. "Revered colleagues." He bowed to the rest of the board members. "Invited guests." He bowed to the audience. "I'd like to begin this debate by stating the community is a horrible, horrible place and that we must do whatever we can to—"

"Dr. Grubber," Dr. Stanford said. "This isn't a debate. I merely want you to take a few minutes and explain what the scientific literature says about the dangers people with disabilities face in the community."

"A few minutes? Your secretary told me we'd have two hours."

"The meeting is scheduled for two hours. We have many other items to discuss tonight. If you could summarize the literature in four or five points, that would be splendid."

"Four or five points?" Craig shuffled through a stack of overheads a half an inch thick. "Very well. If you insist."

Wendy leaned into Rob. "I don't think you have anything to worry about."

"I still have to convince the board he's wrong," Rob said, clutching his index cards. They were damp with perspiration.

The audience waited as Craig fumbled with his slides. Several fell scattering across the floor.

"Dr. Grubber?" Dr. Stanford prodded.

Flustered, Craig slapped a slide onto the overhead. It had a picture of a young girl with cerebral palsy watching television. Under it were the words: "Protect the cripples!"

"There you go!" Craig announced. "That's all you need to know." He sat with a humph.

Mr. Stanford peered at the screen behind them. "I suppose that summarizes things succinctly." He scrutinized the overflowing boardroom. "Before I open up for comments, I'd like to remind you all that we only have a few minutes, so please—"

Immediately, people started shouting. Some used words like "prison" and "wasted potential." Others called out their support of the school's policies, saying that Elwin Holme cared for their children and kept them safe. Two parents in the first row shoved each other. A man in a jacket and tie cocked his fist.

Wendy patted Rob's knee. "You're on."

Slowly, Rob made his way to the line forming behind the microphone set up in the aisle directly in front of the dais. At least twenty other people were already there, hollering at the board to become more inclusive and to teach their children alongside non-disabled peers.

"Please!" Mr. Stanford hammered his gavel. "Please. One at a time. One at a time!"

Wendy yelled, "Let Dr. Chudinski speak!"

There was a swell of agreement as the line melted away. Rob suddenly found himself standing before the board.

"Ah," Mr. Stanford said pleasantly, "Mr. Chudinski. I trust we won't have to have you escorted off our premises this evening."

"Well…" Rob examined his notes one last time, then slid them into his breast pocket. "The night's still young."

Somebody chuckled.

"Look," Rob said into the microphone. His voice blared throughout the room. He retreated a pace. "There's a great deal to discuss and evidently very little time. We could talk at length about all the bad things that can happen in the community as Dr. Grubber intended to do."

Craig sprang out of his chair, opened his mouth, and then—finding nothing objectionable about this statement—sat.

"What we need to keep in mind is—"

"Let me stop you there," Mr. Stanford interrupted. "To be clear, you admit that people with disabilities face numerous and sundry dangers in the community."

"Of course, but—"

"Then why would you expose them to these dangers? Don't you have any decency, Mr. Chudinski? Don't you care for individuals with disabilities at all?"

Rob fought the anger rising in him. "I'll have you know, Mr. Stanford," he said coolly, "I am a very decent person. That's why I'm here."

"Decent?" Mr. Stanford repeated disdainfully. "Mr. Chudinski, people are taken advantage of in the community. They are exploited. They are raped, beaten, and abused."

"That's true for everybody," Rob replied sharply.

Smiling, Mr. Stanford spread his hands as though Rob had made his point for him. "Exactly. And if the world outside these walls is perilous for individuals as competent as you and me, how do you expect our residents to survive?"

"You teach them!" Rob retorted. "You teach them the skills they need to be as successful as possible!"

People applauded and cheered. Mr. Stanford waited for the commotion to quiet down.

"That's pie-in-the-sky ivory tower talk, I'm afraid. Our residents are severely disabled. They have intense and pervasive needs. They simply cannot learn."

"You're wrong!" Rob told him.

There was an outpouring of voices, some agreeing with Rob, a good many who did not.

"Quiet, please!" Mr. Stanford pounded his gavel. "Mr. Chudinski, I think we've heard enough—"

"During the past fifty years," Rob said, "we have developed more effective techniques for teaching individuals with cognitive and behavioral challenges. For example, my research has found that students taught using a system of self-identified reinforcers are far more likely to acquire the desired target behavior *and* maintain that behavior longer than individuals—"

At this, Craig bounded to his feet. He waved papers vigorously over his head. "I happen to have Dr. Chudinski's so-called research right here! And I would like to submit into evidence that his findings are based upon only seven people! Seven! How can there be—" He checked something written on his hand. "—*generalizability* with such a small sample size? There's a lack of—" He checked his palm again. "—*statistical power*! His study is hopelessly and utterly flawed!"

Everybody looked at Rob.

"Craig…" Rob sighed.

"That's Dr. Grubber to you!"

"Dr. Grubber… First, it's called single-subject research for a reason. And we don't worry about statistical power. There are no regression analyses in these types of investigations."

"Ah-ha!" Craig cried. "See! He doesn't know what he's doing. He's a fraud!"

"That study," Rob replied with some heat, "won an award from an actual organization. Not something fake like 'OFM'!"

Craig huffed. "How dare you!"

Mr. Stanford banged his gavel. "Order! Take your seat, Mr. Chudinski. We've heard enough from you."

"Fine. But before I sit down, I want to say one thing." Rob searched the crowd behind him and found some of the faces he was looking for. He waved them forward. "I understand that you believe my views on this matter are driven by some sort of misguided liberal agenda. So perhaps you'd like to hear from people who have taught your former residents."

He stepped away from the microphone.

"What do you want us to say, Dr. C?" Justin Averill asked.

"Tell them what you learned." Rob patted Justin's shoulder. "And be sincere."

Rob made his way back to Wendy and Sid.

"Good job," Wendy said as he sat next to her. She nodded to the students standing in front of the dais. "What's this?"

Putting his clammy hands together in prayer, Rob replied, "A hail Mary."

"Order! Order!" The room quieted as Mr. Stanford glared down at the students. "We don't have time for all of you. We have other things—"

"We'll be quick, sir," Justin said. "We promise."

Mr. Stanford exhaled heavily. "Hurry up."

"My name is Justin Averill," Justin said into the microphone. "I'm one of Dr. C's students at EW-U, that is, at Eastern Wisconsin University."

There was an awkward pause as Justin struggled to think of something else to say.

"Last semester, Dr. C gave us this assignment. He gave us a list of parents who needed help with their kids. Kids who had disabilities. And we were supposed to help them learn stuff. I really didn't want to do it. But I needed the extra credit."

The audience shifted uncomfortably in their seats. Many checked their cellphones.

"Anyway, I was hired by these parents who had this kid. I can't tell you his name because of confidentiality and all, but—well—he is, as we say, pretty involved. He has a profound intellectual disability. He communicates mainly by kicking and pinching and biting. I mean, the little dude can be really scary! I still have bite marks on my arm from him!"

Justin rolled up his sleeve, but nobody seemed interested in looking at his bruises.

"To be honest," he said. "I didn't think the kid could learn. All he did was scream and bite and grab. But, you know, I tried—and I found that he *could* learn. And, well, I'm proud to say that I got David, I mean—the child—he's now potty trained. And his inappropriate behaviors have decreased a bunch. I'm not saying he's perfect or anything like that, but he's really made excellent progress."

Mr. Stanford leaned forward. "Thank you for your anecdotal—"

"What I'm trying to say is—" Justin indicated the students around him. "What *we* want to say is… Dr. C's method of least restrictive prompts and systematic, self-identified reinforcers, well, it works. It's difficult at first, and it requires a lot of planning and consistency, but it works! These kids can learn."

Katie Bletchley stepped in front of the microphone. "I taught a teenager with autism to use a communication wallet. I didn't think he could do it, but he learned. And his bad behaviors have gone to almost zero."

"It's all about looking at the data," Chloe Biel said.

"And about being systematic," Katie added.

"Right! You have to figure out what's going on and then be consistent in how you change things."

"This is all very nice," Mr. Stanford said. "Clearly, Mr. Chudinski is exceedingly adept at indoctrinating his—"

"He's a terrific teacher!" Katie said. The other students agreed. "The best we've ever had. He knows what he's doing."

Wendy elbowed Rob. Rob smiled.

"I'm sure you believe that he does," Mr. Stanford said, "yet—"

"One last thing, please," Amy Collins said. She was so short, she had to stand on tiptoes to get close to the microphone.

Mr. Stanford begrudgingly let her go on.

"Before I took Dr. C's class," she told the board, "I thought being a teacher meant I taught my students things. But Dr. C showed us that we first have to learn *from* our students. He showed us how to find out how they communicate and to see patterns in their behavior. He taught us how to determine what motivates them and why they behave the way they do. Once I allowed myself to learn from my student—that's when I truly became a teacher."

Craig glowered at the far wall; his arms folded tightly in front of his chest. Many of the other board members, however, appeared to be listening with great interest.

"Well put," Mr. Stanford said. "And with that, I'd like to bring the discussion on this item to a close. Thank you all for your comments. Let's move to the items we skipped. May I have a motion to accept our meeting minutes from February?"

Chapter 88

"Hey, Laura." Rob let his former real estate agent into the foyer. It was the day after the so-called debate, and he'd become resigned to the fact that he was going to have to find a job elsewhere. But first, he had to sell his house. "I appreciate you coming over on such short notice."

"Thanks for having me." She looked about the front room. "I love what you've done here. It's very homey."

"Thanks."

She inspected the pristine parquet floors.

"I'm glad you went with the light honey color rather than the darker coffee. It makes all of the other wood pop." She handed him a gift basket of wine and cheese. "And this is for you. Sorry I couldn't bring it sooner. Things have been beyond hectic."

"Thanks." Rob set the basket on his dining table next to a stack of job applications he was preparing to mail. "Things been busy in the real estate market?" He asked hopefully.

"Crazy busy."

"A lot of people are buying?"

"Oh, heaven's no! That's why I have to scramble to find every buyer I can."

Rob groaned. That wasn't what he wanted to hear.

"Say," she continued, "do you know anybody at the university who is looking for a house? Maybe somebody who has had a baby and is looking for a bigger place? Or someone who has gotten tenured and wants to move out of their old apartment?"

"I'll ask around."

"Great! Every referral helps." She admired the grandfather clock. "This is gorgeous. I love grandfather clocks. They add such charm and character. And this one is perfect for a Craftsman-style home like this."

"Glad you like it."

Rob's basset hound waddled into the room.

"Oh, how cute!" Kneeling, Laura scratched him behind his floppy ears. "What's his name?"

"Guster."

"Hey, Guster! You're such a cute boy! Yes, you are!"

"Actually," Rob said, wondering how to raise the topic he wanted to discuss. "I invited you here for a reason. You see—I need to sell the house. Fast."

Laura started. "Why? Don't you love it? Look at these floors? And high ceilings? And all of this wood? The banisters are hand-carved. You can't find that kind of workmanship in new houses."

"Of course, I love it. It's great! But my job isn't going as well as I'd hoped, and I need to move. Think you could sell it quickly?"

The grandfather clock chimed the half-hour.

"Rob—" Laura glanced longingly at the wine in the basket. "It took me years to sell this house."

"Years? I thought it was only on the market three months."

"That specific listing was only posted for three months. The owner had tried to sell it for five or six years before that. She used it as a rental." Laura looked around them, her shoulders sagging. "I can try to sell it, but… as I was saying, it's a down market, and this house requires a certain type of buyer."

"What do you mean?"

"First off," she said, "it only has two bedrooms, which limits its draw. Nobody with a family will want it. It'd mainly appeal to a single person like yourself or maybe a retired couple. But older couples don't want to mess with the large yard or live on the corner or have a second floor. They usually prefer one-story ranches. And there's a lot of driveway and sidewalk to shovel. Then there's the spring."

"What about the spring?"

"Laura grimaced. "One of the issues with being this close to the lake is there's a little problem with lake flies."

"How little," Rob asked, preparing himself for the worst.

"For about two weeks in May, the place is swarming with them."

"Why didn't you tell me?"

"I worked for the seller. You knew that."

Rob stared at the bay windows, imagining them covered with flies. "You're saying I won't be able to sell?"

"Not right away." She added, "Maybe you could rent it out to some college students. It's close enough to campus. In fact, most of the houses in this neighborhood are rentals."

The thought of drunken college students throwing beer bashes on his newly stained hardwood floors made Rob cringe.

"What if I took a loss? I could probably sell it for five thousand dollars less than what I paid for it."

She shook her head.

"Ten thousand!" he said louder.

"If you were to buy a house and then sell it a few months later—at a loss nonetheless—people would think there's something wrong with it."

Rob sat on the sofa and put his head in his hands. "Jesus Christ!"

"Are you sure you can't stay?" Laura asked. "It's such a lovely home!"

Chapter 89

Rob clutched his Yebisu beer. It was early Wednesday evening and, other than a quartet of frat guys eating a pizza and drinking Budweiser a few tables over, Vino's was empty.

"Are you sure neither of you wants to buy a house?" he asked Wendy and Sid. "I'll give you a great price!"

"We already discussed this," Wendy said crossly. "Not before we're tenured."

"Sorry. I didn't mean to be a pest."

Frank Sinatra's *That's Life* came on the jukebox.

"I know you're frustrated—" Wendy said.

Rob took a drink and grumbled, "That's a bit of an understatement."

"—but things will work out. You'll see."

Gazing out the window, he watched a group of students pile out of a blue Toyota Prius. Under their knee-length coats, knit hats, and long scarves, they looked like mounds of laundry shuffling through the blowing snow.

"She actually told you it was unsellable?" Sid asked.

"She didn't say that exactly," Rob admitted. "But she said it required a special type of buyer who doesn't come around very often."

"Special type?"

"An idiot who only needs two bedrooms and doesn't know about the infestation of lake flies every spring."

The students from the parking lot entered the bar. Shedding their many layers, they slid into an adjacent booth.

"I can't believe she didn't tell you about the flies before you bought the house," Wendy said, appalled. "That's criminal!"

"It's not criminal," Rob replied. "Realtors don't have to disclose anything about the community. They assume it public knowledge. I was too stupid to know about it."

Sid nursed his beer. "Somebody told me about it when I came to interview. Showed me pictures and everything. That's why I got a place on the west side."

Rob lifted his head. He was afraid of the answer but had to ask. "Was it really that bad? In the pictures?"

"It was like a black cloud. Some of the houses were completely covered."

"Jesus Christ!" Rob groaned. "I thought I was getting such a great deal!"

"You did!" Wendy told him. "The flies only last a week or two. Get a hotel room or go on a trip every year. You won't even have to see them."

"Why don't you rent it out?" Sid asked. "It's what—? Seven blocks from campus? You'll have plenty of renters. And the students won't care about the flies. They'll be on summer break when they hatch anyway."

"I'm afraid I'll end up spending more money repairing the place after the tenants leave than I'll make." Then Rob said, "Plus, I won't have an income. That's my biggest problem. I need a job."

"Any leads?"

Rob took a long pull from his beer bottle. "My doctoral advisor knows of a few positions coming available in the fall. One of them is for a tenure-track faculty member. It isn't exactly in my area of expertise, but I might be able to get an interview. Maybe…"

A few more people came in and sat at the bar. A woman stood in front of the jukebox, analyzing her options.

"What are you going to say when they ask why you're leaving here?" Wendy asked.

Rob watched the snow swirl in the parking lot. "I have no clue. I thought I'd tell them I wanted to be closer to my family, but that'd only work if I moved near Chicago."

"There're tons of schools around Chicago! I'm sure several of them will have openings."

"But they have to be hiring in special education. Not only that, but they also have to be wanting somebody with my background. It's a pretty specialized field. Not many schools even have courses covering severe disabilities."

Guns and Rose's *Welcome to the Jungle* blared over the speakers.

Wendy winced. "Sorry."

"Me too," Sid said.

Rob took a drink, then sighed. "I'm such a failure."

"You're *not* a failure!" Wendy told him. "Don't say that! Didn't you listen to all those students who came to speak at the board meeting? My god Rob, you reached them. You reached all of them!"

"A fat lot of good it did. Elwin Holme hasn't changed its policy about including kids within the community or teaching them anything worthwhile."

"Give them time. If they don't change, more parents will pull their kids from the school. And believe me, money talks. The board will do whatever they can to keep parents happy."

"Perhaps." Rob rubbed his face. "Then there're my students. When I close my eyes, all I can see is Walrus sitting on that stage, glaring down at Justin and the others. He'll probably fail them out of spite next year."

"I don't care what you say," Wendy told him. "I think you're a hero. Those kids and parents will never forget you."

"Never is a long time."

One of the frat boys called for the bartender to put on ESPN2. The bartender surfed through the channels until he found the correct one. A pre-recorded exhibition game between the St. Louis Cardinals and the Chicago Cubs came on. Arizona was bright and sunny, unlike Wisconsin.

The waitress appeared at their table. "Need anything else?"

"Yeah," Rob told her. "Bring us the next beer on the list. Hell, bring us the next two."

"Will do!"

"Thanks."

Wendy watched him drain his bottle. "Drinking yourself to oblivion won't help."

"It won't hurt either."

"Wait until tomorrow morning and see if that's true."

"Tomorrow…" Rob chuckled miserably to himself. "At least I can stop going to committee meetings. And I'll never have to put up with another irate parent or student again. Craig can deal with them all."

"You're talking like you're quitting."

"Not quitting. Retiring. If I can't get a position at a university, I think I'll return to the public schools. They're always hiring special education teachers. I can't make as big of an impact as I could as a professor, but I can still make a difference."

"Good luck living on what they make," Sid said, watching the game. "I wouldn't be able to pay off my student loans on their salary."

Rob was thinking the same thing. There were also his house and car payments.

"Maybe Mary will come through," Wendy said. "Or the Dean!"

"I don't think Mary has the courage to do anything other than threaten to hold a meeting," Rob said. "She's been pretty upfront about not wanting to go against the department vote. And I can't imagine the Dean caring one way or another."

The waitress set six more bottles in front of them. "Here you go! Let me know if you need anything else."

"Thanks."

Rob took one of the new beers.

"Am I missing anything?" he asked. "Anything at all? Because, if I am—tell me. I'll try anything."

Wendy thought, then shook her head. "I can't think of anything."

"Me neither," Sid said. "Sorry, man."

Chapter 90

"Okay, everybody!" Rob tried to muster as much energy as he could. It was past ten o'clock and, after teaching all day, he was beyond exhausted. He couldn't wait to get home, grab a bite to eat, and crawl into bed. "That's the end of our workshop—*Everything Parents Need to Know About Special Education!*"

The group of forty parents clapped.

"Before we end for tonight, I have an announcement." A wild idea popped into Rob's mind. "Do any of you have any sway with the University President?"

Nobody said anything.

"Or anybody high up in the university?" Rob asked.

"I know Steve Wagner," a gentleman to his right said.

"Who's he?"

"He's a professor in Chemistry."

"No. I need somebody closer to the top of the food chain."

"I know the head librarian," another parent offered. "Her name is Phillis Wellesley."

"I'm afraid she couldn't help," Rob said. "Anybody else? Anybody know anybody who might know the University President? Or anybody in the administration? The Provost? The Vice Provost? The Assistant Vice Provost?"

"Why?" a woman in the front row asked, concerned. "Is everything okay?"

Rob ran his fingers through his hair, then decided to tell them what was going on. "Unfortunately, I'll be leaving Eastern Wisconsin after this semester. They won't be renewing my contract."

Their angry grumbling made him feel a little better.

"Does this have to do with your stand against Elwin Holme?" a father asked.

"Sort of," Rob told him. "My department chair and I don't see eye-to-eye about what's happening there. Different visions for the field, you might say."

"There's no way you can stay?"

"None that I can think of."

A melancholy silence filled the classroom. In the darkened hallway, a custodian began mopping the salt-stained floor.

"At any rate—" Rob attempted to shake the self-pity from his voice. "I wanted to thank you all for coming. I hope you've learned something useful. And please share the resources I've given you with other parents who need them. There's too much ignorance about special education. And I need your help stamping it out. If there's anything I can do for you, please let me know. I'll be using my university e-mail until the end of May." He put on a smile. "Thanks again for coming. And have a great evening!"

There was another round of applause. A woman in the second row stood. Then they all did.

"Thank you. Thank you very much. Be careful driving home!"

When they'd gone, Rob stared at the rows of empty chairs. Then he heaved himself to his feet and turned off the lights.

Going to the main office, he checked his mailbox. Two letters were waiting for him. He opened the one with Eastern Wisconsin's logo. It was from Mary. It began: *"I regret to inform you…"*

She had voted with the department and recommended that he not be reappointed. Even though Rob had been expecting it, it still felt like a kick in the gut. He fought the sob building within him.

Then, wiping his eyes, he looked at the second envelope. It was from NIDR, the agency to which he'd submitted the three-million-dollar grant application. He felt it. It was pretty thick. They wouldn't send a thick envelope to someone who didn't get the grant. They'd simply send a one-page form letter like Mary. And if they awarded him the grant—

Rob ripped open the envelope and extracted the letter.

"Thank you for your submission… Blah. Blah. Blah. *Reviewers awarded your proposal a score of ninety-seven out of one-hundred…"*

Rob scanned the rest of the letter.

"Was not funded…"

His heart crumpled.

"Crap."

He rifled through the enclosed material. Judging from the feedback provided, the reviewers loved his proposal. The only section that was docked points was "University Resources." Had he been at another university, he probably would've gotten the grant. If he wasn't so emotionally drained, he would've laughed at the irony.

Climbing the darkened stairs, Rob tried to feel good about the score. After all, it was his first grant application. Not many people could've done that well. Perhaps he could include the reviews with his job applications. They might help him get an interview somewhere.

He stepped out of the stairwell and immediately stopped. Down the hall, a figure emerged from Craig's office—but it wasn't Craig.

Chapter 91

The following morning, Rob came into work early and purposely left his door open. At a little past eight, he heard Craig clomping along the hall, whistling and telling everybody what a glorious morning it was, despite it being ten degrees outside. He appeared outside Rob's office.

"Here you go, Polly!" He threw empty boxes into the corner. "Some people get gold watches. You get these! I hope they help!"

"Thanks, Craig. I appreciate it. Let me know if you have any more. I'll need them to pack up my house."

Craig's grin gave way slightly. "You brought this on yourself. You know that. You should've never crossed swords with me."

"I didn't bring it on myself! You told me the day I arrived that I wasn't getting renewed. The only thing I did wrong was to accept a position here!" Rob lowered his voice. "I'm sorry. I shouldn't have yelled. But I wish you would've given me a chance. I think I could've helped the program."

"Yes, well—" Craig brushed lint from his bright red tie. "I don't need your type of help here."

"Maybe. But your students do."

As if to reply, Craig stepped angrily into the office. Then he noticed Thelma's black and white photo on Rob's desk. His sneer turned into sudden recognition, then shock. "That's... That's Dr. Larsen's daughter."

"Yeah. Thelma gave it to me before she died. She seemed to think I could follow in his footsteps."

"*His* footsteps? You? Trust me, you are nothing like him, Polly! Nothing!" Craig snatched the picture. "He was a great man. He had this way of making people feel important and worthy of his company. When I was his student, he'd listen to anything I had to say... no matter how puerile or uninformed my ideas were."

He examined the photo with such tenderness, it appeared as though he was about to caress it.

"We wouldn't have this program without him. He fought the governor and state legislature and repeatedly got the funding this place needed to stay afloat. He was tenacious, honorable, and forward-thinking. You, on the other hand—"

Craig turned the picture over and found Thelma's note. He stared at it, then at Rob. For several seconds, he didn't say anything. Then he put the picture back and left without saying another word.

Rob listened intently. From down the hallway, he heard Craig's key slide into the lock. Then the door banged into his desk.

Nothing happened.

Holding his breath, Rob crossed his fingers and prayed.

Then Craig let loose an ear-piercing shriek. "Sons of bitches!"

Bert and Les rushed to him, asking what was wrong.

"They're everywhere!" Craig bellowed. "Everywhere!"

Out of morbid curiosity, Rob went to Craig's office. Thousands of crickets were hopping all over the place. More were pouring out of his desk drawer.

"Ugh!" Craig danced around, trying to avoid the insects springing at him. "Get them out of here! Grab them! Hurry!"

Feeling like spring had finally come, Rob headed to the stairs.

Chapter 92

"I wish to speak with the Dean, please." Rob put his hands in his pockets and rocked on his heels as though he'd ordered a tuna fish sandwich.

The receptionist looked up from her gardening magazine. "He's busy. He doesn't want to be disturbed."

"Oh, he'll want to see me," Rob replied. "Tell him that I know who the jolly prankster is. And I'd love to discuss the matter with him at his earliest possible convenience."

The receptionist eyed him, then put the magazine down. Going to the Dean's door, she wavered, doubt overtaking her.

Rob nodded encouragingly. "He'll want to know. Trust me." He winked.

She knocked and poked her head inside the office. The Dean shouted. She said something. His response was more restrained.

A bit shaken, the receptionist returned to her desk. "He'll give you exactly one minute."

"Splendid! That'll give us time for chit-chat."

Rob strolled into the office, closed the door behind him, and sat in one of the soft leather armchairs. He crossed his legs comfortably.

"What do you want?" the former Marine growled.

"Last night, I was on the sixth floor a little after ten o'clock, and I saw somebody coming out of Craig's office. But it wasn't him. And then this morning, his desk was filled with crickets." Rob uncrossed his legs and leaned forward. "Do you know who I saw?"

The Dean's eyes narrowed. "What do you want?"

Chapter 93

Later that afternoon, as he headed along the sixth-floor hallway, Rob thought he'd heard a cork pop. Voices cheered. Peering into the special education conference room, he found Bert and Les toasting Craig with little Dixie cups.

"Here's to the new Assistant Dean of Teacher Education!" Bert said.

Les cried, "Hear! Hear!"

They drank.

"What does the Assistant Dean of Teacher Education do?" Bert asked.

"Nobody knows!" Craig laughed. "I tell you; it's got to be the cushiest job in the university! Not so high up where people expect results. Not so low down where you have to do anything."

"It couldn't have happened to a better person, Big Guy!"

"Thank you, Bert. And you know what the best thing of all is? After two years as Assistant Dean, I can return to my position here and keep my dean's salary! Can you believe it? What a scam!"

"What are you going to do with all that extra loot?" Les asked.

Craig filled his cup and drained it in one swallow. "Rosie wants to get a bigger house someplace out in the country with lots of trees and land. The dogs would like that too. They need room to run."

"Living like an English gentleman," Bert said, in a bad British accent.

"Exactly! Our own little estate. And, of course, there'll be lots of traveling for the university. The deans go on all kinds of recruiting trips and junkets." Tears dribbled down Craig's cheeks as he gave them more champagne. "I knew this day would come! I knew it!"

"They certainly took their time!" Les complained. "They should've given you the job ages ago. I wonder what took them so long."

"I don't know. The Dean only said somebody recommended me for the position." Craig gazed proudly off into space, his chins elevated. "Clearly, someone high up has finally recognized my abilities."

"Who?"

"I haven't a clue. But I'd love to buy him a drink!"

Rob leaned against the door. "Congratulations, Craig." They turned to him. A wave of annoyance flooded Craig's face. He brushed away his tears. "You deserve it."

"Yes, well," Craig said as though trying to puzzle out whether Rob was making a joke at his expense, "I certainly do."

"I'll let you all celebrate in peace." Bowing, Rob made to leave. "Congrats, again."

"Wait a second."

Rob stopped.

Craig cleared his throat. "After this semester, I will no longer be affiliated with the department. Therefore, somebody will need to take over my responsibilities as chair. Seeing as though Jim is never around and Pete has gone stark raving mad, I told the Dean that, well—you should stay."

"Really?" Rob acted surprised. "That's great! Wow. Thanks, Craig. That means a lot to me. I'll do my best to follow your stellar example."

Craig waved a hand. "I don't care. I'm tired of keeping this god-awful place operational. The department is all yours, Rob. Do whatever you think Dr. Larsen would do."

"I will. Thanks!" Then Rob said, "Oh, Bert and Les. Tomorrow, let's get together and discuss your ideas for enhancing our program."

"Enhancing?" Bert repeated suspiciously.

"Sure. I want to hear your ideas for updating the curriculum and improving how we do things. For example, maybe we can change when classes are offered so we don't have to teach late one night and then early the next morning."

"That'd be fantastic!" Les exclaimed.

"Good. Let's say—ten o'clock, here? Bring a list of your ideas." Rob inclined his head toward the stairs. "Sorry, but I have to get going. I have a Parking Appeals Committee meeting. Congratulations again, Craig."

Bert hurried into the hallway and called, "I'll have that list ready. You won't be disappointed, Big Guy!"

Epilogue

Rob raised his beer. "Here's to the end of our first full term as assistant professors!"

Wendy and Sid clinked their bottles and drank.

Throughout Vino's, drunk college students sang and danced, celebrating the end of yet another school year at Eastern Wisconsin University.

"How's it feel to be chair?" Wendy shouted over the commotion.

"It won't be official until next week. But—" Rob beamed. "It feels good. Really, really good!"

"I bet!"

"Do you have all your curriculum changes in place?" Sid asked.

"All the paperwork is completed and submitted," Rob told him. "But it'll be a while before they go into effect. Do you know it takes five years to change the name of a course?"

"Five years?"

"Yeah, three to go through all the department, school, college, and university committees. And two more for somebody to type it into the course catalog."

Wendy rolled her eyes. "Welcome to EW-U, where change is glacially slow."

"But it does come!" Rob said. "Or it will soon."

They all took a drink as the jukebox began playing Frank Sinatra's *My Way*.

"What other changes do you have planned?" Sid asked.

Rob sipped his beer. He wanted to celebrate all night but didn't want to pay the price in the morning. "We have this class that's supposed to be about collaborating with families. I'm going to have some parents teach it. I think our students will benefit from hearing their perspectives."

"That's brilliant! Are you still having them help kids for extra credit?"

"Not for extra credit. I'm making it a requirement for our assessment course. Students can apply what they learn in class to real-life situations. I think it'll help them master the material. Plus, God knows the parents need support."

A woman with long black hair climbed onto the bar, tore off her shirt, and whipped it above her head. She screamed, "Grad school, here I come!"

Wendy watched as one of the bartenders pulled her down. "Any word about Elwin Holme?"

"Actually, there is," Rob said. "They're telling parents they are going to review their mission statement. They're also going to start giving their residents greater access to the community—field trips and recreational outings. That kind of thing."

"Hey! That's a start!"

"It is. I'm on the team that will be developing a more functional curriculum. The problem will be stripping away the culture there. No curriculum is going to help if their teachers still believe people with disabilities can't learn."

"Speaking of stripping," Sid said, "anything from your former secretary?"

"Tiffani?" Rob asked. "Yeah, I got an e-mail from her yesterday. She says she's now the assistant director of the gallery. Also, she's having an exhibition of her work next month. She's invited us to the opening."

"Wow!" Wendy said. "Good for her! Maybe I'll buy one of her pieces. I need something to put on my apartment walls."

"Me too!" Sid chimed in. "I need to replace my Harry Potter posters anyway."

They all took another drink.

Sid regarded his bottle. "Man, this is good. It's really rich and sweet. I taste licorice."

"And a hint of chocolate." Wendy read the label. "Titanbräu Nera. Where's this from?"

"San Marino," Rob replied.

"Caribbean?"

He shook his head as he drank. "Right by Italy. It's one of the smallest countries in the world."

"It's damn good." Sid took a pull, then smacked his lips. "I wouldn't mind having another."

"Hey!" Wendy poked him. "We still have thirteen countries to go and only twenty-eight hours left. You drink what you want on your own time, mister!"

They laughed as they clinked beer bottles.

THE END

About the Author

From an early age, Meander Swotty expressed a passionate desire to make a positive difference in the world. Unfortunately, he went into academia.

After enrolling in a nearly ivy league university, Dr. Swotty earned his Ph.D. in special education by threatening to date his advisor's teenage daughter. Upon completing his doctorate, he attempted to avoid reality still further by getting a second Ph.D. in economics. But he was soon guilted into accepting a post-doctoral position by his many creditors.

Once mastering the ancient arts of getting coffee and making dual-sided copies, Dr. Swotty was compelled to leave his post-doctoral position and relocate to greener pastures when the department's brand new Xerox machine inexplicably burst into flames while he was attempting to make overheads.

Armed with glowing letters of recommendations that contained such lofty praise as "I can't recommend him too highly" and "You'll be lucky if you get him to work for you," Dr. Swotty searched for a job that could provide a comfortable office chair as well as summers off.

Eventually, he obtained a faculty position at what is euphemistically called "a teaching university." Here, Dr. Swotty taught numerous courses, conducted research nobody ever read, and left countless meetings early because he claimed he had a student waiting in his office. When he applied for tenure, the only dissenting vote contained the comment, "His credentials are fine, but his sense of humor is questionable."

Once young and idealistic, Dr. Swotty is now a haggard and beaten down professor who declines to attend meetings that don't serve donuts. The highlight of his illustrious career was when he threw the Faculty Senate into turmoil by insisting Robert's Rules of Order requires people to use the terms "thee" and "thou." When he isn't regaling his undergraduates about the 1980s, he is writing fiction of dubious literary value.

Dr. Swotty can be reached at MeanderSwotty@gmail.com; however, he refuses to answer any e-mails that refer to him as "Mr."